What News on the Rialto?

The Lost Years of William Shakespeare

Anthony R Wildman

This is a work of fiction. All characters and events portrayed in this novel are either
fictitious or used fictitiously

What News on the Rialto?
Plutus Publishing Australia

ISBN: 978-0-646-99714-8

Chapter 1

Stratford-on-Avon, April 1585

Have you heard the latest outrage that pompous ass has inflicted on our family? Well, he's over-reached this time, by God he has.'

The voice that hurled these words across the taproom of the Old Thatch Tavern in Stratford-on-Avon belonged to a wiry redhead who had shouldered his way through the crowd in search of the cousin who had been sitting at one of the long benches chatting amiably to some friends.

'Calm down, Robbie, for God's sake. Come and sit down and tell me what has happened.'

For William Shakespeare, calming the turbulent spirit of his cousin Robbie Arden had become almost a weekly event. Abandoning his companions with an apologetic shrug, he called for two tankards of ale as his cousin sat down on the opposite side of the table. The other drinkers in the tavern resumed their interrupted conversations, much to Will's relief: the last thing he wanted was for the whole taproom to be eavesdropping on what would no doubt be another Robbie Arden rant.

'So, who is the pompous ass, and what has he done?'

'Sir Thomas bloody Lucy, that's who.' Robbie took a great draught of ale. 'He's been at it again.'

'He's been at *what* again?' Sometimes his cousin could be exasperating.

'Sent half a dozen of his henchmen around and searched the house and stables. Said they had information that there was a Catholic priest in the area, so they were searching every known Catholic household. Smashed up furniture, scared the servants half to death, and drove off a dozen sheep to boot. That's the third time this year one or another of our family have been harassed.'

Sir Thomas Lucy was a powerful local landowner, and a furious Puritan. The Ardens were Catholics. Though the queen had long ago settled the terrible persecutions that had raged back and forth since the death of old King Harry by declaring that she wanted no windows into men's souls, ancient hatreds had still not entirely subsided. And it still remained illegal to celebrate the Catholic rite or to harbour Catholic priests.

That law provided sufficient cover for more fanatically-minded Protestants like Sir Thomas to harass their Catholic neighbours with impunity. The plots against the queen's life which had come to light with increasing frequency over recent years, most of which seemed to revolve around her imprisoned cousin Mary, the queen of Scots, had made the Puritans even more frenzied.

Lucy's campaign against the Ardens, though, had backfired, for he had never found any evidence of wrongdoing, and had been made to look a fool in the eyes of the county. He was a pompous and self-important man, and Will rather suspected that this latest outrage was committed more to demonstrate his authority than to actually catch any priests who might be lurking in the area.

Even so, Robbie and his family had justice on their side, not to mention the sympathy of most of the county, since Lucy was not a popular man.

'You could take him to court,' he said, trying to sound reasonable and calm his cousin down.

'What good would that do? We'd be in the right of it, of course, but Lucy is too powerful. The justices are all in fear of him. He's a damnable louse.'

Obviously nothing much was going to divert Robbie from his furious denunciations, and Will had little option but to listen and drink his ale, chiming in from time to time with his own contributions. In truth, though his naturally cautious nature counselled restraint, inwardly Will sympathised with his cousin's outrage at the casual slights that he and other Catholics regularly had to endure, for he could not understand why neighbour should be set against neighbour over the question of how they chose to worship God.

As the evening wore on, and the tankards came and went, they both became giggling drunk and ever louder and more extreme in their opinions. By then, half the patrons in the taproom had gathered around them, enjoying the flow of ever-more colourful denunciations that emerged from the lips of the two young men, and Will felt himself emboldened by the unaccustomed presence of an audience.

'He's a damnable louse,' Robbie said, for the fourth or fifth time, his inventiveness beginning to flag.

'Lucy is a louse and Lucy is lousy,' Will shot back. *Not an especially clever line*, he thought, but for some reason it got a laugh from the assembled crowd, and he grinned with delight at their amusement.

'A lousy louse. I like that.' Robbie swayed a little in his seat, his eyes unfocussed as he tried to think of a retort. 'But he's a lousy louse who is also a member of parliament and a justice of the peace. Who'd credit that such a thing was possible?'

Will frowned in concentration, the beginnings of inspiration piercing his beer-fuddled mind.

'Tom!' he called across the boisterous room to the tavern keeper, 'do you have some paper and a pen somewhere there?'

When pen, paper and ink arrived at their table, Will waved his friend to silence and set himself to write. After a few minutes, he looked up.

'Here, how about this?' He pushed the paper across to his friend.

Robbie quickly scanned the words and then, with a laugh, he jumped up onto the table, scattering platters and tankards everywhere, and began to read in a voice that carried across the room.

A parliament member, a justice of the peace,
At home a poor scarecrow,
At London an Ass,
If lousy is Lucy as some folks miscall it,
Then Lucy is lousy, whatever befall it!

There was a few moments' silence, then the whole room burst into laughter. Will knew that Sir Thomas was not well-loved among the regulars at the Old Thatch, and within minutes his little ditty was being bawled out at the top of their voices, over and over again.

Will was a little sheepish at this reception; he had been dabbling in writing verse for some years, but always for his own amusement and occasionally for the entertainment of his immediate family. This antic piece of doggerel was hardly a piece of work he could be proud of, yet here it was, being performed in public, albeit to a public of drunks!

His spirit warmed by the friendly camaraderie of his fellow patrons of the Old Thatch, half of whom seemed to want to buy them tankards of ale, he joined in the banter about the shortcomings of Sir Thomas Lucy with gusto. He was a little bemused: his usual position in such crowds was at the periphery, watching rather than participating, so it felt strange to be the centre of attention like this. Strange and quite intoxicating in itself.

But eventually his normal common-sense reasserted itself and he decided that he had had enough to drink. Leaving his cousin in the embrace of the crowded taproom, he made his way out into the cool of the evening, where the fresh night air was a welcome change from the fetid fug of the tavern.

With the cool air came a sudden blast of doubt. What had he been thinking, to compose a verse that insulted the most powerful man in the district? It was all very well to say he had been carried away by the excitement, not to mention the alcohol, but he could not imagine that such arguments would hold much sway if Sir Thomas ever came to hear of his little poem.

Staggering the short way home down the quiet streets of Stratford to the house in Henley Street where he lived with his family, all he could do was to hope that the offending poem would dissolve into the air as the tavern's drinkers poured into the night, and never be heard again.

*

That hope was dashed when, a week later as he walked into the centre of Stratford on an errand for his father, his attention was caught by a paper pinned on the wall of the post-house, its lower edge flapping in the breeze.

Peering at it, he was aghast to read his little piece of doggerel, though he was relieved to see that at least his name was not affixed to the paper. Tearing it from the wall, he stuffed it into his doublet.

Where else, he wondered, had it been distributed? For though the printing was crude, someone had obviously gone to the trouble of having it typeset, which suggested that they intended wide circulation.

Sure enough, as he walked through the town there were copies posted up in prominent places. He began to feel a little uneasy. Unpopular though he might be, Tom Lucy was a powerful man; a friend of the queen's favourite, and he realised that seen in the cold light of day, his harmless little piece of satire might provoke an unwelcome reaction from its target. His only defence, a flimsy one, was the fact that it purported to be anonymous, though anyone who had been in the Old Thatch that night could attest to his authorship.

He didn't have long to wait before the reaction he feared manifested itself. The very next day he received at the hands of a burly and unsmiling

4

bailiff an unceremonious summons to present himself forthwith at Charlecote Park, Sir Thomas Lucy's country residence.

The summons brooked no delay, and the bailiff had been told to accompany Shakespeare back to the Lucy manor, having brought a horse for the purpose. During the five-mile ride, his escort remained grimly mute, ignoring all Will's efforts to engage him in conversation or find out what was behind this precipitous summons.

They approached Charlecote through a broad expanse of open parkland, newly stocked with deer. Once past the gatehouse, the splendour of the house became apparent. Will had been here only once before, as a small boy accompanying his father on a commission for the lady of the house. Sir Thomas had rebuilt it since then in the modern style of red brick, with two great wings connected by the central hall. Its gabled roof and numerous chimney pots were all designed to boast loudly of the owner's wealth and power.

Dismounting, Will gave his doublet a tug, stretched to ease the pain in the small of his back—he was not much accustomed to riding horses—and set himself to face whatever lay ahead.

The door to the manor house was opened by an unsmiling footman who might have been brother to Will's road companion, at least in demeanour, and he was ushered into a large wood-panelled hall, decorated with the banners and arms of the Lucy family along its walls, interspersed with great red and yellow tapestries depicting chivalrous deeds involving knights, damsels, and various mythological animals.

He didn't have long to examine the decorations, however, for within a few minutes yet another Lucy servant, most likely the steward of the household judging from his more sumptuous dress, appeared from a small door at the end of the hall, and looking him disdainfully up and down, bade him follow with a few barked words.

Conscious of his serviceable but undeniably workaday clothes after the haughty inspection of the steward, it began to dawn on Will that he was about to come face to face with power. Some of his natural cockiness evaporated as they approached a small door at the end of the corridor, and he was announced to its occupant.

Swiftly taking in the small room, Will realised that this must be Sir Thomas' private study. One wall was lined with bookshelves, and another covered in paintings—small and large representations of members of the Lucy family. The wooden floor was hidden under well-worn but expensive-looking carpets, and the whole room was dominated by tall windows looking out onto the parkland outside.

Before these stood a large desk, cluttered with papers and writing materials, and a tall, ornate chair, occupied by the manor's owner, who was bent over, intent on a document on the table in front of him, apparently lost in concentration.

The steward emitted a small cough, at which Sir Thomas looked up, an expression of irritation flitting across his face.

'Master William Shakespeare, Sir Thomas.'

Will had seen Sir Thomas Lucy at a distance many times, but this was the first time he had been in close proximity to the district's most important grandee. His immediate impression was of a man of choleric and peevish disposition. A thin nose, sharp cheekbones, and a small pursed mouth, barely visible through the fashionably pointed short beard and similarly short-cropped greying hair combined as the frame through which a pair of close-set grey eyes, narrowing as his brow began to furrow into a frown, regarded him with a cold stare.

Waving the steward out of the room, Lucy settled back into his chair, and for a moment the two men simply looked at each other. Will kept his own eyes steady, determined not to break eye contact, but at the same time trying to minimise any possible offence by adopting what he hoped was an expression of innocence.

'Shakespeare.' The voice was high pitched, almost girlish, and at odds with the stern angularity of the face.

'Sir Thomas.' Will offered a small bow, little more than a slight bend at the waist and a duck of his head. Respectful, but not too submissive, he told himself.

'I am told you have a reputation as something of a poet, is that not so?'

'I did not know that I had such a standing, Sir Thomas, though I am gratified to hear it. In truth, sir, I dabble, no more.'

Lucy did not seem to like the quibbling response, and The grey eyes became even chillier.

He picked up a piece of paper from his desk. 'And as a poet, what, pray, do you make of this piece of doggerel?'

The paper was too far away for Will to read, but he didn't need to, for he knew it was one of the versions of his drunken poem that he had seen posted up around Stratford.

Alarm invaded his mind as he realised that he might be in real trouble. He had known from the minute the bailiff had turned up that his unceremonious summons to attend on the lord of Charlecote Park was related to that wretched poem. He had thrust his previous misgivings to back into the back of his mind, unwilling to believe that what he thought of as a harmless joke would find its way to its intended target, even as the logical part of his mind told him that this was unlikely in a small town like Stratford.

While he stood contemplating the evidence of his foolishness, wondering whether to deny authorship or to confess and hope for leniency, Sir Thomas continued to regard him coldly.

The man's composure collapsed. 'How dare you!' The voice went up a pitch and doubled in volume to a shout of rage. 'How dare you! You might be the son of a former mayor of Stratford, but who do you think you are to write such scurrilous verse about your betters? Oh, don't think I don't know who put you up to it. I know all about your Catholic Arden cousins. I know you waste your idle hours in company with Robert Arden, a troublemaker like the rest of his cursed family.'

Will opened his mouth to try and say something to stem this tirade, but he was forestalled by Sir Thomas, who waved him to silence with a curt gesture. 'Do not try and pretend that you didn't write these wretched stanzas, if you think that is going to be your defence. Did you think I wouldn't know, just because this,' he spluttered, 'this piece of filthy libel was unsigned? You are a fool if you think that I don't know about everything that happens in this district.'

Clearly there was no way out of this, except by an apology. 'Sir Thomas, I am sorry if my poor writings have offended—'

But the enraged courtier was having none of it. Cutting Will's nascent apology off before it had begun, Sir Thomas slammed his hand down on the desk for silence. Regarding his victim for a moment, the fury was replaced with the cold impersonal look of a magistrate passing sentence.

'Were it not for your father, who I hold in some regard, I would have you put in the stocks to be made an example for the whole town of what happens to those who would set themselves above their station to mock the queen's representatives. For that reason, and that alone, I am giving you another option—leave this town and this county immediately. I care not where you go, but I want you out of my jurisdiction within a day.'

Will felt as though a trapdoor had opened beneath him and he was tumbling helplessly into a deep black void. All he could do was stand there in shock as he contemplated his ruin.

Then he thought about the consequences for his wife and three young children. How would they fend for themselves without him? And how would his exile affect his father's standing in the town?

Risking a further explosion, he attempted a plea of mitigation. 'My lord,' he said, using an honorific to which Lucy had no entitlement in an attempt at appeasement, 'this seems a harsh punishment indeed for what was intended as no more than a joke. A foolish one, ill-thought through, to be sure, but nevertheless a joke. Surely—'

Lucy was having no truck with his excuses. 'Do not try to use your silver tongue to sway me. I have decided what your fate should be. Now get out and get back to your home. If my bailiffs find you there in the morning, I promise you, I will prosecute you with all of the power at my disposal.' With that, he picked up a small bell to summon the steward again, who showed him the door with barely-concealed contempt, refusing his meek request for a horse.

He had a long walk back to Stratford, his request for a horse having been dismissed with a mocking laugh. As he plodded along the dusty road, his thoughts veered from outrage to fear and back again. Lucy's threat of prosecution was surely a bluff, built as it was on the flimsy foundation of his alleged but unproven authorship of the offending poem. His sense of justice rebelled mightily against meek surrender, and this, the outraged part of his mind, was telling him to laugh it off. Let Lucy do his worst. The English justice system would look after him.

But there was also a rational, cynical voice that sent shivers of fear through him as it murmured the counter arguments. Lucy wielded great power, power that reached far beyond the borders of Warwickshire: *you know you have little chance of withstanding a legal onslaught,* the voice said. *Your father's standing in the town might bring you some protection, but that will only extend so far.*

By the time he arrived, dusty and worn, at the front door of his father's house, the insistent whispering of that fearful voice had grown ever louder until he could deny it no longer. He knew that he had little option but to flee Stratford.

The house was silent as he entered the big main room. Presumably his mother was out at the markets, and his siblings at school. On the dining table, the remains of the day's main meal reminded him that his interview with Sir Thomas Lucy had also cost him his lunch.

'Hello? Is anyone at home?'

'Will?' His father's voice responded from the other end of the house, where his workshop and shop were located. 'Come on through, lad. I'm just finishing up.'

Amid the familiar smell of leather and fur and wool, John Shakespeare was busying himself at the bench that occupied the middle of the room, covered in scraps of material, off-cuts of leather, half-finished gloves, and scattered sequins, needles, and bobbins of thread. Will settled himself on a bale of wool propped in the corner, and waited until his father, pausing in his work, looked up and seemed for to read the agitation in his son's face.

'You look like you are carrying the cares of the world on your shoulders, son.'

Will shifted uncomfortably on his bale. The citizens of Stratford knew John Shakespeare as a likeable man, with a cheerful disposition and a shrewd judgement which they had valued enough to elect him as an alderman, and then to return him for over twenty years. He had even served briefly as the town's mayor; Will had a dim childhood memory of the splendour of the mayoral gold chain being dangled in front of him by his chuckling father.

But in recent years, after enduring a series of baseless attacks and accusations from those who were jealous of his success in trade, his father had become increasingly disenchanted with the politics of Stratford, so much so that he had stopped attending council meetings. He had become prone to outbursts of anger when the behaviour of his fellow men exhausted his patience, and this had affected his trade so much that his financial position was increasingly precarious.

Knowing his father's uncertain temper, it was with some trepidation that Will told his story, slowly and hesitantly at first, and then finishing in a rush of indignation, with which he hoped to at least recruit his father to his own side of the story.

In this hope he was mistaken. 'William, you are a purblind fool!' When John Shakespeare used his eldest son's full name, it was a bad sign. 'How can you have been so stupid as to let that idiot cousin of yours lead you into this mess? Your mother is the only member of that blasted family who has any judgement at all. I have troubles enough without attracting the attention of Sir Thomas bloody Lucy! You know what he is like—once aroused, he never stops.'

9

Will could do nothing but stand in silence and listen while his father's anger ran its course, though eventually its focus turned away from his son and towards the Lord of Charlecote, whose high-handedness was condemned in the most florid terms.

Finally, when the torrent seemed spent, Will felt safe enough to venture at least a few words in his own defence. 'I am sorry, Father. Of course I was stupid to let Robbie lead me astray, though to be truthful, we were both deep in our cups, and you have to admit that Sir Thomas deserves to be taken down a peg or two.'

That earned him a look of contempt. 'And you think, in your conceit, that a few scribbled words of doggerel will take a powerful landowner like Sir Thomas Lucy down 'a peg or two'? You can add naivety and stupidity to the catalogue of your weaknesses.'

But his father's anger ebbed away even as he spoke. He stood up and came over to join Will at the window, grasping him by the shoulders and looking searchingly into his eyes. 'Will, you are my firstborn son, for whom I have always had high hopes. You have not yet found a path in life that satisfies you, and that has disappointed me. But perhaps that is because Stratford cannot offer you anything more. It may be that this unlooked-for exile is a disguised blessing.'

Will didn't like being reminded of the extent to which he had been a disappointment to a father who had been at pains to try and give him every advantage in life.

When he had needed work to support his growing family, John Shakespeare had used his connections to find him a position with a local lawyer, Tom Richardson. For a while the complexities and subtleties of the English legal system had fascinated him, but he soon realised that the dry-as-dust world of statutes and precedents held little appeal.

Before long, he began to find excuses to escape the confines of the office to wander through the fields and lanes of the countryside, his head filled with the poems of Ovid and Virgil, the plays of Plautus and Seneca, all speaking to him of worlds far beyond the dull confines of rural Warwickshire. Eventually, old Master Richardson had informed him that his services were no longer required. His father had been furious.

Now, in his wise way, his father had also put his finger on the nub of the problem, and pointed the way forward. For he was quite right—Stratford had little to offer him now. It was a worthy enough place, and his family had a certain standing here, but its provincial dullness was suffocating. He was bored, and he knew he needed a broader backcloth against which to live out the drama of his life and realise his dreams, incoherent though they might be.

But merely fleeing to another county would not serve, for what could he gain by living out his life as a clerk or a schoolmaster in some other little town just beyond Lucy's reach?

Then the answer, the obvious answer, came to him.

'I shall go to London,' he said, a new certainty in his voice. 'And I will make my fortune somehow. I swear I will win enough fame and earn enough money that even Sir Thomas Lucy will have to think twice before insulting me. I will make you proud of me, Father.'

John Shakespeare looked at his son for a long moment, and Will felt as if his sincerity was being weighed and tested.

Then his father smiled, nodded his satisfaction, and patted him on the shoulder. 'London. Well, that is not a place for the faint of heart. Yet I have a feeling that you will find your true calling there, as you cannot here. What that may be, I do not know, but go with my blessing.'

Then his mood changed, and he was all brisk business. 'You must stay with Richard Holbrooke; you remember him? My supplier of fine cloths? I make no doubt he will happily give you lodging and help you find your feet. I will write a note to him now, while you go and break the news to Anne.'

That was an interview he had been dreading from the minute he left Charlecote Park. Leaving his father to resume his work, he went next door to the adjoining cottage, which his father had fortuitously purchased a few years before as an investment and which now provided a somewhat cramped home for his family.

The front door stood open to admit the sunshine, and he stood on the threshold, his presence unnoticed, and enjoyed the tranquillity of the small domestic scene before him.

His eldest daughter, Susanna, who was approaching her second birthday, and who was already showing herself to have a solitary, self-contained nature, sat by the fireplace at the back of the room happily playing with a bolt of cloth discarded from her grandfather's workroom.

The twins, Hamnet and Judith, barely three months old, were sleeping peacefully in their crib, watched over by their mother, who sat at the table repairing one of his old shirts that had mysteriously acquired a hole.

11

When Anne looked up, his throat caught, as it always did. Eight years older than her husband—a fact that had caused a minor scandal when they had married—she was a woman in her prime, tall, willowy and beautiful still.

He had been so much in love with her when they met in the summer of 1582. And he still was, though their relationship had cooled under the weight of disappointment in her husband. For, mad with desire, he had painted her such a picture of their future together—they would live in a house of their own, she would have clothes of the finest silk and they would have a position of respect in Stratford society. In short, he had promised her the sun, the moon and the stars.

Quite how all this was to be achieved Will had never mentioned, airily talking of his prospects in the business of the law and neglecting to mention how much he hated his work with the long-suffering Richardson.

With most people, Will thought he was capable of dissembling, hiding his emotions behind what he thought of as his solemn look. But not with his wife, who instantly sensed his every emotion. 'What is it, Will? What have you done now?'

As always, something about his wife's demeanour demolished his confidence and put a stopper on his usual eloquence. It was typical of her to assume that he was in the wrong, even if in this instance her assumption was right.

Telling his story for the second time that day, he saw none of the compassion that his father had shown. For Anne, this was yet another example of the foolish fecklessness of her husband.

'What, dear Lord, did I do to deserve such an idiot?' she asked, though Will had the sense not to attempt to answer her. 'And what am I to do while you run away off to London? Am I to live entirely on the goodwill of your father? Depending on him for every farthing I need, for food, for clothes for the children? While you, no doubt, pursue your misguided dreams among the stews and ale-houses of London, pretending you are a great poet or some-such.

'None of your pretensions will put food on my table, Will Shakespeare, nor pay for the children's clothes, nor deliver anything you promised me when we married! A day I will regret for the rest of my life.'

This tirade was delivered in a low voice for fear of waking the twins or disturbing little Susanna, who fortunately remained absorbed in her game and barely noticed the fierce exchange between her parents.

By the end of it Anne was in tears, her whole body shaking with frustration. He listened in silence, and when he judged that the first furious storm had run its course, he took her in his arms. She stiffened at first, and then relaxed into his body as he stroked her hair.

'What is going to happen to us, Will? What is going to happen to you?'

'Don't worry, lass' he said softly. 'I know I have been a disappointment to you, as I have to everyone. But all will be well, do not fear.'

He grasped her by the shoulders and looked into her eyes, now red-rimmed and clearly frightened. 'Anne, I swear to you on everything I hold sacred, that I will change this misfortune into success.

'Don't you see? Stratford is too small for me! What can I make of myself here, except to follow my father in his trade? I know I can be greater than that, Anne. I know it! In my bones I know also that London is where I must be, doing what I know not, but only there will I have any chance to find out what is possible.'

She sighed, surrendering again to his enthusiasm and charm, as she always did in the end. 'You are a hopeless dreamer, Will, but I don't suppose you will ever stop dreaming your dreams, and no doubt you would have run off to London of your own accord eventually.'

'I promise you will be in my thoughts every day, as will the children, and I swear that I will make our fortune just as I said I would, and you will have a fine house and will want for nothing.'

Her smile told him that he was, for now, forgiven, though he knew she didn't believe him; why should she?

But Will decided that this promise was one that he would keep for the rest of his life. He would make Anne proud to call him husband, not ashamed.

It was time for him to grow up, to make something of himself. And he would do it by pursuing his dreams, no matter how foolish they seemed to be now, not by bouncing from one stop-gap to another.

It was late afternoon by the time the family gathered again in the front parlour to farewell him on the first stage of his journey to London.

His mother, informed of the situation by her husband, had been a calm presence in the whirlwind of preparations for his departure. She had always believed in her eldest son's destiny, seeing something in him that others did not, and it was she who had insisted that he pack his little library of books into the limited space available in his saddlebags.

13

Finally, he said a tearful farewell to his wife and his mother, received a gruff hug from his father, and was good-naturedly cuffed his brother, Gilbert, whose face was a picture of envy. He said formal farewells to his other brothers, Richard and Edmund, who hid round-eyed in their mother's skirts. Only sixteen-year-old Joan was missing; visiting one of their Arden cousins.

Climbing onto the rented horse, he waved a last farewell and set his face southwards, to Oxford, where he would stay overnight, and then to London.

Chapter 2

London, April 1585

G radually the fields and farms of Oxfordshire and Buckinghamshire gave way to suburbs, as his exhausted horse plodded its way along Holburne Street.

As he crossed a narrow, people-thronged bridge over the Fleet stream, he saw the ancient walls that still enclosed the city proper, and over to his right, high on its hill, the great mass of St Paul's Cathedral dominating the skyline.

His breeches and hose were spattered with mud and he was tired down to his bones from two long and uncomfortable days on horseback. He itched from fleas acquired at the rough inn in Oxford where he had stayed the previous night and he wanted nothing more than to slide down off his equally exhausted horse and find a bath and a bed.

Yet, in spite of his exhaustion, he felt his spirits lift as he passed through the arch of the New Gate and into the thoroughfare of Cheapside. Merchants from London had been regular visitors to his father's house throughout his childhood, bringing samples of fine leather and cloth for making gloves, as well as stories about England's greatest metropolis, which young Will had avidly absorbed at his father's knee. But nothing in those tales had prepared him for the cacophonous reality of the great city.

At this late hour in the afternoon, below a grey and lowering sky into which a thousand chimneys poured their smoke, the street was already cast in gloomy shadows from the houses—three, four and even five stories high, causing Will to stretch his neck as he looked about in open-mouthed wonder.

As far ahead as he could see, the street was lined with shops, many open to the street in an effort to catch the attention of the endless stream of hurrying people. Above, where the upper stories of the houses seemed to lean in towards each other like lovers caught in the act of embracing, washing lines crisscrossed the gap, shirts and sheets hanging limp in the cool and windless air.

After the relatively tranquil surroundings of rural Warwickshire, the noises and smells were overwhelming. The continual hum of the crowd, the

15

piercing, passionate cries of the shop-owners and pedlars marketing their wares, the whinny of horses, and the clanging of workshop tools all combined to assault his ears like discordant music. And though his country-bred nostrils were well used to the sickly smell of horse dung in the country, here it was almost choking, combined as it was with the smell of wood smoke drifting down into the street from the innumerable chimneys, creating a miasma in which he struggled to breathe.

Picking his way down the middle of the street where there were fewer pedestrians to impede him, he remembered his father's directions to continue along until he passed Bow Church, so was relieved to find himself at last outside a modest house on Ironmonger Lane, which was the residence of his father's friend Richard Holbrooke, a trader in fine cloth.

Holbrooke had been a regular visitor to the house in Stratford over the years, and when Will was eventually admitted by a serving girl who looked at him suspiciously, he was exactly as he had remembered—a small and genial man, prematurely grey-haired, soberly dressed in fine black hose and doublet over a simple white shirt. The impression of sobriety conveyed by the clothes was undermined by lively, intelligent blue eyes and wide white-toothed smile.

'Well, young William Shakespeare! What a surprise to see you here, of all places! But don't stand there, man. come on in.'

Holbrooke led him into the house, throwing terse instructions over his shoulder to the girl to arrange for the quartering of his horse and the disposal of his meagre baggage. Once settled in the generous front room overlooking the quiet lane, the merchant listened patiently to Will's stammered explanation of his unexpected presence on his doorstep.

'You do seem to have got yourself into something of a pickle, young fellow,' he said when Will had finally run out of words. 'You know, your little piece of foolishness might have offended the ever-so-high-and-mighty Sir Thomas Lucy, but here it would simply have been a moment's diversion and no more. You have no idea how many such amusing pieces of nonsense are posted up in St Paul's churchyard every day, causing a few days' merriment and then disappearing forever.'

'That may be so, Master Holbrooke, but he left me with little option but to flee. Though it may seem somewhat extreme to have flown this far, since Sir Thomas' demand was merely that I leave the county.'

'No, he is a vindictive man, that one, with powerful friends at court. Getting as far away from him as possible was the only thing to do. Anyway, now you are in London, lad, what do you intend to do with yourself?'

The older man's gaze, though friendly, was intent, and Will suddenly felt much younger and more vulnerable than his twenty-one years. 'That's the question. I am lettered in Latin and Greek, thanks to Schoolmaster Jenkins. I am handy enough at making gloves, though the good Lord forbid that I should take *that* up as a trade! And the half-year spent in the office of the Town Clerk in Stratford has given me enough law to understand that is not my course, either. And that is the full catalogue of my skills.'

'The making of gloves is an honourable enough trade,' Holbrooke said, the implied rebuke causing Will to blush slightly. 'But I can see that following in your father's footsteps is not to your taste. You have education enough to serve as a clerk somewhere, or perhaps a tutor, or schoolmaster. Though I'll warrant that is not where your passion lies, either.'

Something about this kindly man caused him to let down his reserve and talk as he had only ever talked to his wife of his dreams and ambitions. He talked about his excitement at discovering the poetry of Ovid and Virgil, Horace and Lucretius, which he had swallowed whole; the plays of Seneca and Plautus, the great prose works of Caesar and Livy; all staples of his grammar school education.

Every spare moment after he had finished with school, at odd moments of freedom in his working day, and late at night under the flickering light of a guttering candle, had been occupied with yet more reading and writing. He had even, he told Holbrooke with shy diffidence, begun to write a play—an adaptation of a work by Plautus—that he thought had some merit.

'Yet how can I possibly make a living from poetry? Or history? Or drama?' This question had recurred to him over and over again on the journey from Stratford, and it came out now in a voice of despair. 'At best, I might hope to get a post somewhere as a tutor in a great house, teaching a snivelling aristocratic brat the basics of Latin and Greek. Or if I am really lucky, some great lord might engage me to write love poetry on his behalf.'

He stopped, feeling a little embarrassed at his outburst, expecting that Master Holbrooke would dismiss his dreams as mere fantasy. Yet the merchant merely nodded, a sympathetic smile on his face.

'You said you had started to write a play. So perhaps the theatre might be where you could make your mark? Though the Puritans hate the playhouses and the players and have banished them beyond the city walls, the people still

17

love them, and the patronage of the queen and the court have ensured they survive, even flourish. And players need plays...'

This had not occurred to Will.

'I must confess I hadn't thought of such a thing. In truth, I started writing it as a mere exercise, no more. But perhaps you are right. Then again, who is going to want plays written by a country bumpkin whom no one has ever heard of?'

Holbrooke's smile turned into a chuckle. 'Your pessimism is getting the better of you. You are right, of course; the theatre is a chancy occupation. But in the course of my life, I have oft observed that men of passion and determination somehow seem to overcome all obstacles and fashion themselves into whatever shape they require to succeed.'

Will sighed. 'True enough, and perhaps I can find a path to fame and fortune through words, but in the meantime I have a family to support, and so I must do what will make an income, passion or no.'

Holbrooke nodded. 'Aye, family. It's what drives us all. How many children do you have now? Last time I was in Stratford, as I recall, you had just married... Anne, do I have that right?'

'Yes, Anne. Anne Hathaway as was, from over in Shottery. We have three children. Susanna was born two years ago, and our twins, Hamnet and Judith, are just a few months old. We were all living in my father's house, with my own brothers and sisters, so it was jam-packed. Anne hated it; she gets on well enough with mother and father, but told me that she didn't leave one crowded house in Shottery just to live in another in Stratford.

'Things have been better since my father allowed us the use of the little cottage next door, but even so, Anne isn't really happy. She wants a proper house of her own, she says, where the children can be brought up with room to breathe. Servants too, I'd reckon, are part of her vision...' He trailed off, thinking that he sounded like he was whining.

'Women have high expectations of their men-folk, that is for sure. And they oft care little how much those expectations weigh on us.' Rising from his chair, Holbrooke absent-mindedly poked at the embers of the fire before turning back to his houseguest, a quizzical expression on his face.

'I know that the life of a clerk is not for you, but I wonder if you would consider working for me in that capacity for a month or two? I had a good clerk who died a month ago of the flux, poor man, and have been without help since. Of course, I can pay you... not a fortune, but enough so that you can send something back home.'

Will considered that. It would be another stop-gap, and inevitably another dead end. But what else was he going to do? And he had already learned enough of Richard Holbrooke to realise that he would at least be a congenial employer.

'You are kind, Master Holbrooke, and of course I accept your offer. But you are right, I am not made to be a clerk, and I will find some other path in life that will be more lucrative and satisfy my passions. At which time, I promise you I will repay your kindness a hundred-fold.'

Holbrooke merely smiled his kindly smile and put out his hand in agreement.

And so William Shakespeare, glover's son, lately of the small market town of Stratford-upon-Avon, began a new life in the teeming metropolis that was England's capital. He was determined to repay Holbrooke's kindness with a whole heart, and he applied all his intellect and energy to learning the many and varied tasks required of a merchant's clerk in a complex business that turned out to encompass far more than the mere import of fine cloths for the use of tailors and glove-makers. Best of all, Holbrooke paid him enough that he could finally send some money home to Anne.

The weeks passed quickly, and though he was busy from morning to night, he did have the odd hour of leisure here and there, which he spent roaming the capital and drinking in its sights and sounds. On one of those occasions, he found himself drawn towards the great edifice of Saint Paul's.

It had astonished Will to discover that the cathedral, in addition to its sacred purpose, also served as a kind of clearinghouse for the city's news. Lawyers and merchants congregated in the central aisle, exchanging gossip and intelligence. And every spare space was plastered with billboards advertising all the diversions that kept Londoners entertained—plays, fencing matches, bear-baitings, lectures, poetry readings, curiosity shows. Outside, most of the churchyard was given over to booksellers' stalls, where Londoners could browse and buy all manner of printed material.

Unable to resist the temptation to buy yet another book, Will spent twenty minutes haggling with a pasty-faced bookseller for a copy of Ralph Holinshed's *Chronicles of England, Scotland, and Ireland,* newly reprinted and in popular demand. Having settled on a price of sixpence for each of the two volumes, he waited for the books to be wrapped.

Idly looking around, his eye was drawn to the stump of the broad stone base where the wooden spire of Saint Paul's had once stood, having burned down twenty years before and never rebuilt. It was said that the top of the tower afforded unmatched views across London, and on an impulse, he paid his penny admission and climbed the slippery stone steps to join the throng of other sightseers jostling for the best views.

Crammed within the medieval walls, the tightly-packed roofs of the city, pierced by innumerable church spires, stretched away to the east. To his right, the Thames was crowded with watercraft of every description, maneuvering to pass below the arches of London Bridge on the ebbing tide. And at the limit of his sight, the sun lit up the white walls of the Tower behind its grim fortifications at the far eastern end of the city.

As he stood absorbing this vision, he realised he wanted this extraordinary city, with all its noise and confusion, to be his home forever. Having tasted the excitements of London, he could never go back to Stratford, even though his family was there. Though he was but a clerk, the city's pandemonium inspired him, made him even more determined that he would become a famous man.

And he would do so as a poet, not as a clerk, he vowed to himself.

Chapter 3

B loody rubbish.'
The comment came from a slim, well-dressed young man who was standing next to Shakespeare among the press of people in the pit of the simply-named Theatre, in Shoreditch.

It was the latest in a string of critical expressions that had escaped his lips over the last hour, at first barely audible under his breath, then increasing in volume with the speaker's obvious impatience at the onstage goings-on.

Not that the play was being heard in reverent silence; the folk around him were vocal in their approval and otherwise of the performance going on just a few feet away, shouting catcalls and offering advice when the actors tripped over their lines (which they did more often than might be expected) or roaring out their admiration when they approved an actor's delivery.

Between these extremes, there was always a low murmuring as the crowd compared notes, though every now and then a dramatic moment would reduce them to awed silence.

One such moment dragged Will's attention away from his neighbour and back to the stage, where the play—*The Spanish Tragedy*, it was called, by someone named Thomas Kyd—was reaching its bloody climax.

For the last three hours a complex story of revenge had been playing out under the broiling July sun. The crowd of groundlings surrounding Will had been enthralled as Hieronimo, the Knight-Marshal of Spain, agonised over whether to take revenge on Lorenzo, the son of the Duke of Castile, who had murdered his own son, Horatio.

21

He had descended into madness, in which deranged state he devised a cunning plan involving a play-within-a-play that would lure the culprits into an orgy of murder and suicide, each 'death' accompanied by copious quantities of blood produced using some ingenious technique that Shakespeare could not fathom.

Now the play was almost done, and the stage was littered with the corpses of Lorenzo and his sister Bel-imperia, and Balthazar, the son of the Viceroy of Portugal. The other characters in the play—the King of Spain, his brother the duke, their courtiers, and the viceroy—were applauding, not yet comprehending that the stage deaths were real, not feigned.

With a flourish, Hieronimo tore off the turban and threw aside the spangled oriental robe of his disguise as a Turkish pasha. Throwing his arms wide, he turned to the assembled royalty, and in a voice filled with trembling anguish, addressed both stage and real audiences:

'Know I am Hieronimo,
The hopeless father of a hapless son,
Whose tongue is tuned to tell his latest tale.'

A pause, as the actor slowly surveyed the stage, wild madness in his eyes. Twitching open a curtain at the rear of the stage, he revealed the bloodied body of his own son, invoking a collective gasp from the audience and a vague harrumph from the grouchy critic standing next to Will.

As Hieronimo launched into a further oration in which he revealed for all the tale of the murder of his son, Will turned his head to inspect his neighbour. About Will's own height, his slight form was encased in a padded tunic decorated with sequins and jewels, hose and breeches of the finest wool, completed with fine though somewhat muddied knee-length boots.

His face, concentrating intently on the stage, was a delicate oval framed in a great mass of red-brown hair that sprang from a central peak in luxurious profusion. The small, almost pouting mouth, surmounted by the merest wisp of a moustache, was pursed in disapproval.

Will was about to say something when his attention was reclaimed by the stage, where the final appalling scenes of the drama were being played out. Hieronimo, having finished his speech, had bounded off into its far recesses, only to reappear above them on a balcony, placing a noose around his neck, evidently planning on suicide.

The Duke and the viceroy had by now worked out that the staged deaths were real, and demanded in anguished tones why Hieronimo, restrained by soldiers and dragged back down from his perch to the main stage, had murdered their children. Hieronimo revealed his dreadful motivation.

'My guiltless son was slain by your two sons,
Upon whose souls may the Heavens yet be avenged
With afflictions greater far than these!
But by their bloody deaths before you now
Am I at last revenged thoroughly.'

The royal pair, intent on torturing Hieronimo to identify his confederates, seemed to be defeated as the poor madman bit off his own tongue, spitting it out in a spray of blood. Not content to be cheated in this way, the player-king called for pen and paper, demanding that the madman write the names of his accomplices.

Pretending to require a knife to sharpen his quill, Hieronimo, in a final act of revenge, stabbed first the viceroy and then himself. The bodies were borne off the stage to the muted sounds of a dead march, and as the last of the players exited the stage the audience, groundlings and gentry in the balconied tiers of the theatre alike, erupted into raucous applause that swelled as the players returned to stage to take their bows.

Will joined the general approval with enthusiasm. He had seen the occasional travelling player troupe perform in Stratford, and had himself performed in plays enacted at his school—an activity in which had greatly enjoyed—but this was the first time he had been in a proper London theatre, watching a play performed by the professional actors of the Earl of Leicester's Men.

How did it all work? The physical trappings of the theatre were simple enough—a few painted back-cloths, furniture placed artfully here and there and there were clearly many tricks that the performers used to simulate blood and gore, the sounds of wind and storm, even a simulated hanging. Yet with the use of these few prosaic tools, the actors managed to convince the spectators that they were not in cold London, but sunny Castile and the court of the King of Spain.

It was the words, he decided after a few moments of brow-furrowing thought, that were the key to it all, the deft use of phrase and poetry to convey the setting and the story. Without great words, the actors would merely be capering mummers, able to do no more than draw the crudest of emotions from their audiences.

23

Still applauding enthusiastically, he turned to his grouchy neighbour, intending to share his excitement. But that gentleman stood with arms crossed, apparently unmoved by the experience.

'I take it, sir,' Will shouted over the noise of the crowd, 'that you did not approve of the play? It was, perhaps, a little... extravagant?'

The young man turned his head and cocked it on one side as though he had only just noticed Will's existence.

'Not the play, sir. The play is a wonder. And its extravagance, as you call it, is its virtue. No, it is the *players* of whom I disapprove.'

Will's suddenly felt as if he was an unsophisticated rustic. Perhaps, in his enthusiasm, he had not seen the whole spectacle through sufficiently critical eyes.

As the crowd began to move out of the ring-shaped floor of the theatre towards the exits, Will fell into step beside his new acquaintance. 'Yet the performance seems to have pleased the crowd,' he gestured towards the throng, 'so surely it was not so bad?'

His companion sniffed, but his expression softened a little. 'You are, I think, new to the theatrical experience?'

Will laughed. 'New to London as well. I have seen travelling players at home, but none as accomplished as these.'

'Accomplished is not the word I would use. Workmanlike, perhaps, but no more. I am afraid the Earl of Leicester's Men are not what they were since their best players were purloined by the queen last year.'

Will was intrigued. 'Purloined? How so?'

'The story is an amusing one, but first, sir, can I enquire of your name?'

Will stuck out his hand. 'William Shakespeare, late of Stratford-upon-Avon in Warwickshire. I have been in London but two months.'

Taking the proffered hand, his companion introduced himself as Christopher Marlowe. 'But everyone calls me Kit.' He offered no further explanation of his origins or background.

By now, they had left the theatre and passed through a low brick wall; facing them was a ditch that served as a noisome common sewer, beyond which Finsbury Field, dotted with slowly-turning windmills, stretched into the distance.

Turning left, they began to walk down the muddy track south, back towards the city walls. They walked in companionable silence for a while, then Marlowe suggested that, since the day was yet young, they might repair

24

to a tavern for food and drink. Will was intrigued by his new companion, and readily agreed.

Passing through the city walls via the Moor-Gate and into the hubbub of the city proper, Kit led them towards a small tavern, low-browed and propped against the city wall. Inside, the main taproom was already filled with people, the air tangy with the smell of tobacco smoke, a new popular habit among London's citizens.

Finding a small table in a corner of the room that was relatively quiet, Kit waved over the serving girl and ordered ale, cheese and bread.

'So, the actors were "purloined"? How so? Surely they are free agents...'

Kit smiled a knowing smile that might have seemed condescending to anyone who did not possess Will's patient and courteous nature. Rather than taking offence, he simply waited, eyebrows raised, for his companion to elaborate.

'Court intrigue, Shakespeare, court intrigue. Two years ago, Her Majesty decided on some whim to set her various courtiers to compete for the honour of providing a company to play before her at Christmas. As you no doubt know, all London's theatrical troupes are sponsored by one lord or another, else the players could not survive.

'But the queen didn't count on the intensity with which her courtiers would pursue this honour, and before long the rivalry between the earls of Leicester and Oxford became particularly intense, even going to the extent of provoking street brawls between the supporters of the rival companies. This the queen would not tolerate, but in her own clever way, she solved the problem not by commanding that they desist, which would have underlined the competing tensions in her court, but by forming her own company.'

He paused, eyebrows raised, as if to make sure that Will was following the story. Satisfied that he had the full attention of his new friend, he went on.

'This was not something easy to achieve. The various actors were naturally reluctant to leave their own companies, you see, all of which performed to the public. Whereas the new company would only perform at court, and then only on special occasions. So the queen turned to Sir Francis Walsingham.'

Even rusticated William Shakespeare knew the name of the queen's principal Private Secretary, one of the most powerful men in England and, it was whispered, the head of the royal spy network.

'That does seem an odd task to give to the secretary,' he said.

Kit's knowing smile was back again. 'True. But Sir Francis is a most persuasive character, and bone-loyal to the monarch. So by dint of much arm twisting and gentle threats, Mister Secretary Walsingham lured the best actors away from their regular employers to form a new company, The Queen's Men.'

Taking a deep draft of ale, and wiping his mouth with a velvet-covered sleeve, Kit went on. 'The queen's gain is the general theatre's loss, for neither company has recovered from losing their best players. They are left with journeyman actors like those you saw today, mangling poor Tom Kyd's words and over-acting his scenes.'

That prompted Marlowe to launch into a detailed critique of the play they had just seen, explaining with some passion where the actors had gone wrong, how they had mispronounced lines, mangled the playwright's intentions, and bungled entrances and exits.

Will was fascinated by the torrent of theatrical knowledge that his new friend possessed, interrupting only occasionally to pose questions, each of which brought forth a new stream of commentary.

'It is clear, my friend,' he said when the conversation finally ran its course, 'that you have a deep acquaintanceship with the arts and crafts of the theatre, far beyond my poor comprehension! But I am indebted to you for your generosity in sharing your knowledge with me. I doubt I have learned so much in a single session since I left school.'

Kit was clearly pleased with this. 'It's true that I have had the opportunity to see many plays here in London, and so to sharpen my critical faculties, not to mention the chance to meet theatre folk, high and low. And I must confess, I have some aspirations to write for the stage myself.'

Will thought about his own efforts to create a play that lay languishing on his desk, buried under more recent scribblings. He had all but abandoned work on it, uncertain both of its merit and his ability, and so he said nothing of this to Kit, fearing ridicule in the face of that gentleman's more extensive knowledge of the craft, steering the conversation instead back to more conventional channels. 'How did you come to be in London, anyway, Kit?'

Marlowe looked at him and Will had the uncomfortable sensation that his new friend was debating with himself just how much he was willing to reveal. Then Marlowe's face creased into a grin. 'Actually, I should properly be in Cambridge, not London! I am studying for my degree at Corpus Christie College. But I fear I have been something of a trial to the masters of that august institution, and so I have taken a leave of absence. I know not who is more pleased with this arrangement, they or I!'

Which neatly evaded the question, Will thought. 'Is your family from Cambridge, then?' he asked, trying a new tack.

'No, no,' came the wry response. 'My father makes shoes in Canterbury. And before you ask,' he said, 'I am at Cambridge on a scholarship.'

So his new friend wasn't wealthy. Shakespeare's own family was hardly nobility, but his father did have a certain place in Stratford. Clearly Kit's family was poorer than his own. And yet his rich clothes and general air of comfort seemed to belie his origins. Surely he could not be living so well on the mean funds provided by a scholarship?

The more he got to know about Kit, the more he seemed to be an enigma.

'Marlowe! You whoreson, you're back among us, I see.'

These words, emitted at a bellow that turned heads across the room, emerged from an enormous red-haired man, dressed in clothes as homely as his plain and fleshy countenance, which was lit up in a broad smile that robbed his words of any offence.

The target of the greeting visibly winced as the giant dropped onto the bench and clapped an arm across his shoulder, inflicting what was no doubt meant to be a friendly squeeze, but must have felt more like being gripped by a bear. Will could hardly conceal his smile as Kit shot him a grimace before rearranging his features into a smiling look of long-suffering patience.

'And where,' he asked, when his captor finally released him, 'did you spring from, Greene? Have they emptied the gaols for the play season?'

The big man ignored this sally, leaping once again to his feet and waving his arm to beckon across a small group of young men standing in a knot near the entrance to the tavern. 'Lads, over here! See who's back from foreign parts.'

While the others shouldered their way through the crowded tap-room, Marlowe introduced Will to the giant.

'William Shakespeare, meet Robert Greene, sometime poet, gross flatterer of earls and dukes, but above all a scoundrel! I'd keep a firm hand on your purse, Will, while Greene is about.'

Greene bowed and laughed uproariously. 'At your service, Master Shakespeare. I trust you know young Kit well enough not to believe *everything* he says.'

27

Giving Will no chance to respond, Greene turned away to engage in a round of greetings with the trio of young men who had pushed their way across the room to their table and were settling onto the benches and stools arrayed around it. He had clearly decided he was to be the master of ceremonies and proceeded to introduce each of the newcomers.

'Rob Armin, Ned Alleyn, Rich Burbage, meet Master William Shakespeare, my deepest acquaintance of some two minutes! Marlowe, of course, you know well enough.'

The men nodded to Will in acknowledgement of Greene's introduction before turning their attention to Marlowe in a barrage of witty and ribald greetings, allowing Will a few moments to examine his new companions.

Robert Armin seemed more serious than the others. His dark face, which seemed oddly familiar to Will, contemplating the others with a slight frown, not of disapproval, but of concentration, as if competing with such witty companions was taxing his brain.

Alleyn and Burbage sat close together on a bench, both handsome, a little younger than the others; perhaps eighteen or nineteen, fresh-faced and flushed with the heat of the room, engaging confidently in the badinage that was by now flying back and forth across the table and its clutter of ale tankards.

'So why are you back from France so soon, Kit? Were the boys in Paris not to your taste?' This question, hurled at Marlowe by Richard Burbage, elicited laughter from the rest of the table and produced a coy smile from Kit, who seemed not at all put out.

'Pah! I am inexhaustible in that department, as *you* well know, Rich!'

Burbage gave a mock bow in response.

'But the pleasures of the flesh must of necessity be subordinated to the demands of business, which, being done, have led me home, the better to enjoy the dubious pleasures of this company.'

Digesting this exchange, which added two more pieces to the puzzle of Kit Marlowe, Will raised his eyebrows in a silent query, which Marlowe ignored as he turned to face Will. 'These gentlemen, if I can use the term loosely, belong to that strange fraternity of London's citizens called *actors*, although Burbage and Alleyn have barely graduated from playing women's parts. Look closely, my friend, at Armin. Does he not seem familiar?'

Recognition dawned on Will. 'Ah! You were our Hieronimo this day, if I mistake not?'

Armin inclined his head.

'And the only man on that stage who can carry a line.' Kit, in a single sentence, dismissed a performance that Will had rather enjoyed. 'Then well-met, sir,' he said, ignoring Kit's jibe. 'Certainly you seem in good spirits for a man who has just engaged in an orgy of murder, not to mention suicide.'

The words of the play formed in Will's head and, almost without realising he was doing so, he began to recite:

> *'Perhaps you think (but bootless are your thoughts)*
> *That this was fabulously counterfeit,*
> *And that we do as all tragedians do,*
> *We die today for acting out our scene,*
> *The death of Ajax, or some Roman peer,*
> *And, in a minute starting up again,*
> *Revive to please tomorrow's audience.'*

There was a moment's surprised silence, then Marlowe clapped his hands and burst out laughing. 'Well now, my friends,' he looked around the table, 'it may be that here is a new actor in the making. Not so many could have plucked such apt words from a play heard but a few hours hence, and pronounce them with natural skill.'

Shakespeare felt himself blushing, and looked ruefully at Armin. 'Kit flatters me; I have always had a good memory, it is true, but I am quite sure my delivery of the playwright's words does not begin to match your own.'

'Nay, but he is right; you obviously have a natural feel for the theatre,' Armin said with a smile. 'Perhaps you should consider taking up our strange profession? Although you will not make your fortune, I'll say that, unless you have the advantages of being born into theatre royalty, like Burbage here!'

That handsome young man inclined his head. 'Rob speaks true. I do have certain advantages, since my father built and owns the Theatre, the cockpit of Tom Kyd's drama today. But there is much more to acting than simply memorising lines and declaiming them with confidence. Our craft demands physical strength, agility, perseverance and the ability to wear women's clothes with style!'

Marlowe looked speculatively at Shakespeare. 'Now that is something I would like to see.'

'Hush now, Marlowe,' said the hitherto silent Ned Alleyn, coming to the rescue of the by now thoroughly red-faced Shakespeare, 'or else you'll be frightening poor Will away from the stage entirely.'

'I'm not so easily affrighted, I can assure you,' Will rallied. He looked around the circle of faces and felt a sudden rush of affection for them. He wished he could be part of such a group of friends, bound together in the service of an art that could create magic.

'In truth, after seeing the performance today, and meeting with you all, I am fired with a desire to learn much more about your craft. And to one day be up there on the stage with you, weaving your spells and earning everlasting fame.' That came out in something of a rush.

'If it's everlasting fame you want, Shakespeare, you'll not win it by parroting lines and jumping about on a stage to amuse the groundlings!' Greene had clearly been itching to re-join the conversation. 'Writing the words these monkeys speak, telling immortal tales of love and war and blood and revenge, that's the noblest aspect of our art, I say.'

The last words of this provocative speech were almost drowned in the outraged cries of the actors at this blasphemy, and there ensued a lively and incoherent argument about the relative merits of acting and writing, which Will followed with some amusement, finding himself in some sympathy with Greene.

Eventually, when the arguers had talked themselves to a standstill, peace was proclaimed and sealed with the order of another round of ale. Marlowe got to his feet and announced that it was time for him to leave. Will scrambled up also, for much as he was enjoying the company of these men, he was expected back at Ironmonger Lane before evening, which was now fast approaching.

Having made their farewells and extracted themselves from the tavern into the warm air of late afternoon, Kit and Will set off towards their respective lodgings, pledging to meet again in a few days' time.

Will watched his new acquaintance stagger off down the street, weaving expertly between pedestrians, animals and piles of refuse that created an obstacle course that would challenge a sober man. However, it seemed to present no difficulty at all to Kit even in his inebriated state. Marlowe's flamboyance was in contrast to his own sober-suited nature, yet somehow he felt sure they would become great friends.

Later, he found himself sitting at the small table in his garret room that served as a desk, rummaging by the light of a guttering candle through the

30

pile of half-completed, half-discarded poems and essays on which he had been working whenever his work with Richard Holbrooke allowed.

Ah! There it was. A sheaf of cheap paper covered in his rapid, almost illegible handwriting. It had started as a simple translation of Plautus' play, *The Menaechmi*, a tale of separated twins and the confusions that arise when, many years later, they are reunited.

It was a simple enough story, which he had begun translating from Latin to English back in Stratford, in bored or idle moments in the clerk's office or at home whenever he could snatch a few moments' peace in that noisy household. But the simple task of translation he found too easy, and before long he had amused himself by imagining new characters and plot twists.

The result of this intermittent labour was almost a new play, the original work nearly unrecognisable beneath the layers of his own invention. It wanted a new title—*A Comedy of Errors* might work—but on the whole he was dissatisfied with it, fearing it might be too clever, too artificial, and he had almost resolved to commit the whole thing to the flames. For who would be interested in a play by an unknown provincial named William Shakespeare?

As he sat and contemplated the offending pages, he found that his resolve was fired anew by the afternoon spent in the company of Marlowe and his friends. Greene's passionate defence of the importance and essential nobility of the work of the playwright had seemed to him to be as pompous as the man himself but it had struck a chord in Will's mind.

As he had listened to the arguments that had gone back and forth, it had occurred to him that neither Greene nor the actors were wholly right. It was obvious that the only way to achieve both fame *and* fortune in the theatre was to control the whole process from writing to production.

So that was what he would do. He would write great plays and he would produce them, present them, and act in them. Rather than destroy this manuscript, he would finish it, and one day he would see it performed. And it would be the first of many.

Chapter 4

London, June 1585

O ver the following weeks, Kit and Will saw each other whenever his work for Richard Holbrooke permitted, meeting in taverns, browsing the booksellers of St Paul's, or simply strolling the streets of London.

Will was fascinated by Kit, whose surface character of boyish energy and charm seemed purposely constructed to disguise the thoughtful and sensitive layer that lay below. His humorous stories about his travels abroad, laced with earthy and scurrilous anecdotes that frequently brought blushes to Will's face, were interspersed with more serious conversation, usually turning on philosophy and history.

But his greatest passion was the theatre, for which he said he was determined to write 'the greatest play England has ever seen'. It was an extraordinary ambition, it seemed to Will, for such a young man.

It was the theatre that had drawn them together again, for Kit had invited him to join Richard Burbage and his father, James, across the river in Southwark, where the latter was looking at possible sites for a new playhouse. They were accompanied by the raffish theatrical impresario, Phillip Henslowe.

The younger Burbage's habitual air of lazy superiority seemed to dissolve whenever he was with Kit, with whom he debated the merits or otherwise of the actors, playwrights, poems and performances of the London theatrical world.

It was a discourse inevitably punctured by some sharp and wicked comment of Marlowe's, which caused Burbage to collapse into a fit of

32

schoolboy giggles. He seemed almost to worship the older man, and Will wondered from time to time if they were or had been lovers.

Whether or not that was the case, it was clear to Will that this was an intimate friendship into whose territory he might be an unwelcome intruder. But Burbage seemed not at all put out, accepting Will's status as a friend of Kit's with an open heart, so they soon became easy companions; a trio of young literary aspirants. In fact, James Burbage had that very day promised him a position with his new company, on the enthusiastic urging of his son.

So it was in a cheerful mood that, having spent the morning tramping about the muddy fields and lanes that interspersed the low taverns, cook-shops, cockfighting rings and bawdy houses that gave Southwark its well-deserved reputation as a stew of iniquity and vice, Will and Kit approached the southern end of London Bridge.

As it was the only way of crossing the river on foot, the approach to the bridge was crowded with pedestrians, jostling, gossiping and grumbling their way towards the four-story gatehouse that marked the entrance to the bridge proper.

Although Will had visited virtually every other part of London over the last few months, he had not had any reason to visit the south bank of the Thames before that day. Crossing the bridge earlier in the morning, he had passed through the southern gate without giving it a moment's thought. Returning, however, the massive building caught his attention.

As his eye travelled upwards, he stopped in shock. For there, on spikes projecting from the second level at a height clearly visible to the mostly-indifferent crowd below, were half a dozen human heads. They were in various stages of decay, missing eyeballs, grey scraps of flesh still clinging to whitened bone, the wispy bedraggled hair on one looking like a ghastly wig.

Most of the faces were unknown to Will, but one, by some quirk, remained sufficiently recognisable to stop him in his tracks. Kit, chattering gaily beside him, had advanced a few steps before he realised that his friend was no longer alongside and turned, his eyebrows raised quizzically. 'What is it, Will? Never seen the fate of the queen's enemies before?'

Of course; the heads of convicted traitors, preserved with pitch, were always displayed and left to moulder on the gates of London Bridge as a warning to any other would-be conspirators. 'No, it's not that. It's just that... I know one of them.'

Kit sauntered back a few steps, and squinting in the sun, looked up at the grisly trophy rack. 'Which one? They all look pretty much the same to me.'

33

'The second from the left. Edward Arden.'

Kit slipped his hand under Will's arm. 'No point in standing here gawping like some countryman at his first fair.' He tugged on Will's arm to get him moving again into the throng. 'Let's walk and you can tell me how you come to know a traitor.'

Will felt a sudden spasm of alarm; uttering that word in a public place seemed somehow dangerous.

Kit guessed what was bothering his friend. 'Don't worry, Will. I've learned through long experience that sometimes the most confidential matters can be easily talked of in a crowd, for most men are too caught up in their own affairs to pay much attention to others.'

With that doubtful reassurance, Will breathed a small sigh. 'Edward Arden is... was related to my mother.'

'Ah,' was all Kit said as they worked their way along the cobbled road that paved the centre of the bridge. On either hand, shops and buildings towered six and seven stories high, blotting out the morning sunlight and adding to the chill that Will felt as he reflected on the tale that had ended with that rotting head impaled above the bridge gate. A story that was, in a way, the root cause of his present exile.

'Two years ago, was it not?' Kit said encouragingly, after Will had been silent for a minute or two.

'Yes. Edward was a distant relative of my mother. I remember him as being a kindly sort of fellow, a bit starchy and upright, but decent. He was also a Catholic, as are most of the Ardens, but he was like most of his faith, conforming to the laws, attending church regularly. Certainly he never said anything that I know of against the queen.'

'But he did harbour a Catholic priest, did he not? On his estate?'

'Yes, disguised as a gardener. God knows what tempted him to break the law like that: no doubt the priest was persuasive, as fanatics often are. Still, he might have got away with it were it not for his son-in-law, a simpleton called John Somerville. The priest started whispering in Somerville's ear, and before long the loon was wandering around the county waving a pair of pistols and telling everybody how he was going to go down to London and murder the queen.'

'Which didn't go unnoticed by the authorities.'

'No, of course not. He was arrested, charged with treason, and put to the question. In his extremity, he implicated his father-in-law in the plot, such as it was; Arden was arrested too, tried, and suffered a traitor's death.'

'And Somerville hanged himself in his prison cell. Yes, I remember now.'

As they stopped and stood aside to make way for a cart rumbling across the bridge, Will's thoughts flew back to the day that the news of Arden's death had arrived in Stratford. The whole affair had deeply shocked and divided Warwickshire, and had stirred its Protestants to a wave of fanaticism that resulted in the persecution and terrorisation of other branches of the Arden family, not to mention other prominent Catholics in the county, a persecution that had continued off and on over the last two years.

'It was a sham, you know,' Kit said, lowering his voice so that it became hard for Shakespeare to hear him above the hubbub of the crowd. 'Whatever Arden was guilty of, it wasn't treason. At worst, bad judgement and the ill-luck of having a dolt for a son-in-law. Were it not for the fanaticism of Tom Lucy, I doubt he would have been arrested, let alone convicted.'

At the mention of the name of his nemesis, Will started.

'How do you know of Sir Thomas Lucy? A mere country squire, however powerful in Warwickshire?'

Kit waved his hand in an airy gesture that dismissed Will's naivety.

'He is well known at court. Got rich by toadying up to his betters. He's also known to be the mouthpiece for the Earl of Leicester; no doubt Leicester was happy enough to let his hound dog off the leash.'

'But what would the earl have to gain by Arden's death?'

Kit shrugged. 'Power, of course. Though Leicester has had the confidence of the queen these many years, he is yet an insecure man by nature. As long as there are threats against the queen's person, even those as daft as Somerville's, there will be opportunities for her courtiers to cement their favour with the monarch by being diligent in foiling them.

'Somerville was never really much threat to the queen, and Arden was none, but their "plot" could be used to maintain fear at court and in the country, and where there is fear, there is the opportunity for advantage to those who can be seen to be to be most ardent in protecting our state and our queen.'

Not for the first time, Will was struck by the ease with which Marlowe talked about affairs of state and about the court, as if he knew the actors therein well. Unexpectedly, he felt an urge to confide in Marlowe.

'Sir Thomas Lucy is why I left Stratford,' he said.

Kit did not respond, except to glance across with an encouraging look, and so Will poured out the whole story, cousin Robbie's anger at the latest attack on his family by Lucy, the scurrilous poem, the unpleasant interview with the bombastic knight, and his flight from Stratford to London.

Shouldering their way through the throng, the pair were silent again until they emerged at the far end of the bridge, back into the sunlight. Kit took Will's arm again, drawing him aside from the crowd into a small and deserted alley between the buildings. 'Will, I must tell you that you may be in some danger still.'

Will frowned. Surely London was far enough away from Warwickshire to be out of trouble. His friend's bald assertion, delivered in an urgent and conspiratorial undertone, seemed incredible. How could Kit know such a thing? And was he, once again, over-dramatizing?

These thoughts chased themselves through his mind and across his face; though he had said nothing, Kit saw his hesitation and continued. 'I have seen... documents that contain lists of names of those who are being actively watched by the royal intelligence service.'

He was hesitant, uncharacteristically feeling his way. Will had the sense there was something that his friend wanted to tell him, but was holding back. 'And?'

'And your cousin's name is one of those on the list. Oh, I doubt there is anything he has done wrong enough to warrant his arrest as yet, but Walsingham's spies are rewarded for information and sometimes they are none too scrupulous about the veracity of their reports when in pursuit of those rewards.'

'How,' Will asked slowly, 'do you know these things?'

'I suppose I had to tell you at some point, if we are to be friends.' Kit sighed. 'I work for Walsingham myself, as an Intelligencer.'

Some of the mystery that was Kit Marlowe dissolved in Shakespeare's mind. *This* was why Kit could afford to dress as well as he did, to spend money as freely as he did, and why he had been travelling abroad—no doubt on business for Master Secretary.

His mouth must have fallen agape as he absorbed this information, for Kit hastened to reassure him, seemingly anxious to deflect any possibility of disapproval. 'We are not all venal and crooked. Walsingham employs many capable, even brilliant, people to direct his network of intelligencers, and most behave with honour. I myself am held, I believe, in high esteem by the secretary. As you have no doubt guessed, my recent journey to France was on his business.'

This last was delivered with some self-satisfaction, and it was clear to Will that, far from being ashamed of his shadow occupation, he was proud of it.

Will could bear it no longer. Laughter bubbled up and burst forth as he fully comprehended the wondrous vision of Marlowe—popinjay, sodomite, sometime poet, associate of actors and thieves—in the refined and serious company of the Puritan Sir Francis Walsingham.

Kit's face betrayed a moment of offence, but then he too started laughing. 'I know, I know.' He threw his hands up. 'I do seem an unlikely sort of spy. But there again, is that not the best kind?'

'Indeed. But tell me, Kit, why you think *I* might be in danger?'

Marlowe tipped his head to one side in a gesture that Will was coming to know was characteristic when he was considering something serious. 'I don't know that for certain. But Sir Thomas Lucy, though he is a self-important braggart of a man, is both a fanatic and a terrier when he sinks his teeth into the behind of a recusant.

'He does not yet know that Arden's name is on the list that I saw, but he will soon enough, and then I have no doubt he will use it as an excuse to further persecute your cousin. In that pursuit, he may well extend his reach to you, here in London. Don't be fooled, he has some considerable influence at court.'

It all seemed a little far-fetched to Will, but the caprices of the nobility could not be entirely ignored. Queen Elizabeth had been on the throne since 1558, nearly thirty years; longer than Will had been alive, yet still there were real plots against her life. And the eternal enmity of the Catholic world towards England ensured that her polity lived against a background of fear and threat. In such a world, suspicion became second nature to the guardians of the realm.

He, like his father, had always been staunchly Protestant and had never given any cause for even a fanatic like Lucy to doubt his loyalty, but the fact of his mother's Catholicism could easily be used as a weapon against him.

'Curse him. He will hound me to my grave.' His voice shook with uncharacteristic anger. 'What can I do? I have fled Warwickshire to London. Am I to run yet again? And where on earth could I go?'

Kit rummaged in his purse for a stub of pencil and a piece of paper. Leaning against the wall, he scribbled out an address. 'Meet me here, at my lodging, two days hence at eleven in the morning. That will give me some time to make deeper enquiry into this business, and determine whether you are really in any danger. We can decide then what is the best course for you.'

Will looked at the paper. It was an address in Seething Lane, at the other end of the city. He slipped it into the pocket of his doublet. At least he would know in a few days' time whether this supposed threat to his liberty was real or just the fevered product of Kit's over-imaginative brain. He hoped and prayed that the latter was the case, even as he stammered his thanks to his friend for his promised help.

They slipped out of the alley and as they re-joined the throng, Kit took his hand, gripping his elbow with the other hand in a gesture of intense friendship. 'My friend, rest assured that I will be diligent in your interest. If there is any hint, any at all, that you should leave London, you will know in plenty of time to take action. And remember, if you need help, I know many people in low places as well as high! And the former are often more useful than the latter.'

On that point, Will had no doubt that Kit spoke truly.

Chapter 5

S urely this cannot be where Kit lives, Will thought as he stood before a large three-storied house on Seething Lane in the shadow of the Tower of London, whose battlements he could see looming above the rooftops.

He had imagined Kit lodging in some squalid garret above a cook-shop, not living in a fine house like this. He scratched his head and peered again at the short note that Kit had scribbled out a few days ago. No, he had not made a mistake. This was the place named in the note.

He walked up to the big black door and was about to grasp the imposing brass door knocker when Kit's voice emerged from the heights above him. 'Wait there, Will. I am coming down!'

Craning his head, Will was just in time to see his friend's head disappear behind a dormer window, the shutters of which closed after him with a resounding bang.

A moment later, a breathless Marlowe threw open the door, and with a grand sweep, a bow and an ironic grin, he ushered Shakespeare into the house.

'Welcome to my present place of abode,' Kit said, grasping his guest's arm and propelling him up a staircase that materialised out of the gloomy and oddly quiet interior of the house.

Two flights of stairs, and they entered a small but sparsely furnished room overlooking the mounting-yard at the rear of the house. A narrow bed occupied one wall, and the surface of the desk that was propped up against the window was almost invisible under the untidy jumble of paper, pens, ink, paperweights, and a few well-thumbed books; all the familiar detritus of a working writer. The only other furniture in the room was a small stool, presently covered with a pile of clothes that Kit hastily swept to the floor to enable Will to sit, while he himself perched on the edge of the bed.

'Your present place of abode?' Will asked. 'Are you planning on moving somewhere else?'

'Not for the moment but it doesn't pay to become too attached to any single place, I find. Nor to possessions. Poets should be free of such things, for we dwell in the marble palaces and among the gilded furniture of the kingdoms of the mind, do we not?'

Will ignored this piece of high-flown rhetoric. 'The mind's kingdom, however splendid, pays no rent nor puts victuals on the table! For that, poets are like all men—dependant on their patrons if their talents do not produce an income in any other way. So am I correct in supposing that this very earthly mansion is in fact the home of some patron misguided enough to think you worth supporting?'

'Not exactly my patron. My employer would be a better description,' Kit said, a sly smile on his face.

'Your employer...?' Will's mouth dropped open as he realised who this must be. 'Sir Francis Walsingham? This is the home of the queen's principal secretary?'

'Yes, Sir Francis has been most kind in allowing me a room in his house while I am in London. Though how long that will be is moot, for I am likely to be sent abroad again soon on some mission for the secretary whose nature he has not, as yet, disclosed to me.'

The clatter of horse hooves in the yard drew them both to the window, where they watched as a party of richly-dressed men dismounted, handing their reins to the waiting grooms before disappearing into the house.

'They're back,' said Kit. 'Sir Francis has been at Westminster Palace all morning, dancing attendance on Her Majesty.'

The house, hitherto silent as the sepulchre, now filled with noise as the members of the household returned to their allotted working places and resumed their duties.

'Come, Will. Sir Francis said we were to go to him the instant he returned from court.'

'*We?* What have you told him of me, Kit?' This was far more than Will had bargained for when he had confided his worries to his friend the day before. He was unprepared for an interview with one of the most powerful men in England, a man who could protect him or who could as easily send him to prison, if not worse.

'You worry too much. Sir Francis is sympathetic to your plight and willing to give you a hearing. Come, come, he doesn't like tardiness.'

40

Kit grasped Will's arm, hauled him to his feet, and towed him down the stairs once more. Along a wood-panelled corridor, a door opened into a sort of workroom, occupied by three desks, from behind which three industrious heads shot up to examine the newcomers.

'Is he in?' Kit enquired of the room in general, nodding towards yet another door set into the further wall.

One of the three wise men nodded; a blonde fellow wearing eye-glasses that made the orbs behind them seem unnaturally huge. 'Yes, and he is expecting you. But for God's sake, don't vex him, Marlowe. His stomach is giving him trouble.'

Kit assumed a look of innocence. 'And when did I ever vex him, Phelippes? You are overly solicitous, I think.'

This earned Kit a cold stare, which was ostentatiously ignored.

Kit knocked once on the door, and pushed it open without waiting for a response, walking in with the air of one who is confident of his welcome. Will hesitated, but Phelippes' shooing motion left him with little choice but to follow.

The room beyond the door was spacious and generously proportioned. Dust motes danced in the shafts of light emitted by two tall windows facing out onto the lane below.

At one end of the room was a large and imposing black wooden desk piled high with neat stacks of files and papers held down by paperweights of varying sizes and descriptions. Behind the desk was a plain wooden chair, presently unoccupied, and behind the chair stood large, neatly crammed bookshelves, mirrored by their twins at the other end of the room.

The wall opposite the windows was covered with maps and charts of all the countries of Europe and the New World, dense with detail. Turkish carpets, the only luxury in an otherwise plainly decorated room, covered the wooden floorboards.

Ranged along the wall under the windows were a series of wooden chests, over one of which the tall, cadaverous form of Sir Francis Walsingham was bent, peering at a paper he had just retrieved from its interior.

At the sound of the opening door, the secretary straightened and turned, a look of irritation on his narrow face. 'Marlowe! Come in, come in, don't stand there letting in the draught. I feel the cold more than I used to, unlike you young men. And you, I assume, are Master William Shakespeare?'

'Yes, Sir Francis, at your service.'

41

'Well,' said the queen's principal secretary, 'we shall see whether you can be of service in due course. Marlowe seems to think so, else you wouldn't be here. Sit.'

Will and Kit settled themselves onto a couple of stools facing the desk, behind which Sir Francis settled himself, fingers steepled as he contemplated his two visitors.

Returning the older man's gaze with an open and frank expression that he hoped would disguise his nervousness, Will beheld a man in early middle age, forehead etched with frown lines carved by the weight of state business and piercing blue eyes somewhat sunken into their sockets; a man for whom sleep might not come easily. The neat beard and luxuriant moustache were flecked with streaks of grey, though the hair on his head remained pure black.

For such an exalted courtier, he was surprisingly simply dressed, in the Puritan style—a black fur-collared gown over black doublet and white shirt. His appearance seemed to say that, for this man, the exercise of power was more important than its display.

'You seem to have got yourself into a spot of trouble, Shakespeare,' Sir Francis said, breaking a silence that was long enough to be uncomfortable, at least for Will, though Kit seemed entirely untroubled, his gaze roaming around the room; a vacant, beatific smile on his face.

'Not, I assure you Sir Francis, of my own making,' Will said.

The secretary picked up a paper from the desk, holding it close to his face in order to read. 'Sir Thomas Lucy says that you spread libellous poems intended to diminish his authority in the county, that you associate with known Catholic malcontents, and that your loyalties are entirely suspect. Your mother is of course a Catholic, and a member of the family of a proven traitor.'

He replaced the paper on the desk, and resumed his examination of the young man sitting opposite him. 'Marlowe, on the other hand, says that the poetry in question was so poor that it could not fail to have disappeared without trace, and is unlikely to have any seditious effect whatsoever, even among the weak-minded gentry of Warwickshire, so I am sure we can discard that charge without any further thought.'

Will was not sure he was pleased with the offhand way with which his poetical talents were thus disposed; but then perhaps it was better to be perceived as a poor poet than as a traitor.

The secretary's mildly amused expression hardened, however, as he picked up another piece of paper. The blue eyes, hitherto genial, now seemed cold and intimidating. 'Your cousin's activities, I am sorry to say, cannot be so easily dismissed. Robert Arden has, it seems, been making a nuisance of himself and has been widely reported as uttering remarks that are critical of the queen's justice and government.'

Poor Robbie, Will thought, *no doubt his resentment at the world has bubbled up to the surface once too often in the wrong place and at the wrong time.* 'Knowing my coz, Sir Francis, I am sure he was deep in his cups whenever these remarks were made. Catholic he might be, but I would warrant my life that he is loyal.'

'That may be, Master Shakespeare, that may well be. But he has an unfortunate name, and in these dangerous times such murmurings cannot help but be seen as rebellious. This document is a copy of the warrant for his arrest, issued by Sir Thomas Lucy, and by now no doubt fully executed. Your cousin is, I expect, incarcerated as we speak.'

Will shifted on his stool, glanced sideways at Kit, who seemed to have developed a fascination with the wooden beams of the ceiling, then returned his gaze back to the secretary.

'I am sorry to hear that, Sir Francis, but I hope I may trust to English justice to ensure that my cousin is fairly treated.' He had no faith in any such thing, but there was little else he could say. 'I do not understand, however, what his supposed misdemeanours have to do with me? After all, I have not been in Warwickshire these last three months.'

'That is true, and just as well it is so, for I have little doubt that Sir Thomas would by now have you in prison as well. No doubt your foolish cousin can be induced to confess to some sort of charge, and then you would have been indicted as a co-conspirator.'

'But it was Sir Thomas himself who drove me out of Warwickshire,' Will objected. 'Surely it would have served his scheme better if I had remained in Stratford?'

'I cannot explain that. Perhaps he simply lost his temper and forgot what he was about: your little piece of doggerel appears to have incensed him beyond all restraint. Can't understand such extravagant passions myself, but there you are. Unfortunately for you, Lucy is Leicester's lapdog, and his yapping cannot be entirely ignored.'

'And so my name appears on a list,' Will said gloomily.

43

'And so your name appears on a list,' Walsingham repeated. 'A list of men to be watched, men suspected of treason and therefore to be arrested on any excuse that will stand up in the courts.'

Another intimidating silence ensued, during which Will contemplated his predicament, as no doubt the secretary intended.

'Young man,' Walsingham said, before Will could gather his wits to respond, 'tell me how much you know about your father's affairs.'

This was an unexpected tack, and Will was momentarily confused. 'He does well enough,' he said cautiously. 'His trade has suffered somewhat in recent years, it is true, and he has been compelled to retire from public office so as to devote all his energies to it. But things have improved this year. He has been able to employ two new seamstresses and an apprentice. He earns enough to support us all.'

'He has also been pursued through the courts on a number of occasions, has he not?'

'Yes. But the charges were baseless, and seemed motivated by ill-wishers, as the court found.'

Walsingham nodded, seeming satisfied. He picked up a paper on his desk and looked at it briefly, as if to refresh his memory as to its contents, before returning his attention to Will, who was by now feeling thoroughly discomfited.

'Those charges were indeed without foundation. But the men who brought them did so at the bidding of Sir Thomas Lucy.'

'But why would Sir Thomas do such a thing? He claims to be on good terms with my father.'

'Because, according to my reports, your father owes Sir Thomas Lucy a great deal of money.'

Understanding dawned for Will. About a year before, when his father's fortunes were at their nadir, he had come home one day and his habitual gloom seemed to have evaporated. He would not tell anyone why he was so cheerful, but from that day forward his father's business had improved.

It now seemed obvious that John Shakespeare had swallowed his pride and dislike of Sir Thomas Lucy, and had gone cap in hand seeking a loan. No doubt he had offered the house in Henley Street as security.

'So if I were to be arrested and charged with treason,' Will said, bitter anger welling up and threatening to overwhelm him, 'Sir Thomas would use that as an excuse to call in his loan, and since the funds have all been laid out in the business, my father would be ruined and my family would be without a home.'

'No doubt that is Sir Thomas' intention.' Walsingham's tone conveyed a weariness with the sad manipulations of lesser men.

The plan concocted by the Lord of Charlecote depended entirely on Will's being charged on this accusation of treason, flimsy though it was. Clearing his name was paramount but he knew that this would be difficult without the intervention of someone powerful, such as Mr Secretary Walsingham; intervention that would not come without a price. It was time for him to discover what that price would be.

'Sir Francis, you are a busy man, and I doubt you would have taken time to see me if you did not have some means of releasing me from the coils of this dilemma, in return for which, I make no doubt, you will require something from me.'

Walsingham smiled, though Will felt no reassurance from that. *Thus the wolf might smile,* he thought, *before devouring the lamb.*

'You are right, of course. Ordinarily, I would not have spent a moment considering such a case, particularly since doing so might well offend my lord of Leicester, with whom I must work in harmony for the safety of the realm. But you are as fortunate in your choice of friends as you are unfortunate in your relatives. Christopher here has been of good service to me in the past, and because he has asked me to do so, I agreed to at least hear you out.'

Kit, losing interest in the ceiling, returned his attention to the conversation, a bright smile on his face.

Will gave his friend a look of gratitude, and turned back to Walsingham, determined to make his case as forcefully as he could. 'Sir Francis, what can I do other than to protest my loyalty to the country and to the queen? It is true that I am half a Catholic, but it was not so long since all England was wholly Catholic. What man is there in England who can say that he and his family have always been on the right side of these religious questions, except that he be guilty of hypocrisy and cant?

'Her Majesty says she does not want to see into men's souls, and in that she is wise. I am a loyal Englishman, and have ever been so. Yet what kind of England would it be where a man can be thrown into gaol on trumped-up charges simply because he has by some piece of poetry offended a minor lordling? Do the laws of England count for nothing?' Out of breath, and out of words, Will fell silent.

45

Walsingham considered him impassively, and he sensed Kit shifting on his stool to look at his friend with a new eye. 'A most passionate speech, Master Shakespeare.' The secretary's voice was amused. 'Perhaps Christopher is right—maybe you do have the makings of a dramatist in you. Certainly you have convinced me.'

Will heaved an inner sigh of relief. Perhaps, after all, this gamble of Kit's would pay off.

'Even so,' Walsingham went on, seeming to dash Will's moment of hope, 'I cannot, I am afraid, simply wave a wand, Merlin-like, and wash your name off this infamous list of Leicester's. I have a certain amount of credit with the earl, but it must be hoarded against the day I need it for some important bargain that affects the weal of England, not bartered for the welfare of some minor countryman.'

Shakespeare might be a countryman, but he was no fool, and he knew when a bargain was being sought, even if it was unspoken. 'Sir Francis, I know I am of little value in myself, but perhaps if there is some service I can carry out that benefits the state? Something that you can put in the balance, so to speak?'

The secretary raised an eyebrow, his forefinger twitching slightly to tap the black surface of the desk once, twice.

'Perhaps, Sir Francis, you might consider employing Will as an intelligencer or maybe as a courier?' Kit said, startling Will, who had momentarily forgotten his friend's presence. 'Only yesterday Master Phelippes was bemoaning the shortage of well-educated and intelligent men upon whom we can rely. Master Shakespeare may not have a university education, but he is lettered and capable, and quick of wit.'

'That would at least enable me to argue that you are in my employ, and therefore beyond the Earl's remit,' Walsingham said a little too quickly. The suspicion dawned on Will that these two, experienced conspirators that they were, might well have collaborated to place him in a position where he had no choice but to comply. 'Yes, that might serve. But I must think on what mission might be suitable to ensure that Leicester does not push the point too hard. What say you, Master Shakespeare?'

What could Will say? 'Sir Francis, I will serve in whatever capacity I can, though I have no skills as an intelligencer. Indeed, I do not even know what those skills are. But if I am to have a future at all, it seems I have little option but to agree to your proposal.'

46

'Come, Shakespeare, don't be gloomy.' The secretary was suddenly all smiles again. 'The dark arts of intelligencing are not so difficult. After all, even Christopher here has managed to learn them! And Phelippes can teach you all you need to know. You seem to be a shrewd fellow, even if you don't have the advantage of the university education that Marlowe prizes so much, though I have met enough prancing fools who have attended such institutions to know that possessing a degree is no guarantee of intelligence, nor of integrity. Anyway, I am sure you will learn everything you need to know in no time.'

Will could do nothing other than nod. The prey was ensnared and hooked, and further struggle was pointless.

'Now,' the secretary went on, brisk and business-like, 'you will come here daily for an hour or two. You will study our methods of communication, the use of codes and ciphers and such-like—Phelippes is our expert on these matters—and when you have achieved proficiency, we will see what more specific task you can undertake to further the interests of the realm and keep you from the clutches of Thomas Lucy and Robin Leicester! Now, away with you both. I have spent more than enough time on you as it is.'

With a wave, they were thus abruptly dismissed, leaving the secretary's office with a sketchy bow that he half acknowledged, as he glanced down at the papers in front of him.

Back in the antechamber, Kit slapped Will on the back with a force surprising in one so slightly built. 'There you are, Will. I told you it would be all right.'

'Aye, though I have the sense that I have been rescued from the fire in order to be deposited in the frying pan. And that is quite a performing troupe the two of you have going. You should both be on the stage.'

Kit pouted. 'Come now, Will, that is hardly grateful of you! An hour ago you were in danger of being thrown into gaol. Now, here you are, employed by Sir Francis Walsingham no less, and free as a bird. Surely your state has improved considerably as a result of my intervention?'

Will could never remain annoyed for long, and he immediately relented. Though he was certain he had been gulled, he recognised that his friend's motives were honest. And, as Kit said, he was free. So he smiled and embraced him in a hug that probably startled that young man.

'Lord! Don't tell me we have another sodomite in our midst.' That came in an aristocratic drawl from one of the three men whose work in the antechamber had been interrupted by their appearance. Shakespeare felt his

47

cheeks flood and his body tense in anger as he turned towards the offending source of these remarks.

He was about to make a hot retort when he was restrained by Kit's grip on his arm.

'Is that any way to talk to a new colleague, Walter Williams?' Kit purred, his voice soft and controlled in that register Will knew presaged the delivery of a lethal barb. 'Sodomite or no—and no is the answer for your pathetic and prurient mind—Master Shakespeare here is new-appointed by the secretary himself to carry out missions of great importance to the realm, more than has ever been vouchsafed to you, I'll be bound.

'Pay him no mind, Will, he has the soul of a clerk, no more, and he speaks an infinite deal of nothing.' Kit raised his hand and clicked his fingers, as though to dismiss the young aristocrat into thin air.

'Why, you... you popinjay!' spluttered Walter Williams.

'Enough, you two!' This was barked by the tall and thin blonde man who, Shakespeare remembered, was named Phelippes, and who was clearly the master of the workroom. 'We all have enough work to do without having to listen to the yapping of puppies having a quarrel. Master Shakespeare, you are welcome to our fraternity. Sir Francis told me he was expecting you to join us. Come, sit with me and we will begin your instruction. In the meantime, Marlowe, I am sure you have some task or another that needs your immediate attention?'

With a shrug and a grin at Will, Kit turned and left the workroom, managing to knock over a pile of papers perched on the corner of Williams' desk as he did so.

Phelippes sighed. 'Sometimes, Shakespeare, I feel as though I am the ringmaster at a particularly unruly bear-baiting. Now, let us get to work...'

So William Shakespeare Esquire, recently of Stratford-upon-Avon, lawyer's clerk, merchant's apprentice and aspiring poet, became an intelligencer in the household of Sir Francis Walsingham, the queen's chief spy.

Chapter 6

London, August 1585

L ondon was oppressed by a sweltering heat wave that year, and the house
in Seething Lane was sufficiently warm that, for once, there was no need
for the fires that habitually burned in every fireplace for the comfort of its
owner, who felt the cold more keenly than did other men.

Will, doublet loosened and opened as a concession to the warmth, was
slowly and carefully deciphering one of the many coded messages that were
daily delivered by various hands into the workroom that he now shared with
the other three clerks.

Over the last month, he had gradually found himself spending more and
more of his time there, making his excuses to a bemused but tolerant Richard
Holbrooke, to whom he had told the whole story; the merchant had been
surprised, but could hardly object to releasing his erstwhile clerk to work for
one of the most powerful men in the kingdom.

Pausing in his work, he wondered what it was that drew him here, apart
from the obvious fact that the more time Will spent in the direct employ of
Sir Francis Walsingham, the safer he was. There was a certain fascination in
the work itself. Thomas Phelippes, patient and surprisingly kind, had
instructed him in the various coding and deciphering techniques on his first
day, and he had quickly mastered the basic codes.

Sensing his pupil's aptitude, the chief cryptographer had then moved him
on to the more complex ciphers used for encoding the most secret messages,
and soon began to allocate some of the simpler deciphering work to him; for
practice, he said. In truth, the little office was overwhelmed with the sheer

volume of correspondence that flowed in, and Phelippes seemed happy to have an additional pair of hands to deal with it.

But it was proximity to power that really intrigued him. He was fascinated by the way in which power was employed in this place so near the heart of the government of England, how the warp and weft of England's statecraft was woven into a whole. He could see it in glimpses in the documents that crossed his work table, in the daily chatter of his work colleagues and the occasional remarks of Sir Francis as he passed through the room.

That day, the tenth of August 1585, all the talk in the workroom was of Antwerp, England's most important trading partner across the channel, now under siege by the forces of the Duke of Parma, King Phillip of Spain's lieutenant and commander in the Netherlands. He had been placed there to put down the revolt of the Protestant Northern Dutch provinces that had dragged on for nearly five years. Its fall, long-forecast, now seemed imminent.

The chatter and speculation was silenced as the main door opened to admit Sir Francis, accompanied by his cousin, Sir Thomas Walsingham, a handsome and dashing young man who was one of the secretary's most trusted lieutenants.

After a few final words, the younger Walsingham departed for his own part of the great house and the secretary cast his eye around the room. 'Shakespeare, Phelippes, if you please.' The command, unusually peremptory, caused the two men to scramble to their feet and follow their master into the inner office.

'Now, Thomas,' Sir Francis said as soon as they were all settled, 'how does Shakespeare here progress? Is he ready to take on further tasks for us?'

Phelippes was brisk. 'Will has mastered admirably the basic codes and is making excellent progress with the superior codes. We have not yet broached the subject of secret writing and disguisement, which is the next stage of his instruction.'

Sir Francis considered this, then nodded, as if deciding something.

He swivelled his gaze towards the subject of this assessment. 'Master Shakespeare, what I have to tell you must remain secret, though God knows it will be public enough before long. But for now, you must tell no one, on pain of your life. You understand me?'

This was a Walsingham that Shakespeare had not hitherto encountered—steely and frightening. Will nodded, feeling no words were necessary to convey his humble obedience.

'Very well, then. You know the situation at Antwerp?'

Will nodded. He also knew well enough the political problem that the siege presented, for though England's common people were in favour of intervening to support their Protestant cousins across the sea, the government was afraid of provoking a reaction from the league of Catholic countries led by Spain, who looking for any excuse to declare a holy war. And so the queen and her ministers had pursued a policy of steadfast indecision.

'It is now certain,' Walsingham went on, 'that the city will fall to the Spaniards within days. As a consequence, Her Majesty has decided that we can no longer stand by and watch as our Protestant cousins are crushed, and therefore she has this morning, at her Palace of Nonsuch, affixed her seal to a treaty of amity and support for the United Provinces. Undoubtedly the King of Spain, when he hears of it, will regard this as a declaration of war.'

'And Philip must respond,' murmured Phelippes, 'for he cannot allow the Dutch to be reinforced by our armies when the Duke of Parma is so close to victory.'

'Quite so, Thomas. Where and how he will respond, that is the question, which the queen will look to me to answer. So, gentlemen, we must mobilise all our resources to find out. I must know what the King of Spain is going to do before he knows it himself. And that, Shakespeare, is why you are going to Italy.'

Will's jaw dropped open and he forced himself to shut it so as to avoid looking like a complete fool.

Phelippes had the look on his face that he always got when a small puzzle has been solved to his satisfaction. He raised an eyebrow. 'Ah. Venice.'

When Sir Francis nodded, Phelippes turned to Will. 'How much do you know about Venice, Will?'

'Not very much. That she has a great trading empire, and that she is governed as that strange and rare beast—a Republic. And that the city floats on water! Beyond that, I know little.'

'The city is indeed a Republic.' Phelippes nodded. 'La Serenissima, the Serene Republic, she styles herself. But more importantly, Venice remains the only power on the Italian peninsula that is not dominated by Spain. King Philip is also King of Naples, whose territory stretches from that city to the tip of Sicily; Tuscany is an imperial fief, ruled by a puppet duke who is married to Philip's cousin. Spain has governed Milan for the last twenty-five years, and Genoa, though an independent republic in form, is also the King of Spain's principal banker since he sent the Fuggers broke, back in '57. And what banker will go against his client?

'Only Venice, commanding the islands and coasts of the Adriatic and possessing a substantial land-empire, is free of Spanish influence.'

Will nodded, and Sir Francis, with a small gesture of his hand, indicated that Phelippes should carry on.

'So Venice is independent. But to maintain that independence, she cannot rely solely upon her soldiers and sailors, for maintaining a sufficient standing army and navy is a ruinous business, even for the Venetians. So they ever seek to bolster their position by diplomacy. Venice maintains diplomatic missions in all the great capitals of Europe, from which the doge and his Signoria acquire knowledge and influence.'

'Your explanation of Venetian policy is eloquent, Thomas,' Will said, a little bemused but also a little impatient. 'But I still do not see what this all has to do with me, or with this sudden need for me to go there.'

'It is simple,' Walsingham said. 'Until six months ago, we had been in receipt of regular dispatches from an agent who has been serving our interests in Venice for many years. In particular, he has been providing us with information originating from the Papal Curia. Of course, Her Majesty does not maintain any formal embassy in Rome, and so we are reliant on, shall we say, less formal sources of information, such as our man in Venice.

'But I have had nothing from him in months. That may signify nothing, for he might simply have had nothing to report or it may be that his reports have gone astray for some reason. It can be a chancy business, getting dispatches across Europe. In any case, I need someone reliable to go to Venice, find him and deliver new instructions in the light of our change of policy.'

That seems simple enough, Will thought. He wasn't much more than a courier, though he could understand why these instructions could not simply be sent using one of the many private courier services that were routinely used to send letters back and forth across the continent. 'And if I undertake this mission, can I be assured that my difficulties with the Earl of Leicester will be resolved?'

'Naturally. You are protected for as long as you are working here in Seething Lane, and I think I can ensure that your name is cleared in your absence... assuming, of course that you carry out your instructions to my satisfaction.'

Will ignored the implied threat in those words. 'And though I am loath to raise the subject of money, I fear that I must do so. I have, as you must know, a wife and three children at home in Stratford who must be cared for, and I doubt my employer will continue to pay me if I am to abandon even the pretence of working for him.'

An impatient look flitted across Walsingham's narrow face. 'This too will be taken care of. Thomas, I desire some privy words with Master Shakespeare, if you please. We shall talk later.'

Thus dismissed, Phelippes rose and nodded, laying a friendly hand on Will's shoulder as he departed.

When he had gone, Sir Francis contemplated Will, a small smile on his lips. 'William, I know I am asking a great deal of you, and that you probably feel you have been manipulated into a position where you have no choice but to agree to whatever I demand, but I assure you that I would not do so were not the stakes so high.'

Will did not know if he was more startled by the secretary's use of his given name, which was the first time he had ever addressed him in such familiar terms, or by the solicitous tone of voice, which was uncharacteristic in this most spare of men.

'Sir Francis, you are a man of great power, and I am a mere glover's son and would-be poet. Were it not for the unjust calumnies that have been heaped against my reputation, our paths would not, I think, ever have crossed. But I am grateful for the protection you have afforded me, and if I can repay you by undertaking this service I will do so willingly.'

'Very well then,' Walsingham said. 'We understand each other. But there is one further aspect to this, exercise that I have not yet mentioned.'

Will sat a little straighter on his stool, wondering what new twist the old fox was going to impose on him.

'I have in my care a young man; my ward in all except the legal sense. He is the bastard by-blow of the late Earl of Sussex, born as the result of a liaison with the daughter of an Italian musician attached to the court. The earl was fond of the boy, and after his mother died some years ago, paid for him to be raised and educated.

'When Sussex himself died, the earldom passed to his brother, Henry, with whom I have been friends for many years. The new earl did not feel he could continue to support his brother's bastard son publicly, since he has a son of his own, so he asked me to take on this duty out of friendship and respect for his brother's memory.'

Will nodded, once again surprised by glimpse into the human side of his pseudo-employer, whose chilly exterior did not routinely invite confidences.

'Over the two years that he has been in my care, I have become fond of young Tomaso, though he mostly goes by the name of Tom, to be at ease with English society. He is a fine young man, well set up and well-educated, thanks to his father and myself, and he is ready to go to university.

'But he is, I think, somewhat restless. He has expressed a desire of late to see the country of his birth, and it occurred to me that I might knock over two skittles with one ball, as it were.'

'Let me guess. You want me to accompany him to Italy as his, what, tutor? So that he can study at some Italian university?'

Walsingham clapped his hands. 'You have it exactly. And your role as Tom's tutor will provide the perfect disguise for your other tasks. Two skittles with one ball.' This last was uttered with a degree of smug self-satisfaction.

Will wasn't quite so pleased that he, a greybeard of twenty-one years, should suddenly be required to act the tutor and presumably guardian to a ward of Walsingham's no matter how well set up he might be. Young men, he well knew, had a habit of getting into scrapes, and he did not relish being responsible for extracting some illegitimate sprig of the nobility from the results of his own foolishness.

And the idea that he might credibly present himself, with his mere grammar school education, as tutor to a young man who had presumably been exposed to much more learned scholars than he, seemed preposterous. But he kept these reservations to himself; clearly he was going to have this extra burden whether he wanted it or no, so he had better make the best of it.

Then again, perhaps he could extract some advantage from the wily old spymaster. 'I am honoured, Sir Francis, that you think me capable of fulfilling such a role. Though I have some trouble seeing myself as an aged tutor to a young man who cannot be more than a few years younger than I.'

Walsingham laughed. 'Do not trouble yourself on that score, Shakespeare. To a seventeen-year-old, you will seem a greybeard! And Marlowe tells me you have aspirations to be an actor, so I am sure you can counterfeit the gravity of a Socrates should it be required.'

'I am flattered that you should think so, Sir Francis.' Will considered what to say next, though the words had already formed in his head in a flash of inspiration. 'But it seems to me that this impersonation would have more force if I, as the young man's supposed tutor, were to also be undertaking studies of some substance at the same institution.'

Walsingham's eyes narrowed. 'To be paid for out of my purse, I make no doubt.'

'Naturally, Sir Francis.'

Will did not allow his eyes to waver from Walsingham's face, in which he read the beginnings of anger, and he feared that he had badly overplayed his hand.

'You are a bold fellow, Shakespeare, I'll say that,' Walsingham eventually said. 'And something of a huckster, I find. Well, it's fair enough I suppose, and you are right, undertaking studies on your own behalf will add credibility to your pose. But I will pay for just one term, sirrah, no more.'

'Thank you, Sir Francis. And in return, I swear that I will look after the welfare of Master Tom as if he were my own son.'

Walsingham laughed. 'You may well have your work cut out. Tom is an admirable young man of considerable charm and a promising intelligence, but he also has an impulsive side—inherited from his mother, no doubt—that will require restraint from time to time.'

So, as well as playing tutor, he had to make sure that his charge didn't get into scrapes; he, William Shakespeare, who was barely able to avoid getting into trouble himself! 'And at which university do you intend that your ward and I will be enrolled?'

'The University of Padua. It is a fine institution, and I learned much there when I was a young man.' The old man's eyes softened as he recalled those distant years, no doubt golden in his memory, as they must be in all men from whom the flush of youth has long passed.

Then he resumed his usual business-like demeanour. 'You will travel by sea, I think. The land route is arduous and would necessitate travelling through turbulent country. I will have Phelippes find a Venetian ship, since King Philip has rather inconveniently placed an embargo on English shipping throughout his domains.

'Tom is at this moment at my country house. I will send for him to join us here in three days so you can meet. That will be enough time for Phelippes to arrange your passage. Satisfactory?'

55

With that last word, the brusque and forceful personality of the Master Secretary was back, and Will could do nothing other than nod his agreement.

'Then off you go. No doubt you have much to think on and do. And send in Phelippes as you leave.'

Thus dismissed, Will got to his feet and headed to the door. He was about to open it when a cough made him turn around once again.

'Shakespeare, do not think that I am unaware of the burdens that I am placing on you. You will have my gratitude if you are able to complete your tasks well, which I flatter myself is no small thing.'

Will bowed. 'Of course, Sir Francis. I vow I will not disappoint.' With which he left the queen's principal secretary to resume his day's work, while he himself contemplated the turn of fate he now had to confront.

Chapter 7

Within hours of his meeting with Walsingham, Kit appeared at the Seething Lane house, as if summoned by some mysterious messenger, or, more likely, because he was a party to the whole plot; one of the conspirators who seemed intent on manipulating his life.

Will thought he should be angry at being so used, but somehow Kit's sunny presence always banished the hot words that formed in his head, and on this day he was so transparently enthusiastic about Will's impending travels that he had simply burst into laughter.

'Heavens, Kit,' he said, as they settled over tankards of ale and an indifferent game pie at their accustomed tavern, not far from Seething Lane. 'Anyone would think you were coming on this journey with me, were they listening to your giddy, boyish excitement.'

Kit had the grace to look a little abashed. But this lasted only for a few moments, and his irrepressible sense of self-importance took control again. 'I would that I *were* going with you! But, of course, the secretary relies on me and has other missions for me to undertake. No doubt I will be travelling again myself before long. Now, order us some more ale, and let me tell you how to prepare for this great adventure, for I am sure that without guidance from an experienced traveller such as myself, you will suffer calamity after calamity.'

With which Kit launched into yet another series of improbable tales from his travels—although, Will allowed, some may have actually been true—designed to illustrate the perils he faced as a novice traveller.

Entering into the spirit of the game, Will played the wide-eyed innocent, which only encouraged Kit to ever greater flights of fancy, much to his amusement.

At last, when Kit's imaginative and inventive powers seemed to be exhausted, the conversation returned, as it always did with them, to the subject of poetry, play-acting and play-writing.

'I read your play,' Kit said coyly.

Will had given Kit the draft of *The Comedy of Errors*, incomplete and marred with scratchings-out and anxious notes in the margin, feeling the need for someone other than himself to lay eyes on it. A flutter of apprehension jolted his stomach; though he had affected insouciance when he handed the manuscript to his friend, he found himself unable to maintain his indifference as, with a lift of his eyebrows, he invited Kit to offer his criticism.

'I like it. Much more fun than plodding old Plautus! It needs some work, mind, to bring it to perfection. But yes, I can see it on the stage. Finish it, and we'll get Burbage to put it on in his new theatre, though only after they've done my *Tamburlaine*. They'll need some comedy after that.'

Will laughed. How typical of Kit to insist on his own precedence. But then, he was a university man, not a mere country bumpkin, so perhaps that was just. And from what Kit had said, *Tamburlaine*, if he ever finished it, was indeed likely to be strong meat for the play-going public.

He raised his tankard in salute. 'Here's to the two greatest unknown playwrights in London.'

'I'll miss you, Will,' Kit had said, 'as will the others—Burbage, Alleyn, even that great lump Greene. We have all come to enjoy your company. Take care to come home safely.'

So they had parted, slightly tipsy, and Will had gone home to impart his news to Richard Holbrooke, his too-kind and patient host who had received, Will feared, a poor return for his generosity in providing him with lodging and employment of a sort.

Two days later, he had met his young charge—the bastard son of the late Earl of Sussex, Walsingham's ward, the honourable Tomaso Martinelli. He had been deeply engrossed in reviewing a legal contract for Holbrooke when his concentration was broken by a rather breathless boy messenger who he recognised as one of Walsingham's household.

'Master Secretary's compliments, sir, and he desires that you should attend him at Seething Lane as soon as may be convenient, sir,' he said in a treble voice, nervously turning his cap in his hands.

He was, Will recalled, new to the secretary's service, which explained the nervousness. 'Which I presume means immediately.' Will smiled and rose to gather his doublet and hat, flung carelessly across a chair in the corner of the room. 'Come then, lead on.'

Twenty minutes later he was in the familiar vestibule of the secretary's house, but to his surprise instead of going up to the familiar suite of offices

58

above, the boy gestured to the rear of the house. 'They are in the garden, sir. It is this way... I think.'

Will knew well enough how to get into the garden, though he had never been there. It was something of a sanctuary for the secretary, who went there to escape the cares of his office for the odd quarter hour. His staff had learned to leave the great man to his solitude. It was rare, therefore, for any of them to go out there.

Stepping out of the house, he glanced quickly around the garden—a space bounded by a high grey wall that dulled somewhat the ever-present noise of the city. It was not a large area and it was rustic in style. A few trees provided welcome shade and there were flowering shrub beds here and there, clearly well-tended but not laid out to any design or pattern that Will could discern.

Beneath one of the trees there stood a simple bench, on which the familiar figure of Walsingham was perched, listening intently to another man who sat with his back to Will, and who was speaking rapidly and volubly, gesturing with his hands.

Will put one hand over his mouth and coughed gently to announce his presence. Walsingham looked across and, recognising the source of the interruption, raised his hand to beckon Will across the lawn to join them.

'Will, thank you for coming so promptly.' The secretary was, as always, polite. 'Tom here has only a little time before he must go off to see his tailor and I know how important such appointments are for you young men.'

The youth who turned to meet Will's gaze was indeed well-dressed, though not in an ostentatious way. His clothes were made of fine materials and muted colours—black hose, leather knee-length boots, a dark green doublet that matched his fashionably-slashed breeches. A flat cap, also green, with a long white feather and a small ruby brooch, lay on the bench beside him.

The inhabitant of these clothes was broad of shoulder, narrow of hip and possessed of the dark hair and olive complexion of his Mediterranean heritage. His finely manicured hands, now stilled, lay calmly in his lap as he considered Will. The blue eyes, set in the handsome, fine-boned face, were mildly mischievous, as if their owner were laughing at some jest known only to himself.

'I fear, Sir Francis, that my income has not hitherto allowed me the luxury of troubling a tailor for his services,' Will said, intending to make a joke, though it sounded a little stiff even to his own ears.

59

'What, Nuncle, do you not pay your men these days?' The boy's voice was amused.

Walsingham, unperturbed, rose to his feet, forcing his guest to do the same. 'William is well enough paid, but is perhaps more sensible with his money than most young men. Comes of being a countryman, I suppose, and having a wife and... what is it, Shakespeare, three children? Someday, Tom, you'll know what it means to have responsibilities in this world.'

That reproof, if reproof it was, had no effect on the youngster's spirits. 'As well, then, that I will have such a greybeard as Master Shakespeare here to guide me and keep me out of trouble in Italy.'

'Hush, Tom. In the short time we have known each other, I have come to respect William's judgement and intelligence. He may not be old in years, but I sense a man wise in spirit. You will do well to treat him with respect.'

'Of course, Sir Francis,' the young man said, banishing his mockery and adopting an expression of contrition as he extended a formal hand to Will. 'And since you have not formally introduced us, I shall do so myself. Tomaso Martinelli, sir, at your service. I look forward to our voyage together.'

Will took the proffered hand and inclined his head.

'And now I shall leave you two to get to know each other for a little,' Walsingham said, turning back towards the house and the burden of work that awaited him there.

'Shall we walk, Master Shakespeare?' the boy said. 'The garden is not large but I daresay we can take a turn or two.'

'Please, call me Will, otherwise I will think you are referring to my father.'

'And you can call me Tom or Tomaso, which is my real name. My mother always used to call me Maso. So you see, I am used to being called by all kinds of names.'

Was there a hint of bitterness in those last words? The boy's English, though perfect, was delivered with an accent that would no doubt have marked him out among his schoolfellows as a foreigner, and therefore subject to the taunts that the English reserved for all such. 'Tom, then, we are agreed.'

'So tell me, Will Shakespeare, what grievous folly did you commit that caused you to be exiled and sent to nursemaid the bastard son of an English lord?'

The words, though delivered with a grin, startled Will. How much had Walsingham told Tom about his circumstances? Honesty, perhaps, would be the best policy. 'I managed to annoy a knight in my county of Warwickshire, a man who is not so significant in himself, but who has a vindictive spleen and the ear of powerful men at court. And so it is politic that I should leave the country for a while, under the guise of being employed by Sir Francis, whose protection has kept me safe for these last few months.'

Tom's grin now transformed into a laugh, clear, pure, and infectious, so that Will found himself grinning back at the boy.

'I thought as much. There is nothing Uncle Francis does that does not have at least two motives. And I'll warrant he's given you one or two other tasks to boot, to get the fullest value from his investment. He's nothing if not economical. Still, I'm glad my "tutor" is to be someone who is near enough to my own age to remember what it is like to be young, not some grey-bearded ancient whose soul has been emptied out and replaced by dust.'

He liked this young man. Despite his youthful exuberance and outward self-confidence, there was a decided air of vulnerability about him. 'Then we understand each other. But let us try and maintain the fiction that Sir Francis has constructed for us, and play out his play.'

Tom shrugged his acquiescence, though his expression became more serious. 'Why not? In truth though, Will, I am not so conceited as to think that I have nothing to learn from you, or from the world.'

'No doubt we will learn from each other, and share the world's lessons as they are administered. Now tell me what subjects you have studied, so that I may think on the gaps to be filled.'

They chatted amiably for a quarter hour about Tom's previous education, which Will was relieved to discover was not as complete as he had expected. Despite having the benefit of private tutors, his instruction had proceeded in fits and starts, and had started late due to the inconstant attention of his father, preoccupied as he had been with his own affairs.

The sound of church bells announcing noon interrupted their talk, and Tom apologetically took his leave to go for his appointment with his tailor.

They would meet again in two days' time on the dock, where the next phase of their respective lives would begin.

Those days were filled with activity. There was a final round of farewells with Will's newly-acquired circle of friends, whose natural curiosity at this sudden and mysterious journey was tinged with more than a hint of envy.

61

Greene, in particular, had been outspoken. 'How in God's name does a mere glover's son with no education to speak of get appointed as a tutor to a boy-noble? And get to travel to Italy to boot. It defies the proper order of things.'

To tell the truth, Will was beginning to be heartily sick of Greene's pompous insistence on the superiority of all who possessed one of his precious university degrees, particularly since the big man's own literary efforts were of middling quality, at best.

But he held his tongue and laughed it off. 'Jealous, Rob? Sometimes life's path is smoothed less by what you know or what degrees you have than by who you know. And a little effort put into being amenable to others doesn't go astray.'

That remark produced howls of laughter from Marlowe and Burbage, who had joined them for a farewell ale.

'Well, Greene,' Burbage said, 'I fear that if Will is right you will be unemployable for a long time to come.'

Greene looked put out at that, for the outspoken bluntness of which he was inordinately proud, had, as Will knew, cost him several commissions, reducing him almost to penury. Standing abruptly, he shot a withering look of contempt at Shakespeare and marched out of the tavern.

'I fear you have upset our poor Greene, Will,' said Kit. 'And he does hold a grudge.'

'He will have plenty of time to nurse it, caress it, choke on it, and then perhaps digest it, before I come home again.'

'Mind you, I share his envy,' Burbage said, 'but I grudge you not your good fortune. Here's to William Shakespeare and his foreign adventures.'

*

Awaking with a sore head, he had much to do on the following day; his last in England. He had to decide what clothes and other personal belongings to take with him. He was particularly vexed as to which books to take from the considerable library that he had amassed over the last few months, and which were as dear to him as his family and friends.

Then there were arrangements to be made to ensure that the regular remittances from Walsingham were forwarded to his family in his absence. And there was a vast amount of last-minute instruction from Phelippes on those aspects of the intelligencer's craft that he had not yet mastered, as well as specific instructions for contacting Walsingham's agent in Venice.

Overall, he had barely had more than a few hours' sleep over the last few days. It was well past midnight when he finally got to his last, and to him most important task: his weekly letter to Anne. He pictured her opening it, all unknowing that it would be the last she would receive from him for some time.

He could not, of course tell her the whole truth. He could not tell her that his employer was not the young man Tom Martinelli, at least not directly, but that he was being paid by Sir Francis Walsingham. Nor could he confide any of the secret aspects of his journey. And he had to keep from her the threat to his person that continued to dog him as a result of his foolish taunting of Sir Thomas Lucy. That would cause her to fret even more. But within those constraints he could at least offer her some reassurance.

> My dearest Anne,
> This must perforce be my last letter to you for some time, since I am to embark in tomorrow for Venice and other parts of Italy. You will no doubt be astonished by this news, as I was when I learned but a week ago that I was to be appointed as a kind of pedagogue to a young man who, though born on the wrong side of the blanket, is nevertheless of noble blood. He is half-Italian and has a desire to complete his education in the country where he was born. I go with him as tutor and guardian, to ensure he reaches his destination safely and is installed in his new university.
> I owe this unexpected change of fortune to my friend Kit Marlowe, of whom I have written before, who introduced me to certain of his acquaintances, recommending my services, from which this appointment then sprang, all unexpected but, let it be said, not unwanted. For though my exile from Stratford was unlooked-for, my sojourn here in London has opened my mind to so many possibilities and opportunities that I cannot but see it as a good thing. Whatever poor fortune I could have made for myself in Stratford—and only God

knows what that might have been—I believe that my opportunities here are limitless, and once I return from Italy I am determined to make the best of them and to make my fortune, so that you will be proud to call yourself the wife of Wm Shakespeare.

My love, you are the most practical of souls, and I can hear your voice in the inner chambers of my mind asking about that most pragmatical of subjects—money. You will no doubt be cursing me for a light-headed wanton adventurer, and wondering how you are going to make ends meet while I am off wandering the globe. The enclosed draft will perhaps set your mind at rest, for I am to be paid handsomely for undertaking this task; whatever may be said about my employer, he is not niggardly, and he has promised that regular payments will be forthcoming for so long as I am in his service. Give the draft to my father. He will know how to convert it into coin.

My only regret is that I cannot be with you and our children, at least for now. Perhaps, when I have returned and am established, it will be possible for you and they to come to London.

Pray for me as I do for you,

Your loving husband, William.

Signing the letter with a flourish, he carefully folded and sealed it, and applied the delivery address to the outside. He placed it on the corner of his desk. In the morning, he would give it to one of Richard Holbrooke's servants to deliver to the post house. By the time it arrived in Stratford, he would be well out to sea.

As he prepared himself for bed, he smiled a little, thinking of his wife's astonishment, which could, he thought wryly, be scarcely greater than his own.

Chapter 8

B illingsgate Dock bustled with activity, as shoremen manhandled cargo aboard the *Bonaventura* with cranes and poles, grunting and swearing with the effort, exchanging good-natured insults with the ship's crew. Nearby, an anxious-looking clerk clutched his bills of lading, ticking off each item as it was loaded.

Ropes and various kinds of tackle, mysterious objects to Will's eye, littered the rough wooden wharf, creating an obstacle course of some complexity for the unwary. As always, idlers sat on barrels or leant on posts, arms crossed, watching the process with an expertise borne of long familiarity, occasionally offering up acerbic comments when the efforts of the dock workers stumbled or flagged.

Will pulled his cloak more tightly around himself against the bitter wind, unusually cold for August, that ruffled the surface of the river as he stood surrounded by his meagre baggage. He was waiting for Tom to arrive so they could board.

The dockside scene was familiar enough from his various visits running errands for Richard Holbrooke, but he inspected the ship that bumped gently against the wooden pilings of the wharf with greater than usual interest. She was perhaps a hundred and fifty feet long. Her narrow waist was level with the dock, but forecastle and aftercastle towered above it.

His eyes travelled upwards to the four masts, each supported by a profusion of rigging and rope ladders to provide the mariners with a perilous thoroughfare up to the yards in order to furl and unfurl her sails, which were loosely bunted up, awaiting the moment when they would be released to provide the power that would take them down river to the sea.

On the ship's main deck, swarms of seamen worked to stow away cargo, coil ropes, adjust rigging, sweep decks before she could set sail. Their working chatter drifted across the dockside in the polyglot mix typical of seafarers—Dutch, German, Spanish—though the most common language was Italian, for the *Bonaventura* was a Venetian galleon. She was owned by

65

a Venetian nobleman who had been in England for the last few months, ostensibly negotiating trade arrangements, but in reality meeting with the queen's ministers to explore the possibility of a loan from the Venetian Republic. This he had learned from Phelippes at their meeting the day before.

'Francesco Contarini is a senior member of the Venetian Signoria, the council that governs the Republic,' the cryptographer had told him. 'As usual, the queen's finances are at a stretch, and though the good burghers of parliament always express their most profound loyalty to the sovereign, their leaders never miss an opportunity to squeeze concessions from the queen in return for any additional revenues. So Palavicino came up with a plan to borrow money from abroad.'

Sir Horatio Palavicino was the queen's principal financial adviser and, rumour said, her biggest creditor.

'Contarini was in London for his own purposes,' Phelippes went on, 'but he and Palavicino are old acquaintances, so he has been persuaded to convey a request to the Signoria for a loan. For myself, I think it is a forlorn hope, for there is little reason for the Venetians to help us. He is a cautious and guarded man, but if you can make a friend of him during your voyage, he may be of great assistance to you in Venice.'

A day later, standing shivering on the wharf, he wondered how he, ostensibly a mere servant to a junior sprig of the English nobility, was supposed to acquire the friendship and trust of a Venetian patrician. Perhaps the intimacy of life aboard a small ship would break down the social barriers.

His thoughts were interrupted by a carriage emerging from the street behind the dock, the horses neighing and stamping as their driver hauled on the reins to wrestle them to a halt in the narrow space between the street and the wharf.

Almost before the carriage had stopped, the lithe figure of Tom Martinelli jumped out, boots kicking up a muddy spray as they landed in a puddle. He was followed by a rather dishevelled-looking man, presumably a servant, who set about unloading bags from the top of the carriage while exchanging loud but good-natured insults with its driver.

His master left him to it and strode across the cluttered dockside. 'Will! I am sorry you should have had to wait in this wretched wind for us. I fear that I could not shake off the arms of Morpheus this morning.'

Tom's cheerful grin, that of an excited young man setting forth on an adventure, dispelled from Will's mind any sourness he might have felt at being kept waiting. 'You're here now, and I am warmly enough wrapped against the chill, so it was no great hardship. But let us get aboard, lest the captain take it into his head to sail without us.'

Tomaso's eyes went to the ship, taking her in with one swift and appraising glance. Then he turned back towards the carriage, where his servant was struggling across the dock, canvas seabags in each hand, a small chest tucked under one arm, and another lumpy-looking sack slung across his shoulders. He looked like a misshapen tortoise, carrying his whole world on his back.

'Hurry up, Lance, you hopeless lump, else the barky will be at sea before any of us have set foot aboard.'

'As to that, your honour,' said the object of this raillery, his voice emerging from beneath a massive broad-brimmed hat that had clearly seen better days, 'I had to pay the carriage driver, didn't I? But I've seen many a ship sail in my time, an' this barky ain't going anywhere for hours yet. Which I told your honour already three times this morning. But as you is in such an 'urry, I'll aboard directly and get your honour's accommodation shipshape and country fashion.'

The tortoise turned his back on the two men and shuffled up the gangway, loudly exchanging a few coarse words with the sailors, and disappeared below.

'Lance is a good and loyal servant,' Tom said, clearly feeling the need to offer some explanation for his servant's apparent impertinence, though Will had said nothing. 'He is, it is true, a little uncouth. His mother keeps house for me, and since he lacks any other opportunities for employment, being somewhat simple and ill-educated, she begged me to take him as my valet-servant. His tongue is as unkempt as his coat, but he is well-intentioned, loyal and strong, which is as much as one should expect from a servant.'

'It's not for me to criticise your choice of servants, Tom, and as you say, loyalty is a quality that is not to be sniffed at. Come on, let us get ourselves aboard. This wind is finally finding its way through my cloak and I find that my bones are feeling the cold.'

The activity on the main deck of the *Bonaventura* had not slackened while they had been talking, and it did not cease when they crossed the low-browed gangway onto the ship's main deck, where the Italian crew dodged around them, muttering what Will took to be curses.

For a few moments they were completely ignored until a flamboyant, piratical-looking man emerged from beneath the ship's quarterdeck and

67

looked around with a proprietorial air. When his eyes alighted on the two newcomers he beckoned them over to him.

'I am Orsini,' he said in heavily accented English. 'Captain of the *Bonaventura.*'

Tom and Will both bowed, then Tom launched into a short speech in Italian, presumably explaining who they were. The captain's severe expression softened on hearing his native tongue, and after a few further words, he reverted to English to welcome them aboard.

Hardly had he done so before their attention was diverted by a further clamour on the dockside as another coach, this one considerably finer than the vehicle that had brought Tomaso, clattered to a halt. A slight-looking, elegantly dressed man alighted and picked his way delicately between the obstacles that littered the dockside, followed by two servants bearing his baggage.

Captain Orsini abandoned them and hurried over to greet the newcomer as he boarded, with a flourish and a deep, obsequious bow.

'Signor Contarini! *Benvenuto a bordo!*'

So this was the owner of the ship, the Venetian merchant and patrician that Phelippes had told Will he should befriend.

After a brief exchange in Italian, the captain conducted his master over to join them where they stood under the break of the quarterdeck. The impression of fastidious elegance was reinforced by the perfectly trimmed beard and carefully trained moustaches, the spotless white collar standing in contrast to the black velvet of his doublet and the manicured and ringed fingers of the hand that caressed the medallion around his neck.

But the dark and penetrating eyes were anything but soft. Though they were black where Walsingham's were blue, they had the same chilling effect on Will, as if their owner could instantly penetrate any paltry defence he might put up against their investigation.

'Gentlemen, let me add my welcome to the captain's,' he said in heavily accented English. 'I am sure we will have a pleasant voyage together. Now, the captain tells me that we are almost ready to cast off, so perhaps we should retire to the quarterdeck while his crew makes their final preparations. I know from experience that it is best to stay out of their way when they are intent on executing their manoeuvers.'

No doubt to the relief of the crew, the three passengers quickly climbed the few steps to the quarterdeck and settled themselves into what seemed to be the least conspicuous corner they could find.

The work of loading the ship's cargo and stores was now complete, and the sailors occupied themselves with the preparations for departure, loosening and adjusting ropes, tidying away items of gear to leave the decks clear, and swarming out onto the yards in readiness to release the sails from their temporary captivity.

Commands bellowed out from the captain and his officers, and the thick hawsers that held the *Bonaventura* against the wharf were loosed. At the same moment, the topsails were released on the fore and main masts, billowing out and flapping wildly before being sheeted home.

Almost imperceptibly at first, and then with gathering speed, the great ship eased away from the dock, current and wind carrying them rapidly into the centre of the river and its mass of small-craft traffic, which, minnow-like, moved deftly around her. Within minutes they were passing the Tower of London on their larboard side, and the cityscape that had enfolded them gave way to open fields and farms.

So astonished was Will by the turn in his fortunes that had brought him to this ship, so engaged with the details of preparing for departure, that he had not found a moment to contemplate the prospect that lay before him. But now he was gripped by a mixture of elation and apprehension, as everything familiar, known and predictable began to slip away, while what had been an unknown and dimly apprehended future began to take on the outlines of hard reality.

He wasn't, he thought, a natural traveller like Kit. Given his own choice in the matter, he would probably never have left Stratford. Yet he was not immune to the romantic lure of foreign places and things, and browsing among the bookshops of St Paul's Churchyard he had picked up many a traveller's tract and been intrigued, pondering what it would be like to see these breathlessly-described wonders for himself.

Kit's travel stories had also sparked occasional moments of ambition. For why should he, Will Shakespeare, not see something of the world? Surely he could acquit himself on that stage as well as his dear but self-aggrandising friend? Now, standing at the rail of the quarterdeck of the *Bonaventura*, listening to Tom Martinelli happily chattering in a mixture of English and Italian, he determined that he would put aside his apprehension, suppress for

69

now the natural ache for his family, and embrace this adventure, unlooked-for and uncertain though it was.

While these thoughts were going through his head, the had ship settled into its working routine, and Contarini, making courteous excuses, crossed to join Captain Orsini on the other side of the quarterdeck, where they were soon engaged in conversation.

'Come on, Will. Let's have a look at the rest of the ship,' Tom said, taking him by the arm.

For the next hour they wandered over every part of the Venetian galleon, encountering along the way Tom's wayward servant, Lance, happily playing dice with a group of off-duty sailors in the half-light of the tween deck. By the time they re-emerged into the sunlight, the *Bonaventura* was approaching the mouth of the Thames, and Will began to feel the unfamiliar sensation of the decks moving under him. For a man whose life had been hitherto entirely land-bound, this was more than a little unsettling.

Tom on the other hand seemed unaffected by the ship's movement, as if born to the sea. Laughing gaily at the look of astonishment on Will's face as the deck disappeared under his feet after the ship had breasted a particularly steep wave, he led the way up onto the forecastle where they could wedge themselves into a corner and watch as the river merged into the sea.

By the time another hour had passed, England's coast had receded into the distance, and as if each mile had broken another link in the chain that held Will fast to his homeland, any remaining melancholy departed and his sense of elation and freedom from care grew.

*

For the first few days, he found life at sea quite disturbing. To Tom's continuing and heartless amusement, the movement of the ship continued to catch him unawares as it bucked and plunged among the waves, and inflicted bouts of nausea which resulted in the contents of his stomach going over the side on several occasions.

In a ship at sea, he discovered, there was never silence. The ship's hull creaked and cracked as she breasted the crest of each swell, the wind thrummed through the rigging and caused loose pieces of tackle to clatter against the masts or bulwarks, and the sailors' feet rumbled across the deck, shouting jokes in their loud coarse voices as they raced up the rigging to deal with the sails.

Then there were the smells—below decks, the scent of unwashed bodies and the stink of the livestock kept in pens at the forward end of the main deck

70

combined with a dank smell that seemed to come from deep in the ship's bilges to create a fug which persisted even when the ship's hatches and gun ports were open, as they were whenever the weather was fine and the sea benign.

But after a week, having found what the sailors called his sea-legs, and having become accustomed to the sounds and smells of the ship, he began to enjoy the simplicity of this new existence, as it settled into a pattern that was comforting in its predictability. For the first time in his life, he had time on his hands, which he was determined to use as well as he could.

Some of that time was taken up with Italian lessons. In this Venetian ship, English Tom had soon disappeared to become Italian Tomaso, overjoyed to be able to converse in his mother's tongue. He readily agreed with Will's request for instruction in that language.

'Why not? Let's see if we can get you at least passably fluent by the time we get to Venice.'

That seemed to be a tall order to Will, but as usual, having once committed to the task, he was soon immersed in it, and before long they were spending three or four hours every day, sitting in some sheltered corner of the ship, working patiently through the complexities of Italian grammar and vocabulary.

He also read a great deal. His little library included the copy of Holinshed's *Chronicles* that he had bought in St Paul's churchyard, and sundry works of Roman poetry and Greek plays. He also had a copy of Fynes Morrison's account of his Italian travels, which he had bought in preparation for his journey, though both Captain Orsini and Francesco Contarini took great delight in correcting some of the wilder stories that the intrepid Englishman had collected.

Remembering Phelippes' suggestion that he try to befriend the Venetian nobleman, Will did his best to engage him in conversation whenever he could. Though Contarini was, he discovered, a naturally courteous man, he had an air of dignified reserve that was hard to penetrate, and their conversations rarely descended far below the surface. Then, one afternoon a week or so into the voyage, he came into the Great Cabin looking for something, and found the Venetian sitting polishing a set of ivory chess pieces.

'Do you play, William?' he had asked, when Will had exclaimed how beautiful they were.

'I have played a little. Though I would not claim to have any great skill...'

Contarini's smile was wry.

'I am afraid the quality of the chess pieces is far higher than the quality of my own skill at the game. Perhaps we should try them with each other?'

So they had settled down to a game. It turned out that their skills were well matched, and before long the daily match became a part of their routine. It also gave Will an opportunity to get to know the Venetian nobleman a little better, to the extent that the competitive nature of their pursuit allowed him to do so.

Contarini was a dignified man. Always neatly dressed, hair combed and beard trimmed, he talked in a precise way, with frequent pauses as he considered exactly what he wished to say. Yet he was capable of a dry wit with which he delivered such pithy observations ranging across many subjects that frequently found Will trying to suppress his laughter. Despite the disparity in their stations in life, and the differences of culture and outlook, there soon developed an amiable if somewhat formal friendship between them.

And so time passed in these pleasant pursuits as steady and favourable winds billowing under sunny skies propelled the great ship easily south-westwards, across the Bay of Biscay and into the Atlantic, where they should pick up the south-west trade winds. These in turn would take them to that narrow strait between Europe and Africa, called the Gates of Heracles by the ancients, that was the entrance to the Mediterranean Sea.

Early on the morning of their ninth day at sea, Will sat propped against a bulwark reading his salt-stained copy of Holinshed's *Chronicles*, trying to understand the complexities of the Wars of the Roses. Contarini had foregone their daily chess game to retire to the Great Cabin, where he said he had long-neglected papers to attend to.

On the other side of the quarterdeck, Captain Orsini was attempting to instruct Tomaso in the finer aspects of navigation. The young half-Italian had foolishly expressed an interest in the workings of the ship, causing the captain to insist on giving his passenger periodic lessons in its operations.

Tomaso had no ambitions to become a sailor, but he endured Orsini's enthusiastic lectures with a kind of wry stoicism, though he confessed to Will that half the time he had not the slightest idea what the good captain was talking about. Half watching now from his corner of the deck, he was barely

72

able to restrain his laughter at Tomaso's helpless look as Orsini tried to explain the workings of the astrolabe.

At that moment, a cry came down from the lookout perched high on the foremast that land was in sight.

'Come, Tomaso,' the captain said, his facing lighting up, '*Andiamo!* Let us aloft.'

He ran to the rail and swung into the rope ladders that climbed to the mainmast top. Tomaso barely hesitated before following, and Will, with a sigh, dropped his book and went to join them.

Over the course of the voyage, he had climbed into the rigging several times, so the dizzying ascent was not an entirely novel experience. Even so, he found the unaccustomed exercise taxing as he hauled himself up and up, arriving breathless to join Tomaso and the captain in the maintop, a circular basket-like structure which was barely large enough to contain the three of them.

They were afforded a magnificent, if gyrating, view of the surrounding ocean and, far ahead, two grey-blue smudges, barely distinguishable from the horizon's fuzzy edge.

'That, *signori*, is Spain,' Orsini said, gesturing towards the left-most smudge, a look of profound self-satisfaction on his face. 'And that,' his arm swivelled to the right, 'is Africa. We, due to my most excellent navigation, will pass through the middle like a thread through a needle!'

After contemplating his own brilliance for a few moments, the captain disappeared over the side. Leaping alarmingly across the open void to grasp a convenient backstay, he slid down to the deck, leaving the two younger men in possession of their eyrie.

For the next few hours, Will watched with fascination as the two indistinct smears slowly resolved themselves into identifiable coastlines—rocky escarpments covered in scrub, white surf at their foot, distant mountains at their back. By midday, Tomaso was excitedly pointing out the spectacular rock to their north. 'The Moors called it *Jabal-Tariq*, and the Spanish, *Gibraltar*, which means we are now in the *Mare Mediterraneo*, the sea that washes Italy.'

After the long days on the empty ocean, they were close to land again, and Will felt as if their little sea-going community was re-joining the rest of the human race.

*

By early the following morning, the *Bonaventura* was alongside the quay in the port of Malaga, where they were to take on additional stores and fresh water. The familiar dockside scene was rendered strange by the sibilant Spanish language and the presence of Spanish soldiery patrolling the wharf.

From the deck, he could see glimpses of the bustling town beyond, dominated by its vast cathedral and by the great mass of the Moorish fortress—the *Gibalfaro,* one of the ship's crew had called it—that perched on its rock above the town.

Spanish customs officials came aboard as soon as they docked, accompanied by the Venetian agent in the city, a small, precise man who named himself as Don Alvaro Ortega. He made a great show of obsequious deference to Francesco Contarini, bowing deeply with a great flourish and issuing a string of compliments, which Contarini accepted with his usual courtly good manners. The customs officials, having completed their duties, were soon off the ship, and Don Alvaro disappeared into the Great Cabin to confer with his Venetian compatriot and the captain, leaving Will and Tomaso on deck, idly watching the crew take on fresh water and supplies for the next leg of their voyage.

'Our first foreign port,' Tomaso said, as they propped themselves against the bulwark. 'Shall we go ashore and explore? I don't know about you, but I need to feel solid land under my feet.'

Will frowned. He felt more than a little nervous at the prospect of walking unprotected among the Spaniards with whom his country was probably now at war. Yet they were travelling on a Venetian ship, and it was unlikely they would be in any real danger. On balance, he saw little harm in their taking an excursion ashore, though he would have to insist that they leave Lance behind, since his loud and uncouth English voice would undoubtedly attract attention.

He was about to give his assent to Tomaso's plan, in his role as the elder and notional guardian of the younger man, but found his approval was redundant, since Tomaso had already turned and headed for the gangway. For Tomaso Martinelli, thought was always the father of immediate action, and his impulsiveness was hard to restrain. Sighing, he shrugged his shoulders and followed.

He need not have worried. The Spanish soldiers propped on their pikes on the wharf gave them no more than a glance before returning to their conversation. By the time they returned to the ship late in the afternoon, exciting no more interest from the two guards on their return than they had on their departure, the two Englishmen had spent a thoroughly enjoyable few hours wandering through the tangled streets of the town, stopping at a small open-air tavern to drink the sweet Spanish wine and feast on cured ham and hard salty *manchego* cheese.

It was not until the *Bonaventura* was well out to sea that Will had an opportunity to talk again with Francesco Contarini, when they had settled over a small glass of sweet Madeira wine in the snug confines of the misnamed Great Cabin. 'What news did Don Alvaro bring, Ser Francesco?'

The Venetian seemed to order his thoughts. 'Let me see. Perhaps the news of most importance to you is the fact that war between England and Spain has been formally declared. Antwerp has fallen, and the Duke of Parma is making a great show of celebrating his success. But Don Alvaro told me that the general belief in Spain is that the war in the Netherlands is far from over. There are rumours that your English are planning an expedition to the Low Countries within months.'

'An expensive undertaking, I should think,' Will said, remembering that Contarini had been involved in London with attempts to raise money for the English government to use in just such an exercise. He wondered what effect this latest news would have on that mission, though there was no way he could ask that question directly.

'Quite so, William, quite so,' Contarini said, moving swiftly on to other subjects. 'In Italy, the new pope continues his campaign to restore order in the Papal territories; it is said that there are more heads on spikes across the Ponte Sant'Angelo than there are melons in the markets! He seems to have a ruthless streak, this Pope Sixtus. And in Venice, there is a new doge— Pasquale Cicogna was elected this last month.'

That was probably the most important news of all for Contarini, though Will knew that the doge's power and importance was not quite what it might seem.

One evening after they had concluded a game of chess, Contarini had tried to explain the workings of the Venetian government; it seemed hopelessly complicated. The doge was elected for life from among the aristocracy by a convoluted process of ballots and lotteries, and that although he was head of the Venetian state, his power was tightly bounded by the other institutions of the Venetian state—the Signoria, an elected body representing the nobility and the merchant classes, and the Council of Ten, who wielded effective executive power.

'What is he like, this new doge?'

'Don Alvaro took great delight in telling me that he caused a scandal by distributing coins of silver instead of the traditional gold at his coronation.' Contarini seemed deeply amused by this. 'Which surprises me not—Cicogna was always a mean man. Not necessarily a bad thing for the head of our state. It is his other qualities that might be worrying, for he is indecisive by nature, and he is somewhat vain, despite his parsimony with the state's funds. Still, he is elected, and we will see.'

Contarini lapsed into contemplative silence, and Will took this as his cue to leave him alone with his thoughts. Making his farewells, he went up on deck, where Captain Orsini was standing by the mizzen-mast, contemplating the night sky.

'A fine night, captain,' he said, 'and a fair wind, I think?'

'Si, Signor Shakespeare, a very nice night indeed. It is good to be back in the warm waters of the Mediterranean. Your Atlantic chills me to the bone, even when it is calm.'

'Even so, we have had a most pleasant cruise so far. Let us hope our good fortune will continue.'

Orsini nodded, though he also sketched a quick cross. 'Nothing is ever certain at sea, signor, but with God's good will I hope we will have an easy passage to Venice.'

Will nodded, then made his way down below, stepping over the sleeping forms of the sailors, until he found the little screened off corner of the deck where he and Tomaso slept.

Ignoring the gentle snores that came from the young man who had sought his bed long ago, Will dropped onto his rough mattress, and as he drifted off into sleep, his last thought was that, with their journey almost half done, they had so far experienced none of the terrors of sea travel that Kit Marlowe had expounded with such relish back in London.

With luck, they would have a trouble-free passage through the gentle waters of the Mediterranean for the rest of their voyage to Venice.

Chapter 9

The tension among the officers and crew on the quarterdeck of the *Bonaventura* was palpable as, clustered together along the starboard rail, they strained to see into the distant haze.

The sea was glassy and listless, disturbed only by the long slow swell, and the ship's sails hung lifeless, as they had all morning. Without the animating force of the wind, they were helpless against the emerging threat that had been reported from the lookout up in the main-top a few minutes before. He had seen the hulls of two long, low galleys emerging from the haze along the horizon to their south, in the direction of Africa.

'Barbary pirates,' muttered Rafaello, the sailor standing next to Will, confirming the lookout's suspicions. He did not need any further explanation to grasp their peril. The wind having deserted them, they were easy prey for the pirate galleys that, independent of the wind, haunted the north African coast.

'There!' Captain Orsini pointed. Will, squinting in the direction of the captain's outstretched arm, could just make out the two ships, each with a moustache of white water at its bow as the efforts of their oarsmen—slaves—propelled the sleek hulls through the flat water.

The minutes ticked past in an uneasy silence broken only by the creak of the ship's timbers as they worked in the slight swell. Every eye on the ship was focused on those two deadly war machines as they came inexorably closer, until at last the captain, judging that there was no possibility that the pirates would be deterred by the size of the Venetian galleon, turned and bawled out a string of orders.

The ship's crew swarmed into action. The dozen great guns that lined its sides were hauled into position so that they could be loaded with the powder and shot that emerged from the magazines below. Words and daggers were deposited in piles at various points along the upper deck so the sailors could arm themselves in preparation for any assault. Sand was scattered across the planks to better enable bare feet to grip in the event of an effusion of blood

77

rendering them slippery, and grappling hooks were set up along the rail to facilitate boarding the enemy if such an opportunity should arise.

All this activity was carried out with grim efficiency by the Venetian crew, for whom the threat of attack in these waters was not something new. Preparations complete, an uneasy silence settled over the ship.

Will was suddenly aware of Tomaso standing next to him, holding out a scabbarded sword and belt.

'I've never used a sword in my life,' he said, feeling something of a fool. Tomaso, already armed with sword and dagger, as well as a wheel-lock pistol stuck into his belt for good measure, seemed completely at home with the accoutrements of war.

'Then you will probably be more of a danger to your friends than your enemies,' Tomaso said with a grin, 'but put it on anyway; it will make you feel better. Don't worry, *amico mio*, I will protect you from these barbarians.' This last was delivered with a cheerfulness that was the opposite of what Will felt, as his stomach clenched in on itself.

Buckling the sword belt around his waist, he regarded the younger man with curiosity. He would never have thought there was such a martial character hiding in Tomaso's slight frame. He wondered how much was simply the bravado of a youngster eager to prove himself in any arena where he might have a chance to excel.

Nevertheless, he was clearly at ease with the weapons, and Will supposed that he had been given some training in the use of the sword as part of the education provided by the Earl of Sussex.

'In any event, these are precautions only,' Tomaso went on, 'for these pirates are for the most part of a cowardly hue. They have the courage of the lion faced with some lame merchantman, but the *Bonaventura* is a Venetian great galleon, and they will, I predict, behave like the jackal—sneaking up on us, only to run away yelping when they get a taste of our guns!'

Will laughed at Tomaso's fierceness. 'Then all is well.' He clapped his arm around Tomaso's shoulder. 'And since victory is certain we should retire below to drink some ale and await the inevitable outcome. But look, I don't think Contarini shares your optimism.'

That gentleman had emerged from the great cabin fully armed, complete with helmet and breastplate, though he looked about as comfortable as Will in these accoutrements. Martial affairs had not, it seemed, featured greatly in the patrician's otherwise broad experience.

78

By now, the Barbary pirates were racing towards them. Will could see that the upper decks of the pirate ships were crammed with men, most wearing turbans and the flowing robes he had first seen back in Malaga, armed to the teeth with swords and pikes that glinted menacingly in the sun. He could hear the relentless beat of the drums that urged the galley slaves on, each beat followed by a long hiss as the oars cut through the water. And even at this distance the stench of toiling humanity wrinkled his nostrils.

As Contarini joined them, Will glanced across at Captain Orsini, who was paying no attention to the galleys, instead peering intently across the larboard quarter. Following his gaze, Will could see nothing out of the ordinary, beyond a slight fluttering in the glassy surface of the water some few miles distant.

Orsini grunted, then bellowed a series of orders to his crew that resulted in the sails being drawn tighter, an action that seemed entirely pointless to Will.

'Ten minutes,' the captain said enigmatically, then his tight-lipped stern expression was replaced by the more familiar piratical grin. 'In ten, maybe fifteen minutes the wind will come, and we will have the advantage of these sea-carrion.'

With a great flurry as they backed their oars, the pirate ships glided to a halt, barely a hundred yards away, pausing like two hunting dogs sniffing the breeze.

'Fire!' Orsini shouted, with a fierce chop of his arm. An instant later, the six guns on the starboard side of the ship erupted into flame in near-unison, causing the *Bonaventura* to heel with the shock.

A cloud of acrid yellow smoke rolled across the deck, causing Will's eyes to water and his breath to catch in his throat. When it cleared, it was apparent that the first three shots had fallen harmlessly into the sea, sending gouts of spray heavenwards. The fourth by some quirk had whistled through the rigging of the nearest corsair, doing no damage.

But the fifth and sixth shots went home, one ploughing across the upper deck of the nearer ship, and the other smashing into the oar deck of the other. Sharp cries of fear and pain were heard as the pirates hurriedly set their oars in motion to back away from the great ship.

For a few minutes, the battle was at an impasse. The pirates frantically re-ordered their stricken vessels, Shouted commands in sharp-accented Arabic drifted through the tendrils of smoke that lingered in the still air as the pirate commanders determined their next maneuver.

Orsini stared intently at the nearest ship, clearly trying to divine their intentions from the activity he could see on the enemy quarterdeck. All the while he rubbed his hand back and forth across the stubble on his cheek.

Though the pirates made no move to indicate their intentions, the captain seemed certain they were going to attempt an immediate assault, for he bellowed commands that sent the crew into a frenzy of preparation to defend against boarders. Pikes and axes were passed out, arquebuses were loaded and matches primed, and the bulk of the crew were directed to mass in the waist of the ship; her most vulnerable point.

As they did so, the steady throb of drums came across the water, oars stirred into movement, and the two ships separated. Even for a novice in sea-fighting like Will, their enemies' alternatives were obvious—either they would head for the bows and stern of the *Bonaventura*, where their quarry would not be able to bring its big guns to bear as long as she was becalmed, then pound her with their own guns until she was disabled and could be boarded. Or they could swoop immediately, ranging alongside and below the *Bonaventura's* broadside batteries, which could not be depressed far enough to fire into the galleys, then swarm aboard, trusting in their superior numbers to overwhelm the ship's defenders.

It soon became obvious that the pirates had opted for the latter alternative; not entirely surprising, Will realised, for no doubt they too could see the whispers of wind that were beginning to ruffle the sea and had made the calculation that if they did not strike immediately their advantage would soon disappear.

This was exactly the eventuality for which Captain Orsini had planned by massing the ship's crew in the waist. Will looked at the captain with a new respect.

Turning his attention back to the two corsairs, he saw that the most damaged of the pair was approaching their starboard side slowly, allowing its compatriot time to manoeuver around the bow of the *Bonaventura* just out of gunshot range, so that they could mount an assault on both sides of the ship at once. But this would require precise timing, made more complicated by the fact that the two pirate ships would be out of each other's sight once the second ship passed under the *Bonaventura's* bows.

The enemy captains had miscalculated, for their attacker to starboard was closing too quickly, leaving them with a stark choice—hold off long enough to enable their comrades to complete their manoeuver on *Bonaventura's* larboard side, which would expose them to the full weight of the Venetian's broadside guns, or close quickly and hope that they could board in enough force to overwhelm the defenders.

The pirate captain was obviously a gambler, for he did not hesitate; the drums redoubled their urgency and the oars threshed the sea into foam as they drove towards the still-becalmed *Bonaventura*, whose gunners worked frantically to get a broadside in before the pirate ship was alongside. Alas, though they produced a morale-raising blast of flame and smoke, it had little effect on the enemy. One shot parted some stays, but otherwise it left them undamaged. The officers bellowed more orders and the crew surged towards the starboard side of the ship, ready to repel boarders.

Will noticed that Tomaso had slipped away from his side and run down into the ship's waist to push himself among the throng of defenders. Leaving a white-faced and tense Contarini with the grimly determined Orsini on the comparative safety of the quarterdeck, Will muttered a curse and followed his young charge down the companionway, clumsily drawing his sword as he went.

The men ranged along the ship's side, into whose midst Tomaso had disappeared, were silent in those few moments while they awaited the enemy assault; tough and seasoned professionals who felt no need to engage in unnecessary theatrics, saving their energy for the moment of conflict. Will felt a little foolish, afraid that he might trip over his scabbard, which had an irritating habit of tangling itself between his legs. He feared he was more a danger to himself than any enemy, and his presence could make little difference to Tomaso, who had pushed his way through to be in the front rank of defenders. But he felt his honour, not to mention his terror of Sir Francis Walsingham, demanded that he be by the boy's side.

The foreshortened upper masts of the Barbary corsair appeared above the heads of the men in front of him, sliding diagonally towards the ship. At the last minute, they turned and bumped alongside with a gentle grinding crash. The crew found their voices, screaming curses at the enemy in their various native tongues.

A dozen grappling hooks, hurled from the enemy deck below, flew up to lodge in the rigging or dig into the wood of the ship's rail, then turban-clad barbarian heads appeared as they swarmed up the ropes. Knives were tight-clamped in their mouths, swords and guns jammed in belts, ready to be extracted the moment their wearers had a footing on the deck.

This the defenders were determined to deny them. They stamped on fingers with their sword hilts and thrust knives and daggers into snarling faces as they appeared above the rail, desperately trying to cut the ropes that held the two ships together.

Waving his sword uncertainly, Will inserted himself into a small gap that had opened next to Tomaso, who was already engaged in a fierce struggle with a pirate who had managed to heave himself halfway over the rail, and was trying to draw his sword so that he could defend himself against the hail of blows coming his way. But he was too slow for the nimble Tomaso, who, with one quick movement, slammed his dagger into the pirate's neck, producing a spray of blood and sending him tumbling with a howl over the ship's side to collide with those who were still trying to clamber aboard.

Tomaso turned his head and grinned, his eyes flashing with excitement. 'That's one less of the bastards. Look to your front, Will!'

The words of warning were barely in time, for another pirate had hauled himself halfway over the bulwarks and was balanced precariously on the rail. Will's mind had barely registered the threat before the pirate was upon him, leaping down and charging with a roar. They collided with such force that Will found himself flat on his back with the pirate standing straddled astride him, his sword raised above his head, ready to strike.

There was just enough time for him to drag his own sword up and across into a clumsy parry that probably saved his life, though the force of the blow sent such waves of pain up his arm that he lost his grip on the sword, which fell clattering to the deck.

With a curse, the pirate swung his weapon back up again, ready for another attack, as Will struggled to get up, his feet scrabbling on the bloodied deck. Above him, the corsair's swarthy face beneath its greasy turban was fiercely exultant, the eyes glittering with blind rage.

Will realised that he was going to die; an idea that at first seemed ridiculous, then unbearably sad as he thought of his wife and children, and all the promise of his future, about to be extinguished with a stroke of the sword that was poised above him.

Just as his body tensed in anticipation of the killing blow, the look on the pirate's face turned from triumph to pure astonishment as he looked down and saw the bloodied point of a Venetian sword appear through his stomach. He collapsed to the deck, falling half across Will with a thud that knocked his breath out once again.

'Come on, old man!' Tomaso laughed as he extracted his sword and reached down to haul Will to his feet, the fierce light of battle in his eyes. 'Get up, or you'll miss the rest of the excitement.'

He was relieved to discover that the enemy ship was a chaos of bodies, some still trying to climb aboard the *Bonaventura*, but most lying on the deck, dying or dead, or flung back by the bigger ship's defenders.

All along the *Bonaventura's* starboard side, the pirate attack was faltering. Further aft, a small group of pirates had succeeded in getting a foothold on the deck, but even as he watched they were overcome by a party of sailors descending from the quarterdeck to reinforce the crew in the waist. They were led by the fierce and frightening apparition of Captain Orsini in full cry, Francesco Contarini at his side, looking more grimly determined than exultant. Otherwise, that side of the ship was clear of enemies.

Then he felt the wind on his cheek and heard the crack from above as the mainsail flapped and bellied full. The larboard side battery roared out, sending more clouds of smoke across the main deck. When it cleared, the gunners were standing by their guns and cheering themselves hoarse.

Crossing to the other side of the deck, Will and Tomaso saw why—the other corsair was a complete ruin, both masts gone and trailing over the side, decks smashed, and her sides streaked red with the blood of the poor wretches who had been destroyed by the *Bonaventura's* broadside.

As he watched, the pirates succeeded in cutting away the wreckage of her masts, and her oars, much fewer in number than when the battle had begun, were deployed to drag the shattered hull away from the scene of the battle.

The other corsair had also made her escape, cutting through the ropes that had held her fast to the *Bonaventura*, and shipping her oars to get out of range before the big Venetian galleon could fire another devastating broadside.

Little could be done to stop them; the gun crews, denuded of numbers so as to reinforce the defenders on the upper deck, barely had enough men to fight one battery at a time. By the time they had shifted sides, loaded and run out the starboard side guns, the enemy was already at extreme range. Still, they managed one ragged broadside, and a ball ricocheted off the surface of the water into the stern of the pirate vessel. That was the last shot fired in the action, since the two corsairs were now safely out of range.

Cheers broke out aboard the *Bonaventura* and a jubilant Captain Orsini decreed that an additional ration of wine would be issued that evening. But their victory was not without cost, for they had lost four men and another dozen were injured, some seriously. The wind, their saviour, picked up in force, and the captain was busy issuing a stream of orders that sent sailors clambering up to make more sail.

Contarini, back in his accustomed position by the mizzenmast, removed helmet and breastplate with the help of one of his servants. He greeted the two younger men with a tight smile. 'You young men have survived your first sea-battle unscathed, I see.'

'Only just, Ser Francesco, only just,' Will said, still shaken but trying to put on as brave a face as he could. 'Were it not for Tomaso, I fear you would have been without a chess companion for the rest of the voyage.'

'Which would have been an unspeakable tragedy.' Contarini laughed. 'We both owe you a debt, then, young man.'

Tomaso grinned back, shrugging his shoulders as if to say it was nothing. He looked regretfully across the rail at the two corsair ships, now barely visible against the setting sun. 'Why do we not pursue them? We should finish them off so that they trouble the seas no more.'

'A fine sentiment, my young brave,' Orsini said, coming across the deck to join them. 'But we were lucky. If they had been able to board us on both sides, I doubt we would have survived, even with a ship full of young heroes like Tomaso Martinelli, eh?'

Leaving the captain and his crew to the task of setting the ship to rights, the three passengers retired to the Great Cabin to talk over the day's events. Tomaso was still flushed with excitement, reliving every moment of the fight, never considering for a moment the possibility that he might have ended up among the dead or wounded. Contarini listened to the boy's chatter with an indulgent half-smile on his face, sober and thoughtful as always.

As he toyed with his half-full wine glass, Will pretended to listen to the discussion, even contributing a comment here and there. But this was mere playacting, for his inner mind dwelt on the day's events in a different tenor.

Recalling those terrifying few moments when it had seemed that his life was about to be snuffed out like a guttering candle, he felt an involuntary shiver of horror pass through his body. He hoped never to see a sword drawn in anger again.

But even as that thought formed in his mind, it came to him that the world was an unpredictable place, and that having ventured far from the placid surrounds of Stratford, he was likely to encounter violence again, particularly in Italy, whose reputation for gory tales of revenge was well known.

He thought with shame of his own incompetence in the fighting. That at least he could rectify, and he resolved that he would ask Tomaso to teach him how to handle a sword so that next time he would at least be able to defend himself.

Chapter 10

The Coast of Greece, September 1585

Will remembered the days that followed as the most idyllic of the voyage. The wind blew constantly from the west, with just enough strength to propel them through the water with minimal adjustments required to the sails and rigging. This was just as well, since the crew had plenty of work to do repairing the damage to the ship that had been inflicted by the pirates.

He resumed his routines from the earlier stage of the voyage—reading, learning Italian, playing chess with Francesco Contarini. To this was added daily exercises with the sword, Will having made good his resolve to seek tuition in the use of that weapon from Tomaso so that he would never again feel as useless as he had during that short and bitter fight.

They passed across the Mediterranean, sailing along the Sicilian coast and around the heel of the Italian boot, into the fabled Ionian Sea, where Homer's great heroes had lived out their lives and grappled with the gods. It was there, late one afternoon as they made their way north-eastwards, that those same gods, having smiled benignly on them over recent days, decided instead to show their teeth.

Sitting cross-legged on the lower deck and deeply absorbed in his book, Will was startled as the ship lurched violently to starboard, heeling to a blast of wind that howled through the rigging, making a high-pitched whistle that sounded like all the devils in hell had been let loose.

Scrabbling unsuccessfully for a hand-hold, he was thrown against the dozing Tomaso, who let out a yelp as they slid across the deck. They came to rest in a heap between the ship's hull and one of the great guns, surrounded by a clutter of loose objects that had followed them.

The ship's timbers creaked and cracked alarmingly as the hull yielded to the assault of wind and waves. Yet the *Bonaventura* was strong and well-found, and almost before they could catch their breath, she had heaved herself back level, teetered, then began to roll in the opposite direction.

They held on to the gun-tackle with all their strength, and when the ship righted herself for a second time, they struggled to their feet, making their way aft across a deck that was by now awash with seawater flooding in from the open hatch, towards the main companion-way.

Fighting their way up the steps and emerging onto the main-deck, they were roughly bumped aside by sailors intent on securing the ship against the ravages of the tempest.

They staggered their way towards the companion ladder leading up to the quarterdeck, where they would be out of the way. Will was halfway up when another wild lurch to starboard left him clinging on to the ladder's railing as he was drenched by a wall of spray.

A half-heard shout, barely audible over the hiss of water against the ship's side, made him twist around, tossing his head to clear draggled hair from his eyes. There, to his horror, he saw Tomaso being swept towards the ship's bulwarks by the receding wave, scrabbling desperately to grasp for any handhold that might prevent him from being swept overboard.

Luck was with him, and he just managed to get the fingers of one hand around one of the mizzen-mast shrouds. As the torrent poured over him he hung on, most of his body already over the side, his white face turned towards Will with a look of shock and terror as he realised that he was moments away from being swept into the sea.

There was no time for Will to think. Releasing his own grip, he slid and bumped down the companionway, landing with a thump on the main deck. A combination of his own momentum and the force of the still-rolling ship carried him towards the tangle of rigging to which Tomaso clung in desperation. He crashed into the bulwark with a force that left him breathless. But there was no time to recover, and he pushed himself upright, hooked one arm through the rigging and reached out with the other to grasp Tomaso's upper arm.

Aided by the ship, which had at last ended her starboard plunge and was beginning to roll the other way, Will hauled Tomaso out of the water and back over the side, grunting with effort as he did so.

Catching his breath as they huddled in the shelter of the bulwark, Tomaso gasped some incoherent words of gratitude for Will's life-saving intervention, which he, equally breathless, waved away with a grin.

'Thank God, not me. If the ship hadn't rolled back up when she did, I fear you would have been fish food by now, for my arm was fair breaking under the strain. And at least I won't have to explain to Sir Francis how I came to mislay you so early in the voyage. Come on, let's make a run for the quarterdeck before this accursed storm tries again to kill us both.'

Hauling themselves to their feet, they made another attempt on the quarterdeck companionway, this time managing to ascend without trouble. There they were met by Lance who, astonishingly, seemed unaffected by the ship's capers. Each arm was draped with a heavy blanket, and each hand held a wooden cup of wine, which he proffered towards the two wet and bedraggled young men.

'Here, your honours,' he shouted above the gale, 'something to warm yer insides. And by the looks of ye, ye'll need the blankets to warm the outside an' all.'

Anchoring themselves to the reassuringly solid mass of the mizzenmast, they wrapped the blankets around themselves and took a deep draught of the ale. Will nodded his appreciation to the servant. 'You're a rare gem, Lance. Where in God's name did you find dry blankets and good drink amid this chaos?'

Lance's face split into a broad, gap-toothed grin. 'As to that your honour, 'tis best you not ask nor I answer, except to say that I did so honestly.'

Will laughed. 'Then you must be the only honest servant aboard for I see not one other soul who has been so cosseted.'

'Mayhap all the other souls on board had the sense to stay put down below, where they wouldn't need no cosseting. An' mind you, don't try and go swimming again, Master Tomaso. It ain't the season for it.'

'By God, man, you sound like my grandmother. Go on, get you below and out of this cold and rain,' Tomaso said, laughing.

'I will, masters; the 'tween decks seem to me to be much less chancy than up here.'

There was nothing to be said to that, and so they turned to look at the sea, which had been so benign throughout their voyage, but which was now transformed into a grey waste. Under curtains of driving rain, the surface was broken by innumerable whitecaps that decorated enormous waves that seemingly moved in every direction at once.

Above, the cerulean sky to which they had become accustomed had been replaced by roiling, angry grey clouds, pierced every now and then by flickers of lighting. Will had heard the sailors talk of these sudden gales; a common occurrence in the eastern Mediterranean. He had thought they were exaggerating, as mariners do when they wish to frighten landlubbers, but he had to acknowledge that the reality was far more alarming than even their most lurid descriptions.

Yet under the expert handling of her crew, the ship, having yielded to the initial onslaught of the gale, finally began to ride more easily. The sailors had managed to shorten sail, and the *Bonaventura* was now being propelled by two topsails alone, which provided sufficient force to give her steerage way without driving her bows under the waves. So instead of staggering from wave to wave, she rose and fell in a motion that was more like her old self, though still violent and subject to occasional shudders as she hit an unexpected cross-wave.

Looking across the quarterdeck, they saw Captain Orsini standing at the starboard rail with his second in command, a small, self-contained man named Niccolo, swaying easily with the motion of the ship and looking as happy as if he had found buried treasure.

A great, gap-toothed grin split his face as he called across to Will and Tomaso. 'Now *this* is sailing, boys! Nothing like a little wind to show what a fine ship like the *Bonaventura* can do!' he yelled. 'Make sure you hang on tight, the old mare is a little frisky this afternoon!'

This advice, Will felt, was a little redundant as he waved weakly in acknowledgement of the captain's words. As he did so, Francesco Contarini emerged from the great cabin, looking uncharacteristically dishevelled and pale, and staggered across the deck to join them in the lee of the poop, which provided some shelter at least from wind and rain.

Drenched though they all were, remaining on deck to observe the fury of the storm seemed preferable to being enclosed below decks. For a while all seemed to be well, as the captain, ever willing to impress them with his skills as a seaman, kept up a stream of remarks extolling the virtues of the ship and her crew.

But his mask of self-confidence slipped when the screen of rain and mist parted to reveal land, dead ahead and close enough so that they could make out cliffs and the white peril of surf at their foot. His jovial expression gave way to a look of alarm.

'What land is that, captain?' Contarini called.

'It is, I think, the island of Paxos,' Orsini growled in response. 'We should have been well clear of that coast, but the wind…'

He broke off, rapidly scanning the sky and the ship's sails, then issued a volley of orders that sent the crew aloft once again. Yards were braced hard around, and the helmsmen pushed the whipstaff across to drag the *Bonaventura* to a new, north-westerly course.

This work done, the ship seemed to fall silent as the crew, clearly recognising that there was little else they could do to change their situation, watched and waited. For long minutes, there seemed to be no discernible change to their course. The rocky shore came ever closer, and the sound of the death-dealing surf at the foot of the cliffs became a roar that mingled with the chorus of a multitude of sea-birds wheeling above the cliffs. To Will, it seemed inevitable that they would all be dashed on the rocky shore that drew inexorably closer.

Then, agonisingly slowly, the ship responded to her crew's dispositions. Gradually, the *Bonaventura's* bow slid north-westwards, and the sheer cliffs came onto her beam.

This close to the land, the wind, which had been so fierce and unrelenting further out to sea, became fitful, causing the sails to flap and crack alarmingly. Fortunately, the sea was still deep, and though the sound of the waves crashing against the rocky shore was now deafening, they still had plenty of water under their keel.

Time passed slowly, and it seemed for a while that they were suspended between salvation and utter destruction.

The sound of the ship's bell, struck with admirable discipline by the crew member designated to this task, broke into Will's mesmerised thoughts, and he realised that they must have been sailing along this deadly coast for a full half hour. As the peal of the bells echoed against the cliffs and died away, it seemed to him that the ship was at last beginning to draw away from the coast, and that they might perhaps survive after all.

By the time the bell struck again, they were set at last on their course to the north-west, and safety.

'The current sets north-east here,' the captain said, as much to himself as to his passengers, 'so we'll make more leeway than is comfortable. Still, we'll be safe enough so long as the wind does not change direction.'

The next two hours were tense, as the *Bonaventura* bounced her way north-westwards, her motion an uncomfortable corkscrew as sails and rudder fought against the cross seas driven by the current.

Little by little, the menacing, rocky coast receded, and by the time night fell, they had borne away from the island, towards the safety of the open sea.

By midnight, the storm had blown itself out, the last scudding streamers of cloud passing across a moon that illuminated a sea which, though still disordered, was no longer threatening.

Emerging the following morning after a hasty few hours' slumber, Will and Tomaso beheld the island of Corfu, looming up out of a sea that had recovered much of its accustomed composure. Under a sky still grey and menacing, the south-easterly wind, now much reduced in force, carried them slowly up the channel between Corfu and the mainland coast of Greece.

Will watched in wonder as they slid past tiny coves set below forested hills, hardly able to believe that he was looking at the fabled land of Homer, whose writings he had struggled to comprehend back at school, in a Stratford that now felt as if it was in a different universe.

Anchoring mid-morning in the sheltered bay below the two great fortresses that dominated the harbour and town, it was apparent that they were not the only vessel to have been savaged by the storm. Many of the vessels at anchor were trailing damaged rigging and torn sails, while along the shore half a dozen fishing boats had been smashed against rocks and wharves.

Hammers banged on wood and sailors called to each other as they affected repairs to their ships against a background of the harsh cries of gulls, denied their usual feast of fish entrails.

A few hours later, they were comfortably settled in the gubernatorial palace that stood against the inner wall of the so-called New Fortress. Contarini's status as a Venetian nobleman ensured that they were given an effusive welcome from the local officials and conducted through the narrow streets of the old town to the gates of the fortress.

It felt strange to be on dry land, and they walked with a comical rolling gait. Tomaso took himself off to explore the town, so Will was left to enjoy the luxury of solitude, something he found oddly delightful after the long

90

weeks living cheek by jowl with his fellow passengers and mariners on the crowded decks of the *Bonaventura*.

Standing on the ramparts of the castle and looking across the blue vista of the bay below, he reflected on the journey. They were three-quarters done. In a week or two at most, depending on how long it took to set the ship to rights, they would be in Venice. They had been threatened with destruction twice, and were it not for the skills of Captain Orsini and his crew, not to mention Tomaso's skill with a sword, he would no doubt have met his end by now. But he had survived, and he thought that perhaps, after all, Fortune had some use for him.

Chapter 11

Corfu, October 1585

Will was losing, as usual.

Tomaso's thrusts and lunges drove him back and back under the hot Mediterranean sky. His shoulders ached and his right arm was on fire. Sweat poured down his torso, soaking his simple white shirt.

Clumsily parrying yet another offensive stroke, Will wondered, not for the first time, what had possessed him to ask Tomaso to teach him swordplay, for he had unwittingly unleashed the youngster's most competitive instincts. Not content with merely demonstrating his skills, each bout had become a contest the younger man just had to win.

They had started on the ship a few days after the encounter with the pirates, and before long their bouts had attracted a small and critical crowd of off-duty sailors, whose sympathies were more with the apprentice rather than the master. Thus encouraged, and with firm earth under his feet instead of the treacherous footing of a ship's deck, he had made some progress, and over the last few days had begun to feel that he might eventually get the better of his tormentor.

Not that day, however. Despite the warmth, Tomaso's concentration was fierce. He must have sensed that his opponent was flagging, as he launched a new series of attacks that had Will gasping for air. He made a series of desperate parries until at last he felt compelled to end the fight, as he usually did, with a laugh and a shout of 'Pax!' in order to arrest Tomaso's onslaught.

'Enough, Tomaso, enough,' he gasped, leaning on his sword for support. 'One day, I swear, I will beat you, but that day is not today.'

Tomaso went down in a deep ironic bow, sweeping his sword across in a victory flourish. Will took some small satisfaction from the fact that, despite the ease and grace with which he had fought, his young friend was also sweating profusely. As often before, he was astonished by the strength and power that was contained in Tomaso's slim and wiry frame, a contrast to his own stockier, broader shouldered physique.

'You are getting better, Will,' Tomaso said, 'and of course I have been using a sword since I was a boy. It will take more than a few days' practice for you to match me, but I think you have already learned enough to give a good account of yourself against any ordinary Italian ruffian.'

Which, he supposed, was as much praise as he was likely to get.

As they stripped off their shirts and dowsed themselves with water from a pail standing beside the well in the centre of the fortress courtyard, a commotion at the main gate attracted their attention.

Three men and a woman came into the courtyard, escorted by half a dozen Venetian soldiers. One of the men was the port official who Will recognised from their own arrival, a week before. As the group moved across the courtyard, he was in animated conversation with a plump and fashionably dressed young man whose curly brown hair provided a precarious perch for an elaborate red cap from which protruded the longest peacock feather that Will had ever seen.

The other two, trailing a little behind, presented an extraordinary sight. They were dressed in the ragged remains of what had once been fine clothes. The man was tall and gaunt with a shock of wild grey hair, perhaps in his early fifties, though he walked with the slow shuffling gait of a man much older.

The young woman beside him was also dressed in rags, and though her face was smeared with dirt, she was still strikingly good looking. Long, raven black hair framed an oval face that was delicate and yet strong-featured. Most arresting of all were her eyes, which were a startling green, and which at this moment were anxiously watching the older man.

As they approached the ornate arched doorway that gave entry into the palace apartments, the official turned and placed a hand under the elbow of the older man, muttering something and gesturing towards the palace.

This simple gesture seemed to provoke the tall man, who wrenched his arm away, his face furious. 'Take your hands off me! I am a royal duke, and I will not be manhandled by inferior dogs such as you. You will not move me another inch from this spot.'

Will looked at Tomaso, eyebrows raised. What would such an august personage be doing in Corfu of all places, dressed in rags and under military escort? Tomaso looked as puzzled as Will, and lifted his shoulders in a shrug of incomprehension.

'But signor, please, the Governor of Corfu himself awaits you. If you will but come inside…' The port official was clearly flustered.

93

'Begone, I say. Begone! Leave me be, or I will have you whipped until the bones show through your miserable back.' The grey-haired man seemed to draw himself up to his full height, magnificent and haughty in his rage.

'Now brother, calm yourself. These good men are only doing their duty. I am sure that the governor wishes nothing more than that we should be brought quickly to safety.' This from the man in the red hat, in a soft and gentle voice which seemed to calm the older man. The furious expression left his face, he seemed to physically shrink and his voice adopted a wheedling tone. 'Do not let them injure me, brother. I am but a poor wizard, alas, lost, lost.'

As the old man's voice subsided into an inaudible murmur, the girl moved quickly to his other side, and took him by the arm, exchanging a swift conspiratorial glance with the younger man. 'Let us remember our dignity, Father, and who we are,' she said, in a soft caressing voice that barely carried across the courtyard to where Will and Tomaso stood observing the scene.

Much to the relief of the official, the old man nodded his acquiescence, now as biddable as a child, and they all moved off and into the palace.

As they did so, the girl seemed to become aware for the first time of the presence of the two bare-chested men standing dripping by the well. Her eyebrows narrowed for a few seconds, as if she was contemplating what might be the appropriate attitude for the circumstances, then she turned away to follow the little group through the palace door.

*

The governor's apartments were light and airy, opening onto a wide loggia with a fine view across the harbour. It had become customary for them to gather there every evening to observe the maritime comings and goings, in the hour before dinner.

Glasses filled with fine Corfiot wine, they were watching the four galleys of the Corfu squadron as they swept grandly into port after their routine patrol of the approaches to the island. Will was fascinated by these extraordinary craft, with their banks of oars flashing in the last of the afternoon light, their lateen-rigged masts, and their grandly ornate stern-castles, rather like the Barbary pirate ships that had given them a scare off Malaga, but much larger and altogether more formidable.

Turning away from this spectacle to go inside, they entered the dining chamber just as the governor arrived, accompanied by his wife. They were followed by the plump young man and the young woman who he immediately recognised from the scene in the palace courtyard that morning,

94

although the girl had been completely transformed. She had a glow that suggested the effects of a long hot bath and the rags in which she had arrived were gone, replaced by new clothes, not rich but serviceable, presumably purchased in the town during the afternoon.

'Ah, signori,' the governor said, 'My apologies for being delayed. Official matters claimed my attention, and as you know, Francesco, the Republic's business must take precedence over the mere matter of food and drink, eh? But I see you have been provided with our excellent Corfiot wine, and no doubt you have been enjoying the view.'

Will smiled to himself. Governor Friuli was prone to prattling on like this, filling every silence almost before it had begun; a courtier's habit that sat oddly with the fact that, according to Contarini, the governor was a practical and efficient soldier, well-respected by the garrison.

'Now, allow me to introduce Signorina Madalena Adorno and Signor Bassanio Pavoni. They arrived just this morning and will be staying here for some weeks.'

'Messer Pavoni I know,' Contarini said as they straightened from their bows, 'though it is a surprise to see him here.'

Will thought he heard a hint of disapproval in that remark, as if the curly-haired young man was somewhere he should not be. Pavoni's expression, though, seemed unperturbed as the Venetian patrician went on. 'Signorina, I am sure that the governor has already done so, but allow me to add my welcome to the domains of the Most Serene Republic.'

'Thank you, signor. The governor and his wife have indeed been most generous in their welcome.' The words were delivered in the same gentle, beguiling voice that had helped to calm her father earlier that day. Will wondered where that strange man was and why he wasn't joining them at dinner.

'With your permission, Governor, allow me to introduce my companions. Signor Tomaso Martinelli, who despite his name is an English noble, and his tutor, Signor William Shakespeare. They are travelling to Padua, where they will study at the university there.'

Will and Tomaso both bowed once again, and as they straightened Will was amused to see a rather silly grin on his companion's face, his shining eyes fixed on the girl as if he could not tear them away.

'If Ser Francesco will allow me a small correction,' Tomaso said eagerly, 'while it is true that I am English, I am only half an Englishman. The other half, the better half, is Italian.'

'And so does that make you only half-noble, Signor Martinelli?' The girl's eyes were amused and a little disdainful. Clearly she thought her wits a match for an excitable young man like Tomaso.

She could not know that this apparently harmless sally had the power to wound, for though Tomaso wore his illegitimacy lightly for the most part, he did not much like being reminded, however inadvertently, of his status.

The boy's face clouded, and a flush rose to his cheeks. He opened his mouth to make a reply, but clearly thought better of it and offered a small smiling bow of defeat.

The governor gestured towards to dining room, where Will found himself seated between Tomaso and the governor's wife, a rather jolly if plain woman whose surprisingly coarse sense of humour had given him a great deal of amusement over the last few days. Contarini, the young man Pavoni and Madalena Adorno were ranged on the opposite side of the table, with the governor sitting at its head.

Servants bustled into the room bearing trays and platters of steaming, fragrant food, and Will realised he was famished. They began to eat, and soon the room was filled with the general hubbub of polite conversation, fuelled as usual by the governor, who kept up a stream of chatter about the affairs of the island, interspersed with items of gossip gleaned from his dispatches from Venice.

Will was rather pleased that his Italian was by sufficiently fluent that he was able to understand much of the conversation around the table, though when the talk became animated he often had to ask Tomaso or Contarini to translate.

He tried to suppress his laughter as the governor's wife told him a particularly salty joke, involving a group of sailors and their rather improbable sexual exploits. Her husband, firing an annoyed glance at his spouse, which did not seem to affect her at all, raised his voice to get the attention of Madalena.

'Signorina Adorno, I trust that your father is comfortably settled? He was expected to join us, but alas he is indisposed.' This last remark was for the benefit of the table as a whole.

The young woman, who had been deep in conversation with Contarini, switched her attention to the governor, and Will was once again struck by the startling green eyes. 'Thank you for your concern, messire; yes, he is resting, and I have hopes that he will recover from his ordeal soon.' Her lower lip trembled, as if she were about to break out in tears.

Bassanio Pavoni, sitting next to her, gave her a look of reassurance. 'Your troubles are over now, Madalena. And I am sure your father will recover his wits with time and care.'

Realising that his words had excited the curiosity of the table, Pavoni looked at Madalena, seeking her approval to go on. Biting her lip, the girl's nod was almost imperceptible.

'Signor Adorno is a merchant of noble standing from Genoa. Six months ago, he and Madalena set out from Cyprus in one of his ships, carrying a cargo of spices and sugar destined for Venice. But a storm wrecked their ship, and they were cast ashore, along with half a dozen crew members, in a tiny cove, near the southern end of Corfu.

'The only inhabitants of this little place, which is surrounded by steep cliffs and is almost inaccessible, were a fishing family, poor as can be, barely able to catch enough fish each year to feed themselves, let alone the survivors of a shipwreck. The rest of the crew were all badly injured in one way or another, and although the fishing family did their best to make them comfortable, gradually, the crewmen died, leaving only Signor Prospero and Madalena.'

Madalena, who had been looking down at the table throughout, raised her head. Pavoni nodded encouragingly, and she took up the tale.

'My father went mad,' she said baldly. 'The loss of the ship and the fortune that went with it, not to mention the death of his crew, combined to unhinge his wits. You, signori, were in the courtyard when we arrived yesterday and you saw what he is like.'

Will shifted in his seat, a little embarrassed, as if he had been caught eavesdropping. Glancing to his left, he saw that Tomaso, far from sharing his embarrassment, was entranced. His eyes, shining in the late afternoon light, did not leave Madalena's face, and his features were arranged in what could only be described as an expression of rapture.

'Where the fancy came from I have no idea, but he came to believe that he is the rightful Duke of Milan, deposed and set ashore on this island by his evil brother. Perhaps he was recalling an old tale from Genoese history, for there was a doge who bore my father's name a hundred years ago who was deposed and fled to the court of Milan.

'In his delusion, he decided that the fisher family were his servants, and he particularly took to the eldest son, an ugly brute named Calydon. We could barely understand the dialect of these people, for they are much separated from the rest of the island's population, and Calydon was a foolish

97

creature, but my father by turns treated him with great tenderness, as if he had been his own son, alternating with fits of rage, in which he beat the poor boy mercilessly.

'We survived thus for almost six months, with barely enough to eat. Our strength ebbed day by day, and hope with it. My father, in his madness, convinced himself that he was a magician and that he would spirit us out of our troubles by the use of magic spells. Needless to say, none of the charms he conjured from the inner recesses of his mind served any purpose, and he fell deep into despair.

'Then one day, a week ago, Calydon crept up to where we slept, in a corner of the family's hovel, and woke my father. He stared into my father's face with great concentration, as if he had something important to say, but yet could not say it. Eventually after much slobbering and stammering, he came out with it. "Lord Prospero, Lord Prospero, big sea come, come soon." That was all he said. Yet he said it with great intensity, as if it were an omen.

'His words must have touched some chord in my father's fevered brain, for he immediately sat up, seeming stronger than he had for days, and raised his arms as if he was making a benediction. "Yes, Calydon, I know! For I have conjured a storm to destroy my brother's fleet!" This was the kind of nonsense he was always coming out with, and I paid little attention to it.'

'But of course the poor fisher lad was right,' Bassanio Pavoni took up the story again, as Madalena lapsed into silence. 'For a storm did indeed blow up from nowhere.'

'This was a week ago?' Will asked. 'The same storm, no doubt, that nearly cast us up on Paxos.'

Bassanio nodded. 'Yes, the governor tells me that many ships were badly damaged in that storm. As it happened, I was travelling that same route from Cyprus to Venice when we were thrown off course by the tempest. My mariners succeeded—just—in avoiding the rocks of the coast, but our rigging was badly damaged, and we put into the nearest shelter for repairs. Our anchorage was, as you will by now have guessed, the little cove where the Adornos had been stranded for so many months.

'Though the surf was still dangerously high, some chance instinct filled me with the desire to stretch my legs on dry land, so I commanded the services of a boat to take me ashore, where I was astonished to encounter Signor Prospero and Signorina Madalena.'

'My father greeted Ser Bassanio as if he were the usurping brother of his imagination,' Madalena said, smiling at Bassanio. 'I am sure he was both confused and embarrassed at my father's reproaches to his 'brother' for usurping his Duchy of Milan and casting us ashore on that wretched place.'

Her smile found echoes around the table, as they all contemplated the Venetian merchant's bewilderment.

'Indeed, it was most confusing,' Bassanio went on. 'But Madalena made signs that I took to mean that I should go along with this fancy, so I bore his remonstrance with good grace. Then his mood changed completely in the manner that you saw this morning and he decided that he would forgive me for my supposed sins. "Come, brother," he said, "Let us be friends. I see your ship awaits. Let it carry us infelicity to our home in Milan." So we embarked. Unfortunately, we had much work to do to repair the rigging, so we had to remain embayed in that cove for a week and were only able to put to sea yesterday.'

There was silence around the table, broken, rather diffidently, by Tomaso. 'Yet it seems your father's mind is still somewhat... disordered, Signorina Madalena, judging from the scene when you all arrived this morning. What do the physicians say?'

'They think that he will recover in time with warmth, rest, good food and wine. But they cannot say how long it will take. You know what doctors are like.'

Francesco Contarini cleared his throat. 'And what are your plans now, signorina?'

'Signor Bassanio has kindly offered us passage on his ship to Venice when my father is sufficiently rested to travel.'

'Has he indeed? That *is* kind of you, Bassanio.' Will thought he detected an edge of sarcasm in Contarini's voice, an impression confirmed by the look on Bassanio's face, which wore the look of someone who has been caught in an impropriety. 'And do you have lodgings in Venice, signorina? Or has Messer Pavoni arranged that also?'

If the girl also heard the sarcastic undertone in Contarini's words, she chose to ignore them. 'Bassanio has offered his help, yes, but I do not expect that we will need to rely on his generosity in this respect at least. My father has always maintained lodgings in the city, which should be sufficient to meet our needs until we can resume our journey to Verona. Where I am, or was, to be married.'

Tomaso, who had sat listening throughout Madalena's tale in engrossed silence, jolted upright at these last words. Verona, Will remembered, was where Tomaso's mother had been born. Was it that, or the fact that Madalena was engaged to be married that had caused him to jump?

'And of course your fiancé will not know what has happened,' Contarini said. 'Perhaps I can assist. Write him a letter and we will carry it with us when we sail tomorrow. I will arrange when we get to Venice for it to be forwarded to the gentleman by the fastest means at my disposal.'

'That would be most kind, Ser Francesco,' the girl said, in an oddly flat and unemotional voice. 'His name is Ferdinando Nogarola.'

Contarini nodded. 'I know his father, though I have never met the son. They are a fine and important family in Verona. It will be a great pleasure to be able to set the young man's mind at rest.'

The governor's wife had evidently decided that this remark should bring the evening to an end, as she pushed her chair back and stood, forcing everyone else to follow suit. The governor left with his wife and Madalena, saying that the arrival of the Corfu squadron meant that he had a mountain of paperwork to deal with.

Tomaso suggested to Bassanio that they take a walk around the battlements. Will was conscious of odd currents in the air; Tomaso had an air of suppressed excitement that he could not interpret, and Pavoni, as he made his farewells, seemed reluctant to meet Contarini's eyes.

Left alone with Will, Contarini gestured to the last remaining servant who, visibly suppressing a yawn, poured them both a last glass of wine, and they went back out to the loggia, where the distant sounds of the town drifted across the dark and silent harbour.

'What did you think of that tale, Master Shakespeare?'

Will was pleased that Contarini was now treating him, if not as an equal, at least with respect; he had worked hard to project an air of seriousness that he thought would appeal to the older man, who had little in the way of humour. 'It is an extraordinary story. I cannot imagine the privations they must have endured. I am only surprised that the girl did not lose her sanity like her father.'

'She does seem to be a strong-willed young woman. Young Nogarola might be getting rather more than he bargained for!' It was as close as Will had ever seen to him making a joke. 'And then to be rescued by Pavoni, of all people.'

100

'I did notice, Ser Francesco, that you did not seem to view him with great favour.' Will offered this comment with some diffidence, fearing that he might be presuming too much.

'You are perceptive, William. There is no evil in him, though he is something of a popinjay, as I am sure you noticed. But he is pretending to be something that he is not. He does not own any ships, nor any cargoes that I am aware of.

'He is the nephew to Antonio da Mosto, my good friend and a most successful merchant in Venice. Antonio is both generous and shrewd, but where Pavoni is concerned he has something of a blindness, for he is always lending him money for various ventures that promise much but deliver little. I will wager that it is on just such a venture that our Bassanio was engaged when he came upon the Adornos. The ship he is travelling on is one of Antonio's.'

This explained why Bassanio was so uncomfortable in Contarini's presence.

'It does seem, though,' Contarini continued, 'that the young man has had some good fortune at least. Friuli tells me that he has been appointed as First Secretary to the Republic's Ambassador to the Holy See. The position is not well paid, but it carries considerable influence and there are always opportunities for a shrewd man to, shall we say, augment his salary.'

'He is a rather sleek young man, well-suited to court life, I should think.'

They talked for a few more minutes on other subjects of no real consequence, and then Will, pleading tiredness, made his farewell, leaving Contarini alone to contemplate the night sky and the full moon visible beyond the arches of the loggia.

The following day dawned sunny and cloudless, with a brisk southerly breeze that snapped the castle's flags and pennons, promising a fair wind for their departure later that morning.

Snatching a hurried breakfast while perched on the fortress ramparts, Will and Tomaso gazed down at the *Bonaventura*, snugged alongside the port jetty far below. Sailors and shoremen laboured in the morning sunshine to complete the last of their stores under the impatient eye of Captain Orsini, whose occasional roars of disapproval could even be heard on the battlements of the New Fort.

Will had enjoyed their short sojourn on Corfu, relishing the feeling of having solid land under his feet, but he felt that he was more than ready to resume their voyage and complete its last stage to their ultimate destination.

Tomaso, on the other hand, seemed reluctant to leave. His expression was gloomy and self-absorbed, and he was chewed his food in uncharacteristic silence, his unfocused eyes seemed blind to the charming vista before him.

'Where are you, Tomaso? Not here with me, I think,' Will said with a laugh, trying to find a way to break into his young friend's thoughts.

Tomaso looked up and stared as if he had only just realised that Will was beside him. Then he too smiled. 'I'm sorry, Will. I suppose I should be happy that we are finally on our way and that we will be in Venice in a few days. Yet I would wish we could linger here for a few days yet...'

Will thought he could divine the reason for this unwillingness to resume their journey. 'So that you can spend some more time with Signorina Adorno?'

'Is my face so easy to read?' Tomaso replied, a flush mounting his cheeks.

'Perhaps only by me, though your interest in the girl would have been obvious to anyone who happened to look your way last night over dinner.'

'It's true. I find myself unable to stop thinking about her. She is so beautiful, and charming. And what a strange story! She must be a girl of uncommon courage to have survived such trials.'

Will smiled. He had not been unaffected by Madalena Adorno and her tale and could understand the effect of her charms on Tomaso. But nothing could come of it, given the girl's circumstances.

Reluctant though he was to resume the role of older guardian, he felt an obligation to dowse Tomaso's infatuation, lest it lead him down dangerous paths. 'She is spoken for, Tomaso, as you know. Her betrothed will no doubt come hot-foot to Venice the moment he knows she is safe, and that will be that. She will be off and married before you know it. Better that you put her out of your mind, since we sail today, even if you wish it were otherwise.'

Will thought that his words might have provoked an outburst of anger. What young man wants to be told that his love is hopeless? But eventually Tomaso sighed and bobbed his head in acceptance. 'You are right, of course. Come, let us down to the harbour, and we'll speak no more of Madalena Adorno.'

He jumped down and set off towards the gates and the street leading to the port. Will followed, bemused. His change of heart was a little too easy to be believed, an impression that was reinforced when, at the dockside, they

102

encountered Madalena herself, accompanied by Bassanio Pavoni and Signora Friuli. They had all come to farewell their new acquaintances.

Though Tomaso's greetings were decorous, his gaze lingered on the girl, meeting her eyes with a boldness that was only just this side of lasciviousness. She smiled warmly back at him, and for the first time Will considered that perhaps this inconvenient attraction was mutual.

Contarini was already aboard, as was their baggage, and the ship's crew was in the process of casting off the last of the lines that held the *Bonaventura* against the dock. There was time for little more than hasty expressions of farewell and vague suggestions that they might meet again in Venice, before a testy shout from Captain Orsini sent them hurrying up the gangplank.

In a few minutes, the ship was slipping away from the dock, her sails flapping and cracking once or twice before filling as they were sheeted home.

As they gathered way and headed out into the broad bay, Will thought that it was just as well that Contarini's impatience to depart had prevented them from lingering any longer. With luck, his young charge would soon forget this passing infatuation with an unattainable girl once faced with the distractions of Venice and Padua.

Or so he hoped.

Chapter 12

Venice, October 1585

I f London had assaulted Will's senses, Venice seemed determined to seduce them.

The *Bonaventura* entered the Venetian lagoon in the watery sunlight of an early autumn morning, a slight breeze providing just enough power to keep her moving. Their passage through the still water was nearly silent, the only sounds the gentle creak of the masts, the faint chuckle of water being parted under the prow, and the harsh cries of the gulls circling hopefully around the newcomer to the lagoon. Even the cheerful chatter of sailors happy to be home after a long voyage seemed subdued.

Will had been awake since the earliest rays of the sun had burst over the eastern horizon, pacing around the ship in eager anticipation of their landfall. He was a little sad to leave this tiny community of souls with whom he had eaten, talked, laughed, struggled and fought alongside over the last few weeks. But he was also excited to finally be arriving in Venice and a permanent return to dry land. A sailor he would never be, though he had learned a great deal about the mariner's life and the working of ships, knowledge that was now squirrelled away into a corner of his mind to be extracted at some time in the future when needed.

Perched on the forecastle out of the sailors' way, Will was joined by Tomaso, and the two of them watched as a long sandy island, which, he recalled from one of his many conversations with Francesco Contarini, was called the Lido, passed slowly on their larboard side.

After a few minutes, the channel turned away westwards, and Venice herself came into view across the shimmering lagoon. At first it was a mere smudge on the horizon, between the sea and the distant ramparts of the Alps.

104

Gradually the smudge resolved into darkly angular silhouettes, which after a while became identifiable buildings lining a busy waterfront.

As they drew closer, the water traffic increased—small sailing ferries under oar or sail, carrying goods and people from the city to and from the outlying islands of the lagoon. Here and there, larger vessels, merchant cogs and the like, rode at anchor. Darting between the ships were dozens of gondolas, the high-prowed and double-ended boats propelled by a single oarsman that were unique to the Venetian lagoon.

Beyond a marshy spit of land, where long-legged cranes stalked and pecked in search of food among the reeds and mud, the breeze wafted them past an enormous complex of fortified shipyards, from which arose the clangour of hammers and streamers of grey smoke. This, he thought, must be the Arsenal, where the great fleet of Venetian galleys were built and maintained. It was said that the toiling workmen of the Arsenal could turn out a complete galley in a single day, a feat that seemed superhuman when Will considered the half-dozen of these complex and deadly war machines lying at anchor in the roadstead.

The ship's crew were now furling most of the ship's canvas, leaving only topsails set to provide them with enough forward motion to take them up towards a complex of magnificent buildings that lined the waterfront, rosy pink in the morning's sunlight.

'Behold *La Serenissima*. Is she not the most beautiful of cities?'

Will had barely registered the arrival of Francesco Contarini onto the forecastle, so immersed was he in the sights and sounds of the teeming basin into which they were now gliding. In his enthusiasm for his native city, the Venetian nobleman had shed his habitual dignified air and instead wore a grin of unfeigned delight, his eyebrows raised in anticipation of Will's reaction.

'She deserves her name, Ser Francesco, without doubt. I have never seen anything like it.'

That seemed an absurdly inadequate response to Will's ears, but Contarini seemed pleased by it.

'What is that building?' Tomaso asked, pointing at a magnificent brick structure whose two lower storeys consisted of wide loggias, the uppermost of which was in the curious style that he remembered from the governor's palace in Corfu, pointed arches surmounted by trefoils. Above that, the brick façade, faintly pink in colour, was pierced by seven great arched windows, the centremost of which opened onto a splendid balcony overlooking the

105

canal. There were many grand buildings in London, but this was without doubt the most beautiful piece of architecture that Will had ever seen.

'The Palace of the Doges. Not only the home of the head of the Republic, but the meeting place for the Signoria, and the seat of our government.' Contarini extended his arm, pointing at a tall tower near the palace. 'Over there is the Campanile tower of St Mark, the patron saint of Venice. And you see those two columns topped by statues? They are the symbols of the city— Saint Theodore, and the Winged Lion, which you will remember from Corfu.'

The *Bonaventura* had been slowly losing way as they talked. With a rattle of chains, the anchor splashed overboard, and the ship finally came to rest, riding easily in the centre of the basin.

A few moments later, the customs boat arrived alongside. Officials came aboard with a self-important bustle; the chief characteristic of their brethren everywhere. Contarini gave them no more than a brief glance before returning his attention to the scene in the basin and resuming his commentary on the various buildings that lined the shore.

While listening intently to this discourse, part of Will's mind also registered the departure of the customs boat and, a few minutes later, the arrival alongside of a magnificently decorated barge, its blue-painted hull propelled by four strong oarsmen. In the waist of the *Bonaventura*, the ship's crew were piling up their baggage ready to be transferred to the barge, overseen with great officiousness by Lance, who was clearly revelling in reclaiming his importance after the long weeks at sea when he had been a mere supernumerary.

Satisfied that all was in order, he made his way forward and climbed the short ladder to the forecastle. 'The captain asks me to inform Your Honour that Your Honour's barge is alongside and all is made ready for your departure at your convenience, My Lord.' From the first day of their voyage, Lance's habitual air of barely-suppressed insolence was nowhere to be seen when he addressed Contarini, a fact that caused some amusement for Will and Tomaso, subjected as they still frequently were to the saltier side of Lance's tongue.

They made their way to the ship's side and said farewell to Orsini and his officers, Tomaso receiving an affectionate bear-hug from the captain, then clambered down the short ladder into the barge that bobbed alongside. They gathered again in the open-sided cabin decorated with gold leaf and billowing silken curtains that occupied the middle of the barge.

106

With a whistle and a few quick commands, the barge swept easily away from the ship's side and into the traffic of the Grand Canal. The oars swooped and hissed, propelling them away from the shipping basin and into the canal proper, which steadily narrowed until it resembled a watery grand avenue, lined on each side with three and four-story palaces, each with a canal-level water gate, overlooked by balconies and loggias on the storeys above.

Where a terrestrial road would have been jammed with walking people, carts and animals, this aquatic highway was filled with small craft of every description carrying goods and people in every direction, their pilots calling greetings and the occasional sharp warning to their opposite numbers as they obeyed some mysterious code of rules to avoid collisions.

'What a marvellous place.' Will felt that same excitement he had felt when, as a small child, he had been taken to Oxford, where he had been overwhelmed by the splendour of that university town. 'I thought London was a great city, but now it seems provincial, a city of mud and brick, compared with the splendour of your city, Ser Francesco!'

Ahead, the canal was spanned by a high, covered wooden bridge, rising steeply from each bank to a central span crossed by a pair of drawbridges, currently lowered, across which Will could see throngs of people passing back and forth. Contarini told them that this was the Rialto Bridge, the only such crossing on the canal. The Venetians, who didn't like to waste any space that might yield a profit, had lined the covered walkways leading up to the central drawbridge with shops... with disastrous consequences.

'The shopkeepers are not always as careful as they should be,' he said, 'and as a result it has also burned down several times, which is a great inconvenience, as you can imagine. The city fathers have been debating for years whether to replace it with a stone bridge, but the city government moves at a snail's pace.'

Jostling the other watercraft passing beneath the bridge in both directions, they emerged on the other side, passing the grand stone façade of the Fondaco Dei Tedeschi, which housed the trading colony representing the various German merchant houses. A few moments later, the barge slid gracefully alongside a magnificent three-story palazzo.

'Welcome to the Palazzo Santa Sofia!' Contarini boomed, his dignity giving way to apparent pride in this family home. 'Although some vulgar souls have been known to call it the "House of Gold".'

When Contarini had suggested, one peaceful evening as the *Bonaventura* made her way eastwards across the Mediterranean, that he and Tomaso should be his guests for as long as they needed in Venice, Will had accepted gratefully, since it relieved him of the problem of finding lodgings in a new and unknown city.

He had thought little at the time, or since, about what kind of home the Venetian actually lived in; he supposed that it must be reasonably grand, since Contarini was clearly a wealthy man who owned several properties in the city as well as extensive landholdings in the Venetian *terraferma*, but never in his imagination had he anticipated a building such as this.

Three delicate arched loggias, the lowest at water level, soared above them, a fine example of the unique Venetian style of architecture—part Greek, part Byzantine, part Gothic, all faced in blinding white marble, covered with intricate gold leaf decorations that shimmered in the sunlight reflecting off the water of the canal. It explained the nickname, the *Casa d'Oro*. He laughed out loud and clapped his hands in a childlike gesture of delight, earning an appreciative grin from Contarini.

Disembarking directly onto the ground floor of the palazzo, they were greeted by a small party of Contarini retainers, led by the steward of the house, a gorgeously attired man who matched his master for natural gravity. 'Welcome home, signor,' said that dignitary, with a deep bow. 'I trust you had a safe and prosperous journey?'

'Indeed, Bernardo, though not without its share of incident. Now…'

The Venetian nobleman launched into a volley of instructions in Italian that was far too brisk for Will to follow precisely, but which had the effect of launching the servants into action, collecting baggage and ushering the new guests of the palazzo inside and off to their accommodation. In Will's case this was the luxury of a small room entirely to himself, tastefully furnished with bed, writing table and clothes-chest, overlooking the inner courtyard of the palazzo, at that time of day shadowed and cool.

Among the various items pulled out from his bags as he settled in was the leather pouch containing Walsingham's sealed letter to his Venetian agent, along with a small book of codes and various other items of the intelligencer's craft, in the use of which Phelippes had so meticulously and patiently instructed him.

He contemplated them for a few moments, splayed across the desk where he had tumbled the bag open. During the voyage, that strange interlude during between the comfortable certainties of his old life and the unknowable future that had now arrived, he had managed almost to forget this aspect of his journey. Still, the job itself seemed simple enough—find Walsingham's agent and hand over the letter. He was, after all, just a courier, though they had trained him to be more than that as a precaution against any unforeseen complications.

The following day he planned to make a start, for the sooner this simple task was done, the sooner he and Tomaso could leave for the university in Padua.

But getting started did not prove so easy. To start with, Francesco Contarini, discharging what he saw as his responsibilities as a courteous host, was insistent that they should join him at various social functions around the city. Decorous afternoon receptions at the *Ca' d'Oro* led to more eating and drinking at dinners at one or another of the grand palazzi owned by the Venetian patrician's friends or acquaintances. Venetians kept late hours, dining at nine or ten in the evening, before parading up and down the Campo Santo Stefano, laughing and talking, often until the small hours of the following morning.

During the day, having recovered from their nocturnal activities, they went sightseeing, wandering through the maze of tiny canals and narrow crevice-like streets, laughing at the street theatre being performed in the little squares, joining the throng in the vast open space of Piazza San Marco and staring open-mouthed at the gilded ceilings of the Basilica.

These pleasant pursuits seemed to fill every waking moment of every day for a full week after their arrival. And then one afternoon Francesco Contarini baldly announced that he was departing the next day for a tour of his estates in the country.

'I had hoped to have another week or two here in Venice,' he said, 'but it seems that there are some boundary disputes that need to be settled urgently, and so I must leave tomorrow.'

'How long will you be away, Ser Francesco?' Will asked.

'Oh, a few days, perhaps a week or so.' Contarini paused, and looked at Tomaso. 'Perhaps you would like to accompany me, Tomaso?'

'If it is not inconvenient to you, Ser Francesco, I would be delighted!'

'Good. No doubt Signor Shakespeare will appreciate some peace and quiet.'

The raised eyebrow that accompanied that remark made Will laugh. The Venetian had obviously worked out that Will was become a little worn by the high spirits of his young charge.

The next morning, Will saw them off into the barge that was to take them across the lagoon to Mestre, where horses and servants would be waiting.

'Don't get into any mischief while I'm away, old man,' Tomaso said, adopting a mock-serious expression.

'I'll try to stay out of trouble, though it will be difficult without you to restrain my wilder impulses,' he said in the same vein. 'Don't worry, I have plenty to do, and a little solitude will be a pleasant change.'

As the barge disappeared into the stream of water-craft, Will's only thought was that he could, at last, get on with executing Walsingham's mission.

Chapter 13

Venice, October 1585

The big palazzo seemed eerily quiet after Francesco Contarini and Tomaso left. The remaining servants went about the daily routines that kept the house in good order whether or no their master was resident, politely ignoring his presence, an arrangement that suited him perfectly as he slipped down the grand staircase into the courtyard, and out past a bored and yawning doorman who barely registered his passage.

Beyond the gate, he turned away from the Grand Canal, following a narrow brick path alongside a small service canal towards the hubbub of the city. His excursions over the last week with Tomaso and Contarini, having for the most part been on foot, had given him a good sense of the layout of Venice, but even so he found himself lost on several occasions as he threaded the labyrinth of lanes and bridges, backtracking until he found a familiar landmark.

His objective was a small square in the district near the Arsenal, which he reached in the hour before noon, sweating a little from the unseasonably warm October sun. The long narrow campo was a typical Venetian square. In one corner the usual well-head gave the local residents access to the supplies of rainwater captured in the cisterns below, and a modest palazzo, belonging no doubt to a merchant of middling rank, dominated one side of the square.

On the other three sides it was lined with residential buildings of varying heights, half a dozen of which played host to small shops opening onto the square at ground level, awnings extended out over the street to shelter the shopkeepers' carefully constructed displays of their wares.

There were few people about; in front of one shop a wife haggled furiously over the price of her day's supply of vegetables, clearly getting the better of the shopkeeper, and in a corner two fisher boys sat on stools mending fishing nets. Otherwise the campo was deserted.

Digging into the pouch at his waist, he extracted again the address that Phelippes had given him. *The rooming house of Signora Antonia will be found in the square called the Campo Pozzi*, it said, *in the district of San*

111

Martino, near the Arsenale. It is the fourth house along on the opposite side from the Palazzo Pozzi.

That seems to be it, he thought, looking at a tall and narrow building, three stories high and two windows wide, all of which were firmly shuttered. Unlike the buildings either side, this one had no shop at the ground level, just a blank door as determinedly shut as the windows.

Conscious that the two boys had ceased their work and were looking at him with mild curiosity, he walked up to the door and grasped the wooden knocker, rapping firmly three times on the door, making a noise that seemed to echo around the empty square, though it produced no response from inside.

The silence stretched out and Will was starting to feel slightly foolish. His hand was poised to knock once more when there came a shuffling sound from within, the noise of a bolt being withdrawn, then with a creak of protest from hinges in need of oil, the door opened.

Peering out at him from within was a strongly made woman well over six feet tall. The great mass of grey hair that sprang from her temples and fell over her shoulders framed a face that was comely enough, but was set in an expression that was undeniably hostile. Whether that hostility stemmed from being disturbed or whether it was her habitual expression was impossible to tell.

'Bongiorno, signora,' Will said in his politest Italian. 'Can you tell me, please, is this the rooming house of Signora Antonia?'

'Who wants to know?' The voice was as harsh and uncompromising as her expression, though he detected behind the woman's eyes a hint of uncertainty, perhaps even fear.

'My name is William Shakespeare, from England, and I come seeking Signor Andrea Scaramuccia.'

'The Scaramuccia, is it?' The words were followed by a cackle that might have been a laugh. 'There's no man of that name lodging here, though perhaps you might go to Piazza San Marco and ask his friends Arlecchino and Colombina.'

This remark was baffling to Will. Arlecchino and Colombina were characters in an ingenious street theatre performance that he and Tomaso had stood and watched for a few minutes one day when they were wandering around the city. The comedy was crude and broad, the performers, masked and wearing outrageously exaggerated costumes, acting out roles with which the audience seemed familiar. He could not see any connection between the man he was seeking and the street performers.

'My apologies for disturbing you, signora,' he said, trying to mollify her and prevent her from slamming the door shut in his face, which she seemed on the verge of doing. 'That is the name I was given and this is the house where I was told he lodged, but perhaps I was misinformed. The gentleman I seek is, like myself, a foreigner, and I have important messages for him that I must deliver.

'I shall leave you in peace, signora, but if you hear of anyone who knows of this man, my masters have endowed me with sufficient gold to reward their information.'

He turned to leave, all the while hoping that the word 'gold' would have the required effect, which it did, after he had moved only a few steps away from the house.

'Wait, signor. I said only that there was no man of that name lodging here *presently.*' The harsh voice had turned sly. But Will did not want to seem too eager, and having gained the upper hand, he stood and waited, hand on hip and eyebrows raised in a silent demand for her complete surrender.

'You had better come in. And you two can stop gawping and get back to work, lest your master come home and find you idle!' This was directed at the two fisher lads, who, clearly terrified of the woman, averted their gaze and returned their attention to their nets.

Inside, the house was gloomy with an atmosphere of disuse. The only light came from a doorway at the rear of the building, from whence a shaft of light illuminated the dust motes dancing in the close air.

The woman beckoned him to follow her towards the light, and they emerged into a surprisingly large garden shaded by two big trees and overlooking a small stagnant canal. It was furnished with a table and chairs. On the table there stood a bowl half full of peas and next to it a mound of pods waiting to be shelled.

The woman sat down, gestured for him to take the other chair, and absently picked up a knife to continue the task which he had evidently disturbed.

'There was a gentleman who stayed here,' she said after a minute or so of silence. 'Foreign, too, he was. But not, I think, from England.'

'Where might he have been from, then, signora?'

'I am not sure. Perhaps from Spain. He kept to himself mostly. I saw him in the mornings, but then he would be gone until late at night, long after I was in bed.'

Spanish? That seemed strange. It was possible, he supposed, that Walsingham had employed an agent who hailed from the country that was England's arch-enemy, but Phelippes had made no mention of this when he had provided Will with the information necessary to make contact. Apart from the name and address, he had just said that this Andrea Scaramucci was highly placed in the Venetian bureaucracy. 'What was the gentleman's name?'

The hostile look returned to her face. 'You said something about gold...'

'Of course.' He reached into his pouch and extracted a gold ducat, part of the funds he had been vouchsafed by Phelippes when he'd left Seething Lane, intended to cover his expenses and, he supposed, circumstances like this.

He placed it on the table between them and she eyed the coin hungrily, her eyes shifting between him and it as if she didn't dare to snatch it up. 'There is more, depending on what you tell me.'

'His name wasn't Andrea, it was Andres, Andres Gasparo, or that was what he told me. His Italian was all right, but I could tell he was Spanish. I'm good at working these things out; you have to be in my business.'

Which wasn't thriving, judging from the shuttered down state of the house. He guessed that there must have been half a dozen rooms available, none of which seemed to be occupied, unless their occupants were unusually quiet and mouse-like.

'When did he stay here, signora?'

'Three, no four weeks ago was when he arrived. Paid up front in good coin for the best room in the house, overlooking the campo.'

'And when did he leave? Do you know where he went?' Shakespeare was becoming a little impatient with her curt answers.

But her response to these last questions startled him—a brief bitter laugh. 'Where he went was into the canal, a week ago.'

Will put his hand over the coin that lay on the table between them, keeping his eyes on hers, an obvious threat which had the required effect.

'Like I said, he kept to himself mostly. But one day two men turned up asking for him. Rough-looking they were; the types who would bring out a stiletto and carve you up if you so much as looked at them cross-eyed. So it

114

was just as well for me that all I could tell them was what I've told you—he was a Spanish gentleman, and other than that I knew nothing of him, nor where he was.'

Will sensed that, though she affected indifference, the two men had frightened her more than she wanted to admit. 'And then?'

'The next day he turned up dead, floating in the canal,' she gestured towards the rear of the garden with her knife, 'his throat cut from one ear to the other.'

Will schooled his face to stillness in the face of this shocking news, which, if this Andres was in fact the man he sought, was a calamity.

But the woman wasn't finished with her tale. In fact, she now seemed eager to talk. 'Yesterday, the watch turned up, six of them. *Bastardi!*' She turned her head and spat her disgust into the grass. 'Their *capitano* had some document sealed by the *magistrati*, that he said was authority for him to search the rooms of this Andres Gasparo, who was wanted, he said, for crimes against the state. What could I do, signor, except allow them in with their muddy boots to trample through my house and turn it upside down? But they found nothing, I think, for the *capitano* was very angry when they left.'

'Do you know what they were looking for?'

'No, signor, and I can assure you that I was not going to ask that foul-mouthed *puttana* what he was after. He would have had me in a gaol cell in a moment if I gave him any excuse.'

Will slid the coin across the table. The woman seized it and with a quick movement hid it somewhere about her person.

'There is another of those if you will let me see this Andres' room.'

'Of course, signor.' She was instantly obliging, no doubt calculating that there was nothing for her to lose, since the watch had already been through the room and found nothing. 'Come this way.'

He followed her back into the house and up a creaking, rickety staircase that led to the third floor. The room, when she showed him in, was a fine one with two tall windows, now shuttered, a big canopied bed, table, chairs and settle.

The landlady pushed open the shutters to let light into the room, and Will could immediately see it had indeed been subjected to a thorough and violent search. The contents of a chest that stood against one wall had been strewn across the floor, along with books and papers that had presumably been left lying on the table. The fabric of the mattress had been torn and slashed in

115

every direction, the result no doubt of a frenzied attempt to discover if anything was hidden in its straw-filled interior. Even the settle had been dragged away from the wall, presumably in an effort to find out if there was anything hidden behind it.

Will ran his fingers through his new-grown beard. Then he began to gather up the books and the various papers that were lying on the floor and asked the woman to find him a sack in which he could put them. Her compliance with this request was reluctant, and he watched with some amusement as the conflict between her suspicious nature and her desire for more of his gold played out across her face, before, with a few words muttered under her breath, she went downstairs again.

Sitting at the table, he looked through the papers. There didn't seem to be anything of any interest there—mostly unpaid bills and scraps of notes in Italian, all of which seemed innocuous enough at first glance. Still, he would take them with him in case there was something he could glean from closer inspection.

Then he turned his attention to the books. There was a bible, a treatise on the subject of silk-making, a book of poetry and a copy of a book called *Il Principe* by Niccolo Machiavelli. This was a book he knew of, but had never read. It was famous and infamous, since its author evidently argued that a ruler could justify the use of immoral means to achieve their ends.

He remembered Kit Marlowe approvingly quoting a line from it in one of their long and rambling discussions about politics and philosophy—'He who neglects what *is* done for what *ought* to be done, sooner effects his ruin than his preservation.'

The copy he held in his hand, with a portrait of its cynical-looking author engraved on the cover, was well-thumbed, and as he flicked through the pages he saw that there were many passages that had been underscored.

The grey-haired woman reappeared, puffing and muttering at the top of the stairs after her climb, carrying a simple sack. She watched, scowling but wordless, as he collected the papers and the books and swept them into the sack.

'I don't want no more trouble with the watch,' she said, breaking her silence with a tumble of anxious words. 'Their visit has cost me customers as it is. The word gets around when you've been visited by the constables. And what if they come back and want to know what has happened to his things? How shall I answer them?'

116

'I doubt they will come back, signora,' Will said, with more conviction than he felt. 'But if they do, you can say that you burnt his papers and sold his books so that you could let out the room again.'

This seemed to calm her, as did the appearance of yet another coin from his purse, which he tossed on to the table. He left as she lunged to pick up the money as if afraid it would disappear into thin air if she wasn't quick enough, and went down the stairs and into the campo.

A quick look around confirmed that the square was now deserted, the two fisher lads having evidently completed their work, and the shops all closed up for the afternoon; an Italian tradition. Slinging the sack over his shoulder, he made his way out of the square and retraced his steps back to the Ca' d'Oro.

Back in the privacy of his room, he tumbled out the contents of the sack once again, and began to examine everything more carefully, his mind buzzing with questions. Had he found the right address for Walsingham's spy? If so, why had Phelippes given him the wrong name? Perhaps that was a simple error (though in his experience Phelippes rarely made mistakes) or perhaps the spy had had to assume a different name for some reason. And why, and by whom, had he been killed?

All of which led to the biggest question of all—what was he to do now? After all, his task had been simply to deliver a letter, nothing more. He could, he supposed, simply find some way to inform Walsingham of the fate of his agent, then await any further instructions. But that would have its own problems, since he was supposed to be going off to Padua with young Tomaso.

He also thought of the secretary's words when he had given him his instructions, about the importance of finding out whatever could be gleaned about the King of Spain's intentions in the event of war. Time could be of the essence, and if the spy had been killed because he had information that Walsingham needed, perhaps there wasn't the time to sit and wait for instructions.

While these thoughts went around in his head, he sorted through the papers he had taken out of the sack and smoothed out, piling them into a neat stack, which he examined one by one. Most were as innocuous as his first examination had suggested, but one made him pause. It was just a few words in Italian scrawled on a scrap of paper:

La storia inizia con la prima lettera della prima parola

'The story begins with the first letter of the first word'. Was it a quote of some kind? Or perhaps the writer was beginning a treatise, trying out a phrase which he evidently couldn't complete; a frustrating experience that Will had often had in his own attempts at writing.

He turned to the little pile of books. All of them were well-thumbed, obviously much consulted by their owner, but only in one had the text been underlined in dozens of places, on some pages just a few words, in others long passages.

The first letter of the first word...

Taking a clean sheet of paper and a pen from the corner of his desk, he started thumbing through the copy of *The Prince*, writing down the first letter of the first word of each of the underlined passages. After half an hour of laborious work, he had a full page scribbled with a meaningless jumble of letters.

IPBCJPGOKKEMLSSEMTEGRUZPRAPERAPJEMNORCMVESC
OMAMDJEMLRAPORTMOJETARKERGBVAMCAEKNTOROK
ACEKLCSGOVARALSICRKCSBAR

He sat and stared at the page for a while, trying to see patterns that made sense, but nothing did. Picking up the book once again, he began to flick through the pages, double-checking that he had copied the letters correctly.

A new idea came to him as he did so. What if the first letters of each underlined passage in any given chapter represented a word? Taking a fresh sheet of paper, he copied the letters out again, but this time, referring back to the book, he left a space between each group of letters that were contained in one chapter.

IPBCJP GOKKEMLS SEMTEGRUZ PRAPERA PJEM NOR
CMVESCOM AMDJEML RAPORT MOJETAR KERGB VAMCA
EKN TOROKA CEK LCSGOVARAL SICRKCSBAR

Progress of sorts, he thought, but still gibberish. Obviously it was a code of some kind, but without the key it was impossible for him to decipher it. In London, he had been trained in several coding systems to be used for communications back to England should he need to do so. Of these, the simplest to use was a deranged alphabet cipher, in which a keyword was used

118

to substitute for the first letters of the alphabet, with all the remaining letters written in the usual order.

'It has the virtues of simplicity and elegance,' he remembered Phelippes saying, 'for you only need to know the keyword to reconstruct the cipher, so there is no need for code books which might be discovered. On the other hand, once you have the keyword, it is an easy code to break.'

If this was indeed a message, and if it had been left for someone by an agent in English employ, then perhaps he might have used the simplest cipher available to him. Walsingham's spy networks used a variety of keywords with this cipher. The question was, which one had this agent used? Perhaps the most obvious was the correct answer.

On yet another sheet of paper, he carefully wrote out the cipher.

ABCDEFGHIJKLMNOPQRSTUVWXYZ
ENGLANDBCHIJKMOPQRSTUVWXYZ

And so, painstakingly, he deciphered the text again.

KPHILIP COMMANDS SANTACRUZ PREPARE PLAN FOR INVASION ENGLAND REPORT NOLATER MARCH VENICE AMB TOROME IAM DISCOVERED SKIRMISHER

Will's excitement mounted as he worked through each letter group. From the beginning, he realised that it was significant that the message, when decoded, was in English rather than Italian or Spanish, making it more likely that this was indeed a message from Walsingham's agent.

By the end, the implications of the message were profound. King Philip of Spain had commanded someone called Santa Cruz—Will assumed this was a Spanish noble, perhaps one of his military commanders— to deliver a plan for the invasion of England no later than March next year, seven months away. 'VENICE AMB TOROME' was a little more puzzling. Possibly it meant that the source of the information was the Venetian Ambassador to the Holy See.

More alarming was the last statement, that the writer's identity had been discovered. No doubt that was what had led to his untimely death, though at whose hands it was impossible to tell. Who or what 'SKIRMISHER' referred to was also a mystery, though Will presumed it was some kind of identification.

He stood up, flexing his hand to ease the cramp from writing, and walked over to the window, deep in thought. He saw without really seeing the courtyard below, descending into darkness as the afternoon shadows lengthened.

Only a few days ago, Francesco Contarini had told him of some startling news he had heard on the Rialto: that a fleet of twenty-one ships under Sir Francis Drake had attacked and occupied Vigo, a port on Spain's northwest coast, for two weeks, plundering it mercilessly. Since then, the perennial pain in the Spanish king's side had sailed off, who knew where.

England and Spain were now well and truly at war, and for that reason, the dead agent's message had to be transmitted back to Walsingham as soon as possible.

He was tempted to take it himself, abandoning Tomaso to his own devices, and making the journey as swiftly as he could overland. At least that would get him back home legitimately. But on the other hand, he felt he had a responsibility to see that Tomaso was established and settled in his studies, as he had promised Walsingham. It was not perhaps as worthy or important a motive as the security of the realm, but it was still an obligation he took seriously, especially since he had become fond of the young man over the months they had been travelling together.

In another corner of his mind, that bit which had caused his heart to sing as the *Bonaventura* had left England behind and which revelled in each new sight and sound encountered on his travels, he did not want to go home at all.

He also felt he needed to talk to someone. He couldn't carry this entirely alone, even though that was the nature of an intelligencer's role. Unlike Kit Marlowe, he took no joy from intrigue and mystery. Though he liked and admired Francesco Contarini, whose intelligence and integrity he had come to respect, it was obvious that he could not be told about any of this. That left only Tomaso himself as a possible confidant. Was the young man mature enough to confide in? Perhaps not, but he was Sir Francis Walsingham's ward, so his loyalty could not be questioned.

In a few days, Contarini was due to return to the palazzo, Tomaso with him, and he would decide then what to tell the latter.

Chapter 14

Venice, October 1585

I t was a full week before he could talk to Tomaso, days in which he pushed his anxieties about the implications of all he had discovered to the back of his mind, distracting himself by working on his play. But eventually the morning arrived when, having been alerted to their impending arrival by a sharp-eyed boy who had been posted on the roof, Will joined Bernardo, the household steward, at the water landing of the Palazzo Santa Sofia to await the arrival of the Palazzo's master.

The barge had barely come alongside before an excited Tomaso leapt across the narrow gap, grasping Will in a boisterous embrace as if he had been gone months, not mere days. He was followed by Contarini, who wore the bemused but tolerant look of a fond father for a favoured if wayward son. Tomaso seemed to have this effect on everybody.

'Welcome home, Ser Francesco,' he said, forestalling Tomaso, who was obviously bursting to tell him about their travels over the last few days. 'I trust your journey was successful?'

'It went well enough. Fortunately, I have excellent servants who look after my estates from year's beginning to year's end without any supervision from me. Indeed, I suspect my occasional inspection tours are more annoying than helpful, eh Bernardo?'

The steward merely smiled rather absently as he took his master's boat-cloak, wet with spray from the passage across the lagoon and down the Grand Canal.

'You should have come with us, Will.' Tomaso could restrain himself no longer. 'Ser Francesco's horse farms are a sight to behold! I've never seen such rich grasslands, and the horses are magnificent. And we went to Padua, where Ser Francesco showed me the university, and we found Uncle Francis' coat of arms on the wall, among all the other graduates. Why are you laughing?'

'I'm not. Well, yes, I am.' He flung an arm around the boy's shoulders. 'Come on, I'm sure that Ser Francesco doesn't need to hear you recount

121

every minute of your journey. Let's go upstairs and you can tell me all over a glass of wine and some bread and cheese for breakfast. Francesco, with your permission?'

Contarini waved an amused hand and the two of them went off up the stairs to their rooms on the upper floor of the palazzo. Tomaso kept up his happy, guileless chatter about all the things he had seen and experienced over the last few days. It was as if the journey into the Veneto, even more than their arrival in Venice, had made him feel that he was in the land of his heritage, if not of his birth, and he had to soak it all up, lest it escape him.

But even the fiercest torrent must slow, and like a desert spring trickling away into the sands, at last Tomaso ran out of words, suddenly becoming self-conscious. 'I must sound like a giddy maid.'

'You are excited, that's all. It's to be expected, you are new come to your mother's country, which must seem passing strange.'

'It is that. I do feel her presence here. She used to sing Italian songs to send me to sleep when I was a little boy, and she would tell me about how Verona was the most beautiful city in the most beautiful country in the world, and how we would go back there one day. She always missed it, I think, and never really forgave my grandfather for taking her away to England. So I think I want to like it, for her sake.'

Will was surprised and touched by these words, for Tomaso rarely spoke about either of his parents. The earl had been a somewhat erratic presence in the boy's life and his mother had died when he was just ten years old. Left to the care of various governesses and tutors after her death, he seemed to have had little in the way of real parental affection as he grew up, until the earl died and he came into the care of Sir Francis Walsingham. Tomaso spoke of him with far more warmth than he could muster for his father and he seemed to have evoked a fondness in Walsingham that was remarkable in such a severe old Puritan.

'What have you been doing over the last few days?' Tomaso said. 'Buried yourself in that play of yours, I suppose, with no one here to disturb you.'

One evening during their voyage to Venice, Will had told Tomaso about *The Comedy of Errors*, trying to establish his credentials as a man of literature and philosophy. Tomaso had been fascinated and nothing would do but that he should read the draft, by now dog-eared and salt-stained. At the end the boy had been fulsome in his praise, though he had also offered some suggestions that revealed a sharp intelligence and a witty sense of humour.

122

After that, the play had become something of a joint project, Will spending his spare time rewriting and revising, and Tomaso acting as critic for the revisions.

'I did some work on it, yes. But I was distracted by other... events.'

Tomaso's eyebrows lifted.

'You remember, back in London, that you said that Sir Francis never did anything without at least two motives, and that he had probably given me one or two other tasks to boot? At the time, I said nothing, but of course you were right. He did burden me with another mission; a simple enough task, just a matter of acting as a courier, delivering some instructions to his agent here in Venice.'

Will felt slightly sheepish as Tomaso clapped his hands and laughed. 'I knew it! He is a huckster, is Uncle Francis, and I am not at all surprised that he should have extracted a double return for the price of clearing your good name. But I take it from your gloomy countenance that this 'simple task' didn't go according to plan?' Tomaso's eyes were now sparkling with interest; the boy loved nothing more than an intrigue.

'No. When I got there, I discovered that the agent was dead, throat cut and thrown into a canal just a few days ago. His landlady let me look in his room, which had been turned upside down by some toughs of the city watch. I didn't find much, except a few scraps of paper... and this.'

He picked up the volume of Machiavelli from the pile of papers on his desk and handed it to Tomaso, who turned it over in his hands in puzzlement.

'The book contains a coded message,' Will said, explaining with some pride, his efforts at decoding it, ending his exposition by pulling the decrypted message from his desk and handing it to Tomaso.

'I am amazed and impressed, Will. Old Phelippes trained you well. But, tell me, why put the message in a book like this? It seems an odd way of doing it.'

'I don't know, but I think that the agent, this Scaramuccia or Gasparo, or whatever his name was, knew that he was discovered and decided to convey his message this way in the hope that it would escape detection. Perhaps he had a colleague who would know what to do with it in the event of his death. In any event, I have it now.'

Tomaso looked at the decoded message again. 'Scaramuccia did you say his name was?'

'Yes, that was the name I was given in London, though the landlady seemed not to know it. She told me that the dead man was named Andres Gasparo, and that she thought he was Spanish. So I do not even know for certain that this man was in fact Walsingham's spy.'

'I think I can make one point clear, at least,' Tomaso said. 'Do you remember that *Commedia dell'Arte* performance we saw last week in San Marco?' Will nodded. 'There is another character who often appears in these plays, called Scaramuccia. He is usually dressed in the Spanish fashion. He is a boaster and a coward who usually gets beaten by Arlecchino. I remember my mother telling me about all these characters when I was a child.'

The landlady's strange remark about seeking Scaramuccia in San Marco now made sense.

'The point is,' Tomaso went on, 'In English, Scaramuccia means "Skirmisher", which is also the name that he has signed the message with. So I think you can be sure that it came from Uncle Francis' agent. I imagine it must have been some kind of code name, for surely no one would expect to be taken seriously in Italy if that were his real name.'

That seemed quite possible to Will; perhaps he had been given the code name instead of the man's real name by mistake. But it did seem to confirm that the message was authentic.

The more important question was what to do with it. Obviously, it had to get to London as soon as possible, but how to achieve that was another question. He had been given sufficient funds to pay for a courier but could he really entrust such a sensitive message to a courier? It would be better if he could send it home with someone he trusted.

'What were Sir Francis' instructions to this Scaramuccia?'

Tomaso's question was so obvious that it made him feel like a fool. 'I don't know. They are contained in a sealed letter that I was to give to the agent. It didn't occur to me to open it.'

Actually, he wasn't sure he wanted to know what was in the letter, since in the circumstances, it was bound to drag him deeper into this world of intelligencing than he wanted to go. But Tomaso's question was the right one—how could he decide what to do if he had no idea what Sir Francis' intentions were?

With a sigh, he opened the drawer in the desk where he had placed the letter after his return from the dead agent's lodgings. He picked up a knife and pried off the wax seal.

124

'It's in code, of course,' he said, squinting at the closely-printed characters. This was a more complex code than the one he had used for the agent's message, but he recognized it as one for which he had a cipher in the codebook he had brought with him from London. It was locked away in a small chest that he kept under his bed; the key was always around his neck, under his shirt.

Tomaso watched in fascination as Will unlocked the chest and took out the codebook.

'Come on,' Will said, 'you might as well help.'

As Tomaso read out each letter of the coded version, Will used his code book to decipher it and write down the result in plain English. After half an hour of laborious work, they had the result.

> My dear Andrea,
> By the time you receive this, it will be common knowledge in Venice that England and Spain are at war. This has been a conflict long delayed and one that Her Majesty has sought always to avoid, in her constant desire to ensure the wellbeing of her subjects and the peace of her realm. But the enmity of the Catholic powers has always meant that war was going to be inevitable, and now it is upon us.
> Our forces, though gallant, are small against the resources of Spain and her empire. If we are to prevail, we must seek to bend all advantages to our cause, in particular the earliest intelligence about the King of Spain's intentions. Your past services to us in this regard have been most valuable, but I must urge you to redouble your efforts, by employing all of the resources you have to find out what plans Philip might have for the future prosecution of the war.
> I do not need to emphasise to you the importance of the opportunity that your presence in Venice provides. Though the Serenissima is a Catholic state, she is the only

power in Italy not beholden either to King
Philip or the pope. The Republic has
diplomatic missions to both and this has proven
useful to us in the past. I urge you to explore
this avenue again.

You will have received this communication by
the hand of a young man whom I trust, Master
William Shakespeare. He is escorting my ward
to commence his studies at Padua University,
our old alma mater, and so will be in Italy for
some months. You can rely on him to deal with
discretion any information you are able to
acquire, and he has been provided with the
means to communicate urgently with me
should that be necessary.

I wish you good luck and send you my best
affection as your former schoolmate.

Francis W

By the time they had puzzled out the last words of the letter, all levity had
evaporated from Tomaso's countenance and Will was gratified by the new
respect with which the young man now seemed to be regarding him as he
contemplated the implications of the letter.

What seemed most obvious was that the information that had been so
carefully concealed in the book by poor Andrea must be sent to London as
soon as possible. The most certain way of making sure that it reached its
destination safely was for him to take it himself, as he had thought the
previous evening, leaving Tomaso to move on to Padua and establish himself
there without his help... as if that help had ever really been needed.

As the letter made clear, his accompanying Tomaso had never been more
than a convenient fiction, and now that that fiction was no longer necessary
he felt less compunction about leaving the young man to his own devices.
Though he would regret not having the opportunity to join him in his studies,
the concession he had extracted from Walsingham as a condition of
undertaking this mission in the first place.

On the other hand, what was he planning to take back to London? The
fact that the King of Spain had issued a command to one of his underlings to
prepare a plan for the invasion of England was important, to be sure, but Sir
Francis Walsingham had also made it plain in his letter that he was looking

for as much valuable intelligence on the Spanish intentions as he could get, and that he was relying on his agent to get it for him.

Therein lay the rub—Sir Francis did not know that his agent was dead. Yes, he could go pell-mell back to London, deliver the information, and say he had discharged his obligation. But in his mind's eye he could see Sir Francis turning that withering look of contempt on him with which the secretary could quell even the most nobly born of the queen's courtiers. What was more, he had come to both like and respect the old man during his short time at Seething Lane and he did not want to let him down.

If anyone had said in his hearing that William Shakespeare was a patriot, devoted to his country, he would before this day have been puzzled, for he believed he was above all a rational, dispassionate man, and the fire of patriotism was foreign to his nature. Yet his country, the England of which he knew little but loved much, was faced with war and an invasion that, if successful, would rip open the old wounds of religious division and lead once again to good people being burnt at the stake for their beliefs.

For all these reasons, he knew that he had to stay in Italy and at least try to find out more about this proposed invasion fleet, and if possible, recruit a new agent to replace the dead Scaramuccia.

Tomaso sat in silence while Will let these thoughts chase each other incoherently through his head, watching his erstwhile tutor with curiosity. 'So,' he said when he thought that he had Will's attention again. 'What do we do now?'

Will smiled; obviously the boy thought he was going to be allowed to join the English intelligence service. 'You, young man, will be going to Padua University. As for me, I will have to decide how best to get the information we already have back to London, and then how best to further Sir Francis' aims here in Venice.'

'But I thought...'

'Yes, I'm sure. But I cannot allow you to get caught up in these matters any further than you are already. In truth, I should never have even divulged to you as much as I have. So you should go to Padua, and I will join you when I can, unless it seems expedient for me to return to London.'

Unwillingly, Shakespeare softened at the crestfallen look on Tomaso's face. 'Look Tomaso, I really do think it is best for you to go on to Padua and leave me to solve this. This is a dangerous business and Sir Francis would never forgive me if you became involved in it and then were injured or, God forbid, killed.'

127

'And if I refuse?'

The disappointed look had been replaced by a stubborn expression, and Will saw a glimpse of the young man's father in the jut of the chin and the narrowing of his eyebrows into the smallest of frowns, hinting at an aristocratic imperium used to getting its own way.

He was right, of course; Will's authority over him, such as it was, rested on his supposed role as tutor and guardian, and though Tomaso had always been prepared to go along with this fiction in his good-natured and amused way, this time he knew that Tomaso would not submit meekly to his decision.

'Besides, how can you do anything useful for Uncle Francis without my help?' Tomaso pressed home his advantage. 'After all, you know no one in Venice and everything about you marks you out as a foreigner—your clothes, your accent—whereas I can easily pass as a native. And surely two minds at work on this will be better than one?'

They stared at each other in a silent tussle, before Will capitulated, throwing his hands in the air. 'All right. Perhaps you are right; the sooner we can get what Sir Francis needs, the sooner we can both get on to Padua, and I can go home. But mark you, we must take care in this business. It has cost one man's life already, at whose hands we do not know, and from the fact that the watch came looking for Andrea, it seems obvious that the Venetian Republic is aware of his activities, so we must tread carefully with Ser Francesco.

'If either the Venetian authorities or whoever killed Andrea, assuming they were not the same people, learns that we have taken papers from his lodgings—and I'll be bound that the landlady's mouth will be un-stoppered quickly enough with the merest application of gold—they may well come after us.'

'Then it's just as well I can defend myself and I've taught you enough swordplay that we can at least be sure you will do more harm to your enemy than to yourself.' Tomaso's grin was irrepressible.

Will smiled in response. Nothing was going to daunt this young man, that much was clear, and his old-mannish caution had done no more than provide a whetstone to the blade of his excitement. 'So then, first order of business, Master Intelligencer Martinelli, how do we get Skirmisher's message to London as quickly and as safely as possible if I am not to take it myself?'

'Did Phelippes not provide you with the means to communicate information back to him? By a courier perhaps?'

128

Will had already thought long and hard about this. Courier services were maintained by all of the major banking houses, for whom the secure transmission of information about their clients was essential to their financial success. And there were other private services, though these were often less reliable.

Phelippes had indeed given him sufficient funds and the means to engage just such a courier, one who he regarded as both swift and reliable, and who could be used to send routine reports back to London. But Will hesitated; the information he had to transmit was far from routine, too important to be entrusted to a mere courier.

'Yes, but what if the courier meets some mishap on the road? It happens often enough, and were this a mere ordinary letter, it might be a risk worth taking. But do we dare take such a risk with a document of such importance? We need to find someone we can trust, someone who we can be sure will do everything in his power to make sure that the letter gets to its destination.'

Tomaso nodded. 'What about Lance?'

The question seemed to be such a non-sequitur that Will was taken aback. 'What about him?'

'We could send him home to London with the message. He would defend it with his very life, that I'd swear.'

Since they had arrived in Venice, Will had seen very little of Tomaso's uncouth retainer. He lived with the other servants in the upper reaches of the building, and Will had only encountered him occasionally as he came and went from Tomaso's rooms. Though they'd greeted each other with the natural affection of strangers in a strange land, Lance's natural impish insubordination had been, it seemed, overawed by the grandeur of their new surroundings.

Will had last seen him that morning, disembarking from the barge with the rest of the Contarini retinue, looking a little harassed, as if the task of looking after his master's needs on this particular journey had been particularly taxing.

The idea that Lance could serve as a trusted courier seemed on the face of it to be outlandish. But Will had to admit, the man's loyalty was undoubted, and the outer garment of his rude manners clothed a surprising wit and intelligence that had flashed forth from time to time aboard the ship, often catching him by surprise. 'Yes, that might serve. Why don't you go and find him while I write a letter to Sir Francis?'

129

Alone once more, Will sat at his desk and, after a few moments' thought, applied pen to paper.

> Sir Francis,
> Greetings. If you receive this message, it will have been delivered by the hand of a loyal servant, who I beg you will reward as seems appropriate. As per your instruction, I attempted to deliver your letter to your agent in Venice, but on discovering that he was dead, by foul means, it would seem, I took it on myself to search his lodging. The enclosed message was discovered therein and I am sure that you will understand its import immediately and why I chose to send it to you in the saddlebags of said trusted servant rather than via courier.
> I also took the liberty of opening your further instructions to your agent, and since they cannot be enacted by him, I have resolved to do my utmost to procure the information you require by my own efforts. I trust that this course of action meets with your approval.
> Tomaso is well, and we are now at Venice, where Ser Francesco Contarini is providing accommodation, but I hope soon that we will move on to Padua where Tomaso can commence his studies.
> Your faithful servant,
> Wm. Shakespeare.

Will had completed his letter, encoded it, and was in the process of sealing it when Tomaso reappeared, with Lance in tow. When Tomaso had explained that he was to be sent back to London, taking with him some important documents, the servant's expression barely changed. Apart from the slightest widening of the eyes and the faintest twitch of a smile, he might as well have been receiving instructions to shop for supper, rather than being presented with a change in his immediate future, and the prospect of a long and arduous journey home through Alpine passes in wintertime.

130

'And where do your honours wish me to deliver this document?' was all he asked.

On being told that he was to go to Seething Lane and deliver the papers into the hands of Thomas Phelippes, and no one else, he smiled and tapped the side of his nose knowingly. 'I sees, your honour. Well you don't have to worry, old Lance knows what's what, that he does, and your message will get to Seething Lane safe and sound, that I swears.' He went on, in a low, almost inaudible monotone, as if he was talking to himself. 'There's a party of Burgundian merchants leaving the city tomorrow, going back to the low countries. I could travel with them as far as Bruges, and then take passage across the Channel. Slow, perhaps, but safe and secure.'

How Lance knew the movements of the merchant-folk who thronged the city was a mystery, and how he was going to insert himself into this Burgundian caravan was even more so, but Will was comforted by the man's no-nonsense practicality.

Lance and Tomaso having departed, he settled down for bed feeling confident that his dispatch would reach London safely. For the rest, he would have to think hard about a strategy to take things forward. Though Phelippes had equipped him with many skills, they did not include the techniques necessary to successfully identify and recruit agents in a foreign country.

Will felt at a loss as to how to proceed. Little as he liked to admit it, he realized that Tomaso was right—he would not be able to do anything without his help. He was not sure how comforting that thought was as he finally drifted off into sleep.

131

Chapter 15

I s that not Bassanio Pavoni? Over there, at that jeweller's stall?'
They were in the Rialto, the complex of buildings that served as
Venice's principal mercantile exchange and marketplace.

He and Tomaso had spent most of the morning browsing among the
booksellers ranged on one side of the square, buying up the books that
Tomaso would need when he commenced his studies at Padua in the new
year.

Ever since he had first learned to read as a small boy, books had been his
chief source of pleasure, and in London, Will had spent every one of his few
spare moments haunting the booksellers in St Paul's churchyard, spending
what meagre funds he had acquiring books and pamphlets on all manner of
subjects that he then read over a guttering candle deep into the night alone in
his attic room. In the three months that he had been away, one of the things
he had most missed was the joy of hunting among the booksellers' wares for
hidden treasures, and so that morning was something of a special treat.

He had been in the act of adding one more book to the tottering pile held
in the arms of one of Contarini's household servants when Tomaso's remark
caused him to turn and look across the heads of the noisy crowd that
thronged the courtyard. Sure enough, there was the familiar shock of curling
brown hair, the red cap with its preposterously long peacock feather, no
doubt Pavoni's favourite hat, atop the fur-swathed form of the young man
they had last seen on the dockside at Corfu. He stood at the stall of a silver-
merchant under the canal-side loggia of the market, handling a small gilded
casket that he turned this way and that.

Without waiting for Will's response, the ever-impulsive Tomaso pushed
his way through the crowd, waving his arm to get Pavoni's attention. Shaking
his head with a tolerant smile, Will turned to the bookseller, slipped a few
coins across his counter in payment and commanded the servant to go back
to the Palazzo Santa Sofia with their purchases, an instruction that was
obeyed with evident relief.

By the time he had forced his own way through the crowd, Bassanio and Tomaso were embracing each other as if they were long-lost friends with that Italian effusiveness that he, still the phlegmatic Englishman, found discomforting. Their greetings completed, Pavoni turned to Will and offered a graceful half-bow, and they exchanged rather more restrained courtesies.

'What have you there?' he asked, looking at the small silver casket, Spanish in style, entirely covered in elaborate and finely chased designs representing flowers and leaves, which Bassanio seemed to have forgotten that he was still holding in his hands. 'It's exquisite.'

'Yes, it is rather beautiful,' he said, before handing it back to the shopkeeper with a regretful sigh. 'But I fear a little beyond my means, at least for now. Perhaps in a month or so...'

Will smiled inwardly, remembering what Contarini had told him about Bassanio Pavoni during one of their conversations over the chess board on the voyage from Corfu.

'The boy is a spendthrift,' he had sniffed. 'Oh, I like him well enough, but he seems never to be able to keep hold of a single ducat for any length of time; always spending on half-baked commercial ventures, on clothes and jewels. If it were not for his Uncle Antonio, whose generosity seems to have no end, he would be in the prison for paupers.'

Will held his tongue as Bassanio shook off the importuning of the disappointed shopkeeper, suggesting that, since it was close to midday, they all retire to one of the small cook-shops that were tucked here and there among the other stalls and shops that lined the porticoes of the marketplace, a proposal that Tomaso, whose youthful appetite was voracious, took up with enthusiasm.

'So tell me, Signor Bassanio,' Tomaso said, having devoured a bowl of bean soup and half a loaf of bread, 'does your presence here also indicate that Signorina Adorno and her father are also in Venice?'

The question, seemingly artless, took Will by surprise. Clearly Tomaso's brief infatuation with Madalena had not been exorcised by the passage of time and the distance from their last encounter.

'Indeed they are,' Bassanio said, 'Signor Adorno recovered his wits entirely with a few weeks' rest, praise God, and we were able to continue our journey here without further delay. Both he and Madalena are now staying as guests at the palazzo of my uncle, Ser Antonio da Mosto, who was most affected by the tale of their shipwreck and rescue, and who insisted that they abandon their own lodgings to stay with him.'

133

'Will they be staying long in Venice or do they go on to Verona immediately?'

'Of that I am not certain. You will recall that Madalena is to be married to Ferdinando Nogarola, from Verona. He has been advised, by the fastest courier, that the Adornos have arrived here, and I understand that he and his father will be arriving in Venice at any moment. I expect that they will all go back to Verona after a suitable interval to resume their marriage plans.'

'Ah. Ser Francesco and I called on the Nogarola household when we were there a week ago,' Tomaso said, earning himself a look of astonishment from Will, for Tomaso had said nothing to him of any such visit. 'Ser Ferdinando was not at home, but we conveyed the happy news of Madalena's survival to his father, who seemed overjoyed.'

'And yourself, Bassanio?' Will asked, forestalling any further questions on the subject of the Adornos from Tomaso, 'Do you remain in Venice for long? I seem to remember Ser Francesco telling me that you are to take up a post in Rome?'

Tomaso looked up from his wine glass, a sharp expression on his face. 'Yes, I have had the good fortune to be appointed as Secretary to the Ambassador of the Most Serene Republic to the Holy See. But I am remaining here in Venice for a while yet. The ambassador does not leave for Rome until after the Christmas festivities are over, which is as well, since I have some affairs of my own that I need to take in hand.'

'It would take more than mere good fortune, I'll be bound, to be entrusted with such an important position. No doubt the Signoria recognized your considerable talents as well.'

This was laying the flattery on with a trowel, he knew, given that they were barely acquaintances. But Bassanio barely seemed to notice. 'There were others vying for the post, for certain. And my uncle was helpful. But yes, I think that I owe my appointment to merit, mostly.'

'But tell me, what does the Secretary to the Ambassador actually *do*? Forgive me, I ask out of ignorance.'

'Oh it is not such an important position,' Bassanio said, affecting a modesty that Will felt was mostly false. 'Mainly I will be responsible for managing the correspondence that crosses the ambassador's desk—opening daily dispatches from Venice, composing reports for his signature, that kind of thing. It is an honourable position, but humble; a start on the ladder of my career, I hope.'

134

Seeing the disappointed look on Will's face, which was not entirely contrived, Bassanio hurried on. 'Of course, much of that correspondence is highly confidential, so the Secretary to the Ambassador must be trusted to deal with it sensitively, to know what is important and what is not, to sort the wheat from the chaff. And the ambassador requires eyes and ears beyond the embassy walls, so it would be normal for the secretary to get out and about, talking to the kinds of people who would not normally come into the ambassadorial presence. So you see, it is more than a mere clerk, this position.'

'I never doubted it, dear Bassanio,' Will said. 'It is a weighty position indeed. You will be a great success, I make no doubt.'

Bassanio nodded, causing the peacock feather to form an arc in the air. 'I hope so. My only desire is to do honour to the Republic, though she is a demanding mistress.' The self-satisfied expression gave way to gloom. 'But there are substantial expenses that I will have to meet—tailors for the clothes that I will need if I am to present an appropriate figure in Rome, suitable lodgings, food and wine with which to entertain. In short, signori, it is an expensive business, acquiring a position of honour in the Venetian Republic.'

'But surely there is a salary attached to the position?' Tomaso asked.

'Yes, of course, but it is, I am afraid, rather modest, and it is always in arrears.'

Will nodded in sympathy. The Venetian Republic sounded as parsimonious as the English monarchy.

'But enough of this gloomy talk of money. Besides, no doubt Uncle Antonio will lend me whatever I need until my salary arrives,' Bassanio said, though he did not sound entirely certain. 'The future will be whatever it will be, and in the meantime life is to be enjoyed to the full, is it not?'

He raised his glass in a toast, and the conversation moved on to other subjects, mostly gossip about prominent figures in Venice and Rome. Bassanio had a diverting way of telling stories, embellishing them with details gathered from all sorts of sources and people, from grand Venetian patricians to lowly stablehands. He wove them into an amusing and entertaining whole that kept Will and Tomaso entranced for a full hour. With his disarming demeanour and his air of universal friendliness, Bassanio was the kind of man in whom people were willing to confide all sorts of secrets; a useful trait for a would-be diplomat.

'Oh, I almost forgot,' Bassanio said as they paid the cook-shop owner and stood in the street preparing to go their separate ways. 'Uncle Antonio is holding a reception at the Ca' da Mosto two days hence in celebration of his birthday, to which you are both invited. The written invitations will be sent to the Palazzo Santa Sofia this day, but since we have met so fortuitously, I do not imagine he will mind if I tell you now.'

As Bassanio walked off towards the wooden arch of the Rialto Bridge, Tomaso jumped in a little skip of excitement, a broad smile on his face.

This prompted a quizzical look from his companion. 'It's just another party, Tomaso. I can't see why you would be so excited by such an invitation. Unless it is because you are on fire to see Madalena Adorno again. Could that be the cause of this strange levity?'

'What are you suggesting, Will?' Tomaso's feigned outrage convinced Will that his shaft, launched on nothing but an instinct, had flown true. 'Certainly I am looking forward to seeing her again, for I found her company enchanting at Corfu. But what is wrong with that?'

'She is engaged to be married, and to a Veronese nobleman, that's what is wrong.'

'I know, I know. But still, she was beautiful, wasn't she, and—'

'And nothing! Tread carefully, Tomaso. You know the reputation that your countrymen have for hot-bloodedness and I have no desire to have to extricate you from a duel just because you looked at a girl the wrong way.'

Tomaso threw his hands in the air in a gesture of defeat. 'All right, Will. I promise to be on my best behaviour.'

Will was not at all sure that Tomaso's best behaviour would be sufficient to keep him out of trouble, but there was little else he could say, so he clapped an arm around the youngster's shoulders and gave them an affectionate and forgiving squeeze.

Tomaso's tone became more serious as they walked up the slope of the Rialto Bridge among the throng jostling each other as they were forced into the narrow walkway between the shops that lined each side. 'Do you think he can be bought?'

It took Will a moment to realize that Tomaso had returned to the subject of Bassanio Pavoni. The evening before, having seen Lance off on his journey, he and Tomaso had spent some time talking about how they might further advance Sir Francis' aims in Venice. Finding a new local agent would not be easy, especially since neither of them had ever undertaken such a task, nor had they been trained for it. They had gone to bed without any obvious solution.

'Don't you see?' Tomaso went on, excited. 'Bassanio would be a perfect agent. He will have access to all sorts of correspondence and secret information that crosses the ambassador's desk. After all, that's what ambassadors do, isn't it, spy for their country?'

'Aye, so all we have to do is find a way convince a man we barely know and whose temper we do not understand, to betray his country, putting his position and possibly his life at risk, and give those secrets to us. Nothing could be simpler.'

Though Will's initial reaction was sour, he had to admit that cultivating Bassanio Pavoni had possibilities, though he had no idea how they would go about persuading him to become an informer. Then again, perhaps their encounter with him that day was the fates were pointing them in the right direction.

'He does seem to be short of money,' he mused out loud. 'But the subject will have to be approached with great delicacy. Have you ever been fishing, Tomaso?'

Tomaso laughed. 'No, I could never stay still long enough for the endless amount of time it seems to take to hook but a single fish.'

'Nor could I, but I met a fellow once who was a great expert. John Dennys was his name, and he knew all there is to know about fly-fishing. He used to say that the great trick was to so disguise the hook that the fish barely knew he had swallowed it before it was too late. That is the trick we will have to perform if we are to hook our friend Bassanio.'

Chapter 16

Two days later, they were greeted by the buzz of congenial conversation as they ascended the staircase from the courtyard to the *piano nobile* of the Ca' Da Mosto.

The main hall on that floor ran the length of the building, opening onto an airy loggia, just visible across the heads of the crowd, that overlooked the Grand Canal. They hesitated on the threshold, and Francesco Contarini patted the hand of his wife Giuliana, whose arm was threaded through his. She was a diminutive and nervous-seeming woman who had recently returned from the country, where she had been recuperating from an illness.

As they moved into the room, they were greeted by a splendidly attired major-domo, who bowed and thumped his staff of office on the wooden floor to announce their arrival. This summoned from the midst of the crowd their host, a distinguished-looking man with an avuncular air who wore a broad smile on his face and held his arms wide in welcome.

'Francesco! How good to see you, my old friend. And Giuliana, welcome. I am glad to see that you have recovered from your indisposition, and that the country air has done you good. You bloom once again, my dear. And these gentlemen, I take it, are the Englishmen that Bassanio has told me about?'

'Quite so, Antonio. Allow me to introduce Messer William Shakespeare of London, and Messer Tomaso Martinelli, also of London, though from his name you will deduce he is Italian by descent, as Pavoni has no doubt told you.'

'He has. Welcome, signori, to Venice, the meeting place of all the races of Europe and beyond, and to my home, where you will find, I daresay, some representative of most of those races.'

A flick of his fingers summoned wine, then Da Mosto led them into the throng, making introductions here and there. Most of the guests were prosperous-looking merchants of one kind or another, many of them elegant Venetians accompanied by their wives.

But also, as their host had said, a sprinkling of foreigners from all over Europe—traders from Bruges and Antwerp, harsh-voiced Germans, an excited and voluble young Frenchman, and even in one corner surrounded by admiring ladies, an Arab dressed in a turban and flowing robes. He was a reminder that though Venice was a longstanding leader in the struggle to defend Europe against the depredations of the Ottoman Empire, her prosperity also depended on commerce with the Muslim world.

Seeing some young men of his acquaintance across the room, Tomaso excused himself with a muttered farewell and a sketchy bow, pushing through the crowd in the direction of the loggia. Then Giuliana Contarini deserted them for the company of other wives, leaving Will and her husband to talk to a lean, unsmiling Dutchman; a trader in spices whose conversation seemed to extend no further than the details of his business.

Before long, he and Contarini were deep in discussion about the subjects that fascinate traders everywhere—prices and rumours—and they barely noticed when he too excused himself.

Will wandered through the big room, feeling a little awkward, not yet willing to engage in the kind of witty small talk that still taxed his Italian, and he eventually he found himself standing alone against the wall, empty glass in hand, a small smile playing around his mouth; an observer rather than a participant in the scene.

'It is a pretty crowd, is it not, Signor Shakespeare?'

Will turned, startled out of his reverie, smiled and bowed to Madalena Adorno, who seemed to have appeared out of nowhere to stand next to him, toying with an empty goblet of blue Venetian glass as she too contemplated the congregated throng.

'Signorina Adorno,' Will said, making a small bow, 'it is a pleasure to behold your countenance once more. And in happier circumstances. How is your father? Can we hope that his condition has improved?'

'Thanks be to God, yes,' she said, crossing herself. 'In fact, his recovery seems to be almost complete. He is over there, talking to Ser Antonio.'

Will looked across the room, and sure enough, there was the tall figure of Prospero Adorno, laughing at some joke, seemingly as free from care as any bird, though he still looked a little frail to Will's eyes. 'And you, Signorina, the rigours of your ordeal have left you unmarked, I trust?'

She laughed, a silvery chime that drew an answering smile from Will. 'Believe me, Signor Shakespeare, I am completely whole. My father says I am tougher than the toughest sergeant that he ever encountered in his military

139

days. I am not sure I should be flattered by that comparison, particularly coming from my pater.'

'Can you not see her, armoured with cap and brigandine, terrifying the daylights out of raw recruits? I am sure she would terrify me.'

There was a hint of mockery behind these words, delivered with a smile by a stocky, russet-bearded young man who emerged from the crowd to join them, slipping a possessive hand through the girl's arm.

It prompted in her a momentary a look of annoyance. 'Really Ferdinando, there is no woman on earth, I swear, who could terrify you. Signor Shakespeare, this is my betrothed, Ser Ferdinando Nogarola.'

The exchange of formal greetings gave Will the opportunity to examine Madalena's fiancé more closely. Elegantly but soberly dressed, he seemed to be a physically powerful man, the muscles apparent under the velvet sleeves. His face was square and blocky, the beard disguising and softening a prominent chin.

But the most remarkable feature of his face were the eyes, which were the bluest and coldest that Will had ever seen. They regarded him with a cool, appraising stare. 'You were in Corfu,' he said, blunt to the point of rudeness.

'You remember, Ferdinando, I told you last night,' Madalena said before Will could respond. 'Will was travelling with Francesco Contarini.' Was there a hint of warning in the way that she emphasised Contarini's name? As if to caution her betrothed that he should take care how he dealt with Will.

'Ah yes. You are a pedagogue of sorts, yes? Accompanying the son of an English earl who has an Italian name?'

'Yes. Tomaso Martinelli. His mother was Italian, from Verona. Both parents are now dead, and since I was planning to study at Padua myself, his guardian asked me if I would accompany Tomaso and see him safely installed in his studies.' A small lie, justified in Will's mind by Nogarola's dismissal of him as a mere pedagogue.

'It is a fine university, one of the oldest in Italy. And what will you be studying there?'

'Tomaso follows his guardian into the study of the law. For myself, philosophy and literature. I am a poet, you see.' Will liked the sound of that claim.

The expression on Nogarola's face softened. 'I have studied poetry a little myself. There is no finer form of literature, and Italy has produced some of the finest poets in the world. Petrarch, Dante, Tasso... were it not for the fact

140

that my rank commands me to a more practical life, I too might have delighted to call myself a simple poet.'

'Though a poet may be simple, poetry alas is rarely so, I find. I sometimes wish that I too had been commanded to a practical life.'

'We must all plough whatever furrow is destined for us, Signor Shakespeare.' Nogarola was genial, the earlier, frostier aspect of his personality having dissolved. 'And when do you and Signor Martinelli depart for Padua?'

'In the new year, I expect. The teachers do not commence their classes until February, which is as well, since Signor Contarini seems determined that we should remain here for the Christmas festivities.'

'Then we will most likely encounter each other again. There are some matters to be resolved between my father and Signor Adorno before our nuptials can proceed, and so we too will remain in Venice until the new year.'

'Ferdinando, it grows close in here.' Madalena was abrupt. 'Perhaps we could all go out onto the loggia?'

'Of course, my dear, whatever you wish.' Nogarola was all solicitude.

The loggia of the Ca' da Mosto was as broad and deep as that of the Ca' d'Oro, and at this time of day the weak and watery sunlight reflecting off the canal made dappled patterns on the tracery of the ceiling above the heads of other guests who had similarly sought escape from the warmth inside. Over in one corner, Will saw Bassanio and Tomaso, deep in conversation. As if sensing his gaze, Bassanio looked up at that instant, and, seeing Will, took Tomaso's arm and pushed through the crowd towards them, whispering in the boy's ear.

Bassanio's bow was deep and courtly, the formal greeting addressed to Nogarola and Madalena delivered with dignity combined with just the right amount of obsequiousness.

'Pavoni.' The aloof aristocrat was back as Nogarola conveyed his obvious disdain for Bassanio in a single word. 'I hear you are to join the ambassador's staff in Rome. Congratulations.'

'Thank you, Ser Ferdinando.' Bassanio was unperturbed. 'I hope I can do the post honour. Allow me to present Signor Tomaso Martinelli.'

This produced the merest of nods from Tomaso, barely polite enough to leave him on the right side of insolence, as he switched his attention to

Madalena. 'Signorina Madalena, I am glad to see you looking so well. And fully recovered from your troubles. As is, I hope, your father?'

'His mind seems fully recovered; for once the doctors' predictions were right. But he is still somewhat frail in his body. His strength will no doubt return with time.'

'He's well enough to be driving a hard bargain with my father in negotiations for your dowry, my love. I tell you, he is as fierce as any huckster and as sly as any Jew, my father says.' Nogarola's words were delivered with a grin, as if it were a great joke.

Madalena's scowl indicated that she did not think this indelicacy was at all humorous. 'Ferdinando! This is not a proper subject to be spoken about in public.'

'Of course, Madalena my dear.' Nogarola's expression was not in the least contrite. 'Tell me, Signor Martinelli, how does an English nobleman come to have an Italian name?'

'My late father was the Lord Chamberlain of England, the Earl of Sussex, and the queen's trusted adviser. It is from him that I get my first name, which is Thomas in English. But my mother was Italian, and it is from her that I get my surname.' Tomaso's response was defiant, daring Nogarola to give voice to the salient missing fact in this description—his illegitimacy.

'There was an Alessandro Martinelli, if I remember rightly, a musician, who left Verona and went to England some twenty years ago.'

'My grandfather. He was a senior court musician, much honoured by the queen.'

'Then he flew high, your grandfather. It is a wonder of our age, is it not, that a mere musician can in time produce nobility. Even if on the wrong side of the blanket.'

Tomaso's eyes widened in shock, then narrowed in anger. Red spots appeared under the stubble of his cheeks, rapidly spreading into a flush of indignation. His hand dropped to the dagger he wore at his belt, an instinctive gesture that might have led to the fatally dangerous act of drawing had Will not casually dropped a hand onto the boy's arm, seizing it with a hard grip that caused Tomaso to wince and transfer his angry gaze to his friend.

'Ferdinando!' Madalena's voice was sharp. 'That was unforgivable. Tomaso is a fine young man, an honoured guest of our host and my friend. I will not have you talk to him so.'

Nogarola raised a single eyebrow as he contemplated his wife to be for a moment, then gave a small laugh. 'Of course Signor Martinelli, Madalena is right. I apologise for my indiscretion.' The apparent sincerity of the words were undermined by the expression on the Veronese aristocrat's face, a look of amusement that said that he was apologising only to please his betrothed, not because he felt any real regret.

Tomaso had no choice but to accept this faux-apology, which he did with a graceful nod.

The small silence was broken by the sound of a gong, struck three times, announcing the arrival of food into the banqueting room that stood just off the main reception room of the palazzo.

'At last!' Bassanio exclaimed, a bright smile on his face that belied the anxious look in his eyes. 'I am, I find, amazingly hungry. Shall we go in?'

He slipped between Madalena and Ferdinando Nogarola, taking them each by the arm, to the horror of Nogarola, who visibly shrank from the touch, and chattering brightly about nothing very much, steered them inside, turning his head as the trio was about to disappear through the door, and bestowing on Will and Tomaso such a broad grin that Will burst out laughing.

Tomaso's good humour, however, was not so easily recovered. 'By God,' he growled, 'if you hadn't stopped me, I swear I would have had his blood.'

'Then it's just as well I did stop you. The last thing you and I need is for you to become embroiled in a feud with a Veronese nobleman, no matter how justified your cause. Think, Tomaso! We need the goodwill of these Venetians if we are to serve our country and Sir Francis.'

'Even so, he is an insufferable prig. Who is he anyway? Verona is but a subjugated client state of Venice, and has been so for over sixty years, its nobility reduced to serving as bailiffs and the like. He has no business looking down on me, the son of an English earl.' Just as it seemed his anger would burst forth anew, he sighed in resignation. 'But you are right of course, Will. As always.'

'Come on, let us inside; the hour draws on, and I fancy that Contarini will be calling for his barge before long, anyway.'

Inside, the crowded ballroom had indeed begun to thin out, some heading for the big doorway that led to the stairs down into the courtyard, others busily engaged with the consumption of food in the banqueting room next door.

143

They spotted Francesco Contarini, reunited with Giuliana, near the door, looking around the room, clearly preparing to leave. Seeing them enter from the loggia, he raised his arm in a languid summons.

'Time for us to depart, I think,' he said as they joined him. 'Do you join us or do you wish to stay a little longer?'

'Oh, I think we are ready to go,' Will said. 'But perhaps we will walk. 'Tis not so far, and a little exercise won't go astray.'

'Very well. We've made our farewells to Antonio, so there is nothing to detain us. Come, my dear.' They disappeared through the door and out onto the staircase down into the courtyard, from where they could board their barge, lined up with several others awaiting the arrival of their owners.

Will and Tomaso scanned the room, looking for their host so that they too could make their farewells. But da Mosto was nowhere to be seen, and so they too made their way down the stairs.

At the foot of them they turned away from the water and went out onto a narrow path that ran alongside a small service canal. After a hundred yards or so, it intersected with a wider street, carried over the canal on a hump-backed bridge.

Pulling their fur-lined cloaks more closely about them against the cold, they joined the stream of pedestrians making their way between shops and stalls.

'She does not love him, you know,' Tomaso said. 'It is an arranged marriage, according to Bassanio. Adorno's trade has had a series of misfortunes, he says, wrecked cargoes and the like, and even before this last misadventure he was in serious financial difficulty. The marriage with Nogarola was to be the solution to all his troubles; the Nogarola clan become members of a famous Genoese family, in return for which they advance sufficient funds to rescue Adorno. But now...'

'But now that Ser Prospero has lost another cargo, his situation is even more parlous. And so the negotiations have been reopened.'

'It is foul that Madalena's happiness should be sacrificed just for financial gain. As if she were a mere milk-cow.' Tomaso's outburst was bitter.

'That is the way of the world, Tomaso.' Will was hard. 'It may not be just, but women have been being used in this way time out of mind. No doubt when the time comes, Sir Francis will arrange a suitable match for you with someone of appropriate station and means. Whether the girl finds your person attractive or not will be of no relevance whatsoever. And you, my

144

young friend, will no doubt marry her willingly, bed her incessantly, and give not a thought to what her desires might have been before she ever heard of you.'

'And I shall tell Uncle Francis precisely what he can do with his arranged marriage.' Tomaso was vehement, his cheeks flushed once more. 'I shall marry for love, or not at all!'

'The son of an English earl marrying for love! Whoever heard of such a thing?' said the man who had indeed married for love, over the objections of his family, and who knew too well how passion could override every other consideration before it cooled, leaving consequences that could linger for a lifetime.

In his own ears, Will knew he was a hypocrite, though Tomaso was ignorant of the extent of his hypocrisy, he never having confided the full story of his own marriage.

'Anyway,' he said, a mischievous note in his voice, 'when was the last time that you saw any of Sir Francis' plans disrupted? Why, I'll wager he will have you trussed up and at the altar before you are even aware that the chosen girl exists.'

'There's truth enough in that.' Tomaso was rueful. 'Be that as it may, it does my heart no good to think of dear, sweet Madalena yoked to that oaf.'

Madalena seemed well able to manage that particular oaf, but Will knew that voicing this thought would do nothing to soothe his young friend.

Besides, they were now at the land gate of the Ca' d'Oro, which meant he could change subjects. 'Come on, let's see if Francesco and Giuliana are here yet. I have been telling him for weeks that it's faster to walk than to take the barge over such short distances and now we can find out whether I am right.'

Chapter 17

Venice, December 1585

Under a weak and watery winter sun, the chattering crowd, for the most part bundled up against the cold in colourful cloaks and furs, swirled and eddied around the marketplace.

The women were intent on getting to the morning markets to buy their vegetables, fish, meats, fruits, spices and all the cornucopia that the Venetian maritime empire delivered to their doorstep. The men gathered in knots to chat and exchange the latest rumours on the Rialto, the cargoes arriving and departing, the prices being quoted for silk and woollen cloth and wheat and silverware. Thus the commercial heart of Venice began beating for another day.

It was a scene now thoroughly familiar to Will as he made his way through the crowd. Over the last month, he and Tomaso had visited the markets every day, sometimes together and sometimes separately. Their purpose was to gather as much information as they could for the report that Will planned to send off to Sir Francis Walsingham in London.

At first, neither of them had the slightest idea how to gather intelligence that might be of use: indeed, they were even hazy about what might constitute 'useful' information.

'The Rialto,' Tomaso had eventually said, after they had debated the subject fruitlessly for an hour. 'The merchants and traders there know about everything that happens in Venice.'

It was one of those insights that, once made, seemed blindingly obvious. The Rialto was a clearing house for information, where the bankers and financiers gathered news and gossip and rumour and negotiated their exchange rates. When he was working for Richard Holbrooke back in London, Will had been a daily visitor to the Royal Exchange, which served a similar function in the English capital. There he had learned how to sift and sort fact from rumour and speculation to compile reports for the merchant.

'No doubt you're right,' Will had said. 'But we aren't merchants, and have no business there, so why would anyone tell us anything?'

146

The answer to that question, it turned out, was Bernardo, Francesco Contarini's steward. Feigning boredom, they had asked to accompany him on one of his daily visits to the Rialto. Bernardo, surprised but flattered by this request, was happy to oblige. The steward was well known in the markets, and he had introduced them to several merchants and minor officials with whom Contarini had business.

Tomaso then set about building on this slight foundation, doing small favours, telling jokes and long, humorous stories. Before long he had developed a network of regular contacts among the merchants and brokers, the minor public officials, the shopkeepers and tavern owners, lawyers and notaries: in short, all the diverse array of people who did business on the Rialto.

From these encounters, Tomaso had extracted a steady stream of gossip, rumours, and the occasional hard and verifiable fact. Collating, annotating, and classifying the information thus acquired was a painstaking task for Will in the evenings, using the skills he had learned in London to decide what was important enough to go into their report, and what should be discarded. The art of 'intelligencing' was, Will reflected with some inner amusement, nowhere near as glamorous an activity as Kit Marlowe had made it out to be.

Will's other task was the cultivation of Bassanio Pavoni, and it was to meet Bassanio that he had joined the crowd that, like a broad stream constricted by a ravine, pushed and jostled up the ramp of the great wooden bridge across the Grand Canal. The canal itself was invisible behind the shops and stalls that lined each side, prized real estate for the jewellers and silversmiths vying to get the attention of the bridge-crossers.

'Guglielmo! Guglielmo Scrollalanza! *A qui!*'

Will smiled at the Italian form of his name, conveyed in a loud voice that pierced the general hum of the crowd. The silk-covered arm of the voice's owner beckoned him above the heads of a small knot of people gathered around one of the silversmiths' stalls.

Edging his way across the stream, he emerged to receive Bassanio's embrace, accompanied by broad smile. 'Well met, Bassanio. I was expecting to see you at the Ca' da Mosto, but I see that the temptations of the silversmiths have once again proven irresistible.'

A small grimace of annoyance crossed Bassanio's face at this pleasantry; his obsession with all things silver had become something of a running joke between them.

147

But his pleasure in his newest discovery among the silversmith's wares soon overcame his irritation, which he held up for his inspection. 'It's beautiful, isn't it?'

The object in question was a silver medallion, a fine but simple design—a five-petaled rose surrounded by a wreath of laurel, hanging from a simple silver chain.

'It would look well on you, Bassanio. Does the rose have any special significance for you?'

'Not of a personal nature, no. But in times past, a rose suspended from the ceiling of the council chamber pledged all those present to secrecy. An appropriate symbol for a diplomat, do you not think?'

Will laughed a little uncomfortably, for Bassanio's remark, though he could not have intended it to do so, underlined the challenge he had ahead of him to prise any secrets out of this otherwise garrulous young man. They had met several times before today, on one occasion borrowing Antonio da Mosto's barge to go on an expedition to the more remote islands of the lagoon. He had proven to be a gossipy conversationalist, sharing all sorts of rumours and stories about the city's wealthiest and most important citizens with a wit and humour that had Will laughing until his sides hurt.

But his indiscretions stopped short of anything that might relate to his official role as Secretary to the Venetian Ambassador to the Holy See. And though Will was becoming an expert at dangling bait to extract information, he had seen no crack in the defences of this particular target through which he might slip a tempting morsel. Not yet, anyway.

While he was absorbed in these thoughts, Bessanio had been turning the medallion over in his hands, looking at it in different lights, clearly wanting to purchase it. Then he sighed, turning to return the casket to its place in the stallholder's display, with a regretful nod at the trader. 'But of course, I can't afford it. At least not until one of my uncle's ships comes home and I can prevail on him, again, for a loan.'

'Speaking of your uncle, Bassanio…'

'Yes of course. Let's go.'

They made their way across the bridge into the narrow street behind the Fondaco dei Tedeschi, barely avoiding being knocked over by a group of German apprentices making their noisy way out of the compound into the city.

148

A quarter of an hour later, after threading a maze of small lanes and canal bridges, they arrived at the land entrance to the Ca' da Mosto, passing through the familiar ornate gates and running up the broad staircase to the *piano nobile* floor.

Shedding coats and furs, they were warming themselves in front of a roaring fire when Antonio da Mosto arrived.

'How is my favourite nephew today?' he asked, grasping Bassanio by the shoulders and offering him a kiss on each cheek, in the Italian custom.

'Your *only* nephew, uncle,' Bassanio said with a wry and affectionate grin, 'is as healthy as a fish, though cold.'

Antonio patted him on the shoulder. 'And you, William, I hope you are well also?'

Will nodded, set at ease as always by da Mosto's charm and open generosity of spirit. 'Very well, Ser Antonio, though much as I am enjoying the charms and entertainments of Venice, I find I am beginning to be impatient for the commencement of the new scholastic year at Padua so that Tomaso and I can get on with our real purpose in being here in Italy.'

'That is commendable in you, though I do wonder whether Tomaso shares your impatience; that young man seems to be enjoying Venice a great deal. Shall we sit?'

They settled into the comfortable chairs arranged around the fireplace, a single servant handing them beakers of mulled wine.

The previous week, Bassanio had invited Will to join him and Antonio for what was evidently their well-established weekly routine, an exchange of news and rumours heard on the bourse and elsewhere. Will had been flattered by the invitation, though a little mystified as to why it had been extended. Bassanio had simply said that Antonio always enjoyed meeting foreigners, and that he thought that Will and Antonio would find each other's company congenial.

So it had proved—Antonio's genial curiosity about England and all things English had charmed Will, and his answers to the merchant's questions seemed to be sufficiently interesting to prompt an effusive invitation to return the next week.

'So, Uncle, what is the news on the Rialto this week?'

The news, it seemed, was the menace of piracy.

'In this week's *aviso*,' Antonio waved his copy of the handwritten newsletter, produced each week and distributed to subscribers, 'there are

149

reports that the Uskok pirates have captured and ransomed five ships in the last month and have raided several small towns in Istria. It seems that they are becoming bolder than ever, despite the best efforts of the navy to control them.'

Will thought of the pirates they had encountered in the Western Mediterranean, and he treated his hosts to a rather over-dramatized account of that short sea-battle, emphasising the cowardice of the pirates, the heroics of the captain and crew, and ending with a gently humorous description of his ineptitude with sword and dagger that greatly amused his host.

'It's surprising that they had the temerity to attack a Venetian great ship,' Antonio said as their conversation reverted to a more sober tone. 'The Barbary Pirates are almost a spent force in the Middle Sea. The Uskoks, on the other hand, have been plaguing Venice for a hundred years and more, and they are supported, it is believed, by the Habsburg emperors who created them in the first place. They are a curse and a constant source of worry to anyone in Venice involved with shipping.'

'Are *you* worried, uncle?' asked Bassanio, 'I know you had a cargo coming up from Crete, but wasn't that due yesterday?'

Antonio nodded. 'It has not yet arrived. I am not worried yet—a ship that is two days overdue is hardly to be labelled late—but it is true that I will sleep more soundly when it is safely landed.'

'I am surprised you sleep at all, Ser Antonio,' Will said, 'given the number of cargoes and ships you have at sea. Ships run aground, are subject to tempests, can be attacked by pirates. If it were me, I swear I would be spending every waking hour, and most of my sleeping hours too, worrying and wondering about the fate of my wealth.'

Da Mosto smiled. 'That, my dear Will, is why I *can* sleep soundly at night. You see, the cargo from Crete is but one of a half-dozen ventures. I have a ship going to and from Mexico, another cargo bound home as we speak from England, and yet another at Genoa.

'Therein lies my strength, for though one project may fail, a single ship founder, I am not wholly dependent on the success of any one of my ventures, and thus I am insured against total ruin.'

Will nodded, though he was not entirely convinced by Antonio's serenity. Catastrophe could, he knew from the stories told in London, strike at any time, although in truth he had never encountered anyone in London whose commercial interests were as extensive as those of the modest-seeming Antonio da Mosto.

'But enough of such dull subjects,' Antonio said, turning his gaze on his nephew. 'You go to Rome in a week or so, don't you, Bassanio? What do you hear about the new pope?'

'Sixtus is, it seems, a most vigorous man, contrary to all expectations.' Bassanio adopted what Will had come to think of as his 'serious' look, with which he had presumably convinced the Signoria to appoint him in the first place. 'You will remember, uncle, that it was said that he feigned decrepitude in the conclave so as to convince the cardinals that, if elected, he would not last long, thus clearing the path for one of them to ascend the Throne of St Peter. But it seems that he is far from decrepit, and since his coronation he has been very active indeed.'

'How deceitful of him!' Antonio laughed, placing a hand on Will's sleeve. 'There is nothing, my dear Will, quite so devious as a cardinal pursuing the Triple Tiara.'

Bassanio frowned at this pleasantry, seemingly not quite decided whether to join in the laughter, or maintain his serious demeanour. 'He may not have given offence to anyone before his election, but anyone who knows his record should have realised he would be a wolf in sheep's clothing. Twenty-five years ago, he was here in Venice as Inquisitor General, but was so high-handed in his execution of that office that the Signoria asked for his recall. And in the years since then, he made as many enemies as friends in the Curia, not least of whom was Pope Gregory, who forced him into retirement.'

'And since his elevation?' Will asked.

'In the last eight months he has been ruthless in suppressing the brigands who have infested the papal territories for years, something his predecessor seemed incapable of dealing with. Thousands of them have been brought to justice and executed, and the roads through the Romagna are now safe for travellers.'

'Something for which you will no doubt give thanks when you go south, Bassanio,' Antonio said.

Bassanio nodded. 'Yes, indeed. But the real scandal in Rome, my informants tell me, is the Accoramboni affair.'

Will had heard something of this story from one of his friends on the Rialto. It had started when Vittoria Accoramboni, a celebrated Roman beauty, had married one Francesco Peretti, a man of no consequence or means, other than the fact that he was a nephew of Felice Peretti, Cardinal Montalto.

151

She was also an extravagant woman, and the couple were soon plunged into debt, from which her brother sought to rescue her by the extreme means of having her husband murdered so that she could marry Paolo Orsini, the Duke of Bracciano, one of her many admirers. To add more scandal, it was rumoured that the duke had been complicit in the murder of young Francesco.

Still, the story might have ended there were it not for the fact that Cardinal Montalto, the murdered man's uncle, had since been elected as Pope Sixtus V! The vengeful pope had launched a vigorous persecution of the duke and his paramour. They had fled from Rome, first to Venice, and then on to Salo, up on Lake Garda, where the duke had died a month ago.

'Oh?' Antonio's interest was piqued. 'Has something more happened since Bracciano died?'

Bassanio had the pleased look of a cat that has just deposited a particularly juicy titbit onto the doorstep. 'The duchess was overwhelmed with grief and, unable to bear remaining near the scene of her husband's demise, took herself off to Padua.' He paused for dramatic effect; the dramatist in Will silently applauded the performance. 'And there, two weeks ago, she was murdered.'

'So the pope's promised revenge is complete!' Antonio said. 'But did the pontiff have any hand in the murder? It would be outrageous if it were so.'

'No, not the pope. It seems she was followed to Padua by one Lodovico Orsini, a relation of the dead duke, who hired a band of ruffians to do the deed. His motivation is not known, though there are some rumours that her husband died at his wife's hand through poison, so perhaps revenge again.'

Will wondered whether this story should be included in the dossier for Walsingham. Like so much of the information they gleaned from their intelligencing efforts, it was hard to categorise. Though it had no intrinsic connection to England's interests, it did nevertheless serve to underline the ruthlessness of this particular pope. He would have to discuss it with Tomaso.

'What a tale!' he said. 'Perhaps I will make it into an epic poem or a play one day, when I am back in England. You are very well informed, Bassanio, considering that you have yet to take up your office.'

Bassanio made no reply, contenting himself with a quick smile at Will, before he shifted in his seat and cleared his throat. 'Uncle, I fear I must raise another, more uncomfortable subject with you.'

Antonio merely raised an eyebrow, as if he knew what was coming but was unwilling to make his nephew's task any easier.

'This new position of mine is one of considerable honour, as you know. It is also an opportunity for me to make my career, to establish myself on a path of service to the Republic that will, I am sure, eventually secure my future.

'But it is also expensive; the stipend paid by the Signoria is a pittance, yet I will be expected to maintain myself in a style suitable to the importance of the position. No one takes seriously a diplomat who cannot entertain, dress well and, where necessary, make the small and discreet payments necessary to ensure the flow of information such as that which I have just shared with you.'

'And so you need money,' Antonio said, his voice level.

'And so I need money.' Bassanio nodded. 'A loan only, for I believe my expenses will be most substantial only to establish myself in Rome, and thereafter my salary should be sufficient for my needs.'

Antonio gave him a long, considering look. 'Nephew, you know the love I bear you. Since your parents died in the late plague, you have been as my own son, and I would have you want for nothing. But my ventures are as I said, all at sea, and for the present my funds must be husbanded. I fear that I cannot, for now at least, be of service. In six months, perhaps, but not right now. I am sorry.'

Bassanio looked as shocked as if he had just been foretold the date of his own death. Clearly he had never contemplated the possibility of a refusal from his so-indulgent uncle. Will felt more than a little embarrassed to be witnessing this unexpected confrontation, and did his best to seem invisible.

After a few moments' silence, Bassanio let out a long, low sigh, and nodded. 'I understand, uncle, of course. I would not have asked if I had any other alternatives. There are always the Jews, I suppose.'

'Be careful, Bassanio, in your dealings with the Jews,' Antonio said tartly, 'lest you find yourself lighter by a pound of flesh!'

The two Italians spontaneous laughter at this remark dissolved the tension, though it left Will puzzled.

'It is an old story,' Antonio explained, taking pity on his guest, 'which I am sure Bassanio will tell you later. Now, I must go; the counting house calls.'

He rose, prompting the two younger men to scramble politely to their feet.

153

Antonio placed his hands on Bassanio's shoulders and looked at him affectionately. 'Nephew, if you *must* deal with the moneylenders of the Ghetto to finance your needs, go and see Silas da Ribera. He and I have done business most amicably in the past. He should be accommodating. But do be careful in your dealings with him, please!'

'Thank you, uncle, I will send a messenger today to arrange an appointment. And I promise you, I will be cautious.'

Antonio nodded, and after a few more pleasantries, departed to harass his clerks in the counting-house.

'Will, why don't you come with me to see Silas?' Bassanio said as they made their way down the stairs and into the courtyard, bundling themselves up again against the cold. 'Tomaso always tells me that you are cautious to a fault, which might be a quality that would be most helpful should I find myself straying into dangerous waters.'

'Yes, of course, though I don't know how much help I can really be.'

'By the way, I had a letter from Madalena Adorno yesterday,' Bassanio said as they arrived on to the street and prepared to part. 'They have all arrived safely in Verona, and are installed at the Nogarola palazzo. The date for their wedding has been set for one month's time.'

Neither he nor Tomaso had laid eyes on the Adornos since that uncomfortable afternoon at the Ca' da Mosto, though Bassanio had told them that they were preparing to depart, Prospero Adorno and Nogarola senior having finally reached agreement on the terms of the betrothal. Tomaso had received that news in silence and had not said a word about Madalena since, though Will sensed that his infatuation with the girl had not yet abated entirely.

'I will tell Tomaso.' He stamped his feet. 'It's cold, standing here. Send a messenger when you have arranged a time to meet Silas.'

As he headed back to the Ca d'Oro, Will found himself deep in thought, for though he had remained impassive at the name Silas da Ribera, in fact it was familiar to him. Back in London, Phelippes had provided him with a letter of introduction to this same Silas, which would allow him to draw funds if he should need them. 'Silas is reliable and discreet,' Phelippes had said, though he had not mentioned that he was of the Jewish faith, 'and we prefer to use his services rather than the Italian banks when we need money.'

A plan to recruit Bassanio Pavoni as a spy for England began to stir in his mind.

154

Chapter 18

Tell me this story of the pound of flesh,' Will said two days later, as the gondola slid out of the traffic of the Grand Canal and into a narrow side canal, his words echoing off the walls of the houses as they passed.

'It is an old story, from a book of tales called *The Simpleton*. A young Venetian named Giannetto whose godfather, Ansaldo, equipped him with a richly-laden ship with which to make his fortune. On his first voyage, Giannetto came by chance to the port of Belmonte, which was ruled by a mysterious, beautiful and very rich woman. This woman had issued a standing challenge to any merchant entering the harbour—she would offer herself in marriage and all her possessions, to anyone who could successfully seduce her.'

'Why would she do such a thing?' Will asked.

'Because there was also a penalty—if the suitor failed, he must lose his ship and all his goods. So far she had resisted the charms of all of her would-be suitors, and since no one had succeeded, she had amassed a considerable fortune.'

Will nodded. 'And Giannetto, of course, is sure that *he* cannot fail.'

'You have it. Things proceed as you would expect, and Giannetto was sure he was going to be the first challenger to win her. But the lady had a trick up her sleeve. She invited Giannetto to drink with her before taking her to bed; the drink was drugged, and he fell asleep immediately, thus falling at the first hurdle, and forfeiting his ship and its cargo.

155

'You would think this would be lesson enough for the young man, but he had fallen in love with the lady, and, undeterred, he persuaded his godfather to fund a second ship for another try. But again he fell for the same trick, with the same result; the loss of another cargo.'

'I can see why the story is called *The Simpleton*,' Will said, laughing.

'Well, a slow learner at least,' Bassanio said. 'But perhaps it was the gambler in him, convinced that enough throws of the dice must eventually throw a six. In any event, he was determined for a third try but by then he had exhausted his funds. Returning home, he begged Ansaldo to fund him for a third voyage to Belmonte. Poor Ansaldo, however, had also run out of money, and so he turned to a Jewish money-lender, who was prepared to lend him the required sum, provided that he posted a bond as security. The deal being completed and the bond signed, Giannetto returned to Belmonte.

'No doubt he would have suffered a third loss, were it not for the intervention of the lady's serving-girl, who warned him that the drink is drugged. Giannetto only pretended to drink the wine, and so was finally able to have his way with the lady, which did not displease her, since she had by now fallen in love with Giannetto. The two wed, and Giannetto becomes the lord of Belmonte.

'Some time passed, Giannetto and the lady were living in harmonious matrimony, until the feast day of San Giovanni comes along, which was also the day on which Giannetto suddenly remembers that Ansaldo must repay the Jew, or else forfeit his bond.'

Bassanio turned to give the gondolier instructions, for they were now deep in the labyrinth of small canals that connected the various islands on which Venice stood.

'And of what did the bond consist?' Will asked when he had Bassanio's attention once again.

'Can you not guess? The bond that the Jew demanded was that if Ansaldo failed to repay the ten thousand ducats by San Giovanni's day, his forfeit would be a pound of his own flesh, to be cut from wherever on Ansaldo's body it should please the Jew.'

Will was horrified. 'But surely such a bond must be a death sentence!'

'Yes of course. So, knowing this, Giannetto hastened back to Venice. But though he was armed with sufficient funds to redeem the bond, had not reckoned with the stubborn determination of the Jew, for whom this had become a way to exact revenge on all those gentiles who have slighted the Jewish race over the centuries. In his hatred, he insisted that, since the debt

156

had not been discharged at the required time, he must have his due by way of the flesh-bond. Giannetto, in desperation, offered to pay ever greater sums to secure his godfather's life. Each bid was rejected by the Jew, even when the sum offered was as high as one hundred thousand ducats!'

'But this cannot be the end of the story?' Will said.

'No, indeed not. Rescue came from a most improbable source. It so happened that an eminent doctor of laws, trained at Bologna, had arrived in Venice at the same time as Giannetto, and had made it known that he would advocate for any dispute in Venice that was brought before him, however hopeless.

'Here was a ray of hope for Giannetto, and he prevailed upon the Jew to put the case before the courts, which the Jew reluctantly agreed to do, confident nonetheless that his bond contract would prevail. That confidence seemed at first to be well placed, since the lawyer immediately conceded before the court the validity of the contract and caused Ansaldo's shirt to be stripped from his body so that the Jew could extract his penalty, much to Giannetto's horror.

'But, just as the Jew was about to make the fatal cut, the lawyer intervened, saying, "Take care what you do; for if you cut away more or less than a pound of flesh, you shall lose your own head. And I tell you, moreover, that if you let flow a single drop of blood, you shall die, for your bond says naught as to the shedding of blood. It simply gives you the right to take a pound of flesh, and says neither less nor more. Now, if you are a wise man, you will consider well which may be the best way to compass this task."'

'A cunning lawyer!' Will interjected.

'Yes' Bassanio continued, 'and since there was no way that the Jew could extract his pound of flesh without shedding blood, he saw the trap that he was in. Relenting, he offered to accept the promised one hundred thousand ducats in discharge of the bond, but the doctor of laws, sensing his advantage, rejected this, and rejected again and again the Jew's ever-decreasing offers, making it clear that he would get nothing, until at last in rage he tore up the bond contract, thus freeing Ansaldo from his debt, to the general rejoicing of the Venetians gathered in the court.'

Will clapped his hands in joy at the cleverness of it all. But there was one question that begged to be answered, though he had some idea what that answer might be. 'And might I hazard a guess that the identity of the so-

157

clever lawyer is none other than the mysterious and beautiful Lady of Belmonte, disguised as a man?'

'Bravo, Guglielmo! You are most perceptive,' Bassanio said. 'That was indeed the case. The lady, as well as being beautiful, was clearly intelligent. Fiorentino's story ends with some nonsense involving a ring, by which the lady's identity is eventually revealed, but the essence of the tale is that they all live happily ever after.'

'Except, presumably, the Jew,' Will said.

'The story does not record what happened to him, but for certain he would have been vilified throughout Venice. In any event, the tale of the Lady of Belmonte is a salutary one for all who would do business with the Jews, for they are a greedy and rapacious race who, though they have their uses, are not to be trusted.'

The gondola entered a long, straight section of canal, along which ran a blank wall, pierced here and there by small gates that gave onto water landings, where various people, most of them wearing a uniform red cap, embarked or disembarked from boats and gondolas.

'I am curious, Bassanio,' Will asked, 'are there many Jews still in Venice? We have very few of them in England since they were last expelled.'

Bassanio shrugged. 'There are, I suppose, some thousands. But you will not see many of them on the streets of Venice, for about seventy years ago, the Signoria decided that all of the Jews should be confined here, to the Ghetto Vecchio,' he gestured at the long walls, 'and here they have made their own colony. They are locked in at night and their movements during the day are restricted. The state taxes them severely, as befits a race of heretics. They are only permitted to work in certain occupations and they must always wear a red cap when they leave the Ghetto.'

'And yet, you will forgive me of for observing that gentiles such as yourself are not averse to doing business with them?'

'They have their uses, like all the creatures in God's creation,' Bassanio said with another shrug. 'Though they lend at interest, which the Church forbids Christians, they are sometimes the only alternative available, and so their rapacity must be suffered. As is my case, although Antonio's warning is well given.'

Will pondered this. Bassanio's attitude to those of the Jewish faith seemed to him to be hypocritical at the very least. Clearly he despised them as a race, and yet was willing to avail himself of the services that only they could provide.

158

The recent history of his own country was one of endless religious strife, as Catholic and Protestant vied to impose their religious views on each other, often with great savagery. He himself found it impossible to hate those who held beliefs different from his own, though in truth it was difficult to discern just what those beliefs were. A nominal Protestant he might be, but his sceptical nature took little on faith. Certainly this segregation and vilification of an entire race of people purely on the grounds of their religion seemed to him to be both pointless and unjust, though he said nothing as they alighted at one of the water-gates.

As Bassanio paid the gondolier with a few coins, Will looked around with curiosity at the people bustling around in the entrance to the Ghetto; they seemed to him to be indistinguishable from all the other Venetians he had ever met, except for the peculiarity of the red caps.

As for Silas, he was not at all what Shakespeare had expected. The man whose pudgy hands poured him tea from a delicate porcelain teapot was as soft of manner as of physique. Of medium height, the body disguised beneath the elegant silk of his robes, though not really fat, was all rounded bulges, as of one accustomed to living well but remaining a stranger to physical exertion.

Otherwise, the general impression was of darkness—black eyes, a swarthy complexion, betraying perhaps origins in Spain, where intermarriage between Jew and Moor was not unknown, and black hair, peppered with sparks of grey.

They sat in a small receiving chamber on the first floor of Silas' comfortable house in the Ghetto Vecchio, overlooking a small canal through windows shuttered against the cold. A brazier in the corner emitted enough heat to keep the room warm.

A servant had brought them the tea and a small tray of cakes before retiring to his position of respectful attentiveness near the door. Silas gestured to the cakes, inviting Will to indulge. With a tinge of regret he shook his head, resisting the temptation of his own small vice of gluttony. Bassanio, on the other hand, scooped up his cake with no hesitation at all.

The tasks of hospitality complete, Silas regarded his guests calmly from his comfortably padded chair. 'How does my good friend Antonio, Messer Pavoni? He is well, I hope?'

'He is, and he sends his greetings.' A small nod of acknowledgement. 'His business prospers, though he has many cargoes at sea at present.'

'So he does indeed. This is common knowledge on the Rialto. And you, Messer Shakespeare? What brings you here to Venice? From your name I take it you are English?'

'I am, Signor Ribera. I am on the way to study at Padua, but since the new term does not begin until February, I linger in Venice, enjoying its pleasures while I can.'

'Ah. I have never been to England, though I have done business with many Englishmen. They are, on the whole, a reliable risk, I find. Honourable to a fault. But pleasant though it is to pass the time of day with you gentlemen, I must assume your arrival here at my house, all unheralded, is more a matter of business than pleasure.'

Silas' gaze settled on Bassanio, clearly assuming that it was he rather than Will who had need of the moneylender's services.

Bassanio shifted uncomfortably in his seat, clearly not sure how to start. 'Yes. I have been appointed as secretary to the Republic's Ambassador to the Vatican Palace, a position of prestige and honour, but alas one that also carries with it some considerable expense.'

A slight lift of his eyebrows was Silas' only response.

'One must be properly equipped for such a role, if the dignity of Las Serenissima is to be upheld. Clothes, servants, lodging, all are expensive in Rome.'

'But surely, Messer Pavoni, the Venetian state will pay you a salary to support all this expense?' Silas was wry, as if he knew what the answer to his question would be.

Bassanio looked pained as he was forced once again to explain his predicament. 'The difficulty is the cost of establishing myself. The salary, though far from munificent, will be sufficient for my needs after that. With some economies, of course.'

'I see. And so you need a loan. How much, if I might ask, do you seek?'

'Five hundred gold ducats should be sufficient to meet my needs.'

This was a large sum of money indeed; surprisingly so. Clearly Bassanio wished to maintain himself in some style in Rome.

'You have security?' Silas seemed to be untroubled by the size of the loan being sought, the genial smile never leaving his face.

'No, I do not. Though Ser Antonio will, I am sure, be prepared to offer his good name as security if I asked him.'

160

Antonio had, Will recalled, offered no such thing. He wondered whether the idea had come into Bassanio's head prompted by the story of the pound of flesh that he had told with such relish in the gondola, though one would have thought that such a tale would be cautionary, if anything.

'Antonio da Mosto is a most excellent man; on that I am sure we are agreed. But you know and I know that his ventures are all at sea at present, and that he has some risk to his fortune. Though I am sure he would be willing to post bond for you, I am less sure that I would, in these circumstances, be prepared to accept it.'

Bassanio's smooth mask dissolved to reveal a look of pure, patrician anger. 'Look, da Ribera, do not trifle with me. You know full well that Uncle Antonio's fortune is safe enough. In any case, you should be prepared to accept my word alone as your bond, the word of a Venetian patrician of good standing.' Bassanio came to an indignant halt, as if he could not believe that the simple statement of his status would not be sufficient to sway the argument, yet conscious that he had no other way of making his case.

Silas hands came up in a placatory gesture. 'Of course, Messer Bassanio, in a simpler world, a more honest world, I would have no hesitation in accepting your promise. But alas, the world I must live in is not so perfect.

'You would be astonished if I were to be so indiscreet as to tell you the names of some of the fine Venetian citizens who have come to my door asking for my poor services, who I have obliged, only to be disappointed when they tear up their bonds when the time came to repay me. They come to me in their extremity, but when the crisis has passed they remember that they are Venetian nobles and I a mere Jew. And so I find I must insist on security.'

Bassanio could find no answer to this and simply sat open-mouthed, as if searching for some new argument that might compel the moneylender to look on him favourably.

This was the moment, Will thought, for him to intervene. 'Perhaps, Signor da Ribera,' he said, adopting a respectful tone, 'if Messer Pavoni could make do with a lesser amount? Might you be able to accommodate him then?'

Silas said nothing, looking at Bassanio in silent query.

Various expressions crossed Bassanio's face in succession—annoyance at Will's intervention, then hope, and finally calculation as he tried to decide by how much he could reduce his demand. 'I could, perhaps, make do with four hundred gold ducats.'

161

'With security,' Will said, before Silas could respond.

Bassanio looked at him in puzzlement, but Silas merely smiled.

'So now we come to it, eh, Messer Shakespeare?' he said. 'And what security did you have in mind?'

'This.' Will withdrew a paper, carefully folded, from within his doublet, and handed it to the moneylender.

Silas opened it, scanned the contents, and then gave Will a long, careful look of appraisal. 'Yes, this will be sufficient, I think. I will need to have a notary draw up the necessary contract, which you will have to sign, but otherwise this will serve very well.'

'You seem to have been expecting to see this paper, or something like it?'

Again, the conspiratorial smile appeared on Silas' face. 'Oh, I know who you are, Messer Shakespeare. Thomas Phelippes sent me word by courier that I should be ready to assist should you need it.' He turned to Bassanio, who looked mystified. 'You are fortunate in your friends, Messer Pavoni. When the contracts have been drawn, you may have your four hundred ducats—due in six months, mind. And out of respect for Ser Antonio, at a moderate rate of interest.'

'And no pound of flesh?' Will was mischievous.

Bassanio looked mortified, but Silas gave a great, long laugh. 'You have heard Ser Fiorentino's tale, Messer Shakespeare. It is a cautionary story for both Jew and Gentile alike, I think. No pound of flesh. Now, gentlemen, if you please, I have work to do. Come back in two days' time, and the contracts will be ready.'

Back out on the street, Bassanio's confusion was complete. 'I think, Will,' he said carefully, 'that you need to explain some things to me.'

Now for the most ticklish part of the business, Will thought. 'Yes, that is fair. In here.'

They were opposite a small tavern, crowded with noisy drinkers. Shouldering through the crowd, they found a relatively quiet corner in the back, where they ordered wine, over which Will took a deep breath and fixed his most earnest gaze on Bassanio.

'I am for the most part what you always thought I am—a sometime poet and pedagogue, going to Padua with Tomaso. But I am also, against my own desires, something else. The paper that I showed to Silas was an authority for me to draw funds, should I need then, against the credit of the English Crown. It was provided to me by Thomas Phelippes, who is the chief clerk in

162

the office of Sir Francis Walsingham. Silas will use it as security against your loan.'

'Walsingham is the private secretary to your queen.' Will was not at all surprised that the well-informed Bassanio knew exactly who Walsingham was, though his name was unknown to many, even in England. 'And why would William Shakespeare, poet, pedagogue, or whatever you are, have such a paper on his person?'

Will took a deep breath. 'Because Sir Francis is also the head of the queen's intelligence service.'

'So you are a spy.' The look of puzzlement was replaced by something like disgust.

'Originally I was to be no more than a courier,' Will said, feeling an obscure need to justify himself, 'delivering instructions to one of Walsingham's agents. But circumstances changed, and I find myself obliged to do my best to fulfil the instructions myself.'

'And Tomaso? He is aware of all this?' The thought that Tomaso too might have been deceiving him seemed to be even more distressing to Bassanio.

'Yes, though it was never intended that he should know what I was doing. After all, my task was simply to deliver a letter, nothing more. There was no reason he should know about it, until things went awry, and then I had no choice but to tell him.'

'And so now you seek to buy *me*, taking advantage of my financial embarrassment to place me in your debt. I thought you were my friend.'

'So I am. Do you think Sir Francis provided me with these funds so that I could use them to enable you to live in luxurious style in Rome? If he finds out, or worse, if you fail to repay and the security is drawn, I do not know what the boundaries of his anger will be. Do you not think that it is the act of a friend to take that risk on your behalf?'

This seemed to mollify Bassanio. 'All right, all right. I promise you that the loan will be repaid. You heard Antonio—in six months he will be able to fund me for this amount, and more. But what do you want from me in the meantime? I will not betray the Republic, I tell you that—'

'Nor would I ask you to,' Will said, relieved; the hardest part of the conversation was now behind him. 'You know that England is at war with the King of Spain. Sir Francis' instructions to his agent were that he should cultivate any sources that might provide information about Spanish intentions. The late pope supported Philip in his efforts to defeat the Protestant Dutch, and no doubt this new pope will be as enthusiastic in his support for this latest effort by the Spanish king to topple the queen off her throne.'

Bassanio's nod was tentative, cautious.

'All I ask is this: if you come across any information that might relate to either Papal or Spanish intentions towards England, pass it on to me. As an accredited diplomat, you are in a position to observe, shall we say, communication between the king and the pope. And you will no doubt hear things—gossip, facts, rumours, from your own informants.'

'That is all?' Bassanio seemed relieved that Will's demands were relatively light; clearly he had been fearing that he would be asked to do much more.

'That is all. Look, I regret having to ask you to do this, for I think we are friends, but I really do have no choice. I said that I was in this business somewhat unwillingly, which is the truth. Sir Francis has some power over me, and if I do not serve him well, I may face prison... or worse.'

It was this that seemed to persuade Bassanio more than anything else Will had said, as if he drew some comfort from the fact that Will too, was subject to forces he could not control. 'All right, I will do as you ask. If you had asked me as a friend and as a patriot, and if you had explained all the circumstances, I think I would have agreed anyway.'

Though Will offered up a sheepish look of apology at this remark, he didn't believe it. Though he had not wanted to coerce Bassanio into this, he did not believe that, without some further leverage, he would have agreed.

'But nothing from within the Embassy, mark you,' Bassanio went on, applying another fig leaf to his surrender. 'I will not share confidential documents that come across my desk there.'

'Of course. Nor would I expect you to. Come, we had better get going. The gondolier will not wait forever.'

Both were silent as they started their journey back through the watery labyrinth between the Ghetto Vecchio and the Grand Canal, but after a while, Bassanio's natural good humour began to reassert itself. By the time they arrived at the Ca' d'Oro, they were talking with nearly all their old lack of restraint, as if their difficult interview had never taken place. For this, Will was grateful, for he did genuinely like Bassanio.

164

Of more importance, he felt he had achieved his most important goal—recruiting a source who was in a position to supply him with a steady stream of useful information from the papal court. And that meant that he and Tomaso could depart with an easy conscience to Padua and the university there.

Chapter 19

A nd so, gentlemen, Aristotle summarises the youthful character thus—
they overdo everything. They love too much and hate too much. They
think they know everything, and are always quite sure about it. If they do
wrong to others, it is because they mean to insult them, not to do them actual
harm. They are ready to pity others, because they think everyone an honest
man. They judge their neighbour by their own harmless natures.

'And finally, they are fond of fun and therefore witty, wit being well-bred
insolence. Which, if the quality of wit demonstrated by the members of this
class is any guide, might suggest that you gentlemen are poorly-bred indeed.'

There was a moment's silence as the twenty or so students sitting at
benches in the lecture hall registered the fact that their professor, a man
whose character they had long ago assessed as being terminally dry and
serious, had made a joke. Then the room erupted in laughter, and a few of the
more boisterous students, mostly the Germans, banged their hands on their
desks. William Shakespeare contented himself with a small smile, scribbling
a few notes. *Wit is well-bred insolence.* He liked that.

The professor—Antonio Riccobono, for the last ten years sole professor
of Latin and Greek Humanities at Padua University—held up his hands for
silence, resuming a serious demeanour that did not quite banish the ghost of a
smile that lingered on his lips.

'Tomorrow, we will move on to part thirteen, in which the philosopher
considers the character of the elderly—men who he says have lived
many years. They have often been taken in, and often made mistakes, and for
whom life on the whole is a bad business.'

Riccobono paused, as if considering whether another sally into the realm
of humour was justified; evidently deciding it was not, he waved vaguely
towards the door. The students broke into noisy chatter and gathered up their
notes and books. Spilling out into the early summer sunshine that striped the
broad loggia overlooking the central courtyard of the Palazzo Bo, the
building that housed the University of Padua, they split up into groups,

166

chattering happily and noisily in their native languages—the various Italian dialects, German, French, and Dutch—and descended the stairs on their way to an hour or so of freedom before the afternoon lectures began.

Weaving his way through the knots of students gathered in the courtyard, Will headed for the main gates and out into the hubbub of the city of Padua. Dodging in front of a donkey-drawn cart that was rumbling along the muddy cobbles of the street, he ducked into a narrow lane overhung with houses.

At the end of it, he emerged into a broad, irregularly shaped piazza, dominated along one side by the enormous bulk of the Palazzo della Ragione, Padua's town hall. It being the middle of the day, the fruit-sellers, to whose trade this piazza was dedicated, were in full cry, hoping to sell all of their stocks before the heat of the afternoon.

Picking his way among the stalls, he eventually came to the stall where he had appointed to meet with Tomaso, who was in laughing conversation with the portly woman who was its owner.

'Here, try one of these.' He handed Will a strawberry plucked from the pile at the front of the stall. 'Signora Gianozza says they are the best in the market.'

Will took a bite, dutifully agreed that it was indeed the best strawberry he had ever tasted, and stood waiting impatiently as Tomaso haggled over the price of a bag of them. Eventually, their business concluded in the Italian way with many flowery compliments.

They set off in the direction of their lodgings, two rooms in a modest house that overlooked the piazza, which they occupied with three other students. The five of them shared the thirty ducats that it cost to rent the house for the academic year and pay the two servants who cooked and cleaned for them. Two of their fellow lodgers were Italians studying law, while the third was a German from Dusseldorf, like Will, a student of the humanities.

When they arrived, the house was empty except for the cook, Maria, who had prepared a meal of pasta, bread and salad greens, accompanied by a beaker of wine.

'So how was Aristotle today?' Tomaso asked as they sat down at the table that dominated the small parlour at the back of the house.

'Somewhat tediously labouring the deficiencies of youth. Though Riccobono managed to make a joke at the end, which almost caused a riot, it was so unexpected.'

167

'Even a poor joke would be welcome in my law lectures. But I can't see any of the dried-up old sticks even thinking about making a joke without first subjecting it to such a vigorous examining that it would shrivel up and die in preference to emerging into the lecture room.'

They both laughed. This was a constant refrain among the students, particularly the younger ones, whose natural high spirits were oppressed by the solemnity of their professors.

Will's mockery, though, was half-hearted, for he actually rather liked Antonio Riccobono, who at forty-four years of age was considerably younger and more human than the other professors who taught the courses he was taking in Logic and Moral Philosophy. Both taught in such a determinedly plodding style that they were frequently interrupted in the lecture hall by the sound of snoring emerging from some unfortunate soul no longer able to sustain consciousness.

'How are your new poems coming along?' Tomaso asked between mouthfuls.

As well as his formal studies, Will had also taken up the study of Italian poetry, with which he had become fascinated as his mastery of the language grew.

'The sonnet, you mean? Slowly, to say the least. In Italian, it's a perfect form, but I'm trying to write in English. I'll never be a Petrarch, I fear.'

Tomaso laughed; he had, Will thought, little understanding of poetry, and less interest. In the evenings, when Will settled down to read and write, Tomaso went off to frequent the taverns that lined the city's piazzas. Padua was a lively town during term-time, and every evening boisterous parties seemed to erupt, only ending in the small hours of the morning. Will had often been wakened by Tomaso staggering home long after curfew.

When he could, Will attempted to moderate these impulses, conscious always of Walsingham's injunction to keep the youngster out of mischief, a task he frequently found wearying.

Thoughts of Walsingham took him to the particular reason why he and Tomaso had arranged to meet. That morning, a courier had arrived, discreetly scratching at the back door of the house to deliver a packet. The seal, a simple cross enclosed within a circle, though nondescript to the casual observer, was one of several used by Thomas Phelippes.

Though he was excited that at last there was some communication from London, the first such that they had received since they had despatched Lance from Venice, Will was late for his lecture, so he had stuffed the

168

envelope in his pocket, telling Tomaso about it as they parted to go their separate ways.

As they finished up the last of their meal, he retrieved the packet and broke open the seal.

There were two papers inside the thick outer cover. The first was a short note, written in the clear and precise hand that Will recognised as that of Sir Francis Walsingham.

> My Dear Shakespeare,
> I am gratified to hear that young Tom has settled into his studies. The legal training he will get from Padua is second to none, and his future will be all the more assured when he completes his studies, for the skills of the law can be widely applied. I am sure he is enjoying the student life to the full, and thinking of it brings back the joy of my own time there as a young man in the fifties.
> Though I am sure that his professors have prescribed many texts for his studies, I have enclosed a further list of works which I believe it would be most beneficial for him to examine. Most should be available in Padua, and unless you have been reckless with the funds already provided, there should be sufficient monies to pay for them.
> As for yourself, William, I hope that your own studies are proving fruitful, and I look forward to seeing their fruit being put to good use when you return.
> Take care of your persons, both of you, Tom for the love that I have always borne him, and you for the affection I have developed for you since you came into my employ.

The note was simply signed *Fra. Walsingham* in the secretary's familiar looping hand.

The second sheet of paper appeared to be nothing more than the list of books to which Sir Francis had referred, written in a different hand. This, Will knew, would be but a disguise.

Taking up a flask containing coal-dust which he had retrieved from his room when they arrived at the house, he turned the paper over and sprinkled it with the dust, which he then gently rubbed into the paper using a cloth. In a few moments white letters began to appear, written in a neat characters which Will immediately recognised as the handwriting of Thomas Phelippes.

Looking up from his work, he laughed at the astonished expression on Tomaso's face. 'Written with a solution made of alum and vinegar,' he explained. 'The words disappear within seconds of being written and are usually recovered by dipping the paper in water and then holding it to the fire. This new method is surer and simpler.'

Unsurprisingly, the text was in code, though it only took a few minutes for them to render it into clear English, so adept had they become at using their standard cipher.

> My dear William,
> Firstly, please accept my apologies for making so tardy a reply to your correspondence. Your servant suffered some misfortunes on the road back to England. He eventually succeeded in getting to London, but he was much delayed, so that your second message arrived hard on his heels. This letter therefore responds to both of your communications.

'I wonder what troubles Lance fell into,' Tomaso muttered. 'I hope he was not injured. I have become fond of the old curmudgeon.'

> Based on the intelligence gathered by our unfortunate late agent, we have launched several shafts aimed at finding out exactly what the Spanish king intends. These enquiries may take some time to bear fruit, and in the meantime I beg you to continue your efforts to acquire any information you can that may shine a light on this subject. In this context we

170

approve entirely your recruitment of the agent
Peacock you named in your second report.

Will and Tomaso had been pleased with their choice of code name for Bassanio, whose surname meant Peacock in English. Bassanio had been true to his word, sending them coded bulletins every month, mostly containing gossip gathered at the papal court, things he had heard in conversations or which his various informants had told him.

> The information he has provided so far is most useful, particularly the news that William Allen and his accomplice Robert Persons have arrived in Rome. This we did not know from any other source. What their objectives are we do not know, but it is probable that they are plotting again for the pope to renew the excommunication of our sovereign lady, the queen. Any further information he can glean on their activities would be most welcome.

William Allen was the head of the English College, based at Rheims, an institution whose chief business was the training of Catholic priests to send into England. Persons, according to Bassanio's report, was a writer of Catholic tracts, though he was rumoured to have been involved in various plots against the queen.

> Peacock's views on the disposition of Pope Sixtus with respect to King Philip's ambitions was also of great interest. More on this would be greatly welcomed.

This item had come from Bassanio's second report, in which had told them of a conversation he had had with a cardinal. The fellow had evidently been rather tipsy, and in his cups he had confided that the pope, though as fierce in his determination to defeat the forces of Protestantism as his predecessor, was yet suspicious of King Philip's ambitions.

The pope, the drunken cardinal had said, knew that King Philip was planning to invade England, and fully expected to be asked to contribute financially to such an undertaking, something he was most reluctant to do.

Which brought them to the most important clause of Phelippes' letter.

But it is the news brought by your servant that has us most vexed, and is of the highest importance. Your report tells us that King Philip has issued an instruction to the Marquis de Santa Cruz to prepare a plan for the invasion of England, but we know no more than that. As I said, we have launched a number of enquiries through our diverse channels to find out whatever we can, but Peacock is in a unique position to acquire the information we need.

We know that the Spanish king is in contact with the pope on this matter, and it is well known that the Vatican is a leaking vessel at the best of times. I will leave it to your judgement as to how hard you can press him, and if you need more money, I am authorised to make it available through the channels you know of.

At the end, Phelippes repeated Sir Francis' warning.

Do take care of yourselves in Italy. This business can be dangerous, as you well know.

Will pushed the letter aside, and looked at Tomaso.

'At least we know that our reports are getting through,' he said.

The long silence from London had been a source of some anxiety to them. Though they had faith that Lance would prove a faithful message-bearer, they had entrusted their second report to a private courier service and there was always the possibility that couriers could meet mishaps on the road.

'When do you expect to hear from Bassanio again?' asked Will. They had agreed that Bassanio's communication with them should be through Tomaso, on the basis that letters between the two Italians would be less likely to attract attention than one addressed to William Shakespeare.

They had concocted a coding system whereby the key messages were hidden among gossipy news items, which Tomaso could then decode using a codebook of their own devising. The system was cumbersome, required considerable ingenuity on the part of the sender, and took time to decipher,

172

but Bassanio had seemed to take great delight in the whole process and they felt it was worth the effort to protect both Bassanio and themselves.

'Within the week, if he stays true to his past habit. He is returning to Venice from Rome with the ambassador, according to his last note. So I expect he will send something from there.'

Will nodded and rose from the table. 'We had better clear this mess up before Maria comes in.'

They busied themselves for a few minutes sweeping away the residual coal dust and destroying the message by burning it in a small bowl. The ashes were scattered out the window, from where they drifted away into the ether.

'Will, have you given any thought to what you will do when the term ends?' Tomaso asked as they went back out into the piazza, saying a quick hello to Maria as she came back from shopping at the market.

Will frowned; he had not given the question very much thought, though the end of the academic year was only a few weeks away, at the end of June. Daily life was so busy that he had little space in his head to spare beyond his studies, writing poetry and their intelligencing work. 'No, not really. I suppose I shall go home, since there is nothing to hold me here.'

As he said it, he realised how much he was going to miss this life, a short few months though it had been. But of course it was impossible for him to stay—Tomaso was settled and would not be leaving Padua until his studies were complete, several years hence, and with Bassanio established as a source of intelligence in Venice, that part of his mission was finished. Certainly he had done enough to clear his name in England, and it was time for him to resume his life, and perhaps get a career in theatre started, if the fates allowed it.

'I think I shall go and visit Verona,' Tomaso said, though he sounded tentative about it, as if nervous of Will's reaction. 'It is, after all, the place of my mother's birth...'

And it was also the home of Madalena Adorno, now the wife of Ferdinando Nogarola. They had heard about the wedding in one of the gossipy notes within which Bassanio disguised his despatches.

Though hardly unexpected, Tomaso had seemed particularly affected by the news, and for several days had been uncharacteristically moody. It had occurred to Will that Tomaso was still infatuated with the Genoese girl, an obsession that he had thought dead and buried.

173

His gentle suggestion that Tomaso should forget her had provoked the young man into a rage, and they had almost come to blows. Since then, they had both avoided mentioning Madalena's name, by mutual consent declaring a truce on the subject.

'Yes, of course,' Will said. 'It's only natural you should want to go there. Perhaps we might travel there together, since it is on the road that leads to the Brenner Pass, whose heights I must thread to go home to England.'

The suggestion seemed to take Tomaso by surprise, prompting Will to become a little mischievous. 'Perhaps I might even stay a week or two. I am told it is a very fair city, and there is no hurry for me to go home.'

'Mmm. Yes, perhaps. Look, there's Tebaldo. I promised him I would give him my notes from yesterday's lectures. I'll see you tonight.'

He disappeared up the stairs that led the lecture halls devoted to the faculty of law, at the top of which he embraced a handsome, fair-haired youth. Tebaldo Pindemonte was a native of Verona who was studying at the university and with whom Tomaso had formed a close friendship of which Will was a little jealous. The pair disappeared out of sight.

There was something going on that Tomaso was not telling him, of that he was convinced. It would not hurt if he did indeed stay in Verona for long enough to ensure that Tomaso stayed out of trouble.

But all that would have to wait until another day, since he was going to be late for his afternoon lecture by the esteemed doctor of moral philosophy, Giason de Nores.

174

Chapter 20

D ottore, dottore, dottore del buco del cul. Vaffancul! Vaffancul!'
A dozen students danced gleefully around a newly graduated
Doctor of Philosophy, who was garlanded with an outsized laurel
wreath, befuddled with drink and grinning idiotically. They were singing the
traditional scurrilous ditty which Tomaso had translated for Will's benefit
from the Venetian dialect as 'Doctor, doctor, doctor of the mouth of the arse.
Fuck you! Fuck you!'.

The little group swayed happily through the middle of the Piazza dei
Signori, attracting new adherents as it went, so that by the time they reached
the far side of the piazza the dozen who had started out were trebled in
number, and at least doubled in volume, the words of the song echoing off
the houses that lined the northern side of the square.

The townsfolk of Padua laughed and smiled and applauded, outwardly
tolerant as always, but perhaps thankful that these scenes heralded the end of
the academic year and the return of a period of peace and quiet until the
university recommenced in December.

This was the fourth or fifth such graduation party that Will had witnessed
that day, as doctorates were awarded to graduating students. Though their
antics were amusing, particularly when, following another tradition, they
forced the poor graduate to perform some debasing ritual, Will preferred to
stand on the sidelines and watch.

Tomaso, on the other hand, could not resist joining in all the fun, and Will
hadn't seen him since he whirled off with a particularly noisy group headed
in the direction of the market square next door to the Palazzo del Ragione.
He had left him with a group of their student friends who, being older and of
a more sober disposition, were content to drink wine poured from a big glass
flask provided by the proprietor of a nearby tavern while they watched the
antics of their more boisterous colleagues.

The sound of the big clock on the tower of the Capitano's Palace striking twelve prompted Will to drink up the last of his wine, say goodbye to his friends and make promises that they would meet later in the day for dinner.

As he made his way back to their lodging, he had a moment of sadness as he realised how much he was going to miss this life. In a week or so, he and Tomaso would both be leaving Padua. Will would return to England. Tomaso would spend a few months in Verona, the city where his mother had been born, before returning at the end of the year for his next term, aiming eventually to be paraded around the piazze of Padua as a newly-minted Doctor of Laws.

He would miss Tomaso. Though he was not susceptible to the physical charms of his own sex—if he had been, he would long ago have found himself in bed with Kit Marlowe—Tomaso, his near-constant companion for most of the last year, had brought forth in Will a kind of protective affection for the young man, chaste but no less emotional for all that. Their approaching separation would be a painful moment.

His thoughts turned to the reunion he would have with his friends in London, Burbage, Greene and the rest. How he would impress them with his newly-acquired learning! He saw himself at the centre of one of their debates, deploying his knowledge like a rapier, making delicate probes and deadly thrusts. No longer a mere grammar-school boy, he could truly claim to be as well educated as they were.

And he would resume the career in the theatre: his mind was teeming with ideas for plays and poems when he finally got back to London. He would show them what a glover's son from Warwickshire could do.

These pleasant thoughts were interrupted by his arrival at the house, which was quiet as the sepulchre, the servants enjoying a day off, and the other students no doubt immersed in the end of year revels.

In the common room at the back, one end of the big communal table was littered with the detritus left after the departure of the occupants that morning—half a dozen plates containing the remains of the morning's meal were scattered among dog-eared books, notepapers, quills, and ink pots.

In the middle of the table, a green cap lay draped jauntily over a candlestick holder. A black cloak had been flung over the back of one chair, and a doublet, faded and with frayed cuffs, sagged despondently over another.

176

Will's eyes flicked over the familiar squalid scene, and as he turned to leave the room he spotted a letter propped against an inkpot at the nearest end of the table.

He instantly recognised the script with which the letter's originator had addressed the letter to *Signor Tomaso Martinelli* as belonging to Bassanio Pavoni. It must have been delivered, he realised, after he and Tomaso had left that morning. Presumably one of the other students had accepted the delivery, though this was against the protocol that they had agreed with the couriers who carried their dispatches back and forth between Padua and Rome.

He frowned. Bassanio's next report was not expected for another week or two, so perhaps this letter contained information that could not wait that long. And Tomaso was most likely out for some time yet; he decided he might as well undertake the decryption of Bassanio's letter himself.

He climbed the stairs to Tomaso's room, which, as he surveyed it, resembled the 'tween decks of the *Bonaventura* after their encounter with the storm. He picked his way through the clothes and shoes tumbled on the floor to the small desk that sat under the window with its view down into the piazza below. This too was piled high with books and papers, and Will wondered how Tomaso managed to concentrate among this wreckage. For himself, a man given to neat orderliness in most things, working in such an environment would drive him to distraction.

Still, he knew where the items he needed were kept—securely locked in the desk drawer, to which only he and Tomaso had a key. Sliding the drawer open, the decoding sheet that he sought was on the top of a pile of other papers. He lifted it out and turned to go.

As he did so, his hand swept across the desktop, dislodging a small pile of what looked like letters, sending them fluttering to the floor. With a curse, Will bent to pick them up. Though he'd had no intention of reading them, the signature at the bottom of the topmost letter caught his eye.

Written in a clear hand, simple and without embellishments of any kind, was the name Madalena Nogarola. What, he wondered with a frown, was the former Madalena Adorno, now a married woman, doing writing to Tomaso? Involuntarily, he shifted his eyes to the top of the page and began to read:

> My dearest Tomaso,
> I hope that my letter finds you in good health,
> and that your studies at Padua prosper. How I

envy you the life you must be leading there, studying the greatest thinkers and enjoying the opportunity to discourse with others engaged with the same pursuits.

Such excitements are denied to us mere women, though why this should be so I do not know. Perhaps men fear that women, equipped with the same learning, might begin to forget their place and dispute with them as equals. Then might the world be truly turned upside down.

Your last letter, which I have burned, for prudence' sake, says that you will come to Verona as soon as your studies have ended. You are a free man of means, and you can go where you will. And I understand your desire to come here, to the city where your mother was born, and to reacquaint yourself with such relatives as you still have here.

But dear Tomaso, please understand that you cannot meet with me except when I am in the company of my husband. Anything else would be most improper, and would incur Ferdinando's extreme displeasure, something that you will not want to experience, I assure you. You know I bear you the greatest goodwill and affection, so nothing would give me greater pain than that you should suffer at my husband's hands.

Dear, sweet Tomaso, had we met before my fate was determined, perhaps we might have become more than friends, though the estate of friendship, carrying its own freight of selfless love, untainted by the confusions of physical desire, does sometimes seem to me the higher rather than the lower order of human relationships. And I confess that the passion that you express in your letters so immoderately does not go entirely unrequited.

178

But the world's rules are stern and unbending,
particularly for women, and so I must beg of
you, put your emotion aside and think of me as
you would a sister, nay perhaps more a female
cousin, and so in that state we might be able to
continue in the traffic of friendship.

There were half a dozen other letters in the little pile he held in his hand,
and given the content of the first, he felt he had no option but to look through
the others. A brief scan showed that they were in much the same vein,
answers to what had apparently been expressions of undying love from
Tomaso.

Read in order, it seemed that Madalena had not quite known how to
respond to this furious assault. In her first letter she seemed to encourage
him, giving more than a hint that his feelings were returned. But in the
subsequent letters she seemed to cool markedly, perhaps realising that it
might be dangerous to allow Tomaso's obsession free rein.

Yet she never quite cut him off entirely, and there were hints here and
there that her marriage was not a happy one, that her husband had a violent
nature, and that she had suffered at his hands.

What to make of this? That Tomaso had been attracted to Madalena had
been apparent from the first, but Will was surprised at the depth of that
attachment, not so much in these letters as in their invisible counterparts,
Tomaso's impassioned protestations to Madalena. Missives that Madalena,
with commendable prudence, had destroyed rather than risk them falling into
the hands of her husband.

With a sigh, Will realised that, yet again, he would have to take steps to
protect Tomaso against the consequences of his own youthful folly. He had
told Tomaso, half in jest, that he would come with him to Verona and
perhaps stay there for some time. Now, he felt he had no alternative but to
make good on that proposal, even if that meant a further delay to his own
departure for home.

Placing the letters back where he had found them, he went to his own
room next door, closing the door behind him, and settling at this desk to
begin the tedious task of decrypting the message from Bassanio. The code,
having been devised by Tomaso and Bassanio, was not familiar to him, and
the work proceeded slowly. Fortunately the message was,
uncharacteristically for Bassanio, quite short.

Guglielmo, I write in some haste and urgency, for tomorrow the ambassador returns to Venice, and I with him. The ambassador is recalled in order to receive new instructions from the Signoria on a number of matters, and I am to accompany him. We will be in Venice for but a week after our arrival.

I tell you this because I have recently come into information of great importance and secrecy, too important to entrust to writing and the hazards of any courier, however trusted, and so I ask that you come to Venice to meet with me so that I might pass my knowledge on in person.

Meet me at the Gobbo di Rialto in five days' time, at the tenth hour. I know this proposal will come as a surprise and is contrary to the procedure we have agreed for our communication, but there is no alternative, as I am certain you will understand when we meet.

Will looked at the date of the message; it had taken two days to get here, so the meeting that Bassanio was proposing would be in a mere three days' time. It was a day's journey of from Padua to Venice, so if he left tomorrow or the day after that at the latest, he should be able to make the rendezvous in time.

As these practical questions ran through his head, he wondered at the peremptory nature of Bassanio's demand for his presence in Venice. What information could he have that was so important that he dare not entrust it to their usual methods of communication?

The thought also went through his mind that perhaps this was a trap; that Bassanio intended to betray him to the Venetian authorities, though this he soon dismissed. Bassanio had to date proven to be a man of his word, and if he was going to betray them, he would surely have done so before now.

As for the matter of Tomaso and Madalena, he resolved himself to silence for now, for what could he say or do to discourage him that would be any more effective than that young woman's emphatic rejection in her last letter?

And given this urgent need for him to return to Venice, he doubted that there would be an opportunity to even raise the subject with him. Tomaso

180

could never say no to an invitation to celebrate, and his open and charming personality ensured that he was popular, so it was not at all unusual for him to disappear for several days, as one party led to another.

In all probability he would not come back to their lodging until at least the following day, by which time Will would be long gone. He would just have to trust that Tomaso had sufficient good sense to avoid doing anything indiscreet in Verona before Will could return there himself.

Chapter 21

M*eet me at the Gobbo di Rialto'* Bassanio's letter had said. A thin, unseasonal drizzle was falling from a dull grey sky as Will hurried across the familiar arch of the Rialto Bridge to find this famous Venetian landmark.

Just across the bridge, he passed the venerable church of San Giacometto, and then crossed the handsome arcaded Campo San Giacomo, paved in stone with the usual well at its centre. The hour being early, there were few people about. A few merchants ambled along the colonnades deep in conversation, and the occasional black-robed lawyer hurried self-importantly across the square in the direction of the law courts which occupied the corner of the piazza. Otherwise the place was deserted.

Gobbo in Italian meant 'Hunchback.' The Gobbo di Rialto referred to the small flight of steps leading up to a platform from where the city's town criers could step onto the stump of an ancient column and proclaim new laws to the populace. The steps were supported by a statue of a crouching man— not really hunchbacked at all to Will's eye, simply bent under the weight of his burden—that gave the whole structure its name.

Looking around, there was no sign of Bassanio, so, thankful for the opportunity to get out of the rain, he walked into the shadowed space under the arcade that lay behind the statue and settled himself onto a stone bench to wait, hoping that he did not look too suspicious to any casual passerby who might come past in the interval.

Fortunately, he didn't have long to wait. Within a few minutes, the plump form of Bassanio appeared from around a corner, and spotting Will, he hurried over and embraced him, his face wreathed in smiles as he bestowed the traditional kiss on each cheek.

Bassanio had grown in girth, Will's sharp eye noted, no doubt the result of over-indulgence in the pleasures of the table that were so much a part of the life of a diplomat. But Will also detected a certain growth in self-confidence as well; the assurance of a man who had found his place in the world. The jolly, self-mocking demeanour was still there, but beneath it there was a gleam of calculation in his eye that hinted at ruthlessness. For the first time Will felt he should be cautious in his dealings with this man.

'Shall we walk?' Bassanio said, slipping a hand under Will's elbow and steering him out of the arcade and into a narrow and shaded street leading away from the Rialto. 'How was your journey from Padua?'

Will grimaced. 'I shall not, I am afraid, ever be much of a horseman, but otherwise the journey was pleasant enough.' He smiled, remembering Tomaso's observation when they had first travelled to Padua that he sat on his horse with all the grace of a sack of potatoes, a judgement delivered with a lopsided grin that robbed it of its sting.

'In that, my friend, I fear we are kindred spirits.' Bassanio laughed. 'I feel as if every bone in my body was jolted from its housing on the journey here from Rome, though the ambassador travels in a horse-litter, so at least I was able from time to time to get some relief by joining him when he felt the need for my services. And the inns on the road from Rome are villainous! They serve food fit only for farm animals, and every bed is overrun with bugs and lice, so sleep is impossible.'

They came to a small campo, mostly still in shadow except for a shaft of bright sunlight coming between the buildings on the eastern side of the square that momentarily dazzled them as they crossed the piazza and ducked into another narrow lane. Will began to wonder where Bassanio was taking him.

'And how is Tomaso?'

'Last I saw of him, well enough. It is the end of the university term and he was enjoying the revelry and mayhem that seems to be the lot of the poor citizens of Padua at this time of year.' Exactly as he had expected, Tomaso had not come home the night before he left, so, somewhat irritated, he had left a scribbled note on the boy's desk, explaining that he had gone back to Venice, though without saying why, and that he would meet him again in Verona in a week or so.

'Padua has little else going for it. Were it not for the university it would be a backwater, so I expect they make the best of it.'

Will was beginning to feel a little impatient. After all, he had dropped everything and made haste to obey this peremptory summons to Venice, yet Bassanio was showing no inclination to explain to him why he had asked for such haste.

183

They crossed a small canal, and after passing through a narrow passage emerged into a square that Will recognised as the Campo San Cassiano, dominated on one side by its great church that had stood here since the eighth century, Bassanio gestured in the direction of a tall palazzo that stood across the square, on the other side of yet another little canal.

'That is our destination,' Bassanio said. 'A friend allows me the use of a small suite of rooms for my use when in Venice. I thought we could talk more privately there.'

Will nodded, following his companion across the canal and into the front door of the palazzo, opened at Bassanio's commanding knock by an aged and obsequious retainer who conducted them up a flight of stairs to a pleasant room that overlooked the canal, reflections from whose waters cast patterns on light on the ceiling.

The room was plainly furnished with a settle that nestled beneath the window, a table and half a dozen high-backed chairs in one corner. Two more comfortable chairs were set opposite the large fireplace, in which a fire blazed to ward off the morning's chill. The walls were panelled in dark wood and hung with half a dozen paintings.

The only other exit from the room, apart from the door by which they had entered, was a narrow opening next to the fireplace, which had no door but was instead hung with heavy damask curtains. Beyond, Will assumed, was Bassanio's sleeping place.

Bassanio gestured Will towards one of the chairs by the fire. On a small table between them stood a jug of wine and two glasses. Clearly he had gone to some trouble to set the scene for the next act of his little drama.

As they took their seats, the servant poured wine and then, with a small bow, withdrew. Will raised his glass in a silent toast to his companion, accompanying the gesture with a querulous raised eyebrow. Though he was burning with curiosity, he was determined to play the part of the cool and unruffled spymaster, perhaps unconsciously mimicking the style of Sir Francis.

For his part, Bassanio for the first time that day seemed a little less than self-assured. He fidgeted with the sleeves of his doublet, made a show of tasting and appreciating the wine, a little too sweet for Will's taste, and stood abruptly to grasp a poker, with which he prodded at a fire which needed no such encouragement. This task completed, he turned and, finally meeting Will's eye, nodded as if to say that he was now ready to begin.

'Thank you for coming here at such short notice. I would not have asked you to do so if the need were not urgent. And the matter important.'

Will nodded, conveying no more than a polite appreciation of these sentiments.

'You will recall from one of my letters that the English priests, William Allen and Robert Persons, had arrived in Rome a month or two ago? Well, since they arrived they have been busy importuning anyone who will listen and who might have influence with His Holiness. Their subject is the renewal of the sentence of excommunication against your queen, which has been in abeyance for many years.'

'Yes, this was expected. Are they meeting with any success?'

'No, for the pope is more focused on his building programs and improving the papal finances than he is on foreign issues, so for now their pleas are falling on deaf ears. They have supporters in the Curia, it is true, but there is no appetite just yet for a change to the status quo. But it is not for this information that I asked you to come back to Venice.'

Will's eyebrows shot up again.

'Allen is as close-mouthed and discreet a creature as you could hope to meet, but his companion is not. Knowing of my position, and hoping to influence the Ambassador through me, thereby adding another twig to the bonfire he and his master are trying to build, Persons found an occasion to bend my ear over copious jugs of wine. Cheap wine. My head was ringing for days afterwards!'

The serious air dissolved as they both laughed at the image of poor Bassanio with a hangover earned in the path of duty.

'Anyway, after delivering his routine diatribe against the sins of the English queen—a catalogue of which I was already well aware, since these two have wearied every diplomat in Rome on the subject—he began to talk about his own history. He is a boastful man, full of his own self-importance, and before long he was bragging of his intimacy with the various great men he has met on his journeys through Europe. Among them was the Duke of Parma, at whose court he spent some months a few years ago.'

Will sat up a little straighter at the title of the King of Spain's governor in the Netherlands, and his most capable general.

'It seems,' Bassanio continued, 'that he is still in contact with his friends at the Ducal court, through whom he claimed to have been receiving continual intelligence on the goings-on there. Though his company was

185

becoming somewhat tedious, I did not discourage him from talking on, seeing it as my duty to glean whatever information I could for the ambassador.

'Much of what Persons had to say was just court gossip, of little interest. But then he started to talk of the new campaign that the King of Spain is planning against England. Knowing your interest in this subject, I plied him further with wine and eventually, with many conspiratorial nudges and whispers, he told me what he knew of the Spanish intentions.'

Bassanio looked a little smug, knowing that he now had the full attention of his audience. *He would make a fine actor,* Will thought, *with that sense of timing.* 'Which are...?'

'The duke has proposed to the king that he be authorised to build a fleet of barges, with which to send thirty thousand battle-hardened troops across the channel on a moonless night. Once in England, they would join with rebellious Catholic subjects of your queen to sweep all before them. No doubt Master Persons sees himself in a leading role in the revolt.'

Will frowned. The information gathered by Walsingham's dead agent was that King Philip had instructed the Marquis of Santa Cruz to prepare an invasion plan, not the Duke of Parma. Was this, then, a competing proposal? If so, which plan had the Spanish monarch chosen to adopt? Or was he as yet undecided?

'A bold stroke indeed,' he said. 'But I am puzzled—how does the duke expect to be able to cross the channel with his great mass of barges and remain unmolested by English warships?'

Bassanio shrugged. 'Persons did not say, but the duke is a soldier, not a sailor. No doubt he under-estimates the difficulty. He would not be the first general to misunderstand the importance of control of the sea-lanes, as we Venetians well know.'

Will nodded. He too was neither soldier nor sailor, and he knew nothing of military strategy by land or sea, but what Bassanio said seemed to make sense.

'In any case,' Bassanio went on, 'that question is irrelevant, for it appears that this plan was rejected in Madrid, much to the duke's annoyance. It seems that the Spanish king has been considering several alternatives, including those of Santa Cruz.'

Will felt himself becoming impatient again. 'This is all very interesting, Bassanio, but I fear that a tale about a rejected invasion plan told by a

186

drunken, self-aggrandizing priest is not likely to be of much interest to Sir Francis Walsingham.'

'No, I did not expect so. But Sir Francis would, no doubt, be much more interested in the final plan that *has* been approved by the king.'

'Of which we have a copy.'

This astonishing statement came not from Bassanio, but from the familiar smooth voice of Francesco Contarini, as he emerged from the curtained doorway beside the fireplace.

Will jumped to his feet, his heart hammering in the cage of his chest, his mind in turmoil. What did the Venetian patrician's presence here mean? Had Bassanio betrayed him, informed Contarini of his activities as an intelligencer? If so, he could be in mortal danger, for a spy betrayed could soon come to an untimely end, as the fate of Andres Gasparo demonstrated.

His fists bunched and he fought down the urge to strike out at his betrayer. The anger must have been apparent in his face, for Bassanio flinched and took an involuntary step backwards.

'*Pace*, William.' Contarini was as urbane and unperturbed as ever, calm as a judge mediating in a quarrel between two village oafs too far below his station to warrant such a vulgar thing as passion. 'You are in no danger. Bassanio has had the difficult task of steering a middle course between his loyalty to you as a friend and his natural loyalty to the Venetian state that he serves.'

'Ser Francesco has the right of it,' Bassanio was eager, his soft eyes pleading for understanding. 'I said to you from the start that I could not and would not betray Venice, and I have not done so. All of the information that I sent you over these last months was common gossip in Rome, rumours and facts that you could have got yourself, had you been in the city. I saw no harm in sharing these snippets with you, in discharge of our agreement, and doing so could in no way harm the Republic.'

Reluctantly, Will acknowledged the justice of this with a grim nod; a glance at the impassive face of Contarini revealed nothing.

'But what I heard from Persons was more difficult to reconcile with my conscience. I could not fathom where the interests of Venice lay—in passing this information on to you or in withholding it. And so I turned to Signor Contarini. He is, as you know, a senior member of the Signoria, and a good friend to my uncle, and so I felt he would be able to guide me.'

187

'And betrayed me, your friend who helped you get out of a financial mess, at some risk to himself.' Anger, bitterness, and contempt laced his voice as he turned to Contarini. 'And so I assume you will have me thrown into the *Prigione Nuove*, signor?' The New Prison, right next door to the Doge's Palace, was where prisoners of the state were incarcerated.

Contarini just laughed, and spread his hands to placate the angry Shakespeare. 'You have a flair for the dramatic, William. As I said, please calm yourself. You are in no danger of being escorted to the state prison or anywhere else.'

Indifferent to Will's confusion, Contarini settled himself into one of the chairs, gesturing for him to sit in the other. Bassanio was left standing beside the fireplace, watching.

'What young Pavoni here has not yet told you is that this drunken, self-regarding priest, as you so aptly described him, had more to tell. His informants in Brussels had also told him that King Philip had written to Pope Sixtus, detailing his final plan for the invasion of England.

'Knowing this, we set our own agents to work, and they bribed one of the pope's gentlemen of the bedchamber to obtain a copy for us. This he did by stealing the key to the pope's writing desk while he slept, extracting the letter and copying it, and returning the key before the old man woke the next morning. Quite a neat operation, wouldn't you say?'

Will stared at the patrician face, self-satisfied as its owner contemplated his coup. 'Who are you, Signor Contarini?'

'Surely you have guessed by now?'

'I know you are a senior member of the Signoria, and a member of the Council of Ten.' This, Will knew, was the body selected from the larger Signoria that wielded effective authority over government affairs. 'But I imagine you are also the head of intelligence for the Venetian Republic.'

'Bravo, Messer Shakespeare, bravo! You are quite correct. But like your master Walsingham, I keep this aspect of my official duties quiet.'

'And how long have you known I was in the employ of Sir Francis?'

Contarini laughed. 'Since the day you boarded my ship, of course. Your colleague Phelippes made the arrangements through a third party, intending to disguise the true nature of your journey, but naturally nothing happens on the docks of London that is not known to Sir Horatio Palavicino, and since that gentlemen and I are good friends, he naturally did me the courtesy of ensuring I knew the true identity of my passengers.'

188

Why would Palavicino do such a thing? He and Sir Francis were colleagues, ostensibly, yet perhaps they were also rivals, each trying to outdo the other in demonstrating their zeal in protecting the queen.

Contarini had been engaged in the delicate matter of arranging a loan for the English government, Will remembered. Perhaps Palavicino was simply anxious that these efforts should not be sabotaged if Contarini discovered Will's connection to Walsingham by some other means.

Will's mind was now a mess of fears and uncertainties, out of which a new suspicion formed. He turned to Bassanio, his eyes narrowing with anger. 'I suppose you have been working for Signor Contarini all along.'

'No, no Will, I swear.' Bassanio looked genuinely offended by Will's assertion that he had been betraying him from the start. 'It was only when I realised the importance and scale of Persons' story that I sought out Ser Francesco. Before that I had no knowledge, none at all, of his other, more secret role.'

'What Bassanio says is true, and that's the end of it.' Contarini was now brisk and all business. 'Though I could well wish that he had come to me sooner. Let us get to the immediate matter in hand. Which is this—I want you, Will, to take the plans back to England and ensure that Master Walsingham gets them. Which I imagine would present no difficulty, since it must conform with your own wishes.'

This was a turn he was not expecting the conversation to take! The Venetian spymaster was quite right to say that a return to England, particularly bearing such useful information, was at the heart of his own desires. He had had enough of travelling, and though he had learned much, since the university term had ended he had increasingly felt the tug of home. Yet questions remained.

'Yes, of course. I will most willingly do so. But tell me, Ser Francesco, why you are disposed to send this information to England rather than hold onto it yourself? After all, England is a heretic country, and Venice risks the pope's displeasure, or worse, if it were to be discovered that you are aiding my country against the leading member of the Catholic League.'

'The pope! He is as distrustful of King Philip as we are, and for the same reasons. Moreover, though he must of necessity appear to support Philip's plans, I am told that, far from sharing the Spanish king's obsession with overthrowing the heretic Queen of England, he rather admires her.' This somewhat startling proposition brought a brief smile to Will's face.

'Alas there are those in the Signoria who are full of fear—afraid to offend the pope, afraid of the power of the Spanish Empire—who would be appalled if they knew what I am doing.' This was said with the secret smile of a man who clearly enjoyed intrigue. 'But there are others, of whom I am one, who believe that the King of Spain's shadow is already too long. He controls virtually all of the Italian Peninsula, with the exception of Venice and our land empire, much of Germany, and he has the enormous resources of the New World with which to extend his ambitions further. Anything that distracts him and weakens him, undermines his ability to further expand here in Italy.'

Will nodded. The Venetian's words were an echo of the briefing he had received from Phelippes in London.

'For the moment, the Signoria is split on foreign policy as on many other subjects, and Doge Cicogna, though worthy, is something of a ditherer, unable to arbitrate between the various factions. In the meantime, we of the Council of Ten must do our best to advance Venetian interests. In my judgement, those interests are best served by supporting, albeit clandestinely, the cause of England.'

Contarini leaned forward in his seat, looking Will earnestly in the eyes. 'William, over our acquaintanceship I have come to respect your honesty and intelligence. It is because of this that I am entrusting this task to you. You will appreciate that I cannot commit what I know to writing and entrust it to any ordinary courier. I need someone I can trust to ensure that it arrives safely at its destination and, who, moreover, has the ability to ensure that it is delivered into the right hands. Will you do this for me?'

Will remembered being asked a similar question by Sir Francis Walsingham, to which there had only been one acceptable answer. 'And if I will not?'

'Then I will have to find another way. I will not threaten you, William, though I could; by any definition your activities here have been those of a spy. But that is not my way.'

Will smiled and extended his hand. 'Then I am your man, Ser Francesco.'

'Excellent! I am glad that we are friends and allies again. Now, Bassanio, if you will…'

Bassanio, who had stood silently by the fire throughout, went across the room to a small chest that sat on the table. Fumbling in a pocket, he extracted a small key and proceeded to open it.

While he did so, Will decided he would explore another suspicion. 'Ser Francesco, did you order the murder of our agent, Andres Gasparo or Andrea Scaramucci or whatever his name was?'

Contarini looked pained. 'His name was, in fact, Andres Gasparo, and he was a Spaniard. No, I did not order his death, though I did know that he was an agent working for your government. But he slipped past my men one night, and by the time we found him again, he was dead, by whose hand I do not know.

'He could have been the victim of common thieves or it is possible that he was killed by the agents of the Spanish if they also knew that he was a spy. Naturally, we ordered the watch to pay his rooming house a visit, just in case he had left anything behind that was of interest. Not surprisingly, those oafs were not as astute as you, William, and they failed to notice the book-code that you so cleverly identified and decrypted.'

Bassanio had now extracted from the strong box a small bundle of papers, which, receiving a nod of permission from Contarini, he handed to Will.

The text was difficult to make out. Though written in familiar Latin, the handwriting was a shaky scrawl, as if the writer had been in a great hurry. Holding the letters up to the light of the fire, Will soon worked out that this was indeed a copy of a letter written from the King of Spain to the pope, explaining in some detail the plan that he had settled upon for what he called 'The Enterprise of England'.

It seemed that Philip, faced with competing alternative proposals, had chosen a compromise plan—a vast naval expedition, over one hundred and fifty ships, was to carry troops and artillery to make a landing in southern Ireland, which the Spanish saw as fertile ground for the incitement of a supporting uprising of the Irish. Then the fleet would sail into the Channel, sweep aside the English navy, and provide protection for the Duke of Parma's force of thirty thousand men to cross and land in Kent.

'And thus, Holy Father,' the letter concluded, 'when my armies have overpowered the puny English forces and taken possession of London, the heretic Jezebel will be deposed and her league of ministers executed, to be replaced by England's rightful queen, Mary of Scotland.'

The two Italians waited patiently while Will worked his way through the letter. Looking up, he met the cool and appraising gaze of Contarini.

'This is a vast undertaking,' he said. 'Can it succeed, do you think?'

'It has some risks, to be sure. Timing the coordination of the actions of the invading fleet with those of Parma's army might be more difficult than

191

the Spanish expect, and there are the usual vagaries of wind and tide. And it relies on surprise.'

Which would be lost if the English government had forewarning of the Spanish plans. The document in his hands did not specify exactly when this *armada*, as the Spanish king called it, would be launched on its mission, but it would at least alert Walsingham and the rest of the Privy Council and ensure that they would devote sufficient resources to watching out for the telltale signs that an attack was imminent.

'There is something else,' Contarini said. 'We estimate that it will cost at least four million ducats to execute this plan. This is an enormous amount of money, and the Spanish exchequer is already deeply in debt. No doubt Philip will send his fiscal agents out to seek further loans to finance the expedition.

'When you return to London, you should convey this information and suggest that he sends out agents to the banking houses of Genoa and Florence and use whatever means he can to discourage them from extending further credit. I cannot, alas, guarantee that the Venetian bankers will be similarly reticent, but I intend to do my best to discourage them.'

The English Crown, Will remembered, had been seeking to use Contarini's services to negotiate a loan from those same Venetian bankers. No doubt he had some financial interest in keeping Venice on England's side as well.

'I am sure, Ser Francesco, that you will be most persuasive. Well, there is little left to be said. I will leave Venice today and begin my journey back to England.'

Contarini nodded. 'Excellent. You will travel by sea? I am sure we can arrange passage without any difficulty.'

'No, this time I think I must go by land. I cannot simply abandon Tomaso Martinelli without saying goodbye and ensuring that he is properly settled. He intends to go to Verona, and if he is not already there, I will accompany him. It is on my way, after all.'

Will took his leave of the two Venetians, his mind boiling with conflicting thoughts and emotions. He was excited at the prospect of finally setting his face towards home, apprehensive at the weight of responsibility that now lay on his shoulders to get this vitally important information back to London, and had a lingering suspicion that he was being used by the Venetians for their own purposes.

Within the hour he had crossed the lagoon, retrieved his horse and was on his plodding way to Verona, and Tomaso.

Chapter 22

I t was late in the afternoon when Will's horse clattered across the causeway leading to the Porta Nuova, the imposing gateway that pierced the forbidding modern fortifications protecting the city of Verona.

Ahead of him a mule train plodded its way through the gate, the heavily loaded animals braying in the afternoon heat. Their protests were ignored by the muleteer, who shouted curses and flicked his whip at his recalcitrant charges.

Will tried to muster some patience, sorely tried by five days on horseback and nights spent in the vile, cheap inns that were all he could afford, since he was now compelled to hoard his funds against the long trip north.

Slipping finally into the welcome shadow of the gate's tunnel, he handed to the guards the pass that had been provided by Francesco Contarini. They made a rather comical performance of carefully reading every word and shooting suspicious looks from under their helmets at this Englishman, an unaccustomed nationality this far from Venice and therefore worthy of scrutiny. Eventually, duty satisfied, they waved him into the city.

His horse, its head drooping with fatigue, trudged steadily along the broad avenue that stretched beyond the gate until they reached another wall, older and taller and flanked by towers. A splendid double arch, topped by a clock that told him the hour was approaching six in the evening, led into a broad and irregular open space lined with shops, taverns and townhouses.

But it was the structure that dominated the far side of the piazza that caused him to start with sufficient violence to disturb the complacency of his horse, which turned its head with a quizzical look and whickered a mild

193

protest. Tomaso had told him about the arena built by the Romans to hold gladiatorial games and spectacles for the entertainment of the masses; one of the few in Italy that had not been demolished as generation after generation mined their walls for stone to build their houses and palazzi. Yet Tomaso's description had not prepared him for the sheer scale of the building in front of him.

A flick of the reins got the horse moving again and he passed at a walk around its perimeter, gazing up in awe at the two graceful tiers of arches, at least a hundred feet high.

He stopped at a workshop, one of the many that occupied the arched entryways to the arena. A pottery, judging from the wares piled up under an awning that was flapping and twisting in the breeze. Dismounting, he asked the potter for directions to the address that Tomaso had given him in the scrawled note that he had left in Padua.

Deciding to lead the horse through the narrow streets of the town, he eventually arrived at another busy marketplace, which the potter had told him was called the Piazza dell' Erbe, the city's main food market, though it was nearly deserted at that time of day.

From there, a short walk down a narrow street brought him to the address he sought, a tall and narrow five-story house, a little larger and grander than its neighbours, with an arched gateway that led through a short tunnel to a small, deeply shadowed courtyard.

Sitting on the steps that led up to the main entrance to the house was a plump, jovial-looking woman, a big bowl of peas nestled in the folds of her skirt, which she had been in the process of shelling when his arrival interrupted her.

'*Buona sera*, Signora, ah, Cappelletti,' Will said, assuming that she was in fact the owner of the house as per Tomaso's note. 'My name is Shakespeare. I believe I am expected?'

'I've been keeping your room for this last week and more in expectation of your arrival, Signor Shakespeare.' The tartness of her words were undermined by the broadness of her grin as she put the peas aside and hauled her considerable bulk to her feet.

'My apologies for the inconvenience, Signora. I was delayed somewhat upon the road by an encounter with some vagabonds who seemed intent upon relieving me of my purse.'

The smile was replaced by a sour look. 'You came from Padua? That road is notorious, infested with thieves and outlaws who make life a misery

194

for the honest folk who must travel along it, aye and it has grown worse in these last sixty years since Venice has been Verona's master.' Her frown deepened as another possibility occurred to her. 'I trust, signor, that the efforts of these outlaws were not successful and that you have sufficient funds to pay for your lodging?'

'Of course, signora.' Will laughed. 'We had hot work of it for a bit, my companions and I, but we beat them off in the end. So we chose to take a somewhat more indirect route to avoid any further unpleasant encounters, hence the delay in my arrival. But never fear, I and my purse are still joined together.'

The landlady's cheeriness returned as she turned and put her fingers to her lips to give a piercing whistle. 'Nicola, you lazy bag of bones, come and take the gentleman's horse!'

A skinny, ragged boy emerged from the ramshackle wooden stable that leant against the wall on the opposite side of the courtyard and led the horse away to a well-earned feed, while Shakespeare turned to follow the landlady into the building and up four flights of stairs, which the woman climbed surprisingly nimbly considering her bulk.

On the top floor, she showed him to a small but comfortable room that had the luxury of two windows, one overlooking the street and the other giving a view of the courtyard. The space was almost filled by a good sized bed, leaving just enough room for a table under one window, on which stood a basin and water jug. A couple of chairs and a small chest completed the room's furnishings.

'My last room, signor,' the landlady said, as if anxious that he might not approve of it. 'Signor Martinelli was most insistent that I should keep it for you, even though I could have rented it out three times over.'

'And you have my thanks that you did so.' He drew a small purse from within his doublet and counted out some coins in payment of a week's rent.

With a bob of gratitude, the landlady left, closing the door behind her.

With a sigh, Will threw himself onto the bed, and within minutes was insensible. When his slumber was interrupted by a crash as the door was flung open and an excited Tomaso hurtled into the room, it felt as though he had only been asleep for a few minutes, an impression that evaporated when he realised that the late afternoon sun had almost completely given way to darkness.

'Here you are at last, Will!' Tomaso boomed, causing Will to wince. 'I was beginning to think you had abandoned me entirely.'

195

A flask of wine appeared magically from behind Tomaso's back, from which he took a deep swig before handing it across. He had clearly been drinking for most of the afternoon.

Struggling into an upright position, Will took the flask and swallowed a mouthful. 'Good to see you, too,' he said, sourly. 'I came as soon as I could.'

In fact, for a man supposedly hurrying home to London, he was making slow going of it. He had left Venice and made good time to get to Padua late the following day. There, he had found a short letter from Tomaso, posted from Verona. The letter simply said that he had arrived, having left Padua the day after Will had gone to Venice. He said he had found lodging for them both at the guest house of Signora Giovanna Cappelletti, directions for whose address were scribbled on the reverse.

Though Will had intended to depart for Verona immediately, it took him almost a week to arrange to convert into cash the last of the promissory notes that Phelippes had given him to cover his expenses, since the Padua agent of the Genoese bankers against whom the draft was drawn was out of town. Then there was the matter of finding a group of travellers to which he could join, for the road between Padua and Verona was notoriously infested with outlaws and vagabonds, so that travelling alone was inadvisable. In the end, it was a fortnight before he finally set out, with half a dozen other travellers, along the narrow and rutted track that led west across the plain towards Verona, three days' journey away.

It was on the morning of the second day that they ran into trouble, as he told Tomaso.

'We had just got started, and we were passing through a patch of dense forest when a band of ruffians attacked us from both sides of the road. They were a pretty motley lot, ragged and armed with rusty old swords. They seemed to want us to stop and hand over our money and valuables.'

'Which you didn't?'

'No. They made a mistake in picking on us, for we had among our number some pretty tough men-at-arms that the merchants had hired to protect themselves against just such a possibility. And we were armed ourselves. So we just charged them, and after a few blows were struck, they disappeared back into the brush. And that was that.'

'Bravo, Will!' Tomaso clapped his hands with joy when he had finished relating this tale. 'All those lessons put to use at last.'

'Aye, well, I gave good account of myself, I think,' Will said modestly, though in fact he was proud of his contribution to their little victory in the

196

forest. 'But caution dictated that we proceed with rather more care after that, for they could have come back in greater force at any time, and we decided to take some back roads that took us through less dangerous open country, all of which added another few days to our journey.'

'Anyway, you're here at last, and safe and sound. Tell me, though, what was it that had you hot-footing off to Venice in such a lather? I must confess that I was surprised to come home and find you gone, with no more than the briefest of notes in explanation.'

'I know, and I am sorry. But I could not risk committing to paper the reasons I had to go so suddenly.'

He proceeded to tell Tomaso everything that had happened in Venice, enjoying immensely the moment of jaw-dropping surprise on Tomaso's face when told of the sudden appearance of Francesco Contarini. 'And so I must return as soon as I can and advise Sir Francis directly of the plans for this armada and the invasion of England.'

Tomaso's face fell. 'But surely you can stay for a day or two? Verona is such a fair city, and I have much to show you.'

A few days would not, Will thought, make much difference, considering that the journey ahead of him would take at least a month, and he nodded his acquiescence.

'Good! And in any case, you must stay for the great public banquet and ball to be held at the Palazzo Giusti in three nights' time. It will be the biggest social event in Verona for the year. All the city's noble families will be there, and I have been invited.'

'Oh? How did you arrange that? You've only been here for a few weeks, and here you are, going to a society ball.'

Tomaso looked smug. 'Through Tebaldo Pindemonte. We travelled here together from Padua, and of course he introduced me to his father. Tebaldo never told me, but his father is the vicar of the House of Merchants, the most senior elected magistrate in the city.

'He knew my grandfather and my mother before they went to England. For their sake, and because of Tebaldo, he seems to have taken a liking to me, and so when the great ball was announced he made sure I was given an invitation.'

Will was unsurprised at this further demonstration of Tomaso's ability to charm everyone around him and to make new friends so effortlessly. There was a guilelessness about him that new acquaintances found disarming.

197

However, that same quality could lead him into questionable friendships, such as with Tebaldo Pindemonte, who struck Will as being rather arrogant and overly sure of himself, loud in his opinions and quick to provoke a fight. The fact that he was now revealed to be the son of Verona's leading magistrate—its mayor, in effect—probably explained the self-assurance that had often been on display in Padua and which would no doubt be exaggerated now he was on his own turf.

'I expect that Sir Francis will forgive me a few days' dalliance. Assuming, of course, that you can get *me* an invitation to this ball?' A vigorous nod. 'Then of course I will stay until then, though not a day longer. But tell me, what is the occasion that this ball is celebrating? It is not, so far as I can recall, any religious holiday. Though I am no Catholic, so it is possible there is some saint's day I have forgotten. Or is there some local Veronese tradition that it celebrates?'

'Only the tradition of *vendetta*!' Tomaso was clearly proud of his knowledge of the city's politics. 'The old families of Verona, who used to be the aristocracy of the Republic before the Venetians took over, have been at feud with each other for years, squabbling over grudges that go back to the days of the della Scalas.

'Recently it has become so bad that the streets were not safe, because of the fights that broke out almost every day between the supporters of the various families, in particular the Nogarola and the Bevilacqua. Nobody knows what started their feud, but Tebaldo says it is the fiercest of all; the families really hate each other.

'But the Venetians have finally had enough, and the Podestà has imposed a peace, threatening proscription if it should be broken. It is to celebrate and cement this agreement that the great ball is being held.'

Will recalled from a conversation with Bassanio Pavoni that the Nogarola were indeed one of the oldest families in the city. A Nogarola had been a confidante and supporter of Cangrande I, the greatest of the della Scala family who had ruled Verona for more than a hundred years. The Bevilacqua pedigree was just as storied and ancient, but where the Nogarola had declined in political influence under Venetian rule, the Bevilacqua had prospered; perhaps another source of enmity between the two families.

And the Nogarola were also the family into which Madalena Adorno had married. 'So I imagine that Ferdinando and Madalena will be there?'

Tomaso's feigned look of surprise, as if the suggestion had never occurred to him, might have convinced the casual observer, but it did not fool

198

Will for a minute and it was all he could do to stop from bursting out laughing.

'Yes, I expect so. Leonardo Nogarola, Ferdinando's father, and Alvise Bevilacqua are the principal guarantors of the peace, and at the command of the Podestà they will be held responsible for any further outbreaks of violence. So they must be there, and so I suppose Ferdinando and Madalena must come too.'

'I saw Madalena's letters to you,' Will said, broaching the subject more abruptly than he had intended.

He could not tell from Tomaso's silence whether he was angry or embarrassed.

'I'm sorry, I didn't mean to read them. They fell off your desk when I was looking for a cipher, and I read them by accident when I picked them up.'

'I know what you're going to say, that nothing good can come of pursuing her, even more so now that she is married.' Tomaso's voice was tense. 'But I love her, Will. I have done ever since I first saw her, all that time ago on Corfu. And she is so unhappy, married to that brute. He beats her! Can you imagine? It is agony to think of it, and know there is nothing I can do.'

Tomaso turned his face away, trying to regain his composure. An image came into Will's mind of his own younger self, hot with love for his Anne, a woman ten years his elder of whom both his parents disapproved, a woman they saw as being wholly unsuitable as a potential wife. They had been vocal in their opposition to his courtship of her, and he, with all the stubbornness of a young man in hopeless love, had become even more determined to have her.

Yet had it really been love? Or mere lust? He had asked himself that question many times, once the passion had finally subsided, and he found himself loaded down with the burdens and responsibilities of parenthood at exactly the moment that he wanted nothing so much as freedom from care.

What he also knew was that no amount of hectoring by his parents had had any effect on him whatsoever, and that he would similarly have no effect on the young man in front of him if he tried the same methods.

'I know. And you know, probably better than I, what the consequences of pursuing her might be. Ferdinando Nogarola did not strike me as a forgiving man, and should he ever find out about your letters to Madalena, I would fear for both you and she.'

199

'I am not afraid of Nogarola. But I would not want to be the cause of Madalena suffering any further hurt at his hands, and for that reason I promise I will be cautious.' That did not sound like a capitulation to Will's ears. 'In any event, Madalena has already made it clear that I must stay away from her.'

'Oh? Then you have seen her? Here in Verona?'

'She was in the Piazza dell' Erbe, three days ago, with some of her serving women. I tried to talk to her, but she was very cold, and said that I was on no account to speak with her in public again. Her women were scandalised, and all but chased me away.'

Will's imagination had no difficulty reconstructing the scene—the alarmed Madalena, all too aware of the watching faces and listening ears, not only of her servants but of all the other bystanders and gossips in this most public of places. The importunate young suitor, throwing caution to the winds, declaring his passion, but finding his boldness rewarded with a harsh rebuff, perhaps harsher than she had intended. The clucking women shooing him away like hens defending their chicks against the depredations of a fox.

Though Tomaso was making light of it now, Will had no doubt he had felt badly shamed at the time. Yet what alternative did Madalena have? 'Then there is an end to it. You must respect her wishes, Tomaso, though it breaks your heart.'

'Oh, I understand why she had to chastise me in public. It was foolish of me to accost her so in such a place. I knew it at the time, but when I saw her, I could not stop myself. But I know she cares for me, I know it!'

'And so you hope to see her again at this ball? And pursue her further, even though it is an even more public place? Surely you know it will be hopeless.'

'I'm not a fool, Will.' Tomaso was scathing. 'Of course I will be careful. But if she gives me any signal at all that she has feelings for me, then yes, I will pursue her, as you put it, though the chase will not be long, for the quarry will want to be caught.'

'And when you catch her? What then? I don't know why, but it seems to have escaped your attention that Madalena is married, in a bond that cannot be undone, no matter what your feelings for each other.'

'Better that we run away together to somewhere where she will be safe from the brutalities that man inflicts on her than that she should stay here. I care not a fig for convention, and neither does Madalena!'

Will was not so sure about that, but the defiant look on Tomaso's face told him he was not going to win this argument, at least not that day.

But neither was he going to allow Tomaso to pursue his reckless course, and that would mean that he would have to stay close to the boy over the next few days, and go with him to this ball, to try and ward off the inevitable dangers. Which meant yet more delays before he could resume his journey.

He felt a mild irritation at Tomaso. Why could the boy not see what danger he could be in? But it was clear that he was not going to give up on his hopeless quest to win her over, and Will felt that he owed a duty to Sir Francis to do his best to make sure that Tomaso did not come to any harm. He knew that if he did not keep a watch on him he would commit some indiscretion that would lead to injury or worse.

So he would stay, he decided, at least until the ball was over. After that, he would have to leave Tomaso to his own devices and return to his higher duty and more urgent mission—ensuring that his intelligence about the armada got to England as soon as possible.

'Time will tell,' was all he said, realising that he could do no more, though he could not resist a final word of warning. 'Romantic as it might sound, exile is not a pleasant experience, and you might think on that before you do anything rash.

'It must be time for supper, and I would swear that is the smell of venison pie coming from the kitchen across the way. Let's say no more on this, and instead bend our persuasive energy to extracting a meal from the good Signora Cappelletti, eh?'

Chapter 23

A s well as endowing the city with an amphitheatre, the ancient Romans had also built a theatre into the side of the hill overlooking Verona. It was from here that Will found himself contemplating the city not long after dawn on the fifth morning after his arrival.

Below, the river Adige flowed vigorously between the five arches of the San Pietro bridge across which a solitary priest hurried, late to take his place in church in time for mass. Beyond the bridge, the city was a mass of red roofs punctured by towers. Wisps of smoke emerged from chimneys as the city stirred into life and the townspeople began another day. The scene was tranquil, the melodious chiming of church bells summoning the faithful to mass the only sound disturbing the quiet.

It was already warm, despite the early hour, and he knew that by midday the heat would be brutal under the unforgiving blue sky. Perhaps a thunderstorm might descend later from the mountains to break the heat and cool everything down.

Sighing with the realisation that his moments of abstracted and peaceful contemplation of the scene had to come to an end, since the day beckoned. He swung his legs across the wall, and picked his way through the ruined walls of the theatre, long disused and crumbling away, steadily being devoured by weeds and trees growing between the stones.

Scrambling down a steep path, he crossed the red brick bridge, passing through a gatehouse manned by a sleepy and thoroughly bored-looking guard who didn't give him a second glance, and into the shadowed maze of lanes and streets of the city. Ten minutes later he was back at the guest house of Signora Cappelletti.

'*Buongiorno*, Signor Shakespeare.'

'*Buongiorno*, Madonna Giovanna, how do you do on this fine day?'

'Ah, signor, for me there is always work. Not like you young gentlemen, with your leisure.' This ritual lament was delivered in good humour; a line she had offered up without fail every morning for the last week.

'And we are all grateful for the work you do, signora, believe me.' Flashing his most winning smile, he went in the door to head up the stairs to his room on the top floor of the house, throwing over his shoulder a request that Giovanna should, if she would be so kind, send Nicola up with some breakfast of bread and cheese when her duties permitted.

Pushing open the door to his room, he surveyed his little domain, which by now looked thoroughly lived-in. The bed was rumpled, and a much-mended shirt hung from the back of the only chair. A doublet—his best, though it, too, was faded—hung from a hook on the wall. On the table, the stub of a candle was testament to his late-night writings, which lay strewn across the table's surface, while on the floor there lay crumpled up, discarded papers, mostly poems.

Settling at his desk, he decided to distract himself by resuming the project he had been working on back in Padua—attempting to write a series of sonnets in the Italian style, but in his native language. Thus occupied, he passed a pleasant few hours, as the day's heat slowly invaded the room until he was obliged to discard his sweat-soaked shirt and open a window so that the slight breeze might cool his naked torso.

He was re-reading the result of his efforts, quietly pleased with himself, when he heard the sound of Tomaso whistling some tuneless air and bounding up the stairs two at a time. The youngster had an energy that made Will feel ancient, though he was but twenty-three years old.

'Done with your scribbling for the day? Come on, it's much too fine a day to be lurking inside. I'm going to meet Tebaldo at the Inn of the Fig. Come and join us.'

Though they had been casual friends at the university in Padua, since arriving in Verona Tebaldo had attached himself to Tomaso as a limpet attaches itself to a rock, infatuated to the point of obsession. Will had not much liked him at first, but his devotion to Tomaso was endearing, and he had slowly warmed to the boy, who had also become their indefatigable guide to the city and its people.

One of his favourite haunts was the Inn of the Fig, an establishment off the Piazza Brà, the big square in front of the old Roman arena, where he and Tomaso often went to play dice games and drink ale. The prospect of joining them seemed, at that moment, enticing.

'Why not?' He retrieved his shirt from the back of the chair and pulling it over his head. 'It's too hot to think, let alone write.'

203

The tavern, when they got there, was already buzzing with conversation. It was a simple place—beyond an arched entrance opening to the street it consisted of just an open courtyard, with long table in the centre that was lined with benches and stools on which the inn's patrons sat talking, playing dice and drinking from the jugs of wine and ale that littered the table's surface.

The wall on one side was covered with the big, crude mural of a spreading fig tree that gave the inn its name. Below the tree the artist had painted a buxom smiling woman who winked lasciviously as she poured wine from a jar. The opposite wall was rough-plastered and painted white, a perfect canvas for the wits of Verona, who had covered it over the years with scribbled poems and scurrilous epithets.

At the far end of the courtyard, the enticing smell of cooking meat emerged from an open-fronted kitchen, in front of which meat and vegetables, cheeses, bread and oil were piled up on another table, from which the patrons could help themselves for the payment of a small fee.

On their appearance at the entrance to the Inn, Tebaldo jumped to his feet, abandoning for the moment his drinking companions, and came over to greet them. He moved like a cat, Will thought, graceful and swift, with a coiled energy contained in the smoothly functioning muscles of the athlete that he was.

Tebaldo was an accomplished swordsman who revelled in all kinds of physical activity. His blonde good looks, colouring that was common in the north of Italy where the native Italian stock intermingled with the fair-haired and fair complexioned blood of the south Germans, nevertheless had a dissolute air, that of a man who, though still so young, had already acquired the habits of overindulgence in food and wine.

'Tomaso! And Will! He dragged you away from your labours, then? I knew you would not be able to resist. Come and join us. We are about to start another game of hazard.'

Tebaldo introduced his two other friends, skinny youths both dressed in the livery of the household of Leonardo Nogarola, the patriarch of the Nogarola clan and Ferdinando's father. The taller of the two was named Gregorio and the other, a freckled redhead, Simone.

Settling around one end of the long table, they poured ale for everyone from two big jugs, and immediately launched into a new game of hazard, or, as they called it in Italy, *Zara*.

204

Though Will usually had no appetite for gambling, this simple game had become an agreeable way of passing the time, and he enjoyed the raucous sessions in which the protagonists declared what number they thought they would throw with three wooden dice.

In the middle of the table was a chequered board, on which stood various pieces—squares, circles, stars—and the total score thrown from the three dice determined how far each player could move his piece. But if a player threw seven or less, or fourteen or more, they forfeited their turn. When thus blocked, they shouted '*Zara!*' usually accompanied by an oath or two and the ribald teasing of their companions.

And so the afternoon progressed, amid good-natured laughter and jokes, the consumption of copious quantities of ale and food, and much teasing of the poor serving girls who periodically removed plates, goblets and jugs from the centre of the table.

They played for small amounts of money, and by the middle of the afternoon Will had, pleasingly, accumulated a small pile of winnings from several games. He had just completed a throw of the dice, which fortunately had given him a twelve, and was moving his counter when he felt a sudden chilling of the atmosphere in the tavern courtyard, a drop in the volume of the patrons' voices, and an uneasy shifting of backsides on seats.

Looking up from the board, he beheld a young man of medium height and willowy build. Everything about him was dark—black hair and ebony eyes, a swarthy complexion, all encased in black doublet, close-buttoned in spite of the heat, black breeches and black hose. All this darkness made him seem menacing.

Behind, a gaggle of half a dozen youths, clearly followers of their saturnine leader, blocked the arched entrance to the courtyard, engaged in a silent shoving match for precedence which the dark man ignored.

Will felt Tebaldo, sitting next to him on the long bench, stiffen at the sight of these intruders. 'Piero Bevilacqua,' he whispered, as much to himself as to Will. 'Here is brazenness—to come here in the middle of the day.'

Which explained the sudden iciness that was cooling the afternoon air. Though the Podestà had imposed a peace between the Bevilacqua and Nogarola families, Verona was still divided into quarters wherein the two factions dominated, and into which the other did not go unless they were looking for trouble. The Inn of the Fig was in the area of the city that the Nogarola regarded as their own, and those of the Inn's patrons who were not neutral were supporters of that family.

For Piero in particular to appear there was indeed brazen, for Will had heard he had been the architect of the latest round of violence between the two factions, causing the ancient grudge between these two families, otherwise equal in their antiquity and honour, to burst anew from the tamped-down ovens of their fury. For a mere wager and for the devilry of it, he had attempted to seduce one of the daughters of the Nogarola family; failing in his suit, he had resorted to kidnap, stealing the lady off and locking her in a castle out in the countryside.

Besieged by furious adherents of the girl's family, he had eventually surrendered her, but not before several men had died on either side in an attempted breakout from the castle. Though a peace between the factions had been imposed by the authorities, it had failed to hold, and Piero had become the chief general in what amounted to a civil war waged on the streets of Verona, only recently suppressed by the will of the Podestà and the soldiery of the Venetian Republic.

'Well lads, there's a rank smell in the air this day, wouldn't you say?'

The words were delivered in a surprisingly high-pitched voice, accompanied by a startlingly white-toothed smile that, far from being reassuring, seemed quite menacing in that still, dark face. It was the look of a tiger enjoying the prospect of tearing apart its prey. The young men behind the tiger laughed out loud, wrinkling their noses as if they had just caught the offending scent.

'Ah! It's the stink of the Nogarola flower, for certes,' one of them said.

'Bravo, Marcello, bravo. But it is a wilting flower, it seems to me; a flower that droops at the first sign of heat. For see you how they tremble in fear of us.'

A spasm of anger went through the crowd and several men leapt to their feet, hands going to hips, where daggers and swords hung ready for use. Yet none were drawn, for fear of the penalties they would suffer if they broke the newly-imposed peace.

'What do you do here, Bevilacqua?' Tebaldo's voice was barely under control as he called across the heads of those patrons who were still seated. 'You know this place is Nogarola territory.'

'What is this talk of "territories"?' Piero laughed, his voice full of mockery. 'Surely since the Podestà has commanded that all strife be erased in Verona, we can all consort with whom we will wherever we will. I myself have just come from exchanging the kiss of peace with my lord Ferdinando. I am surprised that you didn't know that, Pindemonte, inserted as you usually are up his arse.'

This was clearly news to Tebaldo, who seemed momentarily at a loss. Then his face reddened at the gross insult that Bevilacqua had delivered so casually and so mockingly. His hand went to the dagger hanging at his waist, the knuckles white as he gripped the pommel.

Will gently laid a hand on his arm. 'Take care Tebaldo. Do not be the first to draw in this fight, else the law will go ill with you.'

This seemed to penetrate the red fog of the young man's rage, and though his body remained tense, his hand released the hilt of the dagger, and he simply stood and stared at his antagonist in mute fury. By now, the half-dozen young toughs had made their way through the constriction of the arch and had ranged themselves on either side of their leader, staring at their opponents in mute challenge.

In the silence, Gregorio hauled his lanky frame to its feet, and slowly and deliberately put his thumb in his mouth, bit it, and then flicked it contemptuously at Bevilacqua, with whose gaze he had locked in silent combat.

Anger contorted that saturnine face. 'Do you bite your thumb at me sirrah? Do you?'

Gregorio just smiled the sweetest of smiles. 'Nay, I do not bite my thumb at you, though I do indeed bite my thumb. 'Tis but an affectation.'

'Aye, it is so,' red-headed Simone piped up from his friend's side. 'He has affected to bite his thumb on many an occasion before this, I have seen him do it. But he did not bite his thumb *at* you, Bevilacqua, for the Podestà has decreed that no man shall insult another in Verona, on pain of imprisonment, and Gregorio here is a law-abiding man.'

A menacing growl arose from the throats of the Bevilacqua retainers.

'Do not bandy words with me, sirrah!' their leader shouted, his sword rasping in its scabbard as he drew it. Taking this as a signal, his followers did the same, prompting those of the tavern's patrons who had come armed to retaliate by drawing their own swords and daggers.

Tebaldo leapt up on the table from Will's side, pointing his rapier at Piero Bevilacqua, and screaming incoherently with rage. Then, to Will's astonishment, Tomaso also climbed up on the table, his sword also out and weaving a deadly arc.

207

Plainly the heat had got to them and they had all gone mad! Frantically, he pushed his way through the crowd on his side of the long table, shoving men aside until he found himself standing in front of Piero.

'Hold! Signor Bevilacqua, you know that the law is against you, since you and your men drew first. Put your sword up, I beg you, and do not allow bloodshed to mar this happy day, when you have kissed the cheek of Ser Ferdinando in signal of your reconciliation with him and his family.'

Piero looked curiously at Will, a man unknown to him who yet had the temerity to speak to him with this voice of authority. With a flick of his wrist, the point of his sword came up to hover in front of Will's face. Slowly it drifted down until it came to rest on his collarbone; one thrust to the throat and Will would have been done for, a fact that he tried to ignore as he kept his eyes locked on the black, depthless orbs of his antagonist.

'And who are you, sir?' The high voice glittered with menace. 'By your accent no native of Verona, of that I am sure.'

'No, I am a knight of England on a diplomatic mission from Her Majesty to the Doge and Signoria of Venice, from whence I am returning with urgent dispatches for the queen.' Will did his best to counterfeit all the haughtiness of an English aristocrat. 'Doge Cicogna would be most displeased should he learn that I have been impeded in my journey, as would Podestà Morosini, with whom I am to sup tonight.'

Which was ladling it on with a big spoon, since he had never done more than meet Morosini at one of Antonio da Mosto's gatherings, and that briefly. Certainly he was not having supper with the podestà, the Venetian governor of Verona and its highest power, that evening or any other.

But his assumption of arrogance seemed to do the trick, and Bevilacqua looked uncertain for the first time since he had walked into the tavern. His eyes wavered and he looked around the courtyard, perhaps belatedly recognising the truth of Will's words, for the authorities would indeed not look kindly on whichever party had started the affray, and perhaps wondering whether this proud-seeming Englishman might in fact be well connected to the Venetian establishment.

Either way, he seemed in that moment to recognise defeat. His sword went back into its scabbard, and after a few moments of hesitation his followers also sheathed their weapons.

'Your name?' Though he had backed down, Piero had lost none of his arrogance.

208

Will proffered a deep bow, just this side of mockery. 'Sir William Shakespeare, sir, at your service.'

'Then, Signor Shakespeare, we will see you at Saturday's festivities, which no doubt you will be attending, as you are such a great friend of Signor Morosini.'

Will just nodded.

'As for the rest of you, I can well see that we are not welcome here, though we come in peace seeking nothing more than ale to quench our thirst. Shame on you, I say, for not offering the hand of friendship to one who is a peacemaker.'

With this piece of cant, he abruptly turned on his heel and pushed his way through his retainers out into the street, leaving them to follow with backward scowls towards the inn's patrons.

Will was surrounded by people thumping him on the back and wringing his hand in congratulation for his stance. He smiled absently; in truth, he had been scared witless that Piero would run him through without another thought. Now that the moment of danger had passed, he felt a trembling in his knees that he brought under control with an effort, narrowly avoiding the ignominy of falling to the floor.

Tomaso and Tebaldo presented him with yet another mug of ale, laughing themselves silly.

'Jesu, Will, even I believed you must be a representative of the emperor himself, so haughty were you.'

'And no doubt Tommasino Morosini is preparing a great feast for your supper as we speak.' Tebaldo was even more gleeful. 'That was a master-stroke!'

'Enough! I fear I have made an enemy of that one, particularly once he works out that I am nowhere near the august personage that he now thinks. It's as well I am leaving straight after this blasted ball.'

Though he joined in the laughter that ensued, and got progressively drunker on ale after ale. He knew that he had indeed made an enemy that he could ill afford, and he prayed that he would be able to avoid any further encounters with Piero Bevilacqua in the few days that remained to him in Verona.

Chapter 24

Verona, August 1586

I'm looking forward to seeing the face of old Alvise Bevilacqua when he has to exchange the kiss of peace with my lord Leonardo. I don't doubt the old bastard's visage will split in two with the pain of it!'

The words were uttered loudly enough to draw some sharp looks and muttering under the breath from others in the crowd of people crossing the Adige by the elegant and arcaded Ponte Nuovo.

'Peace, Tebaldo, I beg of you,' said Tomaso, saving Will the trouble. 'I know you adhere to the Nogarola faction, but this is not the day to make fun of your opponents, not when the Podestà has decreed that any who cause the old quarrels to flare again will be thrown into the deepest dungeons beneath the Castelvecchio.'

Tebaldo shrugged, though he did lower the volume of his voice a little. Since the incident at the inn, his fury at the Bevilacqua had known no bounds and he never seemed to tire of talking about their perfidies, a subject that Will found increasingly tedious.

He eased the conversation into less contested channels as they reached the end of the bridge and crossed the small island that had been formed when, long ago, a channel of the Adige had cut its own watery path to the east. The *acqua morto* they called it, 'dead water', and that description seemed apt as they crossed by another bridge, for the channel was as still and black as the Adige itself was bubbling and lively.

Beyond, the evening crowd that had been pressed together by the confines of the bridges dispersed to their various destinations, most heading for their various homes after the day's labours. But there was still a sizeable group who were, like Will and his companions, heading for the Palazzo Giusti, over in the eastern half of the city. It was there that the great public banquet and ball were to be held to celebrate the podestà's peace.

Like many Italian palaces, the Palazzo Giusti presented a fairly modest face to the world, a blank wall in a narrow street relieved only by a row of first-floor windows, their shutters thrown open to let in the evening air. From these apertures a soft yellow light was thrown by the chandeliers and the pleasant sound of the hundreds of chattering voices within.

The centre of the façade was pierced by a splendid arched gateway through which the crowd passed, their invitations checked carefully by liveried servants. Beyond was a courtyard surrounded by a loggia on three sides and bounded on the fourth by a crenellated wall. Here, long tables were piled high with food—steaming platters of lamb and beef, piles of whole roasted chickens, sweetmeats, vegetables, great bowls of pasta from which the hungry guests were already busily helping themselves.

In one corner of the courtyard, a fountain spurted wine in half a dozen jets, from which the thirsty filled and refilled glass and pewter goblets. Though it was early, barely nine o'clock, the city's good and great were in high spirits, enjoying the rare treat of such largesse provided at the expense of the state.

Behind the crenellated wall lay the palazzo's chief glory—its gardens, laid out only five years before, but already famous throughout Italy. Nearest to the palace itself, nine formal garden squares were planted with hedges woven in sinuous patterns around the fountains that tinkled and shimmered in the afternoon sunlight.

The whole was bisected by a long avenue of poplar trees climbing up the hill to a wide terrace, above which more trees and gardens could be seen. Just beyond, the grey city walls marched protectively up the hill. Guests could be seen here and there, wandering among the hedges in chattering groups or sitting on benches with plates of food perched on their knees and goblets of wine in their hands.

The two younger men attacked the food tables with enthusiasm. With his customary abstemiousness Will contented himself with a couple of pieces of roasted chicken and a glass of wine. Thus fortified, he and Tomaso decided to make their way up the grand staircase leading to the ballroom on the first floor, Tebaldo having deserted them on seeing some of his cronies out in the garden.

The great hall, when they entered it, was a high and vaulted room that occupied the entire width of the first floor, overlooking the street on one side and the courtyard on the other. A low hum of conversation from the crowd provided the background against which an occasional raised voice or laugh could be heard, but for a social event that was supposed to be the happy occasion signifying the end of conflict in the city, the room had an oddly subdued air.

211

It seemed obvious that, peace or no, the two families and their adherents had little intention of mingling with each other, for Will immediately perceived that the room was divided into two. At the far end of the room, crippled old Alvise Bevilacqua leaned heavily on his cane, surrounded by his kin. Among them his nephew Piero was prominent, dressed again in his deep black, leavened only by a magnificent gold chain hung over his shoulders.

At the other end of the room, on the courtyard side, was the vast bulk of Leonardo Nogarola, swathed in silk; a cheerful, ruddy-faced man who Will remembered from Venice, where he had been a tough and wily negotiator against Prospero Adorno for the hand of the latter's daughter.

The patriarch of the Nogarola too was surrounded by his adherents— among them the retainers Gregorio and Simone—and was deep in conversation with his son, Ferdinando. Standing politely to one side was Madalena, radiantly dressed in the height of Venetian fashion yet seeming detached from the whole scene, as if she were merely acting a part.

Between these two formations, in the middle of the room, was another that was grouped around the podestà, Tommasino Morosini. As a senior member of one of Venice's most aristocratic families and as the civilian governor of Verona, he was unquestionably the most powerful man in the room.

The podestà represented civil authority, acted as chief justice, controlled and instructed the police, and managed the civil administration of the city and its surrounding countryside. Admittedly, he relied on the local aristocrats to form the city's council and fill key elected magistracies. The soldiery, fortifications and the treasury were all controlled by his counterpart, the capitano of the city, so that in the usual Venetian way all authorities were checked and balanced.

Nevertheless, Morosini was for all practical purposes the master of Verona. And like all powerful people, he was surrounded by lesser lights, such as Fiorio Pindemonte, Tebaldo's father, who was deep in conversation with several of his fellow *proveditore*, the members of the city's council.

Between these three groupings there seemed to be little traffic, other than the liveried retainers of the Giusti family, who bore trays of yet more food and drink. Instinctively, Will headed towards the group around the podestà, steering a middle course between the Scylla of Piero Bevilacqua and his father, and the Charybdis of the Nogarola clan. This dangerous whirlpool was even now sucking in Tomaso, whose regretful glances in the direction of

212

Madalena were interrupted by Will taking a firm grip on his arm and steering him towards Fiorio Pindemonte.

'Ah, young Tomaso. Welcome!'

The vicar of the House of Merchants was an older version of his son, still wiry and athletic in build, though with the suggestion of a pot belly under the robes of his office, blonde hair with an undertone of grey, classically handsome face and pale blue eyes, cheerful and welcoming.

'Messer Pindemonte, may I present Messer William Shakespeare, a compatriot of mine from England.'

'Messer Shakespeare, I am pleased to meet you. Tebaldo has spoken of you. Mostly as an impediment to his more extreme adventures while at Padua, something for which, as a father, I thank you.'

Will laughed and inclined his head in a small bow. 'Sadly for me, restraining the exuberance of youth seems to be my principal occupation at present.'

'And you such a greybeard,' Tomaso mocked. 'Would you believe, Messer Pindemonte, that William is but twenty-three?'

'For myself, I have often thought I was born middle-aged,' the vicar smiled, 'and have spent my entire life waiting for my physical self to catch up. Perhaps Signor Shakespeare shares this cast of mind.'

That, Will thought gloomily, had the ring of truth.

'Pindemonte, will you introduce these gentlemen?' The voice, deep and authoritative, came from behind him, causing him and Tomaso to turn.

'Of course, my Lord Podestà.' Pindemonte was deferential. 'Signor Shakespeare and Signor Martinelli are visiting Verona from Padua, where they have been studying at the university there, with my son.'

'Ah.' The podestà's square and regular features creased into a frown, and one hand went to stroke his beard. 'I have met these gentlemen before, I think. In Venice, at the Ca' da Mosto? Am I right?'

Will was astonished at this feat of memory, for he had met Tommasino Morosini only for a few moments, introduced by Antonio da Mosto among a group of others at a large party.

The podestà looked smugly pleased with himself when Will confirmed that this was indeed so. 'And, if my informants are truthful, it was you, Signor Shakespeare, who averted the outbreak of an affray yesterday at one of the city's taverns. Correct? You have my thanks for that service, signor.'

'And mine,' Pindemonte added smoothly, 'since my own son was also there, and if I know my Tebaldo, he would have been at the forefront of any quarrel.'

Will nodded, wishing to appear as modest as he could, and feeling uneasy that his actions had brought him to the attention of the authorities in Verona. More than ever, he wished he could be quit of the place and on his way back to London.

'That your son needs to learn to control his temper is no news to either of us.' Morosini's smile was sardonic. 'But that is a fault shared by too many of the young men of Verona. They seem determined to perpetuate the quarrels that their elders have long forsworn.'

His genial expression turned grim. 'Well, we will have no more of it. As I have made clear to both Nogarola and Bevilacqua, any further outbreaks of violence, by either side, will be dealt with, sternly and with the full force of the law.'

'In which endeavour you will be applauded by every one of the *proveditore*, my lord. Even if my own son, God forbid, should fall foul of your justice.'

'Let us hope that Tebaldo is always in the company of prudent men such as Signor Shakespeare, eh?' The podestà's mood lightened again. 'Speaking of Tebaldo, is he here this evening?'

'He is in the gardens, I believe, signor,' Tomaso said.

'If you see him out there, send him to me. I have a task for him.' The podestà nodded their dismissal from his presence and turned to talk to another group of courtiers who had approached while they were talking and had been waiting patiently to get his attention.

As Tomaso and Will walked away from the group, turning towards the knot of people paying court to Leonardo Nogarola in the corner of the big room, Will's eye momentarily held that of Piero Bevilacqua, who had, it seemed, been staring across the room at them for some time. One saturnine eyebrow rose and a small smile played about his lips as he mockingly half-raised a goblet in greeting.

A group of musicians occupying a small stage erected on the street side of the room were making preparations to play, the muted and discordant sounds as they tuned their instruments alerting the guests that the evening's ball was about to commence.

214

Will, no dancer, would have been happy to use this as an excuse to leave the ballroom and go out into the fresh air once more, and thereby steer Tomaso away from the Nogarola clan, and Madalena. But his impetuous young friend was having none of it and, seizing a goblet of wine from a passing servitor as he went, he plunged into the group swirling around Leonardo and Ferdinando Nogarola.

Though he had no eyes for either of the men, his gaze locked with that of Madalena, still standing slightly apart, her emerald eyes cool and appraising. With an inner sigh of frustration, Will decided he had little choice but to follow Tomaso. He could not prevent the lad from meeting with Madalena, but perhaps he could thwart whatever mad impulses were driving him that evening.

Fortunately, he saw that Madalena was likely to aid him in this self-appointed mission, for, seeing Tomaso approach, she moved to her husband's side and slipped her arm through his, interrupting the conversation he was having with his father and causing him to jerk his head around as Tomaso, closely followed by Will, joined the knot of retainers and clients gathered like planets circling the Nogarola sun.

Ferdinando's angry frown at his wife's interruption disappeared as he recognised Will. 'Signor Shakespeare! I had heard that you were here in Verona. You should have called on us. And you too, Martinelli.'

The last words were offhand, dismissive of the younger man, who immediately bristled with anger. Why, Will wondered, did Ferdinando always manage to find ways to irritate Tomaso? Did he suspect the latter's infatuation with his wife, even if he had no certain knowledge of it? Or was it simply a casual arrogance that was ignorant of its effect on others?

'The earl, my father, used to say that, on his many missions on behalf of the queen, when in a foreign city it was always prudent to call upon the most senior members of the local aristocracy first. No doubt we would have got to you in time.'

Bravo, Tomaso, Will thought. Returning barb for barb and reminding Nogarola of his own rank. He waited for the usual outburst to which he had become accustomed in Italy.

But Ferdinando surprised him by responding with laughter. 'And that puts us firmly in our place, eh, Madalena? Even so, you are both welcome at our house when the press of demands on your time permits. And you might find, when you have fully surveyed the ranks of the "local aristocracy", that the Nogarola do have some seniority in Verona.'

215

The jovial tone did not match the coldness of his eyes, though they softened a little when he turned his attention back to Will. 'If my servants are not all outright liars, a possibility not to be dismissed, I believe I owe you something of a debt of gratitude for stopping some of them from ending up in the podestà's prison cells yesterday.'

Again Will nodded his humble acknowledgement of a feat that seemed to be the talk of the town, though he felt himself that it did not warrant such attention.

'It was a scuffle, Ser Ferdinando, no more, over before it had started.'

'Oh, it was a little more than that,' Tomaso said. 'Piero Bevilacqua intended to do murder yesterday, have no doubt, and he would have been as happy to run Will through as anyone. It took real courage to stare him down.'

'Piero has always had a devil in him,' Ferdinando was mild. 'And he has caused great grief to my family, but the podestà has decreed peace and I have exchanged kisses with him, so we must of necessity do all we can to maintain civility. Verona has had enough strife in these last years.'

'I for one am glad that Signor Shakespeare prevented any bloodshed yesterday, especially his own.' Madalena's smile was radiant; she really was a beautiful girl. 'Now let us talk of less sombre subjects. At our last encounter you were both leaving for your studies at Padua: I trust that they have been fruitful?'

Thus redirected, their conversation flowed into the amiable channels of art and poetry and philosophy, subjects on which both Madalena and Ferdinando were well-versed. Ferdinando was particularly passionate about the art of Torquato Tasso, the Italian poet whose epic poem, *Jerusalem Delivered*, had been a sensation when it was first published a decade before, and who had until recently been imprisoned as a lunatic in a madhouse in Ferrara.

It was like being back in Padua, Will thought, as they debated the merits of a work that had given him many hours of pleasure and challenge as he attempted to understand it in his rudimentary Italian.

Even Tomaso abandoned his touchy pride and joined in the talk as it went back and forth, though Will noticed that he became puppy-like every time Madalena spoke, eyes shining and eager to agree with her opinions. If Ferdinando also noticed he gave no sign, his aristocratic demeanour altogether abandoned.

Their talk was interrupted by the little orchestra, which burst suddenly into a loud fanfare announcing the commencement of dancing for the

216

evening. The centre of the ballroom was rapidly filled by guests, the separate groups perforce breaking up as they made space.

'Duty calls,' Ferdinando said. 'I am afraid we will have to cease our discourse and join the dance. It would not do for the heir to the house of Nogarola to be seen to hold back in these circumstances. Shall we, my dear?'

They swept off to join one of the lines that were forming on each side of the ballroom, and in a few moments were moving gracefully through the dance steps of a slow pavane. With the dancers warmed up, the next dance was a sprightly galliard performed to laughter and cheers from the spectators as the pace became ever faster and the various leaps and turns more athletic.

To Will, whose exposure to the art of the dance had been attendance at one or two masked balls in Venice, the entire spectacle was an exciting mystery. Tomaso, more versed in the art, applauded enthusiastically the more accomplished performers. His eyes, though, never left Madalena.

After another two dances, Ferdinando and Madalena re-joined them, flushed and laughing, appearing to Will's eye like any happy married couple. He wondered again about the strange nature of their marriage. If what she had told Tomaso was true, that he was violent towards her in private, there was no sign of that fact in their public appearances nor had Will detected any sign of damage on that beautiful face, even disguised beneath the layers of paint and powder with which women customarily hid even minor blemishes.

But perhaps Ferdinando's cruelties were more of the mind than the body, something Will could well imagine, for there was an underlying ferocity about the man that was always present, even when discoursing on such mild subjects as poetry.

'Ferdinando, I think I must get some air,' Madalena said, her voice breathless.

'Of course, my dear.' Ferdinando raised a hand and snapped his fingers, summoning Gregorio, the young retainer who had no doubt been the source of Ferdinando's information about yesterday's events. 'Escort my lady out into the garden, Gregorio, if you please.'

It pleased Gregorio very much, it seemed, as he took his mistress' arm and walked out of the hall, a grin stitched from one ear to the other. Tomaso was less pleased, a half-scowl forming on his face as his eyes followed the couple's progress towards the door and the stairs to the courtyard below.

'Now, signori, if you will excuse me, I must return to my father and his guests.'

217

With a small bow of farewell, Ferdinando went in search of his father, leaving the two Englishmen alone at the side of the hall. The orchestra was preparing to start again, and the dancers were re-forming their lines in anticipation.

They watched for a while, but Tomaso was restive and Will soon grew bored, so by an unspoken agreement they made their way through the crowd and down the stairs into the courtyard. There, they met Tebaldo Pindemonte and his father, who were picking over the remains of the feast.

The courtyard was almost deserted, most of the diners having either gone upstairs to the dancing or wandered out into the gardens, lit only by a full moon that was obscured from time to time as streamers of cloud scudded across its face.

'The podestà appears to have got his wish—the Nogarola and Bevilacqua clans seem to have buried their animosities,' said Fiorio Pindemonte, clearly feeling pleased to be on the side of the angels of peace. 'But tell me, Signor Shakespeare, something of the commerce of your country. I have met few Englishmen, and I am most curious about your customs and trades.'

While Will did his best to satisfy the senior Pindemonte about subjects on which he was not very conversant, Tebaldo and Tomaso grew bored and drifted off out into the gardens. By the time their conversational well had run dry, half an hour had passed, and neither of the younger men had returned.

When Pindemonte's attention was claimed by another of his fellow town councillors, Will took the opportunity to slip away and pass through the arched gate into the gardens beyond. Though the hour was late, there were still many guests lingering, sitting on benches beneath the nine fountains that still shimmered in the moonlight or wandering in pairs through the ornate pattern of hedge-lined paths, drinking and talking.

Tebaldo he quickly spotted, perched on a bench deep in conversation with a young woman he did not recognise. But Tomaso, he realised with a frown, was nowhere to be seen.

Without seeming too frantic about it, he searched each of the gardens, and as he did so, a suspicion formed in his mind. During his conversation with Fiorio Pindemonte he had not stirred from the foot of the stairs, so it would have been impossible for Tomaso to have passed him unnoticed if he had gone up into the ballroom. The same would be true of Madalena.

And if neither of them were in either courtyard or lower gardens, he had to assume that they had gone up into the upper gardens, which were reached via a poplar-lined path that went in a straight line up the hill. At the top, there was yet another small fountain set into a retaining wall, flanked on either side by stairs.

Climbing these, Will found himself in an untamed wilderness of trees and shrubs; not entirely wild, but planted in a way that artfully suggested wildness, in contrast to the formal gardens down below. This part of the garden sloped upwards, and beyond the trees he could see the town walls rearing up against the black of the night sky.

He had barely walked a few yards along the sketchy path that led into the garden when the sound of familiar voices stopped him in his tracks. They were coming from a small copse to his right, and the speakers were entirely hidden from him, though their voices carried clearly in the night air.

'…but Madalena, my heart, you don't love him!'

'What does love have to do with it?' Madalena was scornful. 'You know my situation, you have always known it.'

There was a pause, before she went on in a softer tone of voice. 'Tomaso, what would you have me do? I cannot just run away with you! Where would we go? How would we live? We would be fugitives.'

'We could go to London. My father left me enough land and money to allow us to live in comfort for the rest of our lives. And not even Ferdinando could harm you there.'

'You are not being realistic, Tomaso. I would still be married, even in your heretic England. And what about my father? The shame alone would kill him.'

'Madalena, I can't leave you to his mercies. You have told me enough of what he does to you that I am in fear for your life.'

'Your fears are exaggerated, Tomaso. He won't kill me, of that I am sure. And the rest I can bear.'

'Even the beatings?'

'Even the beatings. Though his temper has much improved of late. I don't know what drove him in the past, but whatever the demons were, they have left him, at least for now.'

There was a pause. Though Will could not see them, he sensed that there was an impasse, could visualise them staring at each other, each waiting for the other to back down.

'Tomaso, you are a dear, sweet, beautiful young man, and if I had never been fated to marry Ferdinando, marriage to you might have been the delight of my life. But you must give this up. I cannot, I will not, run away from everything I know, every place that is dear to me, from my own father, in order to live the life of an exile in England, even with you. There, it is said. Let that be the end of it, for both our sakes.'

Silence, and then a low sob, a half-cry quickly choked back. The sound, Will thought, of a proud heart breaking. Then, without a further word from either of them, Tomaso turned and left, now visible to Will as he walked away in the opposite direction.

Will turned, hoping to leave this sad scene unnoticed, but in his haste he stepped on a twig, which cracked with a noise loud enough, in his ears at least, to wake the gods.

'Who is there?' Madalena's voice was querulous and fearful. He stepped out from behind the bush that had hidden him from view.

In the moonlight, relief flooded the girl's face as she recognised him, quickly followed by anger. 'How long have you been skulking there, Messer Shakespeare? Eavesdropping is not an endearing habit, in anyone, let alone in someone who I have hitherto considered a friend.'

'I assure you, signora, that I had no intention of listening to your conversation.' He was not intimidated by her display of fury. She was, he knew, more frightened than angry. 'I was simply looking for Tomaso.'

'You're hardly likely to find him by sneaking about in silence among the bushes!' She was scornful. 'How much did you hear?'

'Enough.' He paused, trying to convey his sympathy without using words. 'Madalena, you did the right thing, though I fear his heart is quite broken. I have tried many times to warn him off a passion that, as I look at you now in the moonlight I can entirely understand, but which could have no future, as you well know.'

Her annoyance dissolved, and she slumped, sitting down on a small stone bench. 'You do not know, William, how difficult these months of my marriage have been.' She looked up at him, a small, rueful smile on her face. 'I have, as my father would tell you, a strong will and a mind of my own. But for Ferdinando, I am simply a shrew in his eyes, an unruly possession to be tamed into obedience. The fights we have had! You would not credit it.

'There was no one I could turn to, no one I could confide in, and when Tomaso first wrote to me, in terms so kind, telling me of his love for me, I was touched somewhere deep in my heart. And so I wrote back. Before long, I was confiding everything, all my woes and pain. And it is true that were circumstances different, I could have happily married Tomaso; in that I do not lie.

'But he took my confidences as evidence of something deeper, an expression of reciprocated passion that I did not intend. From that, it seems he has built this fantastical notion that I would simply run away with him, to England or somewhere else. You do see how impossible that is, don't you?'

In a few sentences, Madalena had gone from imperious, angry aristocrat to confused and hurt girl, on the edge of tears. He resisted the urge to join her on the bench and take her hands in his, instead remaining standing.

'Madalena, I love Tomaso as well as any man on this earth, and it pains me to see him suffer. But it is suffering at the hands of his own passions, for which you can have no responsibility. Believe me, destroying his fantasy is a kindness, though neither of you will think that is so for a long time to come, I am sure. Your decision was the right one.'

She nodded, though the misery did not leave her face.

'Come,' he said, offering her his arm as she stood. 'Let me escort you back down into the gardens. If anyone asks, we have simply been taking the air and admiring the view from above.'

As they walked along the path in the direction of the steps down into the formal gardens, Will thought he heard the rustle of bushes and the sound of feet on the carpet of dead leaves and brush that lay below the trees. But the noise was faint and could have been nothing but the wind, fanned to greater significance by his nervousness.

The gardens, when they emerged from the poplar-lined avenue, were all but deserted, the hour being late and the food and wine exhausted. Ferdinando, when they found him, seemed barely to have noticed his wife's absence, and accepted Will's explanation that they had been wandering the gardens with a nod.

Tomaso was nowhere to be seen, so Will made his farewells, promising to call on the Nogarola household before he left Verona, and made his way towards the ornamental front door of the Palazzo, assuming that he would find Tomaso when he got back to their lodgings.

At the gate, he found his way blocked by Piero Bevilacqua, accompanied by a couple of his henchmen. A tired anger welled up inside him. He had had more than enough drama for one evening, and another confrontation with Bevilacqua was the last thing he needed. 'Ser Piero, we meet again. And once again you seem to be between me and the gate. Kindly allow me to pass.'

Piero smiled his dark, arrogant smile and Will prepared himself for a verbal, if not physical assault. But the Bevilacqua prince surprised him. 'Of

221

course, Sir William, I would not impede your passage in any way. I merely hoped to catch your attention before you left in order to invite you, and your friend the Martinelli boy, to the Palazzo Bevilacqua tomorrow afternoon. Allow me to make amends, in the spirit of this night of reconciliation, with you and Tomaso, by the breaking of bread and sharing of wine.'

There was something in this invitation that Will found disturbing, even though it seemed to be offered in good faith. Either Piero was an extraordinarily good actor or he genuinely wanted to make amends for his behaviour the day before. The latter was not entirely impossible, he reflected, since it was obvious that the whole affair was well known throughout Verona, and Piero's part in it was not seen in a flattering light.

'Very well, Ser Piero, I will be there. I cannot speak for Tomaso, since he appears to have departed, but I will communicate your invitation, and he can decide for himself whether to accept. Now, if you please...'

With another smile, and a deep bow, Piero stepped aside to allow Will to pass. As he walked down the street away from the Palazzo Giusti, he could feel those mocking eyes following him. But he was bone-weary, and all he wanted to do was collapse into his bed. Tomorrow could look after itself.

Chapter 25

I t had been, all the Veronese said, unusually hot that year, a statement Will could easily accept as he struggled out of the deep well of sleep and back into consciousness on the morning after the great ball.

Though it could not have been later than the eighth hour of the morning, his room was already stifling, a condition he relieved at least a little by throwing open the window shutters on each side of the room, thereby capturing at least a little of what breeze there was.

His head ached, the consequence of consuming too much wine over the course of the previous evening. Cursing, he pulled on hose and shirt, and went out into the narrow corridor that separated his room from Tomaso's and led to the staircase down to the common rooms below.

The door to Tomaso's room was open as he passed it, the interior a familiar jumble of clothes and belongings casually flung everywhere, but there was no sign of Tomaso himself. When he got to the top of the stairs, though, he heard the sound of the lad's voice drifting up from below, talking cheerfully to Giovanna.

That was a welcome sound to Will, who had feared for the boy's sanity when he had arrived home in the early hours of the morning to find Tomaso sitting disconsolately on the steps in front of the entrance door, his arms wrapped around his knees on which his head rested, face down. When he heard Will's footsteps, his head had jerked up, revealing a tear-streaked face contorted with misery.

Saying nothing, Will had sat down next to him. He felt a tender sympathy for the young man's agony and wanted to comfort and console him as he would if it had been his own son in such pain.

'I suppose you were spying on me again? And heard it all?' Tomaso's voice was bitter and accusing.

'It might seem that way, but believe me when I say that I was not eavesdropping intentionally. I just wanted to find you so that we could depart. No, I did not hear it all, but I did hear enough to understand why you are distraught. And I am here as a friend to offer what comfort I can.'

With a long look, Tomaso seemed to accept that. 'You've told me often enough that I was doomed to fail. I suppose you have been proven right.' His voice was now gloomy. 'But I love her so, Will, and I do fear for her life with that vicious man to whom her cursed father has her yoked.'

'Oh, I think you underestimate Madalena. And whatever Ferdinando's faults, I doubt he would go so far as to cause her real harm.' Will paused, trying to find the right words. 'Tomaso, I do not profess to know much about love, for I have experienced that strangest and most insistent emotion only once, when I met Anne, though I did not come to her a virgin. The fires of that love have since been banked and have cooled considerably. But when we were in love, it was a lightsome, happy thing, joyous and above all, mutual.'

Those first months with Anne came flooding back to him, the days walking through sun-filled meadows hand in hand, oblivious to anything except each other, the laughter and private jokes that they shared, her solemn, respectful face as he told her about his ambitions, all the wild ideas he had kept from everyone else in his family.

With marriage, and children, all that slowly disappeared under the weight of financial worry and the continuing disapproval of his parents, his mother in particular. He would always be loyal to Anne, he knew, but he regretted intensely the loss of that happy, carefree feeling of being in love.

'My parents disapproved of Anne,' he went on. 'But they would not, could not, stop us from marrying. And we broke no laws, no customs in doing so.

'That would not be the case were you to have succeeded in persuading Madalena to run away with you. You would have been ostracised and hunted, you would have been breaking the laws of both her church and yours. That would have been a great price to pay even if you had both been in joyous, delirious love with each other. But I don't think either of you have that condition.

'Whatever you think you may feel for Madalena, can you truly say that she has ever given you any sign that she feels the same about you?'

Almost imperceptibly, as if doubtful of his own convictions, he shook his head. 'She said that if she was not married to Ferdinando, she would have come away with me, and gladly.'

Will said nothing, allowing the implications of the boy's own words to sink in, and after a few moments, Tomaso's shoulders heaved in a great sigh,

224

almost a sob, as he fought down his emotions. 'But that condition can never be met, can it?'

And so, with no further words on the subject, they hauled themselves to their feet, and trudged up the stairs to their respective rooms, he to fall into an exhausted sleep, and Tomaso, if he was any judge, to lie awake for the rest of the night replaying the evening's events and cursing his fate.

But perhaps he was wrong, for as he descended the stairs, Will was heartened to hear the happy, bantering voice to which he was more accustomed. Perhaps he had slept, and perhaps that had been enough to apply a poultice to the pain in Tomaso's heart, even if it could never make it go away.

'Bongiorno, Signor Will,' Giovanna greeted him as he alighted from the bottom of the stairs and entered the common room, deserted except for her and Tomaso, though the remains of breakfast plates on the table suggested that the room had been crowded with the other guests until recently.

He sat and gratefully accepted a beaker of cold, fresh water and a platter of meats, cheese and bread. Tomaso watched him eat for a few moments, saying nothing.

'This came this morning.' He slid a folded paper across the table. 'Delivered by a servant in Bevilacqua livery.'

The paper was sealed and addressed to 'Signor Shakespeare'. Using his knife to break the seal, he quickly scanned the brief message scrawled inside.

'Piero Bevilacqua reminds me of his invitation to visit the family Palazzo for an afternoon of music written by his elder brother, Alessandro. He is particular that you should accompany me, Tomaso. He says that Tebaldo Pindemonte "with whom you are known to consort" and his father, Fiorio, have also consented to attend.'

'That seems... unexpected. "Reminds you" of his invitation?'

'Yes, he stopped me at the gate of the Palazzo Giusti when I left. He seemed quite sincere in his desire to make peace after our little encounter the other day. I was surprised too.'

'Though I have no cause to love the Nogarola family, I like the Bevilacqua even less. Must we go?'

'No. In all honesty, I would rather be saddling up my accursed horse and be on my way, but my head aches too much and the day is too hot for that. An afternoon of music might be soothing, and I seem to recall that someone told me last night that Alessandro is a composer and musician of some ability.' He didn't say it, but he also thought that a diversion such as this might be good for Tomaso.

'You don't think it might be some kind of trap?'

'With the vicar of the House of Merchants present? I think not even Piero Bevilacqua would be so foolish as to further provoke violence the day after the podestà has gone to such great lengths to cement the peace between these two accursed families.'

Breakfast over, Will spent the rest of the morning working on his sonnets, leaving Tomaso to amuse himself howsoever he chose until the time came for them to leave for the afternoon's entertainments.

Following the Italian tradition to which he was now well accustomed, he settled down for an afternoon's nap after the midday meal, from which he was awakened by the boisterous sound of the voice of Tebaldo Pindemonte echoing up from the courtyard.

Leaning out of the window, he saw Tomaso emerging from the stables, trailed by the stable-boy, young Nicola; yet another slave to Tomaso's charm.

'Tebaldo! What brings you here?' Tomaso's greeting was puzzled as he embraced his friend. 'I had expected to see you and your father later this afternoon, not before.'

Tebaldo laughed. 'I thought it would be merry for us all to go together, since Piero Bevilacqua—the devil curse him, though I must not say so out loud, since we are now all brothers in the peace of the podestà—insisted that I should come, holding out the fact that you would be there as an inducement.'

'He used the same device to encourage us to attend. Does that not seem a little suspicious?'

'Everything about Bevilacqua is suspicious. Now where is the aged one? Fast asleep and snoring, I'll be bound.'

'He's wide awake and up here, you disrespectful boy!' Will shouted.

'Spying on me again, Will?' The barb lost its sharpness in the face of Tomaso's cheerful grin. 'Come down and let's take some wine to fortify ourselves for this encounter before we leave.'

So, at about three in the afternoon, they left the guest house in a pleasant haze and walked in the direction of the Palazzo Bevilacqua, which Will remembered having walked past during one of their ambles through the city. It had an ornate and splendidly decorated façade not far from the great pile of

226

the Castelvecchio, the fortress erected by the Scala family to dominate and control their unruly city.

The day's heat hammered down, the pitiless sunlight spearing through every gap in the buildings and blinding them as they passed from shadow into light and back again. In moments, they were both perspiring under the formal doublets that they wore over their shirts. Trying to keep out of the sun as much as possible, their route took them through narrow alleys and across several small piazzas.

Entering a slightly broader street, the Via Farina, they suddenly found their way blocked by three men, all dressed in black. At first it was difficult to make out their identity until Will shaded his eyes and recognised the square, muscular form of Ferdinando Nogarola. The men standing behind him were his familiar retainers, Gregorio and Simone.

'Tomaso Martinelli, you son of a whore, step forward and meet your just end!' Nogarola's words, delivered in his powerful voice, were strained with anger, and were accompanied by the sound of his sword being drawn from its scabbard. The two retainers followed their master's lead, though with little conviction, as if they did so only out of a confused sense of duty.

At Will's side, Tomaso's hand went for his own sword, his face a mask of fury. Equally swiftly, Will's hand once again clamped down on his young friend's arm, preventing him from drawing.

'What is this, Ferdinando?' he called. 'Tomaso has no quarrel with you, nor you with he!'

'Silence, Shakespeare!' Ferdinando snarled, the face above his beard red with fury. 'This has nothing to do with you. And my quarrel with this snivelling whelp is deadly, for he has defiled my wife, a crime for which he will pay dearly.'

Will felt a cold fear spread through his body. He knew that Tomaso was guilty of no such thing, but clearly Ferdinando's suspicions had reached white heat in his fevered brain.

'I have done nothing of which I am ashamed!' Tomaso called, shaking off Will's hand, though he left his sword scabbarded for now. 'If anyone should be ashamed it is you for the vile treatment you mete out to Madalena when the mood takes you. No woman should be treated so.'

Ferdinando's face became even more furious, if such a thing were possible.

'Quiet, Tomaso,' Will said, trying to play the peacemaker. 'Ferdinando, listen to me. Whatever you think Tomaso has done, I swear he is innocent of everything except being a friend to Madalena, for which you should honour him, not threaten him with death.'

'Oh? A friend? Is it a "friend" who sneaks off into the gardens in the dead of night to have secret discourse with a married woman?'

'What evidence do you have for such an accusation?' This from Tebaldo, who was thoroughly confused by the whole situation, but whose instinctive loyalty was to Tomaso.

'Evidence enough. He was seen and his dalliance reported to me.'

'By whom?' Will asked, though he was beginning to have a suspicion.

'By an observer unknown, who left an anonymous accusation at my house this morning.'

So there *had* been someone else lurking in the bushes last night, Will realised with a sinking feeling in his stomach. Someone who bore the Nogarola ill-will. His mind immediately flew to Piero Bevilacqua.

'An anonymous accusation seems hardly the stuff by which to convict anyone of such a heinous misdeed,' Will said, though he had little hope that this observation would have any effect on Ferdinando's evident determination to assault Tomaso.

'I need no more proof than that. I am not a fool, Shakespeare! This stripling has been making cow-eyes at my wife since the day they met. It surprises me not that he would take advantage of her to slake his lust.'

This was too much for Tomaso, who shook himself free of Will's restraining grasp and hauled his sword out of its resting place. He stepped forward and adopted the familiar pose of the duellist. 'Enough, you foul-mouthed bastard. We will try this with our swords!'

Gesturing to his attendants to stay behind him, something they seemed most willing to do, Ferdinando also stepped forward, his eyes glittering with contempt, and prepared to strike.

At Will's side, Tebaldo made a motion for his sword, but Will stopped him. For better or worse, this was going to be decided by the two protagonists and no one else.

Looking around, he realised that they were surrounded by a dozen or so people who had been drawn out onto the street by the rising voices, and who now watched in grim silence as the peace of their neighbourhood was disturbed by the all-too-familiar sight of a street quarrel.

With a loud cry, Ferdinando launched himself forward on the attack, and the street rang with the screech of metal on metal as the two swords met.

At first, Ferdinando seemed confident that he would quickly beat his younger opponent. But he had not reckoned on Tomaso's skill with a sword, as he deftly beat back that first flurry of blows.

The Veronese was strong, a strength given extra reinforcement by his anger. Tomaso, by contrast, though slighter of build was fast and agile, and had had the benefit of being taught swordsmanship by the finest teachers of the art in England.

For three or four bouts, Ferdinando's tactic was simple and brutal— charge in with a furious onslaught of blows, attacking his opponent from every angle, as if determined to beat him into the ground. Each time, Tomaso met the assault with cool calculation, assessing where the blows were going to fall and swiftly shifting his sword and his body into the appropriate counter-stroke.

Eventually Ferdinando fell back, his chest heaving. By mutual consent they paused for a moment to gather their strength, Ferdinando glaring across the space between them, Tomaso looking back with an expression that was almost mocking; calculated, Will supposed, to further enrage Ferdinando.

But Will knew his young friend well, and had faced that same lethal blade many times in their practice bouts. It seemed to him that, beneath the bravado, the boy's resilience was being tested in this infernal heat.

As the fight went on, Will sensed that Tomaso's reactions were getting a little slower and his strength was being sapped by the sheer force of Ferdinando's blows. Then, so suddenly that Will almost didn't realise it had happened, Ferdinando crashed through his enemy's defences and succeeded in landing a wicked thrust that pierced Tomaso's abdomen.

The boy's face whitened in shock and his sword clattered to the ground as his hands went to the wound in his side, vainly attempting to staunch the blood that welled through his fingers. With no more than a sigh, his eyes closed and he collapsed to the ground.

As if surprised at his sudden victory, Ferdinando stood over the prone body, breathing heavily, his sword slack at his side. Will shoved him unceremoniously aside as he knelt down and lifted Tomaso's shoulders and head.

Dear God, he thought, *don't let him die,* this impetuous young man who he had come to love like a brother; more than a brother, for he had never had the emotional bond with his siblings that he had forged with Tomaso.

Bending down, he put his cheek to the boy's mouth, and to his relief he felt the soft stirrings of a breath, shallow and ragged. And though his eyelids were closed there was movement behind them. So he lived, at least for now. Only time would tell whether the wound was mortal.

'If he dies, you will pay for this, Nogarola!'

Though the words came from Tebaldo, who stood inches from the Veronese aristocrat, all deference forgotten in his anger and fear for the life of his friend, they might as easily have been uttered by Will himself. He felt a surge of black fury at this arrogant, foolish man who had allowed mere rumour to feed his own suspicion and led him into a fight that might well cost Tomaso his life and Ferdinando his liberty, or worse.

With an effort, Will pushed his anger back down inside himself. There would be a day of reckoning, but it could not be today. 'Stop, Tebaldo! There has been enough bloodshed today.'

He looked around. The little street was now deserted; the residents having fled. Only Gregorio and Simone remained, and they seemed on the edge of flight, caught between fear of the wrath of the authorities and that of their master, Ferdinando Nogarola.

In this moment of uncertainty, Will decided to take command. 'Tomaso still lives and may survive if he can be tended to quickly. Gregorio, Simone—help Tebaldo to take him to somewhere safe where his wound can be bound.'

The three youths seemed happy to accept his authority and moved quickly to lift Tomaso's body upright. Tebaldo extracted a large handkerchief from somewhere about his person and pressed it against the wound in an attempt to staunch the flow of blood, bringing forth a low groan from Tomaso.

'Come on, lads,' Tebaldo said, 'There is a good doctor not far from here, just behind the Piazza dell'Erbe.'

Carrying their charge as tenderly as possible, they departed into the shadows at the end of the street, leaving Will alone with Ferdinando, who had not moved throughout, standing rooted to the spot as if he too was in shock.

'You should hope and pray that the doctor is as good as Tebaldo says he is, for if Tomaso dies...'

Will left the rest unsaid. But what he did say was enough to stir Ferdinando out of his trance. 'My wife's honour, and my own, has been violated. You know nothing of our customs if you do not understand how

230

deeply they are offended by such actions.' Though the words were forceful, they were delivered dully, without conviction, as if Ferdinando was trying to convince himself, not Will.

His voice dropped to a whisper. 'I did not intend to kill the puppy, just teach him a lesson he would never forget.'

'Intend or no, if he dies it will go hard with you. The podestà has made it plain that he will tolerate no new outbreaks of brawling, no matter what the cause. And all because, in your blindness and jealousy, you believe an accusation delivered in secret and anonymously. How do you know that the accuser did not just make it up, to cause you hurt?'

'Because he was there, saw it all, and reported it truly.'

The mocking voice of Piero Bevilacqua as he emerged from the shadows of a side-alley was a shock to the two men standing in the sunlight in the middle of the street. Ferdinando frowned, confused both at Piero's presence and his words. For Will, there was a moment of blinding clarity.

'You, Bevilacqua? It was you? Then Signor Shakespeare is right, I should not believe a word, and have placed myself in peril, and an innocent boy's life in danger, for no good cause!'

Piero just laughed. 'Oh you have cause, Nogarola, believe me, you have ample cause. For I heard them myself, rutting like common animals in the bushes in the gardens of the Palazzo Giusti.'

'You lie! They did no such thing. Ferdinando, I was there too, and I swear that they both behaved with honour. Tomaso, it is true, has long had a foolish infatuation with Madalena, going back to Corfu, but your wife is a woman of great integrity and compassion, and she did no more than tell Tomaso the obvious truth, that there could never be anything between them.'

As soon as the words left his mouth, Will realised that he had made an error.

'You were there too?' Ferdinando's voice was angry again. 'And who else was there, enjoying the privy tale of my domestic life? The rest of the Veronese aristocracy? Am I to be shamed by this whelp and my faithless wife in front of the whole city?'

Piero's look of triumph in Will's direction went undetected by Ferdinando.

'My lord Ferdinando,' he said, presenting an attitude of respect that Will was sure he did not feel in the least. 'We have had our differences, but we have sworn, have we not, to eternal peace between our houses? It is these English interlopers who you should distrust, not I.'

Nogarola looked from one to the other, suspicion struggling with confusion. He had no reason to trust anything that Bevilacqua had to say, but he at least was a known quantity, an Italian and Veronese; these foreigners on the other hand...

Bevilacqua stepped up close to Ferdinando, and put his arm around the other man's shoulders, half turning him away from Will.

'There is more you should know, Ferdinando, that will convince you.' He put his mouth close to the other's ear, and began to whisper. His eyes, looking over Ferdinando's shoulder, were locked on Will's, and they contained a look of pure, horrifying evil.

Ferdinando's body gave a jerk, upwards and backwards, and a small, strangled cry emerged from his lips. Piero laughed and turned, allowing the slumping body of his enemy to slide to the ground, its sightless eyes staring at the heavens above. In moments, Bevilacqua had disappeared whence he had come, leaving an appalled William Shakespeare standing alone above the dead body of Nogarola, from which the gilt handle of a dagger protruded just below the rib cage.

Will dropped to his knees and bent over the prostrate body, searching for any sign of life. But the blank and staring eyes told their story—Ferdinando Nogarola was dead, killed by a deadly accurate thrust of the dagger to his heart.

He did not know how long he knelt there, overcome by this second bout of violence and death within a few minutes, but it could not have been long. His mind was paralysed, uncomprehending, and so it was a surprise to hear the sound of pounding feet and the angry shouts of the officers of the watch as they charged into the little street, summoned no doubt by the local residents.

He was grasped roughly by the arms, hauled to his feet, and his hands were tied behind his back. Words were spoken, questions asked, but his mind, normally so quick, refused to respond, and so they bundled him off, out of the street, and took him to the Palazzo Del Capitano in the centre of the city. There, they threw him unceremoniously into a stinking cell in the gaol that lay beneath the magnificence above.

Chapter 26

He woke in the semi-darkness before dawn, his head pounding, and his nose wrinkling from the smell of urine-soaked straw that pervaded the air. It took him a few moments to recollect where he was, and why. Then he groaned, leaning back against the wall to survey his surroundings.

He was in a small cell, barely a dozen feet square, the flagstones on the floor barely disguised by a thin layer of straw; clean in his case. The bad smell came from the common holding cell next door, where half a dozen prisoners languished. There was no bed, and the only light came from a tiny opening, far above his head, which he assumed to be at street level.

How long had he been here? He remembered that, after the Watch had so unceremoniously dumped him on the floor of the cell and locked the barred door, he had simply lain there for a long time, too stunned by the turn of events to do anything. When was that? Yesterday afternoon?

As he scratched the stubble on his chin, he recalled that the Watch had clearly had no idea what to do with him. It was obvious they thought it likely he had murdered Ferdinando Nogarola, since he was found standing over the body alone in a deserted street. Yet if they had been summoned by the local townspeople, as seemed probable, they must also know that there were other actors in this drama. And so they had likely thrown him into the cell while they referred the whole thing to higher authority.

Eventually, Will dragged himself to his feet and his bellows of protest eventually brought a guard ambling down the corridor to his cell. But Will's protests and demands that the flunkey go and summon some superior to whom he could explain the situation were met with blank stares and a shrug, accompanied by laughter and insults from the inmates of the general holding cell next door. Not surprising, since in his agitation Will had been shouting at the man in English, a fact that he only realised later, when he had calmed down.

As the day went past, he could do little other than reflect on his situation and worry about the future. Of Tomaso he had no word, though he made

233

enquiries of the prison guard when he returned in the morning with some of the thin gruel and hard bread that passed for breakfast, this time in his calmest and most polite Italian. In return, he got nothing more than another disinterested shrug.

For the first time he thought about the consequences for him if the boy had indeed died of his injuries. Even assuming he could escape the charges that were no doubt being prepared against him in Verona and make his way back to England, he could not begin to imagine the wrath that Sir Francis Walsingham would visit upon him. He had been charged with ensuring that his beloved ward stay out of trouble, and instead he had stood by while the young man was murdered.

Could he have stopped the fight between Tomaso and Ferdinando? It was a question he asked himself over and over, and in his heart he condemned himself, for he knew that, had he insisted, Tomaso would have put up his sword, though whether that would have been enough to deter Ferdinando was another question.

And then there was the matter of the secret plans for the invasion of England, which lay carefully hidden in his travelling trunk, back at the Casa Cappelletti. Though King Philip's plans would take many months or even years to bring to fruition, Will knew that it would also take many years for England to prepare herself to meet the projected invasion with a counter-stroke. Knowing the scale and direction of the enemy's intentions as early as possible was essential. And if he died here, executed for murder, what then?

These melancholy reflections, going around and around in his head, were occasionally tempered by his more natural optimism. Surely the truth about Ferdinando's death would come out. The podestà, the city's chief magistrate, had seemed like a fair-minded man, and he had himself said that he owed Will a debt of gratitude for his deterrence of a brawl at the Inn of the Fig. But these reflections were in their turn chased away by gloom, and eventually he fell asleep, exhausted.

Next morning, he woke when the sun sent a shaft of light through the little window. It dazzled him, and spots of light were still dancing across his vision when the flunkey appeared once more and unlocked the bars of his cell. Behind him were two burly and taciturn guards, and the Captain of the Watch, the man who had arrested him two days before, who he had not seen since.

'Come with me,' that worthy said, barely grunting the words.

234

Closely hemmed in by the two guards, Will did as he was told, following the captain up several flights of stairs that seemed to be built into the wall of the Palazzo, until they emerged into an ante-room. Here, he waited while the captain knocked on the door that was set into the far side of the room. Though there was no reply from within, he pushed open the door, and with exaggerated courtesy, gestured that Will should enter.

The room beyond was plainly furnished, just a desk and a few chairs, though it boasted a fine tall window that overlooked the Piazza below and washed the room in a light that Will found welcoming and cheering after the gloom below.

Sitting on an ornate chair behind the desk was the podestà, Tommasino Morosini; otherwise the room was empty. At a gesture, the two guards withdrew to stand beside the door, and the podestà fixed his gaze on Shakespeare, saying nothing, which made Will if anything more nervous.

'Well, Signor Shakespeare,' Morosini eventually said, 'it seems that you are in serious trouble. The Captain of the Guard tells me that he found you standing over the body of Ferdinando Nogarola, who had been stabbed to death. He surmises that, since there was no one else in the vicinity, you must have been the murderer, and hence he followed his duty and had you conducted to the cells below until the matter could be further investigated. What do you say to this charge?'

The podestà had been cold and precise as he levelled the accusation, with no hint of warmth towards his erstwhile prisoner.

Will restrained the urge to cry out his innocence, instead trying to match Morosini's own dispassion. 'Sir, I know how it looks, but I did not kill Ser Ferdinando, with whom I have—had—always had the most cordial relations. What motive could I have for such an act?'

'The motives of men are always opaque,' Morosini said dryly, 'so we must proceed on the facts of their actions, which we can at least observe. Other witnesses have said that there was an altercation in the street at which you were present, in which swords were drawn and blood was shed. Your friend, Tomaso Martinelli, was badly injured. Is it not possible that, left alone, you could have attacked Nogarola in a rage and killed him?'

Will opened his mouth to respond, but no words came, for he suddenly realised how plausible such a scenario was. And there were no witnesses.

He put himself in the podestà's shoes and realised that, no matter how he might feel personally, it would be difficult for him to take the side of this Englishman against one of the most powerful families in Verona, who must

235

be howling for his blood. And the truth would be even more difficult for Morosini, since it would reignite the very feuds that he had worked so hard to stop.

Yet the truth was the only defence he had. 'Ser Morosini, there was a witness. The real murderer. Piero Bevilacqua.'

'Bevilacqua? Well, I can believe almost anything of that young devil, and God knows he has caused mischief enough in the few years he has been on this earth. But, to ask your own question, why? What would be his motive? He above all knows the penalties for breaking my peace.'

Though Morosini's words were sceptical, something in his demeanour suggested to Will that he did not dismiss the possibility altogether. So he decided to take a gamble, and lay out for the podestà everything that had happened, including the source of the trouble, Tomaso's infatuation with Madalena.

Morosini listened in judicious silence until the end, never taking his eyes off Shakespeare's face. At the end he sat back in his chair and folded his hands across his stomach, evidently thinking through the implications of what he had just been told.

'I will, I think, curse the name of all Englishmen from this day forward,' he finally said. 'If your story is true, and I arrest Piero Bevilacqua, that touchy family and its host of retainers will be armed within a day, and we will have mayhem on the streets. Yet if I do not produce Ferdinando's killer in a reasonable time, the Nogarola will do the same. I could, of course, avoid all this by having you executed outright.'

Thus the master of Verona confirmed Will's worst fears.

'My Lord Podestà,' he said, thinking rapidly, the words transmitted to his lips the instant they appeared in his mind, 'when in Venice I was once taken to The Hall of Advocates, in the Doge's Palace. As we went in, an inscription above the door was pointed out to me. It said—*"Before anything else, always investigate thoroughly in order to establish the truth with justice and clarity. Condemn no one, except after an honest and balanced judgement. Judge no one on the basis of suspicion but seek out evidence and let the sentence be compassionate."*

'Venice is rightly proud of the impartiality of her judges. I beg of you, though I am a foreigner, give me the benefit of that Venetian justice which is so ably administered throughout your empire by noble patricians such as yourself. At least question Piero Bevilacqua and test my claims against his testimony.'

Morosini considered that, then came to a decision. 'You are eloquent, Messer Shakespeare. Very well, I will order that Piero Bevilacqua be taken into custody and we will try this issue in a closed court. I do not want this to become a circus upon which the fickle and easily distracted public can feed.'

With a gesture, he indicated that the guards should take Will back to his cell. But Will stood his ground as they grasped his arms. 'Signor Morosini, you told me that Tomaso was badly injured. But you have not told me whether he yet lives.'

'Oh, he lives, though he is very weak and has not regained consciousness these two days past. The doctor to whom young Tebaldo Pindemonte took him proved to be a wise choice, for he has served on the battlefield, and well knows how to deal with sword cuts and the like.

'He is optimistic that your young friend will recover, but, like all his kind, he hedges his bets with "it's too early to say", and "all depends on God's will".'

Will nodded his thanks for this information as relief flooded through his mind. He turned to leave, but a word from the podestà to the guards caused him to turn again. 'Take Messer Shakespeare to the apartments above and find him a room there, with some light. You will still be under lock and key, Shakespeare, but I see no reason why your incarceration should not be a little more comfortable than the common cells for the few days it will take to resolve this matter one way or the other.'

And so it was from a small but far more pleasant room on the third floor of the Palazzo del Capitano that Will waited to hear word of his impending trial. He was well enough treated, and his food was improved considerably over the vile gruel that had been his lot down below, but he was a prisoner nonetheless.

Though he could at least watch the comings and goings in the piazza below, his impatience mounted as the promised 'few days' became a full week, and then stretched halfway into another. The only communication that he had from the podestà was a short note delivered with his midday meal, to say that Piero Bevilacqua seemed to have disappeared, and that a search of the city and the surrounding countryside was underway to locate him. If this precipitate flight changed the podestà's view of the likely truth of Will's story, he showed no sign of it in his note.

He did have a visit from Tebaldo Pindemonte, who brought some news from the outside world, most importantly, that Tomaso had recovered consciousness at last and was slowly gaining strength.

He also said that Ferdinando's murder had caused an uproar in the city, and though the peace had so far been kept with the help of an increased presence of soldiery on the streets, gangs of the two rival families were again roaming about, looking for trouble. People knew that the podestà had taken someone into custody for the crime, but the identity of the supposed murderer was unknown.

'And Madalena?' he asked, knowing that Tebaldo would have been in touch with his friends Gregorio and Simone, retainers in the Nogarola household. 'How does she fare?'

'Simone says that she is in mourning, as a widow should be, but that she remains for the most part dry-eyed, a fact that has been noticed by some of the sharper-eyed of the household servants. The household is a sad place—old man Leonardo has taken to his bed, and will see no one, even leaving the arrangements for his son's funeral to his steward.'

Madalena, he had reflected as he sat on his bed after Tebaldo's departure, would not mourn for long the loss of a husband for whom she had had little respect. She would be free, once the mourning period was over, and if Ferdinando and Leonardo had followed the usual custom and provided for her as a widow, she would have sufficient means to do what she chose. Though no doubt her father, now far away in Genoa, would have something to say about that.

Then at last, a full fourteen days after his arrest, word came from the podestà that he was to be arraigned for trial the following morning. Will assumed that Piero Bevilacqua had been found and dragged back to Verona, though the message from Morosini said nothing of that. He would no doubt concoct a story to exonerate himself, and all would depend on whether Morosini and his fellow magistrates believed a native of the city and a member of one of its most prominent families over the testimony of a mere foreigner. The odds, he thought as he drifted off into a fitful sleep, could not be much better than fifty-fifty.

The next day, he was conducted down the stairs into a small chamber, where Tommasino Morosini sat in full state behind a long table, flanked on each side by two magistrates, one tall and gaunt, the other plump with the face of a cherub. A clerk sat at a smaller table to one side of the room, fussing with paper and quills. Otherwise the room was empty.

Will was kept standing, his two guards just behind him, as Morosini cleared his throat and began to speak. 'This court is convened, in camera, to test the respective claims of Signor William Shakespeare, a foreigner from

England, and Ser Piero Bevilacqua, of the house of Bevilacqua, with respect to the murder of the late Ferdinando Nogarola.

'I have judged that the trial should be held in secret because of the atmosphere of unrest that pervades Verona. Nevertheless, secret or no, its deliberations and its judgements will have the same force as any judgement delivered in open court.'

The clerk scribbled hurriedly to record these words, a task he was still completing as a door to one side of the room opened, and two more guards entered, escorting Piero Bevilacqua, who, though he was dressed in his customary fashionable black, looked a little the worse for wear. There was a bruise under his right eye, his hair was dishevelled, and he was unshaven.

'Good. Now that you have graced us with your presence, Signor Bevilacqua, we can commence.' Morosini's sarcasm was surprising, given his even-handedness thus far. 'Let us commence with your testimony, Signor Shakespeare.'

So Will told his story again, exactly as he had related it to the podestà, leaving nothing out, however painful it felt to him personally. Throughout, Piero watched him, a smile playing about his mouth, as if he thought the whole process was a sham and that he had simply to say a few words and this upstart Englishman would be condemned out of hand.

And why would he not think that? Will asked himself. After all, it was going to be the word of a noble of Verona against that of a foreigner.

'So that we can be clear,' Morosini said when Will had finished, 'it is your statement, under oath, that Piero Bevilacqua deliberately stabbed Ferdinando Nogarola to death and then ran away from the scene, leaving you alone with the dead man?'

'Yes, my lord, it is.'

'Piero Bevilacqua, what do you say to these charges?'

Piero seemed almost to leap forward, so eager was he to tell his side of the story. 'The Englishman lies.' The statement was delivered in a flat monotone, though his eyes burned as he stared at Will. 'I did indeed inform Ferdinando of his wife's infidelity, and the identity of her abuser. But I did not leave the Palazzo Bevilacqua that day, as any of my servants can attest.'

'And their testimony, should it be called for, will, of course, be entirely impartial,' said the tall magistrate, his eyebrow lifted in irony.

Piero seemed surprised by this intervention, and resorted to bluster. 'Of course they will tell the truth, sir. Without coaching from me.'

'That we will see,' Morosini said. 'But tell me, Ser Piero, if you had nothing to do with this murder and were not in the Via Farina that day, why did you flee the city so soon after the events in question? And have to be dragged back here, most evidently against your will?'

Morosini now seemed to be openly hostile to Bevilacqua. Will had expected a fair hearing, but it was beginning to seem as if Morosini and the other judges were on his side!

As for Piero, the surprise and offence were written in his face, where a scowl had replaced the knowing smile. 'I did not flee the city! I had business at the family estates in the country. And I came back as soon as your officers found me.'

'I am told that it took some "persuasion", as the skinned knuckles of one of my officers will attest.'

So that was how Piero had got his bruise. No doubt he had been dragged forcibly out of some hidey-hole.

'Then there is the question of the dagger,' the magistrate said with the cherubic face, gesturing to the clerk, who stood and carried a small cloth-wrapped bundle over to the magistrates' table. When the magistrate unwrapped and held up the object, Will recognised the knife that he had last seen embedded in Ferdinando's body.

It was a simple steel blade surmounted by an iron handle and crosspiece. The only feature that distinguished it from the blades that could be seen dangling from the hips of any Veronese youth was a small, triangular panel between blade and pommel that was decorated with some kind of device he could not make out from this distance.

The magistrate held the dagger up in front of his eyes to inspect the symbol more clearly. 'A white eagle's wing on a blue background. Your family's emblem, is it not, Signor Bevilacqua?'

'Yes. What of it? It does not prove that the dagger is mine. Any of my retainers could be its owner.'

'Are you saying, then, that a servant of the House of Bevilacqua was the murderer?' The magistrate's voice was as soft as the curves of his face. 'If so, perhaps you can enlighten us as to which of your servants you think could have done this heinous deed? Or do we have to question every one of them, on the rack if necessary?'

Piero said nothing.

240

'So, to summarise, Signor Shakespeare alleges that you attacked and murdered Ferdinando Nogarola following a street-fight that was the result of your providing deliberate misinformation about his wife that was clearly intended to provoke his anger.' The podestà allowed that to sink in. 'Your defence is that you were not at the scene of the crime, despite the fact that a dagger that could have been yours as easily as it could belong to any other member of your household, was used as the murder weapon. We must also consider the fact of your flight from the city, from which you required some encouragement to return.'

'And you, my Lord Podestà, have no evidence against me other than the word of this foreigner!' Piero was almost shouting. 'I am a Bevilacqua, a member of one of the oldest families in Verona. We served Cangrande, and proudly. You should take my word against his, and that should be the end of it if you have any honour!'

'Ah, honour. There is the rub. I am thoroughly tired of the use of this word "honour" to justify violence and rape in my jurisdiction. The ancient honour of the Bevilacqua set in permanent competition against the equally ancient honour of the Nogarola.

'Verona is as fair a city as any in the Veneto, yet its beauty is daily stained by the unending competition between these two "honourable" houses. And you, Piero Bevilacqua, have been at the heart of these disturbances since they began. Do not talk to me of honour.

'As for Signor Shakespeare, this "foreigner" that you so despise has behaved with restraint and forbearance. Only a few days ago, he stopped you from committing another offence against the peace of the city, something he need not have done as a mere foreigner. I find him an entirely credible and honourable man.'

The podestà quickly looked left and right at his colleagues, asking no question out loud, but receiving nonetheless affirmative nods from both.

'Piero Bevilacqua, this tribunal finds you guilty of the murder of Ferdinando Nogarola.'

Will had not realised that he was holding his breath, which now escaped his lungs in a long, low sigh. As for Piero, he seemed unable to believe that his superior birth and position in Verona had been insufficient to sway the Venetian justices.

'You are fortunate in one respect,' Morosini went on, 'for though I would like nothing more than to see you swinging from the gallows, I cannot afford

241

to take any action that might set fire again to the bonfires of civil rivalry between the Bevilacqua and Nogarola houses.

'What I can do is send you, our chief trouble-maker, into exile, and I do so command. You will leave the city within a day, and you will travel beyond the borders of the Venetian Terraferma, never to return. Should you defy this sentence and appear anywhere within the realms of Venice, you will be declared an outlaw, to be hunted down and killed.'

A sneering rage returned to Piero's face. 'You Venetian popinjay! Do you think my father will allow this? He will have you removed from office before you know what has happened.'

Morosini smiled the smile of a man who knew that the dice were loaded in his favour. 'Ah, Ser Piero, there you are wrong. I have already consulted with your father on this question and he has agreed that my sentence is a fit one, should it prove necessary to impose it. He is wiser than you are and recognises that the civil wars in Verona must end. And he has other sons.'

The last words were particularly cruel and they punctured Piero's confidence entirely. He visibly sagged and had to be held up by the guards who escorted him from the judgement chamber.

'Signor Shakespeare, you are free to go. I suggest you resume your journey as quickly as possible, for though these proceedings are supposedly secret, I would be most unsurprised if word of what went on was on the streets within a day.'

'My Lord Podestà, nothing would please me more than being free at last to go home. And I thank you for this demonstration of the famed impartiality of Venetian justice.'

Morosini nodded to his two fellow judges, who, without a further word, rose and left the room, as did the clerk and the remaining guards, so that he and Will were alone.

The podestà's smile when he turned his attention back to Will was sardonic. 'Oh, not so entirely disinterested. You see, I had a visit yesterday from a mutual friend—Ser Francesco Contarini.'

'Francesco is in Verona?' Will's astonishment could not be more complete.

'No longer; he had to depart for Venice this morning. But the delay while we searched for Piero Bevilacqua worked in your favour, for one of your friends here, knowing of your connection with Signor Contarini, sent messengers hot-foot in the hope that he might be able to intervene.

242

'Of course, it took time for them to travel to Venice, and then discover that he was visiting his estates not so far from Verona. When apprised of your situation, he judged it necessary to come here and meet with me privately. He told me that it was important to the security and policy of the state that you should be released and allowed to continue on your journey.

'I will tell you that this advice was welcome. Frankly, I have wanted to find some way to deal with that devil for some time, and this event, tragic though it is, has enabled me to remove the source of much of the hatred between the two houses. There are times when I would happily call down the plague on both of them.'

Sentiments with which William Shakespeare could only concur as he said his formal farewells to the podestà and left the Palazzo del Capitano, out into fresh air and freedom.

Chapter 27

Verona, August 1586

The Nogarola residence was a two hundred years old Palazzo, not far from the Piazza della Signoria and the Palazzo del Capitano in which Will had been imprisoned.

The crenellated wall facing the street was a relic of a more violent time in the city's history, when virtually every house was a fortress, though that day the gates were wide open. Behind them lay a broad courtyard, and beyond that the pile of the residence itself.

From there, William Shakespeare watched through a window as the single watchman employed to guard the entrance grimly scuttled for cover in his little hutch, sheltering from a torrential rainstorm that seemed to have appeared out of nowhere. Though unexpected, the rain was welcome, sweeping away the oppressive heat of the day, washing clean the walls of the palazzo and the flagstones of the courtyard, leaving in its wake the pleasant fragrance of new-washed flowers and the relief of cool, wet air.

He turned away from the scene below as a door opened on the far side of the room to admit Madalena and her father-in-law, Leonardo Nogarola, who seemed to have aged ten years since Will had last seen him at the Palazzo Giusti. With a cane in one hand, and Madalena supporting him on the other, he shuffled his bulky form across the room, settling heavily in a chair before acknowledging Will's presence in the room with a sketchy wave.

Servants appeared, bringing wine and food that they arranged on a small table.

'Welcome to the Palazzo Nogarola, Signor Shakespeare.' The voice was a harsh croak, barely audible. 'I could wish that we were meeting in happier circumstances.' He held his arm out, into which a servitor placed a glass of wine.

'Ser Leonardo, allow me to express my formal condolences on your loss. It was a heinous crime.'

Leonardo eyed him for a few moments, testing, perhaps, his sincerity. 'My son was not without faults, not the least of which was his treatment of

244

dear Madalena, the wife he should have honoured, but to whom he instead offered nothing but abuse.'

Madalena, her hand resting on the old man's shoulder, gave it a little squeeze.

'I will never understand that aspect of him. But in other ways he was an honourable man, not deserving of the end meted out by that scoundrel. And no man deserves to go to his maker without having the opportunity to confess his sins and seek forgiveness.'

The evident affection between Leonardo Nogarola and his daughter-in-law was a surprise to Will, for the man he remembered from Venice was an avaricious driver of hard bargains with little that was sentimental about him. But he was learning that few men are entirely as they seem on the surface.

'Sir, I did not know your son well, but he was always courteous to me.' Will thought it better to make no comment on Ferdinando's treatment of his wife, who confirmed this good judgement with a tiny nod from where she stood, a little behind Leonardo and out of his sight.

'I remember him speaking of you, how he enjoyed discussing poetics with you, that evening at the ball.' He lapsed into silence, staring at the liquid in his wine glass, though his eyes were unfocused. Then he raised them again and looked at Will. 'I am glad, Signor Shakespeare, that you were acquitted of any part on the murder of my son. I would have preferred to see his real killer hanging from the end of a rope, but like the podestà I am tired of the civil strife that has plagued our city, and it seemed to me that another death would not end it.'

There were tears in his eyes as he sat looking helplessly at Will, no longer the grand old patriarch of his clan, just a tired and emotionally exhausted old man.

'Come, Father,' Madalena said tenderly. 'Let us take you to your bedchamber where you can rest for the afternoon. Can you help me, Will?'

With Will's help, she eased Leonardo to his feet and, handing him his cane, supported him under one arm as she walked him across the room, telling Will to wait for her return.

He returned to his vigil by the window, through which bright sunlight now poured, the clouds carrying the rain-storm having dissipated and dissolved.

It seemed that Ferdinando's death had ended not one life, but two, for his father had the look of a man whose remaining tenure in this world had been shortened considerably. Will would be surprised if he was still living in a year.

The clicking of the door disturbed these melancholy thoughts, and he turned, expecting to see Madalena returning. Instead, he was greeted with the very welcome sight of Tomaso, pale and leaning heavily on the shoulder of Tebaldo Pindemonte.

'Tomaso! You cannot know how glad I am to see you.'

His embrace caused Tomaso to wince, even as he laughed with pleasure. 'Careful Will, I am not yet quite mended. The doctor says that Ferdinando's sword managed to crack a rib, a fact to which I owe my life, but it will take a while yet before it is fully healed. In the meantime, he says, not too much excitement.'

'All your excitement is of your own making, you young fool. Tebaldo, when I am gone I shall expect you to take up the thankless burden of ensuring that this idiot stays out of trouble.' *Little hope of that,* Will thought, for Tebaldo was hardly less impulsive than Tomaso. They made a fine pair.

'Perhaps we should both swear to keep each other in check,' Tebaldo said, the serious expression on his face surprising Will. 'I know it would please my father if I too, were to lead a quieter life for a while. But Tomaso said he needed to have some private words with you, so I will leave you alone. I hope your journey home is a safe and comfortable one, Signor Shakespeare.'

'Farewell Tebaldo. I doubt we will see each other again before I depart, but you can be sure you will be in my memories whenever I think of fair Verona.'

When the boy had left, Tomaso settled himself into the chair recently vacated by Leonardo Nogarola, while Will seated himself on a stool taken from a corner of the room. They contemplated each other in silence for a few moments.

'You leave tomorrow?' Tomaso said eventually. 'Over the mountains? Unless you have suddenly learned how to sit a horse properly, that is going to be a very long journey for you.'

Will's grin was rueful. 'I'm not looking forward to it, that is true. But it will be good to be pointed home at last.'

'The report on the armada. It is safe?'

'Yes, sewn into the lining of my doublet by Giovanna last night. It will not leave my person until I get to London and Sir Francis.'

'That's good. Francesco Contarini was anxious to make sure that it was still in your possession.'

'You saw him? When he was here?'

'Yes. It was Madalena who sent for him, you know. She knows nothing of our intelligencing, of course, but she had the good sense to remember that Contarini had been our host in Venice, and that a senior member of the Signoria and the Council of Ten might sway the podestà's judgement in your favour.'

Will nodded. He had guessed that it had been Madalena who had sent to Contarini.

'Madalena is free now...' He left the obvious implications of that fact unsaid.

'Yes, but it is over between us.' Once again Will was surprised, for he had expected that, with Ferdinando dead, Tomaso would immediately attempt to rekindle the fires of the passion he had felt for the girl. 'I thought for a long time, over the last two weeks, while heaven and hell debated which of them was to have my soul. You are right, Will—Madalena never loved me as I was in love with her. She cares for me, that is true, and she paid for me to have the best of care, but hers is the affection of a friend, not the passion of a lover. I know that now.'

'Then you will go back to Padua? I can tell Sir Francis that you are safely installed there for your second term?'

'Yes, I will go back to Padua.' Tomaso grinned. 'And you and Uncle Francis can sleep soundly knowing that I am being guarded against all folly by Tebaldo!'

The door opened to admit Madalena. 'And what are you two laughing like children about?'

'The idea that Tebaldo Pindemonte will somehow be making sure that my Tomaso here doesn't get into mischief when they return to Padua.'

'That *is* a funny thought. So you are going back to university, Tomaso?'

'Yes, Signora, though not immediately. It will be a while before I can ride, and the term does not start for some months yet. So I hope that you might grace me with your company during my convalescence.'

'Signora? Tomaso, are we not friends? Madalena is my name, and I insist you call me by it. Particularly if we are to be spending time walking in the gardens and streets together.' She turned to Will. 'I understand you are

247

leaving in the morning, Ser William? Though our acquaintance was short, I will miss you.'

'And I you, Signora. I believe I owe my freedom at least in part to you, since Tomaso tells me that it was you who sent to Contarini, and he testified as to my character with Signor Morosini. For that, and for ensuring that Tomaso was well cared for, you are in my debt.'

Madalena inclined her head to acknowledge his thanks. 'Now, there are refreshments here, and food. Before you go, let us eat and talk of more important things, like poetry.'

Chapter 28

A nd so we parted. I expect that Tomaso will by now be on his way back to Padua to prepare for his next term there, though naturally I have had no word from him since I left Verona.'

Walsingham's study was, as always, uncomfortably hot; a combination of the October sun streaming through the big windows and the fire that still burned in the big fireplace. Mercifully, since it was the late afternoon, it had sunk to become no more than a pile of glowing embers.

The secretary, sitting unmoving behind his desk, had seemed to Will to have become even more careworn in the year and a month that he had been away. Will had arrived from Ostend only that morning, and had done no more than drop his bags at the Holbrooke home, where Richard had been both astonished and delighted to see him. Changing out of his travelling clothes, he had hurried to the house in Seething Lane.

There, to his chagrin, he discovered that the secretary was downriver attending the queen at Greenwich, so he had been forced to cool his heels in the ante-room for several hours.

Phelippes had arrived but a quarter hour before Walsingham, and had greeted him effusively, but he had done no more than give his colleague the briefest sketch of his adventures in Italy when Sir Francis had arrived and, joining the general astonishment at his sudden appearance, had ushered him into the office.

'This is a tale indeed, Master Shakespeare,' was all he said. 'And these papers that you brought back, sewn into your doublet, was it?'

Will passed the packet across the table. They had cost him the lining of a good doublet, though that was of no consequence considering their importance.

While Walsingham read the copy of the King of Spain's letter to the pope, Will's thought idly about the journey home. As Tomaso had predicted, it was far from comfortable, and he thought that he would like nothing better than to never see the back of a horse's head again.

He had travelled with a small band of traders, fine if somewhat coarse fellows, with whom he had developed a rough fellowship over the four and a half weeks it had taken them to traverse the Alps through the Brenner Pass. Then they had made their way up through the German states, until eventually he found himself in Ostend.

There, it had taken another week to find a ship coming to London; probably the most frustrating week of the entire journey. But there had been no other incidents, no encounters with rogues or bandits, and his worst problems were dealing with thieving innkeepers and fighting off fleas in the beds for which they over-charged.

'Most interesting indeed.' Sir Francis' words broke into his reverie. Walsingham picked up a small bell on his desk and rang it, summoning Phelippes from the outer room. The master codebreaker must have been expecting the call, for he came in almost before the bell's chimes had subsided to silence.

'Read this, Thomas, and tell us what you think.'

Phelippes, ever a fast reader, scanned the document in a few minutes, and looked up at Will, the thick lenses of his glasses making his blue eyes seem huge. 'This is the missing piece of the puzzle, Sir Francis. A bold coup indeed.'

Walsingham grunted. 'My thoughts also. You see, William, we have been collecting all manner of information about this supposed "armada" for well over a year now. It was that German sea-captain, wasn't it Thomas, who first told us back in January last year, if I remember the report rightly, that "the King of Spain had taken up all the available masts for shipping, both great and small".

'Unfortunately, my fellow privy councillors were preoccupied with domestic matters and had no interest in this or the two or three other reports that we received subsequently. My Lord of Leicester said it was all "Spanish brag"!

'But the question nagged at my mind, and it was your first report that set the fire-bells a-jangling. I sent one of my most trusted agents, Tom Heneage's brother-in-law, abroad to see what he could find out. Then, before he could report, we received the most extraordinary intelligence from another agent in Florence. You will recall that your message told us that the King of Spain had instructed the Marquis de Santa Cruz to prepare a plan of invasion, yes?'

250

Will nodded, fascinated to learn how his little piece of information had fitted into the complex web of intelligence that had found its focus in Seething Lane.

'Our agent in Florence was able to get a copy of the Marquis' plans for the invasion and sent them to us barely a week after that had been submitted to Philip!'

Will could imagine the upset that would have caused in this place, and in the government. 'What was Santa Cruz' plan?'

'To send five hundred ships, carrying fifty-five thousand troops up the English Channel to land on the south coast,' Phelippes said.

'And the Duke of Parma's plan?'

'Of this we knew nothing until now, but in any event, it seems that it was superseded by the final decision of the king to combine the two ideas into the plan you have brought us.'

'And which, I am sure, will be sufficient to finally get my colleagues on the council to see the urgency of planning a response.' Walsingham, far from sounding triumphant, seemed grim. 'Though we do not know when the blow will fall, and I do not doubt that some will use the absence of that knowledge to further delay any action. But it is a start.'

'And it is a vast undertaking financially, which could easily bankrupt even such a power as Spain,' Phelippes said. 'Four million ducats! More than three times the annual revenue of our own crown.'

'If I may, Thomas, Sir Francis, Signor Contarini had some advice that he asked me to pass on, which may also be of use.' Will explained Contarini's strategy of trying to limit King Philip's ability to borrow by sending out agents to Genoa and Florence.

'That is the province of Sir Horatio Palavicino, I think, but it seems that it is a sound idea. Thomas, will you prepare a memorandum for him?'

Another Englishman of Italian descent like Tomaso, Sir Horatio was the queen's chief financier, something of a rogue it was said, but a financial genius and trusted by the queen. More importantly, Will remembered from his time working in this office before he left for Italy, Palavicino had an enormous network of financial agents across Europe, a financial intelligence network without equal. If anyone could persuade the bankers of Genoa and Florence to withhold their credit from the King of Spain, he could.

'So, William,' Sir Francis said when they were alone, Phelippes having departed with a bow to return to his paper-laden desk in the next room. 'You have performed your tasks more than admirably. It is unfortunate that young Tom was injured, but you cannot be blamed for that, and hopefully the boy has learned a valuable lesson about curbing his temper. And your country owes you a great deal with this intelligence you have so artfully extracted.'

'Thank you, Sir Francis. It has been an experience that I will never forget.'

'Ah, but I think you must forget at least some of it. You were never more than a temporary intelligencer, set to perform a specific mission. Now that your mission is concluded, you must never mention anything of your activities to anyone again. We have gained an invaluable opportunity to prepare for this coming invasion, but we must keep the secret of what we know and how we found out for as long as possible. You understand?'

'Of course, Sir Francis. But may I take it that I am now in no further danger from Sir Thomas Lucy, or the Earl of Leicester for that matter?' Will had been anxious on this subject for the whole of his journey home, fearing, perhaps irrationally, that Walsingham would never release him from his service, holding the threat to his family over his head.

He need not have worried. 'I think I can safely say you are secure on that score,' Sir Francis said, a smile creeping onto his face.

'Then, Sir, you have my humble gratitude also.'

'So then, you are formally released from my service and you are free to resume your old life. Which, I take it, will not mean returning to Stratford?'

On his journey home, Will had thought often about this question. He dearly wanted to go home and see his children and his wife, not to mention his parents and siblings, all of whom he loved dearly. But this could not be any more than a temporary visit, for more than ever he knew that his future was in London. He had learned so much from his experiences in Italy and his mind was bursting with ideas for plays and poems that needed but a little nurturing to burst into life.

'No, Sir Francis,' he said, 'not on any permanent basis, though I am afire to see my wife and children again. But I will return here, to London, to make my way in the world.'

Walsingham nodded, evidently unsurprised at this declaration. 'Writing plays and poems and acting on the stage, no doubt. It is a profession of which I do not much approve. The more furious among my Puritan brethren would happily banish all of you from the realm entirely, for the theatres incite the citizenry to licentious and bawdy behaviour and distract them from the honest and sober pursuit of thrift and obedience to God's laws.'

Will was surprised at this outburst, for though Sir Francis Walsingham was well known to be of the Puritan cast of mind and was as austere as any member of that sect in his own personal habits, it was rare for him to express his views in such forthright terms.

'And yet, Sir Francis,' Will said, greatly daring, 'the best of our players and the playwrights who create the words for them to say, can also uplift the spirits of the common man, can they not? Help them see the greater truths that might otherwise be obscured?'

'So long as they are shown the truth, and not some fantasy to scramble their weak minds,' the secretary growled. 'In any event, the theatres will never be closed so long as Her Majesty continues to patronise them. And since there will be plays and players, there must be poets and playwrights, among whom will no doubt be Master William Shakespeare. Well then, go to and create your master-works. I wish you all the luck in the world.'

'Thank you, Sir Francis. I promise you, I will write plays that will move the minds of men to such heights that they will see the world anew, as if atop a mountain.'

Walsingham accepted this piece of rhetoric with a nod. 'Your determination does you credit, young man. And perhaps I can give you a little assistance on your way. When you have something worth putting on the stage, send to me. Lord Howard, our new-appointed Lord High Admiral, has a company of players and I have no doubt that I can prevail on him to have your work performed.'

Will could do nothing but stammer his thanks at this generous offer of support from such a powerful man.

'Good. Well then, I have much to do, and I am sure you would like to return to your old life as soon as possible. Speaking of which, I expect that you will find an old friend out in the antechamber.'

The identity of the 'old friend' was immediately apparent the moment he opened the door.

'William Shakespeare, as I live and breathe!' Kit Marlowe's embrace was crushing, surprisingly so for so slight a man. 'You look as though you have been thriving on the air of foreign climes. You must tell me all about your adventures, right now, over a tankard of English ale. And you are paying.'

Same old Kit, Will thought, laughing as they walked through the astonished anteroom and out into the street.

THE END

253

Made in the USA
San Bernardino, CA
13 April 2019